Anywhere
You Run

ALSO BY WANDA M. MORRIS

All Her Little Secrets

Anywhere You Run

A Novel

Wanda M. Morris

HARPER LARGE PRINT

An Imprint of HarperCollinsPublishers

HarperCollins books may be purchased for educational, business, or sales promotional use. For information, please e-mail the Special Markets Department at SPsales@harpercollins.com.

FIRST HARPER LARGE PRINT EDITION

ISBN: 978-0-06-326743-5

Library of Congress Cataloging-in-Publication Data is available upon request.

22 23 24 25 26 LSC 10 9 8 7 6 5 4 3 2 1

This one is for the Elizabeths . . .

Mary Elizabeth
Lila Elizabeth
Mabel Elizabeth
and
Alexandra Elizabeth

All strong and fierce women

I can look back and see sharp shadows, highlights, and smudgy in-betweens. I have been in sorrow's kitchen and licked out all the pots. Then I have stood on the peaky mountain wrapped in rainbows, with a harp and a sword in my hands.

—Zora Neale Hurston,
Dust Tracks on a Road

Author's Note

This book contains certain terms that I would never use or condone. However, as the story takes place in the Deep South of 1964, I wanted to lend as much authenticity as possible to the dialogue and narration. Sadly, such terminology was prevalent during that time.

Anywhere
You Run

Neshoba County, Mississippi
June 21, 1964

All four men passed around a bottle of Jim Beam as they peeled up State Route 19, giddy with excitement about what they'd do once they hog-tied those coons and got them to a tree. The engine revved as they hit the crest of the road, doing 80 mph. Getting pulled over was the least of their concerns because Olen's cousin, Sheriff Bickford, was riding shotgun. Bickford had gotten a tip and rounded up the other three to head from Jackson over to Meridian and then north to Neshoba County.

Olen, sitting in the back seat, threw back a swig and passed the bottle on, assuring the others they were doing God's work. "The last thing anybody needs is for them to start votin'. Bad enough the goddamn government wants us to let 'em eat in our restaurants and sit beside us on a bus. If the Lord had meant for whites to mix with coloreds, he woulda' made the coloreds a hell of a lot smarter. Either we stay all white or we die amongst 'em."

A couple of the other men nodded in silent agreement.

Bickford had explained to the others that his buddy, a Neshoba County sheriff, tipped him off that they'd landed a few of those troublemaking civil rights activists from up north. They'd made "arrangements." The plan was to arrest the men and hold them for a few hours. After nightfall, they'd release the men, tell them to be out of the county before midnight. Fifteen minutes later, the men would find themselves caught in the speed trap out on Rock Cut Road. Bickford's friend told him he could get a piece of the action if he made it up in time.

A few minutes later, the car slowed to a crawl. "I think this is it," Bickford said.

They all went quiet as the car eased up to the edge of a band of trees. Bickford spotted Smite Goody's truck and pointed. They knew they were in the right place. They cut the engine. All four men sat in the vehicle for a moment, polishing off the bottle, Bickford's low wheeze of excitement the only sound among them. The sweltering summer darkness cloaked them all. Voices, low, some laughing, whispered through the cypress trees. The men piled out of the car. Olen and Bickford unloaded rope and pliers from the trunk before they followed the sound of the voices.

By the time they reached the clearing, they found at least six or seven men there, all standing in a semicircle. Someone had parked his car just so and flooded the space with his car beams. The low-lying light cast the men's faces in ghostly angles, their cheekbones and chipped teeth upturned in wicked smiles of accomplishment.

Bickford was the first of his little quartet to reach the clearing, Olen right on his tail. The heavy scent of wet earth and male sweat slinked through the small crowd. By the looks of things, Bickford could see the "arrangements" had changed. The rope and pliers were no longer needed.

They were too late.

All the other men stood over an open shallow grave. And lying at the bottom of it—three young men, two white and one Negro. All three had been shot dead, their bodies oddly contorted, their faces grim vestiges of youth and hope extinguished.

Bickford eased over to his friend and gathered up the details of how the plan had unfolded. According to his buddy, some folks had gotten impatient. Guns this time instead of rope. The blue Ford station wagon the three men had been riding in would be burned and disposed of over at Bogue Chitto. The other men stood around holding conversations, laughing even, and grabbing a smoke. One man stood at the edge of the circle pointing a Brownie camera down into the grave and snapping pictures. There was a new man in their midst, because Bickford heard gagging and vomiting against a tree behind him, probably someone who'd never seen a dead body, or the way Mississippi handled rabble-rousers and nigger lovers.

Now all that was left to do was collect a few souvenirs—an ear, a finger—and head back to Jackson.

PART I
Leaving Jackson

1
Violet Richards

My older sister, Rose, had been dead for almost eight years, and still, she was bossing every part of my life like she did the day she died. After her funeral, I swore I wasn't ever stepping foot inside another funeral. All those tears and heartache to spill over a dead body, the soul of which was long gone. Brown bodies that were tired and worn out, their earthly usefulness ended. Or the other bodies mangled from the wretchedness of living too close to white folks who killed us for sport.

The Richards family had had too many funerals, and I didn't go to any of them after Rose's. That included Papa's death a few years after Rose, and Momma's passing last fall. Even now folks around town still talked about *that shameful Violet Richards gal who wouldn't go to her own momma's and daddy's funerals!* After all those funerals, I was fresh out of tears. I was the reason for all them deaths. And the guilt of it scratched and picked at my heart as if it was a tender scab on a days' old gash.

Now it was just me and my sister Marigold left. Seem like after Momma died, the two of us wandered about aimlessly in the little lives all that death and loss left us with. I dreamed of being anywhere but here. Both of us desperate to leave Jackson but forced to stay by the fear of wandering out in the world without our parents. Even as old as we were, losing both Momma and Papa had left us barely holding on. Death can cut you like that. Everyone—aunts and uncles, deaconesses from church—made promises to be there for us, to fill in and pick up where Momma had left off. But in the days after her death, everybody went back to their own bills and kids and troubles. Maybe they thought me and Marigold was grown women and that we'd figure it all out somehow.

We talked and pretended like everything was okay. But it wasn't.

Last year, after Momma's funeral, everything sorta spun off in a blur. There was the houseful of people sadly shaking their heads and speaking quietly about how there was no finer woman in all of Jackson. But

Momma's upstanding reputation among the neighbors and friends wasn't enough to dull the swollen pain of my having contributed to putting all those people I loved—Rose, Papa, and Momma—six feet under.

A couple weeks after Momma's funeral, I pulled out a bottle of Cutty Sark I'd stashed behind my bed and convinced Marigold to split it with me, liquid courage for us to get through the task of dividing up Momma's things. The scotch numbed us, but it didn't make the task any easier. Marigold kept Momma's Bible, with its worn leather cover, and I kept her old Timex watch, with the mother-of-pearl face. Marigold said it was fitting that I should have her watch, since Momma spent so much time looking at it to see if I would make curfew. I also kept Rose's old diary that we found among Momma's things. I guess if I was the one responsible for Rose's death, I should be the one who kept the reminder of what I'd done.

All them funerals cut a hole deep down inside me that I kept trying to fill up with all the wrong things. For almost a year, I'd been staying out and dancing until all hours of the night at Snooky's Joint, smoking reefer and drinking gin like it could quench my thirst. When Momma was alive, she used to warn me: *Ain't nothing open after midnight except hospitals and legs.* Now Marigold had gotten to the point where she stopped asking where I'd been or who I'd been with. I guess she probably didn't want to hear the answers. Or maybe she was too busy grieving all those deaths I had caused.

Sometimes I think the only thing all that partying did was make me forget my common sense. I guess that's why I didn't even see Huxley Broadus's truck when he pulled alongside me the night I walked home from Snooky's. Before I knowed what hit me, he had blocked my path and was headed round the side of the truck after me. I kicked and fought back the best I could, even left a few fingernails and bite marks in him. But it didn't do me no good. Me, running and screaming like somebody would come and save a colored woman out in the middle of the night. Nobody saves colored women like me. The best we can do is to save ourselves. Too bad for me.

Too bad for Huxley, too.

* * *

Jackson, Mississippi, was a big enough place that if you didn't go to church or work for any of the white families in town, maybe you could hide out, disappear among the crowd. I didn't fit into either one of them categories. I was simply a colored woman who'd killed a white man in Mississippi. It didn't matter that I'd gone to the police about his attack days ago. I needed to get out of town. Fast.

Now, a few hours after I'd killed Huxley, I waited in the humid breeze under a sprawling magnolia in the front yard at 2:30 in the morning and smoked a cigarette. Each puff crawled down my chest and smoothed out my fraying nerves, making me believe I could really pull this off. I might finally be leaving Jackson and all the ghosts I had created. I hadn't even told Marigold what I was planning. If I did, she'd either think I was crazy as a loon or try to help me, and I didn't want no harm to come to her.

I waited. A chorus of crickets, and barn owls rustled and hooted out into the night darkness, restless, like me. Moonlight fell around our old clapboard house in a bright bluish glow. Maybe it was the moonlight or maybe it was all those ghosts hovering over the house and wishing me Godspeed or good riddance. Papa used to call this "our palace," with its chipping paint, squeaking floorboards, and all those ghosts. I closed my eyes and could see the inside, walls covered with the lingering reminders of what we used to be—pictures of Momma and Papa on their wedding day, his bushy mustache, her hands clutching a small bouquet of wildflowers, as they stood in front of a house. There was a picture of Marigold from the first grade, missing two front teeth, and another of Rose dressed for her first school dance with Silas Monteque, his jacket too big and her with a bashful smile. And in the middle of the wall was a picture of Momma, Papa, Rose, Marigold, and me in front of the Greater Saints AME Church.

I gazed up at the porch. Me and Marigold still hadn't taken down that puny string of holiday lights from last Christmas hanging along the porch banister. I hadn't wanted to put up a Christmas tree or any kind of decorations after Momma died, but Marigold insisted, saying it was what Momma would have wanted. I didn't argue with her. Marigold was always smarter than me and it showed whenever we argued.

After Rose died, folks always liked to compare me and Marigold, like we was two different shoes. Like I was a harlot's high heel and she was a sturdy oxford. Marigold was the smart one. I was the pretty one. Marigold was the one who made good decisions. I was the one who made fast decisions. Marigold worked hard at getting rid of what she called her "accent." Me? I just talked the way I talked. Marigold, with all her dreams of going to college and becoming a lawyer. And then there was me. I didn't have no dreams unless I was asleep. So maybe I enjoyed a social outing more than I did a schoolbook. But that didn't make me a bad person. Why people always think things got to be this way or that with nothing in between? Hell, me and Marigold was more alike than we was different.

She would understand my leaving.

I was doing this for both of us. When I got settled somewhere, I would call Marigold and explain everything. Maybe I could send for her, and we could live together again. She'd understand. She was the smart one.

I tucked myself behind the magnolia. There weren't any cars out this late at night, but I couldn't be sure someone wouldn't come along and talk the next morning of having seen me out front. I looked up at Marigold's room. Her light was still on, but I knew she was asleep. She was twenty-two years old, one year older than me, and still afraid of the dark. What ghosts had she created to be afraid of?

Here in Jackson, everything between colored folks and white folks was throbbing hot like a tinderbox about to blow. Marigold told me about that new law the president signed in early July that meant colored folks could go wherever white folks went, and through the front door, too—restaurants, hotels—no more Jim Crow. But the president could sign as many laws as he wanted, it still wouldn't stop the evil inside the hearts of Mississippi white folks. That new law came too late to stop them from probably killing those poor boys up in Neshoba County about a month ago. It came too late for all them colored bodies that had been tossed in the Pearl River, an open grave of warm water and hungry fish. Ever since they assassinated Medgar Evers last year, white folks was bolder now than they'd ever been before. But colored folks were bound and determined to fight back any way they could without winding up dead.

As for me, I was finished with Jackson, Mississippi. I packed Momma's old carpetbag with the few belongings I owned, along with Papa's .38 pistol. The gun Papa showed me and my sisters. He used to say, *All that marching and peaceful protesting is fine. But if somebody come up in here messing with me and mines, they gonna catch a bullet in the ass.* This was the same gun I used to take care of Huxley.

Finally, a beam of light rounded the corner. I ground my cigarette into the trunk of the magnolia tree and quickly pulled a stick of Beemans gum from my purse. I popped it in my mouth and hoped it would do the job. I brushed the front of my green shirtdress and plumped my hair a bit. I'd straightened it and wore it down on my shoulders. That's the way he liked it. Gravel crackled underneath the car as it cut across the driveway. I peeked from around the old magnolia.

Dewey Leonard pulled up in his brand-new Bonneville Coupe, all candy apple red and chrome, beside the house. He flipped a lock of strawberry blond hair from his eyes. Dewey was the kind of guy who always got what he wanted. I met Dewey while I worked at his daddy's feed and supply store. Over the past couple weeks, I'd made him some promises. Dewey was all lit up like he had come ready to collect on every single one of 'em. Marigold would kill me if she knew I had been messing around with a white boy.

I tossed my bag in the back and slipped inside the car. It smelled like new leather seats and Old Spice aftershave. He looked all wide-eyed, full of excitement, as if we were off on our own Bonnie and Clyde adventure.

He stroked my hair. "You are so beautiful," he whispered before he kissed me. "We should be in Birmingham by sunrise. Maybe you should try to get some sleep?" he said.

"I'm fine."

He smiled at me. "I love you, Violet."

I nuzzled my head on his shoulder. "You already know how I feel about you, Dewey, honey." I wasn't no ways close to being in love with Dewey, but I could put on a good show. And just because he was whisking me away up north didn't mean I would start to act any differently.

"Did you tell your sister . . . you know, about us leaving?"

"No, Dewey. It's better this way." I hadn't breathed a word to Marigold or anybody else that me and Dewey was together. Colored folks would think I was crazy, and white folks would kill me with their bare hands. "What about your daddy? Did you tell him you was leaving town?"

"Don't worry about my daddy. I'll take care of him when we get up north. You can be sure of that."

"What do you mean?"

Dewey patted my hand. "Violet, I've got a plan to take care of everything. Just trust me."

"Okay." I nervously glanced around the neighborhood. "We better get going." I didn't have a clue what he was talking about, and I didn't care, either. I just wanted to get out of town, and Dewey was my ticket.

"You pack some sandwiches or something?"

"Uh-uh. Sorry, we ain't have nothing back at the house. Let's just stop and get something along the way."

"Well . . ."

I already knew what he was thinking. We both knew there was no way any restaurant south of the Mason-Dixon Line would let a white man and a colored woman step foot inside as a couple and sit down to enjoy a meal together. It was just the way the world worked down here, no matter how many laws the president signed.

"It'll be okay, Dewey. Really, I don't mind."

Dewey cranked the handle on his door to lower the window before leaning his elbow out. A warm breeze rushed into the car. Dewey squeezed my hand. "Why'd you finally change your mind and decide to marry me?"

"Dew, ain't it enough that I'm here?"

He gave me an understanding nod. He was like every other man, always asking questions and looking for me to tell him what he wanted to hear. The first time Dewey asked me to run away and marry him, I thought he was joking. A white man wanting to marry a colored woman was like a man walking on the moon. Things like that didn't happen in Mississippi, but Dewey said he had a plan for the two of us. He had gone to college up north for a year but came back south right before I met him. Rumor had it he flunked out. He said his daddy had been against his going up north, and after his return to Jackson, his daddy considered him a "solid failure." I knew the real reason Dewey wanted to marry me was because he and his daddy didn't get along. Dewey was always trying to prove something, like he was a better man than his daddy. I didn't want no parts of their family feud. All I wanted was a way out of Jackson, Mississippi.

"I just hope you know how much I love you, Violet. I'd do anything to make you happy. Things will be better up north. Trust me."

"I do."

I hadn't told Dewey what Huxley did to me. Or what I did to Huxley. I didn't need Dewey fighting my battles for me. I just needed him to get me as far away from Jackson as possible.

"You all set?" he whispered.

I took one last look at Papa's "palace" and that string of Christmas lights sagging across the front porch banister. Marigold's light would be on for the rest of the night.

"Yeah, I'm ready."

Dewey pulled off onto the street. I prayed to God to forgive me for what I'd done to Huxley and for what I was about to do to Dewey.

2
Violet

The car quietly hummed along the road, straight out of Mississippi and the white-hot hell that it was. I turned up the radio and we rode in silence for a little while, listening to Patsy Cline warbling out a song about falling to pieces over some man. The country music station finally faded out. Dewey chimed up, talking nonstop about his big dream of the two of us living up north, getting married and having a bunch of sweet brown babies underfoot. I listened and smiled occasionally like that was my dream, too. Men always like to make plans for a woman as if she ain't got dreams and a mind of her own. Nearly every man I'd ever met talked to me like I was four years old and didn't understand English. Maybe men pretend to be smart so they can keep up with the women who really are.

We were probably fifty miles inside the Alabama state line when Dewey's ramblings came to a halt. The whirl of flashing red and blue lights and the wailing siren of a police car right on our tail. My heart darn near jumped up inside my throat. Had they found Huxley's body already? How did anyone know I was in this car with Dewey?

"Shit!" Dewey said.

I blinked back at the bright beams and the spinning lights of the police car. All my plans might be ruined. "Were you speeding? What's going on?"

"Quick! Slide back over to the window. It'll be okay," Dewey said. I coulda swore his voice cracked.

Dewey slowed down. The tires rumbled over rocks and gravel as he pulled the car to a full stop on the side of the road. Dewey ran his hand through his hair and cocked his head toward the window, waiting for the cop. From the wide-eyed look on his face, he was probably as scared as me. Neither one of us had any business in this car together. What we were doing was against the law. He was a white man out in the middle of nowhere, in the middle of the night, with a colored woman. Even he wasn't sure whether he could protect me from the spiteful hate of another white man. All it would take was this cop figuring out we was a couple and Dewey could go to jail; it could be even worse for me.

He turned to face me. "It'll be fine. Just don't say anything. Not a word."

Dewey didn't have to give me no instructions. I had no plans to talk to this cop or any other cop after the last time I stood inside a police station. Momma was the one who taught us girls how we should address the police. But it didn't matter none when me and Marigold went to the police station after Huxley attacked me. The police back in Mississippi wasn't the least bit interested in protecting and serving people like me. And from what I knew about Alabama, it wasn't no different here, either.

The cop took his good and sweet time walking up to the side of the car. Dewey pulled his wallet from his pocket and sat it on the seat between us, ready just in case the officer asked him for identification. I was in trouble if he asked me for the same. By the time he appeared at Dewey's window, my hands trembled slick with the sweat of fear. I sat calm and quiet like Momma had taught us—*No fast moves, don't make eye contact, be polite, yes sir and no sir.* Momma had taught us to become invisible in the presence of white people. In other words, she had taught us to stay alive. *Never give them a reason to harm you, even though they might still hit you over the head with their billy club just for good measure,* she would say.

The officer peered inside the car. "Young man, you realize you were swerving awhile back there?"

"I'm sorry, Officer. Just a little tired, I guess."

"Uh-huh." He pointed his flashlight inside the car and it landed directly on me. "What we got here?"

I suddenly remembered Papa's gun in my bag. *No fast moves.*

"This here is Alberta. She works for our family. I'm driving her over to Virginia to take care of my sick grandmother," Dewey said, as cool as a cucumber.

"Uh-huh," the policeman said flatly. He steered the flashlight across the back seat of the car. "That there's yo' bag?"

My stomach churned and I could feel the first inklings of sweat pop up along my hairline. But I didn't answer him. If he looked inside, I would be off to jail faster than I could blink—unless I got to the gun first. And if I did, I might have to leave more dead bodies. I could feel Dewey staring at me. My only thought now—*Get Papa's gun.*

"Hey, nigger, I'm talking to you!"

"Yes, sir." I never looked at him. *No eye contact.* My heart pounded inside me like a locomotive barreling through my chest.

"I asked you a question. What's in the bag?"

"Just a few things for the trip. Clothes, shoes, sir."

I stared down at my hands. I was scared as hell, but I wouldn't give him the satisfaction of bringing me to tears. I mulled over what to do next once he found that gun. Run? If I could get to the gun first, could I get a shot off? I'd save myself before I let this man cart me off to jail. What about Dewey? He didn't know about the gun or Huxley or who I really was. The cop leaned in toward Dewey, maybe to get a better look at me.

Dewey cleared his throat. "Officer, I'm really sorry. I guess maybe it's been a long drive."

"Where y'all comin' from?" the cop said.

"Jackson, Mississippi. My daddy owns Leonard Feed & Supply." And then Dewey did what he did best. He used his daddy's money to get out of this mess. His voice became lighter, friendlier. He ran his fingers through his hair and smiled at the cop. "Matter of fact, he's planning on opening up a store in Alabama soon." Dewey chuckled and threw the officer a big wide grin. I didn't know if that was true, but I sure as hell hoped it would work. "Like I said, we're just trying to get to Virginia. Get to my grandmother's place. I'll grab a cup of coffee as soon as I can."

"Hmm." The cop flashed the light back in my face again. But at least it wasn't on Momma's bag anymore. I never took my eyes off my hands in my lap. Quiet. Obedient. In that moment, I was a model citizen in the

Jim Crow South. And because of that, I was alive. He finally flipped the flashlight off. "I'll let you off with a warning this time. Watch yourself."

"I appreciate that, Officer. Thank you."

He walked off and we both sat silent. Dewey watched him through the rearview mirror as the cop got back in his car and made a U-turn in the center of the road before speeding away. Dewey let out a long deep sigh. He squeezed my hand. "It's okay now. He's headed in the opposite direction."

Dewey slowly pulled the car back onto the road. Neither of us spoke another word before sunrise. I couldn't tell which one of us was more humiliated by what had happened—Dewey, having to lie and tell the cop that the woman he loved was his maid, or me, with a gun in my bag and a dead body behind me, grateful that he did it so that I got to live another day.

* * *

By daybreak, we pulled into Birmingham, Alabama. I peered out the car window. Steel mills blew curling plumes of smoke and sulfur gas from their huge furnace stacks. The traffic picked up and soon we were amid streetlights and a few people mingling here and there. The pink-orange tint of early day slowly climbed over the top of the buildings we passed. The Municipal Auditorium. The Jefferson County Courthouse. A public library. All places that Dewey could freely go in and out of. Places where I was required to enter through the rear or only on certain days. Birmingham, Alabama, wasn't no better than Jackson, Mississippi, with Bull Connor turning loose fire hydrants and barking dogs on us and the Ku Klux Klan bombing a church with four little colored girls inside.

Was I far enough from Mississippi to risk it?

A few nervous butterflies dipped in my stomach. I decided Birmingham, Alabama, was far enough. This might be my last chance.

"Dew, honey, I'm hungry. Can we stop and get a bite?" I wasn't really hungry. I hadn't had an appetite for anything except freedom.

"Well, uh . . ." Dewey was always thinking about the races and how nobody wanted us to mix. I thought about it, too, I guess.

"Maybe if we go someplace close into town, near a bus station or a train station. Sometimes things are a lil' more pleasant. You know, since folks always coming and going."

"Yeah, that makes sense."

A few minutes later, we pulled into the parking lot of a restaurant called the Eat-in Station. God was looking out for me because the restaurant was located right next to the Greyhound bus station. People milled about, in and out of the place. My guess was that a couple buses were on a layover and people were using the time to stretch their legs a bit and grab breakfast.

Hanging out front of the restaurant was the big, bold sign that greeted every customer in the South, like a lettered guard dog at the door: COLOREDS IN THE REAR. I hated the fact that signs dividing us up was most times bigger than the signs advertising the goods and services inside. Dewey said I'd never have to look at another one of those signs again up north. Apparently, they weren't following that new law Marigold kept talking about, just like back in Jackson. Jim Crow was alive and well here, too.

Me and Dewey spotted the sign at the same time as we stepped outside the car. Even though Papa and Momma tried to cover me and my sisters from the harshest rigors of the South, we knew where we were and what our place was supposed to be. We were young, but we weren't blind. Back in Jackson, we either ordered our things through the Sears catalog or shopped on Farish Street, the black business district. If we didn't have a need to interact with whites, we didn't. Momma used to say she worked in white folks' houses cooking and cleaning so me, Rose, and Marigold wouldn't have to. Momma and Papa provided what they could for us, and if they couldn't, that meant we didn't need it.

"It's okay, Dew. You go on inside. I need to freshen up in the bathroom." I reached inside the car and pulled my bag from the back seat. "You order something for both of us. I'll meet you back here at the car." I squeezed his arm for reassurance before I snatched it away and glanced around to see if anyone was watching. White men could be run out of town for displaying anything close to genuine affection for a colored woman. Dewey didn't seem to mind, though. I watched him walk away. He turned around and gave a brief embarrassed look back at me. I smiled.

Bag in hand, I quickly headed to the rear of the restaurant and scurried past the line of colored folks waiting to order food from the back window of the Eat-in Station, past a couple of women coming out of the dilapidated "colored" restroom. My heartbeat sped up as I crossed the alley, peeking back every now and then to make sure Dewey wasn't following me. I picked up my pace, damn near running as I got closer to the bus station. It was a little hard to run in my heels, but I made do. I scrambled farther down the alley, my head light and fuzzy. *Could I get away?*

A couple minutes later, I stood behind a line of parked Greyhound buses. I glanced back down the alley, nary a living soul behind me.

I wound through a couple parked buses and scooted inside the Birmingham bus station. It was hot, crowded. A frenzy of travelers of all races—some weary, some excited—bustled about. I heard a child screaming and the loudspeaker announcing the arrival of the number 57 from Huntsville. A few minutes later, a crackled voice announced the final call for the departure of the number 28 headed to Washington, DC. I strode up to the ticket counter.

I was practically panting from the run to escape Dewey. "What time's the next bus to Los Angeles, California?" California was as far away from Jackson as I could get. I had a high school friend who lived there, and I could stay put at her place while I looked for a job.

A white man, pale as a cotton sheet, sat behind the counter with a bored expression. "Two o'clock this afternoon."

That wouldn't work. I had to catch the first thing smokin' out of here. And Dewey might come looking for me in the bus station at any minute. I took a quick peek behind me at the entrance. I couldn't spend a minute more in this station than I needed to. I'd have to go north. But I didn't know anybody up north. Besides, the police and Dewey would expect me to head north like most colored folks did.

"Come on, gal. Are you gonna buy a ticket or not? I got customers behind you."

I turned around again. A short brown woman with two small kids hanging on her coattail peered up at me. I smiled at her and turned back to the clerk. "What's the next bus leaving?"

The clerk glanced up at the clock on the wall. "You got about six minutes. Maybe you can make the number twenty-eight. Headed to Washington, DC."

Marigold had gone to the March on Washington last year with some of the people from her job. She was still talking about that city. I didn't know anybody there, but that was good enough for me. "I'll take a one-way ticket."

I reached inside Dewey's wallet and pulled out a twenty-dollar bill. I had caught a lucky break when Dewey left his wallet on the car seat. The money I had in my purse might not carry me as far as Dewey's cash. If the good Lord was with me, maybe he hadn't reached for it inside the restaurant yet and discovered it missing. Hopefully, it would be a few minutes before Dewey even realized what was going on, that his woman and his wallet were missing and that I had stolen it. Restaurants collected the money from colored folks before they even started cooking the food. But white folks in a restaurant could have a full meal, dessert, and a loud belch before anybody thought about collecting their money.

The clerk seemed like he was moving in slow motion. Then another man behind the counter walked over to ask him a question. I only had six minutes to freedom. The longer I stood in this bus station, the faster my heart went to beating. I glanced back at the door. No sign of Dewey or, thank God, the police. The two men finally stopped talking, and the clerk slid my change across the counter, along with a one-way ticket to freedom. "Door seven. Next."

I hustled through the station and back outside. The driver was just about to close the door. "Hey!" I yelled. I hopped on, holding a tight grip on Momma's carpetbag. The bus had a few empty seats in the front. I thought about testing all them new laws Marigold talked about, but I didn't want no trouble. I had brought enough this far along with me. I headed straight to the back of the bus and found a seat next to another colored woman. The driver closed the door. The bus engine whined as we pulled out of the station and I headed for Washington, DC.

Alone.

With any luck, I could outrun Dewey Leonard and the Jackson, Mississippi, police.

3
Marigold Richards

The silver alarm clock rattled on the bedside table at 7:30 with a noisy wake-up call that, lately, set my teeth on edge. For the past couple months, loud noises, strong odors, the least little thing was a reminder. I slammed the alarm clock to silence before I sat up on the side of the bed and turned off the lamp. I waited for the wave of nausea to wash over me like it had been doing every morning for nearly two months. I moved slowly. No fast moves to get out of bed because that only made the nausea worse. A minute later, the familiar queasy feeling eased in, moving up from my stomach and through the back of my throat, my tongue tingling and making way for the urge to vomit. There was no more denying what was there. *We were there.*

I was pregnant.

The house was quiet. No singing. No clanging pots and clattering dishes coming from the kitchen. And praise God, no smell of fried bacon. All the usual tell-tale sounds and smells of Violet being up and about. She must have stayed out late again last night. As usual. I hadn't told Violet about my pregnancy. I would tell her eventually, but not right away. What would she think of me? Women in my so-called delicate condition needed to be mindful of what this might look like. And besides, Violet might gloat over the fact that for all her loose ways, she'd never been stupid enough to get pregnant. I hated keeping secrets from her, since it was just the two of us left now. But I didn't need my sister passing judgment. It was best for me to figure this whole mess out first before I told anyone.

I slid into my house slippers and slowly padded down the hallway for the kitchen. Alaga Syrup. RC Cola. Gingersnaps. I made a mental list of the things I needed to pick up from the Jitney Jungle today. I was down to the last few gingersnaps. Those small brown cookies were the only things I could keep down in the morning.

Sunlight poured in through the red-and-white gingham curtains in the kitchen. Momma had made those curtains the year I started high school. Hanging on the wall over the stove were the big wooden fork and spoon

Momma called decoration. Violet and I used to giggle about how the kitchen looked like a room-size picnic basket. Everything in the kitchen was clean, just like I'd left it the night before. *Where is Violet?* By now she'd have left a sink full of dishes for me to clean up as she hustled out the door, making up some excuse about being late and cleaning up when she got home from work.

"Violet!" I yelled from the kitchen. "You're gonna be late for work." For the past few months, she had been working at Leonard Feed & Supply, cleaning the back room. Sometimes she picked up odd jobs like babysitting Miss Alfreda's kids when she had to travel as a visiting nurse. Violet was probably a fun babysitter, but I sometimes wondered how responsible she was with young kids. I pulled a glass from the cabinet and filled it with water.

"Violet?"

No answer.

"Violet, it's almost eight o'clock." Ever since Rose had died, I had to step up to be the responsible sister, which included making sure Violet got up and off to work on time, even now despite the fact we were both adults. I missed Rose even though she'd been dead eight years this coming August. When she died, there was no one left to prod me out of my shell the way she did. No more big sister to look after me. I became the big sister, and I wasn't any good at it, not like Rose. Since Momma died last year, I didn't offer sisterly advice or even ask Violet where she was going or who she'd been with. I loved Violet. I just didn't know how to show it.

I paced back down the hall to Violet's room and opened the door. The whole room looked neat and untouched in a way Violet never left it in the morning. Her dresser was clear. Her bed had been made, the pink chenille bedspread smooth without a wrinkle. And in the center of the bed—a note.

Marigold,

I'm leaving Jackson. I messed up, but I'll die before I spend my life in a cage. I'll call you when I get settled. I'm sorry. Keep me in your prayers. I love you.

Violet

I scanned the room again. The only evidence of her presence was the faint scent of her Camay soap lingering in the space. I opened her closet. Empty hangers hung from the closet rod like a row of wire skeletons. Every trace of my baby sister was gone, including Momma's old carpetbag.

I looked down at the note again . . . *I messed up.*

I raced back up to the hall closet, as fast as the nausea would allow. I dragged down hatboxes and blankets. Momma's old sewing kit. Me and Violet's graduation caps and gowns. But it wasn't there. I tackled the floor of the closet, throwing shoes and umbrellas out behind me. Nothing. Violet was gone and so was Papa's pistol. I slumped onto the floor.

I messed up.

Another wave of nausea washed over me. I leaned against the closet door and slipped my hair scarf from my head. I knew exactly what she'd done and I was powerless to stop it. We'd both been adrift since Momma died last year. Violet blamed herself for everything that had happened. But I didn't blame her. Who could foretell how one small incident could send an entire family into a tailspin? And now this thing with Huxley Broadus might undo us both.

I knew my baby sister better than anyone. Beautiful. Smart and fearless. A dangerous combination for any man who dared to cross her. Headstrong almost to a fault, she never backed down or cowered to anyone. She so easily did all the things I was afraid to do—go to parties and miss curfew, smoke cigarettes out behind the house, wear lipstick when Momma forbade it. And even when they fussed at her, it seemed to roll off her back like morning dew slipping from a blade of grass.

Momma and Papa had plans for their girls. All three of us were supposed to go to college to become teachers. But none of us were interested in teaching. Rose had confessed to me that she wanted to be a writer. She was well on her way, too, before she died. I wanted to be a lawyer. And Violet? She wasn't quite sure what she wanted to be. And it showed through her grades. College wasn't in her future. Sad, too, because out of all of us, Violet was the smartest. She just didn't believe it.

I got up from the floor, returned to the kitchen, and sat down at the table. I nursed my glass of water and the bad feeling I had about Violet running away.

This thing with Huxley was a whole different ball of wax. To add insult to injury, the Jackson police, lily white and Negro-hating, barely batted an eye when we went to the station to file a police report. *Why were you in that neighborhood at that time of night? What were you wearing? Why weren't you accompanied by a man? Did you make eyes at this man or lead him on?* Questions that made it seem like it was Violet's fault that some man would take out his rage against her. And once the police officer asked her to describe the man, he placed his pen down and rubbed his forehead. *Are you sure it was Huxley Broadus, a white man?! Why would a white man want to rape YOU?*

I closed the bag of gingersnaps, then I did exactly what Violet asked me to do. I prayed for her. I prayed that she would run as far and fast as she could from Jackson, Mississippi. I also prayed that Huxley Broadus understood the depth of his mistake as he went to meet his maker.

* * *

An hour later, the nausea had eased, and I was dressed and ready for work. I'd finally made up my mind that today was the day I would tell him about the baby. But I had to be smart about it. It was dicey, telling a man that you were carrying his child even though you weren't wearing his wedding band. I didn't want him to think I was trying to trap him into marriage. He was a decent guy. He would do the right thing. A good man wouldn't let his own child wander through the world without a proper name.

I remember when our cousin Birdie Mae got pregnant in high school. It was the talk of the whole town until Uncle Bud forced Charlie to marry Birdie. The two of them moved to a small town in Georgia. That's just the way it worked—if you got pregnant, you got married. After Birdie and Charlie got married, the talk settled down. But the town's gossipmongers didn't stop people from having relations without the benefit of a wedding ring or a preacher. Women would just find ways to hide the consequences or make them go away. That's just the way it was too. Now Papa wasn't here to force anybody to marry me. I rubbed my hands across my stomach. Everything would work out. I felt sure of it. There was a child to think about. We'd do what was best for the baby.

I was finishing up my makeup when the doorbell rang. I scurried to the front door and peeked through the curtain. *Oh no!* I opened the door.

"Hey, you ready to go?" Roger Bonny stood at the front door smiling at me, dressed in a blue-and-white box-cut bowling shirt and a pair of slacks. This was what he called his job-hunting outfit. But nobody in Jackson was going to hire a Negro man who wasn't wearing a pair of overalls and a humble attitude. Roger, with all his big dreams, wasn't cut out for working in a city like Jackson.

"Roger?" He leaned in and kissed me on the cheek. "What are you doing here?"

"I thought I'd swing by and give you a lift to work before I go out job hunting."

"Uh . . . oh."

"Now what kind of greeting is that for your favorite chauffeur?"

In high school, Roger was considered a great catch. Tall, handsome, wavy hair, and hazel eyes to go along with all his gold-plated trophies for varsity track and basketball. But now, several years out of high school and no steady job, he had finally worked his way down to dating me. He once told me that his mother thought he was "dating down." Why she said that—and why he told me—was no surprise. Neither one of them was the smartest person in Mississippi. She was light, bright, and almost white, the type of woman who slathered her face in Nadinola bleaching cream every night, afraid of turning darker than a paper bag and thus of a lower class in her mind. They rented the house just a few streets over from us with no visible appearances of living any better than us. It always frustrated me that some people in our race had no interest in standing up for our rights. Roger's mother ignorantly believed that being light-skinned would save them from the white man's bigotry. She was just as misguided as the poor whites who thought they were better than us, all of them too ignorant to realize survival didn't depend on skin tone but on economic status.

He smiled at me quizzically. "You okay?"

"Yeah. Yeah, I'm fine. Just let me get my bag." Roger's arrival had thrown me off. I needed more time to gather my thoughts, to figure out how all this would work.

I locked up the house, and Roger stood at the car, holding open the door to his beat-up old blue Plymouth Belvedere. Today, it was working. I climbed inside and prayed it would make it to the Platinum office building on Farish Street, where I worked for the Mississippi Summer Project. The Summer Project was a volunteer campaign started by several civil rights groups, including the NAACP and the Southern Christian Leadership Conference, the SCLC. Among its many goals, the Summer Project worked hard to prevent Negroes from being forced off jury rolls. To do that, we had to get people registered to vote. If you don't vote, you don't serve on a jury. That's why all-white juries prevailed in the South. We were doomed before the trial even started when we went to court.

Working as a secretary for the Summer Project was the best job I'd had since I graduated from high school. After Papa's death, I couldn't afford to go to college. Being around so many smart and dedicated people now from all over the country gave me a sense of purpose I had never had before. Violet always teased me, saying all those big words I learned in school were finally paying off. Even though we attended substandard schools and used the old torn-up books handed down from the white schools, I loved learning. And now, on my job, I was learning from some of the smartest people in the country. I was saving up my money to move to Washington, DC, one day. I dreamed of going to Howard University and on to law school. Maybe I could go to college one day without it being a national news story like that young man who integrated Ole Miss.

Roger turned the key a couple times before the car engine rumbled to a start and we headed down Oakland Avenue. This was the colored section of town. The houses weren't fancy by a long shot. Almost every house in this neighborhood needed some type of repair and a paint job, necessities none of us had the ownership status or money to do anything about. But most folks did the best they could by planting flowers and keeping their walkways neat and tidy.

"So, what's the count now?" Roger asked.

"Count?" I leaned my head toward the open car window, hoping for a breath of fresh air to help the waning nausea. Instead, I smelled the remnants of someone burning garbage, and another wave of nausea slid through me again.

"How many times have I asked you to marry me

now? Five, six? When are we gonna get married and move up north?"

"Roger, we talked about this. We always talk about this. Now isn't the right time. We're at a crucial point in the project. With the new law and the civil rights groups down here, we're pretty busy."

"Listen to me, the Klan probably killed them three boys that went missing up in Neshoba County, and two of them were white. If they do that to their own, why you think they're suddenly gonna switch up and give colored folks anything? My momma said you and those people you work with are just sending folks into harm's way."

Of course his mother would say that. What other stupidity was she filling his head with?

"So what does your *mother* think we should do?"

Roger went quiet for a moment. Maybe deep in the recesses of his brain, he knew his mother wasn't exactly a vestige of knowledge on the civil rights movement.

Roger just shook his head. "I'm telling you, Marigold, y'all are wasting your time. I ain't met a white man yet that wouldn't take a baseball bat to our head to keep us from voting. I don't care how many laws the government put in place. Once the racists realize we're not voting for them, they'll snatch back all them laws. Just watch."

Despite what Roger and his mother thought, I knew we were on the cusp of something big. And I wanted to be a part of it. All those deaths—bodies hung and burned and buried in pursuit of civil rights for all of us—cannot have been in vain. All we wanted was the opportunity to sit at a lunch counter and enjoy a cup of coffee and a meal or a chance to vote for the people who governed us. Nothing more, nothing less. But white people in Mississippi knew how valuable the right to vote was, which was why they fought so hard to keep it from us. Roger never understood this, and sometimes I grew weary trying to explain it to him.

"Why can't we just get married and move up north?"

"I can't just go off and leave my job. They're counting on me. We've got a stack of court filings I need to type up and—"

"Can't you do more good up north? Why do you want to continue to fight a losing battle down here in the South? Nothing's going to change. It's the way it's always been and it's the way it'll always be."

"What makes you so sure things will be so much better up north?"

"I told you my younger brother, Frankie, is up there and he said up north, colored folks already got it as good as white folks. No riding in the back of the bus. No crossing the street when they walk by. We live just like they live up there."

"Well, here in the South, we are fully entitled to live like that too. And we should also be able to vote. One man. One vote. It's in the Constitution."

"Okay, so the law was passed earlier this month, right? Have you stepped inside the *front* door of a restaurant lately instead of walking around to the back to be served?"

"That's why we have to keep doing this. We have to force them to give us what's lawfully ours now. All that Jim Crow business is over."

Roger shook his head wearily. "Like that's ever gonna happen."

"Let's just talk about it later." It seemed like we had had this conversation a thousand times before. God had given Roger a gorgeous face to compensate for his lack of intelligence.

"C'mon, how long we been dating? Going on two years now." He leaned his hand across the seat and rubbed my thigh. "I wanna make you my wife, take things further." He squeezed my thigh and smiled at me. The guilt started to eat a hole right through me. Roger and I had never had sex and he was getting restless about it. He figured marrying me would put an end to that. I only had so much time before this baby would put an end to a lot of things.

"Stop right here. I can walk the rest of the way. I need the fresh air." He pulled the car to the curb, and I kissed him on the cheek. "We'll talk about it later. Promise."

"All right."

I hopped out of the car and waved back. I hustled up Farish Street and inside the Platinum Building. Ever since Momma died, my life seemed to get more complicated by the day, and not having her here made me wonder all kinds of things about myself. A marriage proposal from one man and a baby on the way by another. Momma would be so ashamed of me.

4
Marigold

The Civil Rights Act of 1964 was signed into law on July 2, and in the weeks following, not much had changed in Mississippi. Change often worked like that—desperately needed, slow to come, and life-altering on its arrival. Despite the law, some white people in the South tried to pretend they were above the law or took extreme measures rather than follow it. The Rialto Theater closed its doors rather than allow Negroes to come and go freely inside. The owner of the Robert E. Lee Hotel closed its doors, too, rather than allow Negroes to stay as guests. Dr. King was right when he called Mississippi "America's shame."

Groups like the NAACP and SCLC and the Congress of Racial Equality, or CORE, as we called it, were sending in investigators—Negroes who attempted to register at segregated hotels or eat inside segregated restaurants. And young people, Negro and white, my age, some even younger, volunteered with the Student Nonviolent Coordinating Committee, called SNCC, to get Negroes registered to vote, especially out in the rural areas of Mississippi. All this change made white people restless and afraid. Since Medgar Evers's assassination last year, we were ramping up to make sure we fought as hard as we could for the right to vote. The Ku Klux Klan could silence his voice, but they couldn't stop his movement.

And fighting just as hard as us was the Mississippi Citizens Council, a group of white civic leaders and wealthy business owners who were staunchly opposed to integration. The Citizens Council was nothing more than the respectable face of the Ku Klux Klan, and much more sinister, too. Slack-jawed monsters draped in seersucker suits and straw fedoras using all their wealth and power to keep segregation alive and strong in Mississippi. They had become the biggest obstacle to getting businesses to follow the new law.

When I stepped inside the Summer Project office, the place was buzzing with all the volunteers and civil rights activists in from different parts of the country. College students, teachers, lawyers, all working toward the same goal—equality between the races. The Mississippi Summer Project had been the most important thing for Negroes in this state. Our office was on the top floor of the two-story Platinum Building on Farish Street. It was a shotgun office space that ran from the front of the building to the back.

The office housed the six of us who regularly worked there, plus the numerous volunteers who poured in and out on any given day. The windows would stick or not open at all and the furniture, a few old metal desks in the center of the room with several lumpy upholstered chairs throughout, had seen its better days. We had a couple rusty metal fans placed about that circulated small tunnels of hot air through the room. But we were grateful to have the space.

I spotted James Scott, one of the NAACP lawyers, standing at his desk talking to a tall, attractive woman I'd never seen around the office. For a moment, a twinge of jealousy ran through me. He handed her a document and I realized she was a "tester," a volunteer who would go out into the local county clerk's offices to attempt to register to vote. Of course, the clerk would find some excuse to deny her application.

Mississippi had no shortage of ways to keep us from voting. The so-called intelligence tests required Negroes to write out sections of the Mississippi Constitution. If you failed to cross a *t* or dot an *i* you were disqualified from voting. Or if you failed to interpret the state constitution to the satisfaction of the circuit court clerk, you were disqualified from voting. Some Negroes with PhDs were turned away for failing that requirement. We'd even heard stories of some people who were denied the right to vote because they failed to correctly count the number of jelly beans in a jar or predict the number of bubbles in a bar of soap. The tester's job was to bring back his or her denied application, along with everything they were told as to why their application was denied. The lawyers used that information for the various petitions and documents we filed with the court.

I settled my things in one of the desk drawers and walked over to James when the woman left. James was a tall, honey-colored man, barely thirty years old. He wore tortoiseshell glasses that gave him the appearance of authority and intelligence. He had left his law practice in New York City to come to Mississippi to work on the Summer Project. His commitment to this work was so inspiring it made me believe every Negro in this country would be able to vote one day.

"James, I need to talk to you." My voice trembled. "You got a minute?"

"Hey, Marigold. Of course. What you got?" A slight

New York accent dotted his speech and always made me think of how exciting it must be to live in a place so big.

"Uh . . . can we step outside . . . to talk?"

James gave me a serious expression. "Sure. Everything okay?"

I stepped out of the office with James behind me. We walked down the hall in silence until we reached the water fountains, careful not to block the ones for the white people.

"So what's going on?" he said.

"James . . . I . . . I don't know how to say this." My hands started to tremble and I wished he'd scoop me up in his arms at that moment. But I knew he couldn't. We had put on such a great act that no one in the office had a clue that we had been seeing each other socially. I looked up into his eyes and nearly dashed away from fear. Was I doing the right thing? Did I have any other choice?

"James . . ."

He lowered his voice and leaned in close. "Is everything okay?"

I lowered my voice to match his. "I'm gonna have a baby." I glanced around quickly, scared that someone might have heard me utter the words.

He slowly stood upright, his eyes opening wide with surprise. He took a step back. "A baby?! What are you talking about?"

"I . . . I missed my cycle . . . I—"

"Marigold, I don't know what to say. I mean . . ."

"I thought you should know." I heard the quiver in my voice again.

"Well, what are you going to do?"

"Me?"

James rubbed his forehead. "I'm sorry. Marigold, you're a nice girl. But . . ." This time *he* scoped the hallway for anyone who might be eavesdropping, his eyes flitting in all directions. "I . . . I didn't mean it that way."

My heart sank. I didn't know what I expected him to say, but somehow this wasn't the reaction I imagined. It wasn't like I was some worthless slut trying to bait him into something he didn't want. I took a deep breath. I decided to be patient. This had to be as much of a shock to him as it was to me when I finally figured out what was going on. "I guess I just thought we could talk and make some decisions together."

"You're right. I'm sorry. It's just that this is hitting me out of the blue." He nodded and smiled weakly at one of the volunteers who passed us in the hall. "Um . . . yeah. We should talk. But not here. Right now, I have to go out to the field with some testers. I won't be back in the office until tomorrow. We can talk tomorrow. Okay?"

I nodded. He patted my shoulder like I was another one of the testers before he walked off. I wanted to cry and scream and plead for him to come back. To hold me like he did all those other times. Instead, I returned to the office. Alone. A few minutes later, I watched James leave the office with the tall, attractive woman. Both of them smiling.

5
Violet

The bus was like a forty-foot can housing human sardines. All the various smells and sounds of the people on board dulled me until I finally fell asleep somewhere outside Leeds, Alabama. I didn't wake up again until the bus pulled into Atlanta. I had heard some good things about Atlanta, with Dr. Martin Luther King Jr. and his work for colored people. But still, Atlanta was in the Jim Crow South. And even though Dr. King fought tooth and nail for equality for us, it wasn't happening soon enough for me. Momma used to say I was impatient, too quick to pass judgment about things that take time. Maybe she was right. Or maybe she was just tired of waiting on all that change that never came for her. All I knew was that I wasn't moving until this bus pulled into Washington, DC.

I rubbed my eyes and yawned; then I thought about Marigold. She'd have read my note by now, probably all confused and angry that I hadn't talked to her before I left town. Talking wouldn't do no good. Nothing would have come of it anyway. Huxley sealed his own fate the night he raped me and left me on the side of that road.

Huxley Broadus.

I had shot a man dead. I didn't know which was worse, the night he attacked me or after, the way he would pop up in different places around town, wherever I was, grinning and winking at me like it was a game to him. Like it was his quiet way of telling me he would do it again and there wasn't nothing I could do about it. Poor white trash like Huxley could come and go as he pleased, do whatever he wanted when it came to colored women. But a colored man couldn't stand on the same side of the street with a white woman lest he be accused of disrespecting her, or worse, get himself killed.

The bus driver yelled into the bus that we had a twenty-minute rest stop in Atlanta. The lady next to me smiled. "This here is my stop," she said. I eased out of my seat to let her pass. I watched her as she gathered up her things and wondered if she lived here in Atlanta or was visiting someone. Maybe I should have chatted her up on the ride into Georgia. Or maybe I knew I couldn't. I was a woman on the run from a bunch of trouble back in Jackson. Making friends was the last thing I needed now.

I slipped back in the seat and took her spot at the window. I didn't need to relieve myself, so I was content to sit on this bus until the driver headed back out on the road. In some small towns, colored folks knew enough not to get off the bus because the whites there had their unwritten rule—NO COLOREDS ALLOWED. But Atlanta was safe. People mingled on and off the bus. Some of them had gone inside to buy sandwiches and drinks. Smelling their hot coffee and hamburgers reminded me that I hadn't eaten anything since yesterday. I thought about Dewey. Poor lovesick Dewey. He'd be okay. In time, another colored woman would come along to help him feel superior to his daddy and he'd forget all about me.

A few minutes later, the driver stepped back on the bus with two white policemen behind him. My stomach tumbled. *How did they find me?* I closed my eyes and tried to think. When I opened them again, I saw the first officer, tall, mean, and ugly, whispering to the other.

The tall, ugly cop spoke first. "Everybody, please remain seated. If you would, take out ya' ticket, we'll need to take a quick look. We just need a couple minutes." I swear he looked straight at me. *Oh God! They found Huxley's body in the woods out behind the Jitney Jungle.* My skin started to itch and I suddenly wanted to scratch it. I wanted to pull my skin off, just to feel something other than fear. I sat there, still as a stone.

Both officers headed straight to the back of the bus. There was only a handful of times I'd been scared in my life. And this was one of 'em. I felt like my head was spinning. How did they find me? Had the police in Jackson called ahead so these two policemen were waiting for this bus to arrive to take me away?

I reached down into my bag and eased my ticket out. I also reached down into the bottom of it and pulled the gun up. I rested it on top of my clothes before I closed the bag again. I would not go down without a fight. I leaned back in my seat, toying with the edges of the paper ticket. The first officer slowly strolled down the aisle, looking directly at each person he passed, like he was making some sort of mental checklist. The other officer, a few steps behind him, checked every ticket. If they were looking for me, they would have to carry me off this bus, 'cause I was never going back to Jackson on my own two legs.

The first officer was only two rows in front of me

when he stopped in his tracks at a young colored man across the aisle from me. The man stared out the window as if the officers weren't hovering over him.

"Hey, boy, where you headed? Let me see ya' ticket."

The young man gently pulled his ticket from his jacket pocket without a word.

"Ain't yo' name Oscar Mosley?"

"No, sir," the young man said, staring down at his hands in his lap. "My name's Jimmie Lee Boone."

"You got some ID on you to prove that?"

"No, sir."

"Let's go. You come on wit me," the officer said.

The young man calmly stood. Before he could slide from his seat, the tall, ugly cop grabbed him, dragging him by the collar of his shirt. The man yelled and stumbled into the aisle. The second cop rushed in, pulled his billy club, and cracked it across the young man's head. The man crumpled to the floor of the bus.

The cop landed another crack across the back of the man's head.

I gasped and yelled, "NO!"

The tall, ugly cop quickly turned and stared straight at me. "Shut up, gal, unless you want some of this too." He gave me a suspicious glare. "You traveling with this man? What's your name?"

Before I could answer, the other cop made a grunting sound as he struggled with the young man on the floor, their bodies tangled together. The cop dashed away from me to help his partner. Both cops dragged the young man down the aisle and off the bus.

Me and my big mouth. I sank back into my seat. I had no place trying to come to that man's defense when I had problems of my own. But I knew the way they was handling that man wasn't right. As soon as the three of them were off the bus, we all continued to watch out the window. Me and everybody on that bus watched the cops with our eyes glued to the windows and our hearts worried for that young man, one of us. A few people stood from their seats to get a better look. I heard an old lady behind me softly whisper, "Heavenly Father, keep him safe."

Oh God. What if the cop came back on this bus for me, thinking I might be traveling with that man? Should I try to get off the bus before they came back? I peered closer out my window, looking for more cops. I didn't see any. I looked out the window across the aisle. The cops had the man down on the ground in handcuffs. One cop stood with his boot squarely on the man's head. The other cop was talking to two other white men in suits. If I could get behind the station, maybe I could make a run for it.

I leaned down to gather my bag from underneath

the seat. But before I could stand, the driver was back. He closed the door with a loud swoosh of rubber and started up the engine. I looked back out the window. This time the cops were pushing the man into the back of the patrol car. One side of his face was bloody. I sank back into my seat, my head throbbing, and started to cry. Like Momma used to say, I was too quick to act and not long on thinking. And because of it, I would be living the rest of my days running—and hiding.

The bus eased out of the parking lot and onto the street. Maybe the bus driver had saved my life. Who knows if I would have been able to make a decent run for it in Atlanta? Now I was too scared to close my eyes and sleep. Too much had happened between here and Jackson. Twice I'd escaped the clutches of the police. Two times God had placed a hedge of protection around me. How many more chances did I have before God gave up on me?

I decided to do what I always did when I was scared.

I ran to my dead sister, Rose.

6
Violet

The bus cruised onto the highway as I pulled a tattered black-and-white composition book from my bag. I ran my fingers along the curlicued handwriting on the cover.

The Very Private Diary of Rose Marian Richards— DO NOT OPEN!!!

The night me and Marigold split that bottle of Cutty Sark and divided up Momma's things, I'd kept Rose's diary. I don't rightly know why this little notebook was so important to me, but it was. I'd read through its pages hundreds of times. Maybe I was looking for some lesson from Rose or maybe I was looking for forgiveness for what I'd done. I turned to a random entry and hoped her words would soothe me.

April 4, 1956

Dear Diary,

Silas said we are going to kiss when we go to the school dance. I just hope he doesn't tell anybody. Momma would kill me if she knew I was planning to kiss a boy. I wonder what it will feel like.

Today, Momma made me go all over the neighborhood looking for Violet. I love my little sisters. God knows I do. But sometimes I wish I wasn't the one who is always responsible for them. In three years, I turn eighteen and I'm moving to New York City to become a writer. When I create stories, it's like Mississippi is a million miles away and color is for painting pictures instead of dividing people.

When I'm gone, my sisters will have to be responsible for themselves.

But it is nice sometimes when Momma makes me the one in charge. She says it's because I'm the oldest and I know things that I should teach them. She always tells me I'll have to be the one to watch over them when God calls her and Papa on to glory. I hate it when she talks about death and dying. But living here in Mississippi under such vicious hate and horrible rules keeps death on our minds all the time. What small mistake might we make or some willy-nilly lie a white person might tell that would be the end of us?

Anyway, I don't think I can teach my sisters everything. How can I teach Marigold to go outside and have some fun sometimes? She's such a serious girl. And how can I teach Violet the opposite? She only wants to play and have fun. Although sometimes I wish I could be more like Violet. Sometimes I get tired of always helping Momma in the kitchen or helping with the wash. But I'm fifteen, the oldest. I'm supposed to be the responsible one.

But when I turn eighteen, I'll only be responsible for myself.

Rose never lived to see eighteen, and I still hadn't become responsible.

7

Violet

The midday sun, bright and hot, beat through the bus window as we crawled to a stop in the parking lot of a Piggly Wiggly grocery store. Another rest stop. I looked down at Momma's old Timex on my wrist. We were almost two hours outside of Atlanta in a place called Chillicothe, Georgia. It wasn't much to look at. The few buildings I could see from the parking lot looked worn and were covered in the red clay dust of Georgia. I peered through the window. People ambled about, not really in any kind of rush. A little boy pushed a car tire down the road as an old man yelled after him. I felt like I was a million miles from home.

I remembered my cousin Birdie Mae lived in this town. I hadn't seen Birdie in years, but I always remembered her as somebody fun-loving, a person who liked to have a good time, like me. Birdie was a few years older than me and Marigold. She and her boyfriend dropped out of high school and got married when they found out she was pregnant. They moved to Chillicothe because he had family here.

Everybody got off the bus for the short rest break, including me this time. Outside, it felt like an invisible blanket of heat had been laid across the entire town and threatened to suffocate every man, woman, and beast. I was still jittery after all that business with the police back in Atlanta. I leaned against the brick wall of the Piggly Wiggly, pondering whether I'd be able to hide out in a town this small. Just long enough to let Huxley's body cool and the heat die down. It wasn't likely for Dewey or the police to find me out in the middle of Georgia.

Fifteen minutes later, I stood at the door of the grocery store and watched the bus pull off from the small port in the parking lot.

Maybe I should have seen that ride all the way through to Washington, DC, but I didn't want to risk running into the cops like the last two times. Hiding from the law, thinking about the law, having to deal with the law—all of it had tired me out. I just needed to lie low for a few days. I needed some time to think and to rest. Chillicothe, Georgia, seemed like it just might be the place to do that.

I pulled a hankie from Momma's carpetbag and wiped my brow before I batted a couple flies away. I had to find a hiding place. I didn't have an address or a phone number for Birdie Mae. Who knew if she even lived here anymore. I was tired. My feet hurt and my belly grumbled.

I stepped inside the grocery store. It looked smaller than the Jitney Jungle grocery stores back home in Jackson. I walked the aisles of the store, determined not to spend more than fifty cents for something to eat. I had a few dollars of my own, along with the money in Dewey's wallet. I had to make all of it last. Some people in the store stared at me a few seconds longer than they should, probably trying to figure out who I was, who were my people. Arriving in this small town where I was new was like walking into a room where everybody was talking about you before you got there but then they suddenly stop, like they can't let you in on all they secrets. This was the first time I'd ever been anywhere other than Jackson. Even though Chillicothe was small, being an outsider made it feel big to me.

I finally landed on a box of crackers and a bottle of Coca-Cola and headed to the cashier at the front of the store.

"That'll be twenty-five cents," the white lady behind the counter said.

I reached inside my bag for Dewey's wallet and wondered if she noticed I had a man's wallet. Maybe I should distract her.

"Excuse me, miss. Do you know a woman goes by the name Birdie Mae Hudson?"

The white lady behind the counter didn't bat an eye. She just stood there, hands on her hips, waiting for my twenty-five cents, looking at me like I was stretching her last nerve.

"I'm related to her and I was trying to find her. I know she lives here. I just don't know where exactly."

"I don't know any Birdie Mae Hudson. Twenty-five cents."

I pulled a dollar bill from Dewey's wallet and handed it to the woman. She waited for me to set it on the counter, seeing as white people didn't want to slip up and touch a colored person accidentally while exchanging money. Afraid that the mere act of touching somebody colored would taint them. Or maybe they were afraid the expression of human kindness to a colored person was a sign of weakness. She counted out my change from the cash register and set it down on the counter. "Do you need a bag?" She said it like packing up my purchase was the last thing she wanted to do.

I shook my head no, picked up the change, and headed for the door.

I stepped outside and looked across the parking lot. The edge of my cotton dress fluttered in the hot summer breeze. All I wanted to do was get out of my clothes and sleep. I coulda slept for days if I had a place to rest my head. I slipped out of my heels and traded them for a pair of black sneakers from my bag. I nibbled on a few crackers before I tucked my breakfast inside my bag and closed it. I peered around again. How would I find Birdie? What if she didn't live here anymore? Maybe I'd made a mistake getting off that bus. *Another fast decision.*

"Excuse me, miss."

I turned, expecting the salesclerk to tell me I'd forgotten something. Instead, a young colored girl, maybe seventeen or eighteen years old, came trotting toward me. Her hair was wrapped in a yellow flowered scarf. Her pretty brown complexion against the brightly colored scarf gave her a fresh-faced look.

"Miss? I overheard you in the line back there. You looking for Birdie Mae?"

"Yes. Do you know her?"

"Everybody know Birdie. She real sweet. I can take you to her house if you want me to. She stay close by my place." The girl's voice was high and keen, like every word was a small bird singing and struggling to be heard.

"I'd appreciate that."

I fell in step with the girl as we headed away from the Piggly Wiggly. She carried a small brown paper sack of groceries with a loaf of Wonder bread peeking from the top of the bag.

"My name's Lilly. Lilly Dukes. What's yours?"

I thought for a second. *New town. New name.*

"Um . . . Vera . . . My name is Vera Henderson." Vera had been my grandmother's name. Grandma Vera always had come to my defense whenever my momma had chastised me for some little thing. She used to tell me wasn't nothing wrong with a strong-willed girl. She said the world could use a few more like me. Grandma Vera had always wanted to be a dancer. She used to tell me how she would sneak off and listen to records by singers like Bessie Smith and Ma Rainey. But her father forbade it, telling her good girls don't grow up to be dancers, shaking and grinding their bodies. I guess I added the name Henderson because it seemed like a good, strong last name. And different enough from my real one.

"You sure are pretty. Where you from? I seen you get off the bus."

I smiled at her. "Well, Lilly Dukes, you don't miss much, huh?"

Lilly smiled back. Two deep dimples sprung up on either side of her face.

"Alabama," I lied, as I looked straight ahead.

"Oh, I think I got some kin in Alabama. What part of Alabama?"

So Lilly was young *and* nosy. "Is Birdie's place much farther?" I asked.

"Just a piece more down the road. You know, I knew we was gon' get visitors to town."

"You did, huh? Why's that?"

"I can see things that other people can't. Things that ain't happened yet. My momma used to say I got a special eye."

I decided to keep Lilly talking. She'd have less time to ask me a bunch of questions if I did all the asking. "So what kind of things can you see with your special eye?"

"I don't know . . . just different stuff. I knew Mr. Nestor's house would catch on fire before it happened. I knew your cousin Birdie was gonna have twins before they was born. And I knew we were getting visitors to Chillicothe. A lot of people don't come here. Most people in town was born here. Chillicothe is mostly for passing through, not staying put."

"Is that a fact?" I said jokingly. "Well, I'm the only one that got off the bus today. Where are the other visitors?"

"Hmm . . . maybe the others will come later. But mark my words, there's gonna be some new people in town."

I let Lilly go on with her girlish talk of seeing into the future. Everybody's got something special about themselves, or at least they should feel that way. If Lilly thought new people were coming to town, fine by me—as long as it wasn't the Jackson, Mississippi, police.

We strolled in silence along Church Street. I remember Birdie telling me once that Chillicothe was so small that you could spit a piece of gum out your mouth, cross the street, and catch it before it landed. There was a diner, a repair shop, and a few small storefronts, but otherwise, the entire downtown hub of Chillicothe was about two square blocks, a far cry smaller than even Farish Street, the colored downtown district of Jackson.

Lilly started up again. She was right in the middle of a story about some local folks I didn't even know when I spotted a black-and-white police car, the words TOLLIVER COUNTY SHERIFF'S OFFICE painted along the side. My heart skipped a beat. I took a couple deep breaths as I glanced inside the car. A fat balding man sat behind the wheel, eating what looked like boiled peanuts. Lilly's chatter continued, but her words were like squeaky little noises in the background. Fact of the matter was, fear had wrapped me up so tight that all the noises around me started to fade. What if the Jackson police knew I'd killed Huxley and were circulating pictures of me? What if this policeman recognized me? Everything inside me focused on that police car. When we walked past it, I turned my head away from the policeman inside, pretending Lilly's conversation was the most fascinating thing I'd ever heard. Maybe he'd paid us no mind, but I was rattled to the core. Everywhere I went seemed like police were around, like I was some kind of magnet attracting them all. Of course I was. I'd killed a white man and robbed another. I must have smelled like Camay soap and guilt.

We walked past a town square with a painted gazebo. The American flag and the Georgia state flag with its Confederate stars and bars hung beside it. On the other side of the square, we entered a pleasant-looking neighborhood. Small, neat bungalows dotted the streets, all named after presidents. Washington. Lincoln. Jackson. Garfield. But I knew better than to think Birdie lived on one of these streets. At the end of Church Street, we walked across a small wood bridge that crossed over a creek. This time, the streets were named after dainty little things like Dove, Starlight, and Honeysuckle. The houses were far from dainty. These streets were lined with rows and rows of dilapidated shotgun houses with peeling paint and dirt for lawns. Some streets contained brick bungalows, but it was clear they had seen better days. Even though I'd never stepped foot inside this town before, I'd lived in the South all my life and immediately recognized the colored section of Chillicothe.

Lilly turned onto Periwinkle Lane, and I followed her to the end of the street.

"That's Birdie's house right there." She pointed to a small frame house. The paint was peeling, but there were curtains in the window. Birdie was giving the house a fighting chance.

"Thanks, Lilly."

"Anytime. I live right around the corner if you ever need anything. Welcome to town. My special eye tells me you'll be staying with us for a good long while." Lilly gave me a big, dimpled smile and walked up the street. So her special eye told her I'd be staying. I shook my head. I think that eye needed some adjustment. I was only staying in this town long enough to let the heat die down.

I walked up the short, crooked steps onto the porch. The sound of kids squealing and playing echoed from behind the door. According to Lilly, Birdie and Charlie had added twins to their family since they left Jackson. I knocked on the screen door. A little girl with big brown eyes peeked from behind the curtains at the front window. I smiled and wiggled my fingers in a wave at her. She stared back with a small brown face of stone, no expression. Finally, she yelled, "Momma, a lady at the door."

A few seconds later, Birdie peeked out the same window before she flung open the door.

"Violet! As I live and breathe." She grabbed me in a big bear hug. Her voice boomed across the entire front porch. It felt so good to hug someone after running from everything—the police, Dewey, all my mistakes—and I lingered in Birdie's grip a little longer than I should have. She was family, and right now, I needed to be connected to someone.

Birdie still looked the same. Birthing a few babies had rounded out her short frame, but she still had the same bright eyes and bubbly personality. She sported a mop of curls pulled to the top of her head with a rubber band. A small gold cross hung around her neck, reminding me of the times we sat in the church balcony, giggling together about some boy until Momma or Aunt Ella gave us the look. Birdie had been like another sister to me.

"Come on in. Girl, what you doin' in Chillicothe?"

"I'm just passing through for a few days." Little kids began encircling Birdie, some small, some a little bigger. Four of them by my count. The house was small and clean, but I smelled the remnants of a diaper that needed changing. Everything in the house seemed a little drab, worn. A room full of hand-me-downs that had been handed down a time too many. The arms of the sofa were frayed from wear, and the top of the coffee table in the middle of the room was bleached a couple shades lighter than its legs from sitting in the sunlight of the window. I looked around and wondered if this would have been my fate if Papa had found out about me and that boy from high school. Would my daddy have forced me to marry into a future like this?

Every single one of the kids looked exactly like Birdie, big brown eyes and sweet round faces that hid a mess of mischief they thought of getting into. I hadn't seen Charlie in years, so maybe I was just missing his resemblance.

"Who is she, Momma?" one of the children asked.

"This here is your cousin; now hush, honey." Birdie shooed the child away. "Violet, come on in and sit down." Birdie brushed off the seat of an old brown chair, the outline of the springs pressing up against the upholstery. She ushered me into the seat like neither one of us saw it.

"How you been?" she asked.

"Good. Real good."

"Momma, can I—"

"Hush up, child. Don't you see I got company? Go outside and play. Take your little brother and sisters with you too."

All three kids followed the older one out the door. They were cute as buttons, but four of them that young had to be a lot of work.

"Violet, honey, what you doing all the way here from Jackson? How's Marigold?"

"She's fine." I wondered what Marigold was doing right now. The guilt of leaving her behind sliced me right through the gut.

"Listen, I'm sorry I couldn't make it back for your momma's funeral. Money been tight. What happened?"

"Doctors say it was a stroke. I think it was losing Rose and then Papa. She wasn't never the same." I guessed the news about me not attending Momma's and Papa's funerals hadn't made it as far as Georgia.

Birdie slowly shook her head. "Such a shame. It ain't right a momma gotta see one of her babies dead."

I quickly changed the subject. I didn't want to dredge up Rose's memory. "Uh . . . Birdie, I was hoping I could stay with you for a few days. Just a few days. I promise."

"Well, honey, we kinda tight in here. I got four babies and two bedrooms. But we can squeeze you in . . . I guess."

"Oh, I didn't know. Well . . ." I never should have gotten off that bus. I never should have left Mississippi. *Fast decisions.*

"Everything okay, Violet? Why you all the way out here from Mississippi?"

"I needed to get out of Jackson. And, look, I don't go by Violet no more. It's Vera Henderson."

"Vera?! Like Grandma's name? What's goin' on with you?"

"Some stuff happened with a man back in Jackson and I needed to just get away for a little while."

Birdie laughed. "You pretty girls always got man problems."

I smiled at her joke. "Speaking of men, where's Charlie?"

The smile melted away from Birdie's face like cream butter across a hot bun. Birdie picked up a paper fan from the table and waved it in front of her face, fast and angry, like she was trying to shake her hand loose from her wrist. "Don't mention that name in my house. That no-good scoundrel up and left me. I ain't seen him in months. And I don't want to either. Good riddance to bad rubbish, as they say."

I never cared for Charlie. He reminded me of Marigold's boyfriend, Roger. Both of them slick and fast moving. "Yeah. So . . . maybe there's a rooming house nearby?"

"Miss Willa lets out rooms in her house. She's close by. But Vio— I mean, Vera. What's happened that you need to change your name and everything?"

"Nothing that's worth spending another minute talking about. Where's the rooming house?"

"Let me put on my shoes. I'll walk you around there."

* * *

Not even five minutes later, Birdie and I were standing on the front porch of Willadene Mason's house, a large brick dwelling with a black-and-white awning in need of repair and the smell of collard greens coming through the front door.

Miss Willa, as everyone called her, was a tall, thin brown woman with a tight smile and strands of gray hair pulled to a bun at the back of her head. She looked like she might have been a stunning beauty in her younger days. But now, time was taking its toll, her edges sharper, her angles pointy and severe.

"Rent is six dollars a week. That includes clean towels twice a week and breakfast and dinner every day. And I *do not* allow men past the front parlor." Willa said the last sentence with a raised eyebrow.

"Sounds fair," I said.

Willa led me and Birdie up to a room on the second floor. The heat on this floor swallowed us whole as soon as we landed on the top step. The room was half the size of my bedroom at home, and it made me realize how much I'd given up for having my freedom. The small bed was covered in clean sheets and a flowered quilt. The bedside table held an old lamp, a transistor radio, and a small metal fan. The window overlooked the backyard and a large vegetable garden. As much as I hated to admit it, this room, Miss Willa's whole house, had a warm, comfy feel that made me miss home. I missed Marigold terribly. I'd left behind everything I loved to seek vengeance on a man who was trash.

"I'll take it." I turned my back to the two women and removed six dollars from Dewey's wallet. "Here's the first week's rent."

Willa gave me a serious glance before she tucked the money inside her bra and headed out the door.

"This ain't too bad," Birdie said as she ran her hand across the foot of the wood bed. "Miss Willa runs a clean place. She's got no kids. Her husband died about ten years ago and I think she run this place more to have folks around than needing the money."

I peered through the lace curtains listening to Birdie. Miss Willa's backyard offered a peaceful view of peach trees and hydrangeas winding up to the neat little rows of vegetables. I could use a little peace in my life right now.

"Violet—I mean, Vera . . . what you running from?"

"Later." I peeked under the bed. Clean, not a dust bunny in sight.

"Whatever that man did back in Jackson must have been pretty bad to make you run to a place like Chillicothe." Birdie sat on the edge of the bed and sighed. "I miss home. I miss having family close by."

"Trust me, you ain't missing much." I opened the dresser drawers, still checking out the room. "Ain't nothing changed in Jackson. Colored folks still living under the white man's rules. The government pass laws, and they still won't abide by 'em. Power belong to the powerful, not us."

"So what does Marigold think about you running off to Georgia?"

"I need to call her. You think Miss Willa got a phone around here?"

"You might be asking a bit much. All this, meals,

and long-distance calls for six dollars a week? You can use mine, but *no* long-distance calls. I can't afford that. Not since Charlie left."

"Thanks for bringing me over here. And like I said, it's Vera now. I'd really appreciate you not telling folks around here . . ."

"Vera. I like the sound of that. You ain't a flower no more."

"What?"

"Your name! Why Aunt Lib name all her girls after flowers anyway?"

"She said she was bringing something beautiful into the world when she gave birth to us." I smiled at the thought. Momma's own little bouquet.

"I guess everybody gotta be called something, huh? Now you know I'm right around the corner if you need anything. I better get back home before them kids burn down the house."

Birdie walked over to me and swooped me up in another big hug. "It feels good to have family around again. I miss everybody back in Mississippi. I don't know why you're here, but I sure am glad you are."

Birdie had landed on the same question I was asking myself. Why *was* I here? And what would I do now?

8
Marigold

I f I was so smart, how'd I wind up pregnant with no husband? I fully understood the biology of this situation, but the logic of my behavior bewildered me. After we got our periods, Momma's only conversation with us about sex was a series of threats and warnings about keeping our eyes open and our legs closed to avoid "big trouble." Momma's voice rattled around inside my head, as if she were standing beside me barking off her platitudes of good-girl advice: *There's plenty of time for lying underneath a man AFTER you're married* or *Keep a man waiting and you'll keep him forever.* Momma was always so busy telling us what *not* to do when it came to boys, she never got around to telling us what we *should* do. What kind of man was right for us? What should we look for in a potential husband?

And who whispered into the ears of all the boys who were encouraged to sow their wild oats? And why didn't anyone tell the girls it could be pleasurable the way they told the boys? Like nearly everything else, it was an unfair system. Secretly, I envied Violet. She did whatever pleased her, and that included being with a man if she wanted to. Nobody, not even Momma or Papa, could tell her how to live her life. Meanwhile, I cowered in fear from almost everything. That is, until I met James.

James Scott was from New York City, Harlem to be exact. I can't even remember how I lost my way with James. I didn't go out with boys all that much before him. If I did, they never got much beyond some hand stuff under my blouse. Rose had been going steady with Silas Monteque before she died. I was pretty sure the two of them avoided all that business. They were barely out of junior high school. And Violet? Well, Violet was Violet, which meant if she wanted to be with a man, nobody's rules, not even Momma's, would stop her. But me? Until James, I had heeded Momma's warnings about the "one-eyed snake."

As I think about it, getting between my legs wasn't the first thing James tried to do when we got together. We'd spend hours talking about the law and what it could do for the Negro people. He asked me what I thought about Dr. King's work and the nonviolent movement. We talked about art and music. We talked about Broadway plays and Lorraine Hansberry, a Negro woman who wrote a Broadway play called *A Raisin in the Sun*. With James, I felt smart. I felt connected to people outside Jackson. And the couple times he did want to go further, I thought it was okay because we had something different. A connection. He was a smart guy. He was my kind of guy. So what if we weren't in love?

I knew he planned to return to New York when the Mississippi Summer Project was over. Did that mean when James and I got married we'd live in Harlem? He certainly had no reason to stay here in Jackson. Neither did I, with Momma, Papa, and Rose all passed and Violet off only God knew where. I'd never stepped foot outside of Jackson, Mississippi. All I knew about New York was that it was cold up there. But I could make it work.

I sat at the kitchen table nursing a gingersnap and waiting for the morning sickness to subside. I closed the bag of cookies. The next thing I heard was a loud pounding at the front door. Hard. Fast. Like someone was trying to bust the door down. I scrambled from the kitchen chair and eased down the hallway to the edge of the living room.

More pounding. Louder this time. I couldn't see

who was there because of the curtains at the door. And I was too terrified to move any closer. It was as if my feet were bolted to the floor. I stood there, praying away whatever was on the other side of the door.

"VIOLET RICHARDS! OPEN UP!" a loud voice yelled through the door.

I peered across the living room and out the front window. A black-and-white police car was parked in front of the house.

Oh God.

I thought my heart would beat a hole straight through the middle of my chest. Should I open the door? What would they do to me, knowing I was Violet's sister?

I couldn't move even if I wanted to answer that door. I stayed right there at the edge of the living room. If the police were here for Violet, they would have to bust down the door because I wasn't going to open it. The pounding started up again. A minute later, it stopped. I watched through the window as the policeman climbed inside the patrol car and pulled away.

God, please keep Violet safe.

* * *

I was still shaking by the time I got to work. I wished I knew where Violet was. When I married James and moved up to New York with him, how would she reach me? How would I even begin to find her? I decided to worry about that later. Right now, I needed to focus on James and the baby. I wanted to be as calm as possible, not all weepy and emotional. There was a child to consider. Deep down, if I was honest, I think I cared more about being out in the world by myself with a baby, instead of whether I loved James or not. Besides, how many marriages were built on a foundation of doing what's right rather than what's in your heart? Of course, over time, we might fall in love. Being married and having kids could do that to you. You build a life together, so how could you not fall in love? Right? Or maybe I was just fooling myself and the truth of the matter was that I didn't want to deal with the stigma of being a pregnant, unmarried woman.

I stepped inside the office. Maria, another typist who worked for the Summer Project, was at her desk, drinking coffee from a paper cup and reading over something she'd just finished typing. She was an attractive woman, about my age, who was still basking in the glow of her recent wedding to Simon Bates of the Bates Funeral Home family, the largest funeral home for Negroes. I wondered if she was pregnant, too, given how quickly they got married. She considered it a major achievement to have married into one of Jack-

son's middle-class Negro families. What she didn't realize was that Simon—or "Simple Simon" as everyone
around town called him—was an overdressed drunk
and most folks didn't give the marriage six months.

"Good morning, Maria. Where is everyone?"

She shrugged. "I'm not sure. Walter's in the back,
though." Walter Anderson was another lawyer out
of Washington, DC. He was a short, thick man with
a gruff demeanor, and he ran the office with military
precision.

"You seen James this morning?" I tried to ask casually, despite the butterflies in my stomach.

"Nope. Not since yesterday morning. Hey, don't
you have a sister? Violet?"

"Yeah. Why?"

Maria rested her coffee cup on the desk. "Have you
seen the morning paper today?"

I shook my head no. "Why?"

Maria didn't answer. She reached across the desk
and handed me the newspaper. The headline: LOCAL
BUSINESSMAN FOUND DEAD. My knees buckled. I could
feel Maria staring at me waiting for my reaction. The
article went on to describe how Huxley Broadus was
found shot dead in the woods, behind the Jitney Jungle
grocery store on Pine Street. The police did not have
any suspects but were seeking a local Negro woman

named Violet Richards for questioning. Of course, it made no mention of Violet's rape charge against Huxley. And calling Huxley a local businessman was like calling a mason jar a champagne flute.

"So everyone's up in arms about that white trash, but people barely batted an eye when those three young men went missing up in Neshoba County simply because they were trying to help us get the right to vote." I shook my head, disgusted.

"Yeah, you're right. But isn't Violet your sister?"

I folded the newspaper and handed it back to her. "Yes."

Maria's eyes widened as she whispered, "Did your sister kill him?"

I didn't respond as I tucked my purse into the desk drawer.

"Well, good for her if she did. I heard that guy was a disgusting beast. A lady that goes to my church said he chased her fifteen-year-old daughter home from school one day. Thank God he couldn't catch her. God only knows what he would have done to that poor child."

I wasn't about to get into speculation about Violet's actions with Maria. Between her husband and all the funeral home staff flapping their loose lips with clientele and church members, Violet's involvement with Huxley's murder would be all over town. I closed the desk drawer. "I'm going back to see Walter for a minute."

"Okay."

I headed for his desk at the back of the room.

"Hey, morning, Walter."

"Marigold. I took a look at the brief you typed up yesterday. Looks good. I just have a few changes." He handed me the inch-thick brief, a filing for an injunction for an upcoming special election. "We should try to get this wrapped up this morning so you can run it over to the courthouse before lunch."

"Of course. Hey, where is everybody?"

"A couple folks are out in the field. And by the way, I'm expecting a new lawyer next week."

"A new lawyer?"

"Yeah. James left last night. The NAACP is sending down a replacement next week."

My stomach tumbled. "James left town?"

"Yeah. Said he had some sort of family emergency and had to get back to New York City right away."

Everything inside me went numb. "I'll . . . I'll get these changes done now." I stumbled backward, forcing myself to get out of Walter's view before I burst into tears.

* * *

I spent the rest of the day at work fighting back my emotions and regretting the day I ever laid eyes on James Scott. He had suddenly decided he had a family emergency back in New York City when he learned he had a new family in Jackson.

I was stupid. Beyond his name and his being from New York City, I knew absolutely nothing about the man whose child I was carrying. Or maybe now I did. Any man who left a woman to fend for herself while carrying his baby was low-class, no matter how many college degrees he had.

Now James was on the run, and I was stuck in Jackson, alone and pregnant.

9
Marigold

E veryone found a way out of their predicament. Violet. James. Everyone except me. What was I supposed to do now?

I was useless at the office after I learned about James's sudden "family emergency" up in New York. I left work and returned to an empty house. The whole place felt like an echo chamber. Every sound in the house—the pad of my slippers against the floor, the soft hum of electricity flowing through the icebox, the rattle of the windows as a large truck passed by—bounced off the walls and fell into my ears, reminding me of the solitude of my life now. My one mistake—forgetting I was a good girl—would forever brand me a slut.

No matter how hard I tried, I was always coming out on the losing end. All my good grades in school were worthless when there was no money for college. All my efforts to be the good girl Momma warned us to be, and for what? To wind up pregnant by a man who left me high and dry. Marigold Richards: The smart, sensible sister. The slut.

I was still sitting on the sofa hours later when Roger showed up on my front porch. I'd forgotten we had plans to go to the movies. I didn't feel up to it. It had been a horrible day. Besides, I didn't want to be forced to sit in the balcony of the theater when I knew that the law said I had every right to sit anywhere I pleased. But on the other hand, I didn't want to sit in my living room all evening, fighting off Roger's attempts to have sex on my sofa.

When I opened the door, Roger stood there, sporting a different job-hunting outfit—this time, a gray-and-yellow print shirt with slacks. What did he do all day, since no one had hired him yet?

"Hey, you ready to go?" Roger asked.

"Sure."

Roger stepped inside and closed the door. "I saw the newspaper this morning. Where's Violet?"

"I don't know. She left without a word. The police came by this morning looking for her."

"So did she kill Huxley?"

I was growing weary of this question. I just stared

at Roger. How could my taste in men run to such polar opposites? James Scott and Roger Bonny. At that moment, both of them disgusted me. I just turned and walked to the kitchen. Roger followed me like an obedient puppy.

"Marigold, I know she's your sister, but it seems to me, she might just drag you into the middle of this thing."

"What do you mean?" I pulled the chain on the light fixture and walked back into the living room, Roger still on my heels.

"Think about it. The police are gonna hang a noose around somebody's neck for killing that white man. Everybody in this town knows he raped your sister, including the police. They'll string up a colored woman long before they charge a white man with something. And if they can't find Violet, you're the next best thing."

I stopped in my tracks. "What?!"

"You know how these folks shell out justice down here. As soon as the white folks start in on how the police are letting a black woman go free while a white man is in a grave, they'll look for anybody to charge with his murder. Might try to say you helped Violet kill him or you helped her get away."

For once, everything Roger said made perfect sense.

Violet might have brought trouble for the both of us. The only reason white folks weren't up in arms about Huxley's murder yet was because every white person within a hundred miles of Jackson considered him trash. But it would be just a matter of time before white folks would be calling for the head of somebody to account for his murder. I was so glad I hadn't opened the front door earlier that morning when that policeman showed up.

"Marigold, let's just get married and get out of here. My brother, Frankie, got a good job up in Ohio working for one of the steel mills. Gets a paycheck every two weeks. Enough to take care of him and his wife. We could get a place up there too. He say colored folks even buying houses and cars, and some of 'em own their own businesses. You know I've always wanted to open up a nightclub, but these ass-backward folks down here too scared to go in with me on it. But up north, I could do something like that. What d'ya say? Let's just get married."

Roger had asked me to marry him more times than I cared to remember, but this was the first time his proposal came with an argument that made sense to me. And now that I was pregnant with James's baby, I started to look at Roger with a fresh set of eyes. By some people's standards, I was already on the older side for getting married. Most of the girls I graduated with were married, some expecting babies, even.

"You smart, Marigold. You can take them classes in college you always be talking about. They got colleges up there. And I bet you won't need the National Guard to escort you inside like they did with that guy at Ole Miss. Let's get married, huh?"

So it wasn't the most romantic marriage proposal. But so far, every word Roger spoke was working in his favor. I didn't have a clue where Violet was. All I knew was that she was never coming back to Jackson, Mississippi. Violet was right in her note. She wasn't much the type for being locked in a cage. Rose was gone. Papa and Momma were gone too. What did I have here in Jackson? Could I really expect to stay here pregnant and unmarried? I would be the talk all around the Negro section of Jackson. And even if I stayed, would I be able to keep my job after I started to show? Maybe there was a better life for me and this baby up in Ohio.

I looked up at Roger. His hazel eyes had a kind of plea in them. Maybe he loved me. Whether it was love or lust, I just hoped it would last us clear across the country. Because right now, Roger's marriage proposal looked a far sight better than the Jackson, Mississippi, police setting up my neck for a noose.

10
Mercer Buggs

Mercer Buggs had worked around the Leonard Feed & Supply Company off and on for five years before the owner's son, Dewey Leonard, even spoke to him for the first time. Mercer could smell his kind a mile away. A big, toothy grin, a hearty handshake, and a slap on the back usually opened doors for guys like Dewey. Mercer figured it was all the elder Mr. Leonard's wealth and the junior Leonard's fancy college education up north that pumped Dewey full of bluster and made the Leonards look down on people like him.

In fact, Mercer did a double take as he watched Dewey drive up to the front of Mercer's trailer in the Oak Tree Mobile Park Village. A few kids played marbles in the dirt nearby. An old lady ambled about, hanging laundry on a line strung from the side of her trailer to a post planted in the dirt ten feet out. The siding on Mercer's trailer had started to rust along the bottom, and still, his trailer was one of the better-looking ones in the whole trailer park. Mercer dreamed of the day he could move his wife and kid into a real house, something solid and connected to the ground. By his estimate, they were living about as bad as the coloreds on the other side of town.

Dewey's brand-new Bonneville convertible, a birthday gift from his daddy, stuck out like a parish priest in the middle of a whorehouse. Mercer noticed a couple neighbors stop talking midsentence to admire Dewey's new toy. Dewey eased the car to a stop and smiled up at Mercer, not a word between them. The car outright gleamed against Mercer's busted-up old gray Ford Fairlane. When Mercer failed to comment on the Bonneville, Dewey slipped out of the car and closed the door.

He strutted up to Mercer, his face all lit up with the afternoon sun. He threw his head back, tossing a lock of hair. "Hey, Mercer! How ya' been?"

This greeting was a first, because Dewey never called Mercer by his first name. It was always "Bug-a-Boo" or "Bugsy," like calling a man out of his name was some sort of joke to him.

"Dewey," Mercer said, civil but guarded. Mercer slid his hand across the top of his dark hair, wrestling with an oily cowlick that always gave him a disheveled appearance.

"I ain't seen you around the supply yard in a month of Sundays." Dewey ramped up his southern accent as if it would build some sort of bond between the two of them.

"I been busy."

"Yeah, Daddy told me about your kid, Rusty."

"Randy."

"Yeah, lil' Randy. Been under the weather off and on, huh? Sorry to hear that."

"Thanks." Mercer was patient, but he knew Dewey was up to something. He hadn't driven this far out to chat about Randy being sick. He wanted something. Ever since Mercer had gotten into that fight at Rally's Roadhouse with the mayor's son, the Leonards had all but abandoned him. Dewey's father told him not to come around the feedstore, and Dewey pretended like Mercer was invisible. The craziest part is that Mercer only got into that fight because the mayor's son said something disparaging about the Leonards, although he no longer remembered the comment. Mercer promised his wife he was finished with Dewey and the whole Leonard family.

"Daddy and the guys have missed you." Dewey quickly realized the error of his statement and tried to clean things up. "Well, me too. Of course, I don't hang around there much these days. I'm trying to set off on my own. You know, start my own business."

"That right?" Mercer said flatly. *Get on with it,* he thought.

Dewey slipped his hands into his pants pockets. "Look, you mind if we talk for a minute?"

"We're talking now."

Dewey gave a nervous chuckle. "Okay, so I'll come right to the point. I was thinking you could handle something for me. Something outside my daddy's business, that is."

"What's that?" Mercer felt his left eye twitch.

Dewey casually leaned against his Bonneville, folded his arms across his chest, and crossed his ankles. He made a big production of it, like it might make Mercer think better of him. "I need you to find somebody for me."

"Who?"

Dewey glanced around the trailer park before he turned back to Mercer. "A woman. I'm trying to find a woman. I remember how you sniffed out that fella who tried to get away with my daddy's feed from the store. Daddy still talks about how you found that guy without a hitch. Said you got the nose of a bloodhound." Dewey chuckled, probably thinking the compliment might lighten things between them.

Mercer took a couple steps closer, narrowing the gap between them, cautious Mary Lou might come from inside the trailer at any minute and spot them, wondering as much as he was why Dewey Leonard was in their front yard asking Mercer to find a woman. "Who's the woman?"

Dewey smiled again. "Well, before we get into all that, I need to know whether I can trust you."

"Who's the woman?" Mercer wasn't working for the Leonards now. He didn't have to be respectful if he didn't want to.

Dewey hesitated for a beat. "Violet Richards. You know her?"

Mercer shook his head. He knew just about everybody in Jackson, even a few of the coloreds on the other side of town. "Where is she?"

"Well, see, that's what I need you to find out, Mercer, buddy."

An old lunker of an Edsel rambled past them and through the park. Both men stopped talking and watched the car pass.

"Why you looking for this woman?" Mercer asked.

Dewey hesitated. Mercer picked up on it instantly.

"That's between me and her. I just really need to find her. So can I count on you?"

Mercer thought it through for a few seconds. Dewey Leonard and some woman. It sounded like trouble. Big trouble. "My kid's sick. I need to stay close to home. I'm not interested."

"I can pay you a thousand dollars, plus any expenses you might have to lay out on top of that."

That was more money than Mercer had ever seen in his entire life. Trouble paid good money. "Seems to me you must really want to find this woman."

"What I need is somebody who can keep all this under his hat too. My business with this woman is just between me and her."

Mercer gave a long, unblinking stare at him before he nodded his chin at Dewey's car. "I see you got a new car. Eight-lug aluminum wheels, huh?"

Dewey stood up from his leaning posture and peered down at the car, then back at Mercer. "I imagine a thousand dollars will go a long way with a sick kid and all."

Dewey was right. The money would go a long way. Mercer finally decided if he was going to take their money and whatever bad business that came along with it, he ought to make it worth his while. "Twenty-five hundred will go a lot further."

Dewey smiled. "My daddy always said you were a cunning one."

Mercer smiled back. "Nice talking to you, Dewey. Nice car, too." He eased away and pulled the handle on the squeaky door to his house. "I gotta get going. Mary Lou's making dinner inside."

"Wait!" Dewey yelled. He stared at Mercer for a beat. "Twenty-five hundred."

"Plus expenses."

"Plus expenses," Dewey echoed.

"What d'ya need me to do?"

"Violet Richards is a colored woman. The last time I saw her was in Birmingham." Dewey pulled an envelope from his back pants pocket. He slid out a small photo and handed it to Mercer.

Mercer stared down at the black-and-white shot of Dewey, his arm wrapped around a tall, attractive colored woman with long dark hair. The couple leaned against Dewey's new car. She was different, this one. Her mouth seemed a perfect little bow with lipstick. She offered up the kind of smile and figure that probably got her all sorts of attention in the right setting. Mercer didn't find colored women attractive, but there was something about this woman. Something about her eyes, or maybe it was that lipsticked little bow of a mouth that could draw a man in.

"Her address is on the back of the picture. She lives over on Oakland Avenue. Has a sister named Marigold. You might want to start there. Can I count on you to keep this between me and you?"

"Wait a minute! Violet Richards? Ain't this the woman the police are looking for? Think she mighta killed Huxley Broadus?"

"Yeah, but I need to get to her before they do."

Mercer stared at the picture and then gave a long quiet glare at Dewey. "Why you need to find a colored gal so bad?"

"Like I said, that's between me and her. You just find her for me."

"I need half the money now."

"That's not a problem. I'll be back with it this evening. We got a deal?" Dewey grinned and stuck out his hand like they were a couple of horse traders sealing the deal. Mercer hated this rich college boy. But he loved Mary Lou and Randy *more* than he hated Dewey. He hadn't worked a steady job in months, and they had a kitchen table full of bills. He needed the money. Mercer took a deep breath and reluctantly shook Dewey's hand.

"What makes you so sure I can find this gal?"

"My daddy always told me you were like a pit bull on a bone, one of the best workers he ever hired. I appreciate you helping me out like this, buddy. Now this is just between us?"

Mercer nodded his agreement. Dewey's father was right. Mercer Buggs was dogged when he wanted something, and right now, he wanted—*needed*—that twenty-five hundred dollars.

Dewey headed for the car then stopped in his tracks and turned back to Mercer. "Oh, there's just one thing." A menacing grin slicked across Dewey's face. "When you find her, don't lay a hand on her. Just let me know where she is. I'll take care of the rest."

11

"Vera"

The day after I arrived in Chillicothe, I woke up with a blinding headache as the first light of day poured in through the window. Miss Willa's lace curtains were pretty to look at, but they did nothing against the sun. Maybe she wanted it that way. Maybe she was one of those rise-and-shine-up-and-at-'em kind of folks who didn't take to her boarders sleeping half the day away.

I had dreamed, deep and vivid and, as always, about Rose. My sisterly ghost that traveled all the way to Georgia with me. I was glad I hadn't remembered the details of the dream. Details only meant more pain. And now all my memories about Rose would be sprinkled with flashes of Huxley Broadus and what happened that night out behind the Jitney Jungle.

Rose and Huxley. Both of them, hovering around in my head, whispering to me tales of who I really was.

I eased out of bed and crossed the room to the dresser. I slid Rose's diary from beneath my clothes folded in the bottom drawer. I climbed back in bed and read a random entry.

April 16, 1956

Dear Diary,

Momma is going to sew a new dress for me to wear to the school dance. She had some pink fabric left over from the Easter dress she made for Marigold last year. I hope she can add some pretty buttons or something to make it look fancy. Annie Pearl Culver always wears the best dresses. I wish Momma would make mine like hers. I would ask her to do it, but I don't want to seem ungrateful.

Yesterday, Papa pulled out the pistol again and made me, Marigold, and Violet watch as he showed us how to load it and take aim. I didn't really watch. I hate guns. But as usual, Violet couldn't peel her eyes away. She kept asking to hold it and asking Papa to let her shoot it for real. Truthfully, I don't think that gun has been fired more than twice. And both times were to get rid of snakes in the backyard. Papa said it's only for emergencies. He said he only bought it after those white men killed that boy Emmett Till up in Money last year after a white lady said he whistled at her.

Momma came home early from a Missionaries meeting at church. When she saw all of us sitting around Papa with that gun, she got so mad. She doesn't like Papa pulling out the gun around us girls. The two of them must have argued for an hour. Me, Marigold, and Violet just sat quiet. As usual, the argument turned to whether we should move up north. Momma wanted to, and secretly I was on her side. But Papa, as the head of the house, always argued her down, saying he had a right to live anywhere in this country and he didn't have to run from anyone. He said he wouldn't let a bunch of mean assholes run him from the place he and his family had called home for generations. Papa always says he won't start a fight, but he won't run from one either. I think Momma worries where his pride and that pistol will land him. But I don't think Papa is prideful. I think he is just a

man who wants all the same things every man is
entitled to if this country were fair.

Sometimes I dream of what it would be like to
live some place other than Mississippi. I wonder
what "fair" would feel like?

Between the lace curtains and Rose's diary, I couldn't get back to sleep for nothing. Everybody told me for years Rose's death was a terrible accident, that I was just a little girl and it wasn't my fault. I didn't believe them. The signs were there long before she died that I was a horrible mess of a person. And even now I was still horrible, leaving Marigold to face my mess. How many times would I keep hurting the people I loved? I closed the diary and placed it back in the drawer underneath my clothes. I slipped on my bobby socks and a bathrobe before I headed down to the end of the hall to use the bathroom.

Miss Willa's boardinghouse was clean, and I had no cause to complain. She had three bedrooms on this floor and another one downstairs where she slept. But clean was no substitute for home. I wondered if Marigold could stay in the house on Oakland now that I had left. The money I earned from the feedstore and my babysitting jobs around town didn't bring in much, but I had been helping out a little with the bills.

I finished my business and clicked off the bathroom light. As I walked back to my room, I ran smack-dab into her. The same young girl from the grocery store. Lilly Dukes with the special eye.

"Vera?"

"Oh . . . hey, Lilly."

"What are you doing here?" She gave me a suspicious glare. "I thought you said you was staying with your cousin Birdie Mae."

I bit my bottom lip and smiled. "Her house is full to the brim. Miss Willa rented me the room just past the stairs there. You live here too?"

"I'm right across the hall from you."

I nodded across the awkward silence between us. "Well, I guess we betta get down to breakfast, huh?" I headed off to my room, hoping Lilly wouldn't be one of those girls who wanted to fly in and out of my room to chitchat or ask to borrow a blouse. I wasn't trying to make a bunch of friends. I just needed a place to sit quiet until I could figure out my next move.

* * *

I decided to skip breakfast and instead ate the last of my crackers and drank the warm bottle of Coca-Cola from the store the day before. I wasn't quite up to going downstairs to breakfast and socializing. The way I figured, I could wait it out in this town for a couple days. If the police were on to me or talked to the bus station clerk back in Birmingham and figured out I had bought a ticket to Washington, DC, they'd be looking for me there. In fact, maybe I was better off staying in this small town in the middle of nowhere for a week or two. Then I could move on, turn in the bus ticket for a different location. But then something about staying here in Chillicothe crossed my mind— why would a colored woman move to town *alone* and then proceed to lie around all day in a boardinghouse? That might bring about the kind of attention I didn't need right now. And I didn't want no trouble with Miss Willa, either. Maybe I needed to get a job or find something to do for the short time I was here in town.

* * *

I was knee-deep in trying to square away my life when I heard a soft knock at the door. I tried to ignore it. Miss Willa didn't seem like the type that would disturb her boarders. Maybe whoever it was would think I was asleep and go away. The knock came again. I figured I might as well answer it. Somebody was determined to see me this morning. I eased off the bed and opened the door.

Lilly. "I guess we missed you at breakfast. I thought you might want something to eat." She stood in front of me holding a plate of eggs, sausage, grits, and a couple biscuits. The smell whisked me away to Momma's kitchen on a Sunday morning.

I took the plate. "Thank you." We exchanged a couple of awkward glances. "You wanna come in and sit for a spell?"

Lilly beamed. "Well, just for a minute. I gotta get ready for work."

She sat in the stiff wood chair by the window.

"Where you work?" I asked before I scooped up a spoonful of grits.

"Over at Birdsong's funeral parlor. That's the white funeral home on the other side of town. I do the cleaning, and sometimes, if they need help getting some of the bodies ready, I do that, too."

"Oh." I needed a job, but I damn sure wasn't working in no funeral home. Lilly must have used her special eye to read my mind because she chimed back.

"So . . . I already know you staying in town. What you planning on doing for work?"

I shrugged. "You and that special eye, huh?" I bit into a biscuit.

"I know somebody hiring."

"Well . . . I'm not much for funeral homes."

Lilly giggled. "Yeah, that's the way most folks is. I think I'm the only one who would take that job at Birdsong's. People told me I was crazy for taking it. But they pay me on time. Dead people don't bother me none. Besides, it ain't the dead people you gotta watch out for. It's the living ones that's scary."

I laughed. Lilly was right. There was something sweet about her.

"I heard that a lady over on Washington Street is looking for a maid. Her last maid, Miss Mamie, died a couple weeks ago. And don't nobody wanna work for her. They say she meaner than a bag of hungry snakes. But it's work. And ain't a lot of that to go around."

"Where she live exactly?"

"Like I said, over on Washington Street, the only yellow house on the street," she said.

"Where you from, Lilly?"

"I was born here in Chillicothe." Lilly hesitated, maybe thinking through what my next question would be. "My daddy kicked me outta the house."

"Why?"

Lilly turned her mouth down in a sad pout. "Listen, I gotta get to work."

Okay, so Lilly didn't want to talk about it. And I was

okay with that. I had a lot of things I didn't want to talk about either.

"Miss Willa said I could only bring up that food if you promise to bring the plate back down to the kitchen. She don't like us to eat in our rooms, but I told her you had a long trip into town and you was probably too tired to come down to breakfast."

"Thanks for doing that. Is Miss Willa mean?"

"Nah . . . I think she's just lived a long time and seen all her friends die. She lonely, that's all. Don't forget to take that plate back downstairs. I'll see you around."

"Yeah, see ya'."

Lilly slipped out the door. I finished up my breakfast. Miss Willa's cooking was as good as Momma's. It also reminded me that I'd never see home again. I might have sat there and cried but for the fact that crying wouldn't help me none.

I finished my breakfast and topped it off with what was left of the warm Coca-Cola. Then I jumped up from the bed and rambled through the dresser drawers. I only had two good dresses. I put on the gray one with the pearl buttons, brushed back my hair into a ponytail, and slipped on my black sneakers. I grabbed the empty plate and dropped it in the kitchen sink on my way out the front door. I was headed to the yellow house on Washington Street. I'd never worked as a maid. Fact of the matter is, I'd never worked at a real job a day in my life, not like Marigold. But the money in Dewey's wallet would only go so far if I was going to get back on the road. And I needed something to do to keep from drawing attention to myself. I'd have to hide out in the open.

I needed a job.

12
Mercer

M ercer Buggs had never held himself out as a detective before, but he had a natural affinity for it. All the years he'd spent creeping in and out of other people's lives, eavesdropping on conversations he wasn't invited into, and standing on the sidelines watching how other people lived had given him all the skills he needed for finding people. Or maybe it was his slim frame and hooded dark eyes that gave him the uncanny ability to slink in and out of places he had no business being. In fact, Mercer's entire body was a laundry list of all the brawls and bad places he'd ever been. His nose was an angled lump of a mess, acquired in a fight in the high school gym after a basketball game. His left eyebrow was pocked with a scar picked up from a knife fight outside a bar over some woman he couldn't even remember the name of now. He had a right pinky bent at an odd angle and a faint limp from a fight he was too drunk to remember the details of. All of it gave him a disturbing appearance that announced he was trouble before he even opened his mouth.

Mr. Leonard, Dewey's father, had once paid him two hundred dollars to find a colored farmer he thought had stolen some feed from the supply store. Mercer lured the old man by promising him a couple of fat hogs at a cheap price. When Mercer brought him to Mr. Leonard and his buddy, he watched as they hog-tied the man and tossed him in the back of Mr. Leonard's truck. Mercer didn't follow them, but he later heard they strung him up from a hickory tree out at Plattsville. Folks passed around pictures in the supply store of that man's limp, disheveled body swinging from the hickory. Sometimes Mercer thought about that old farmer, especially since Mercer wasn't even sure he had the right man. And Mr. Leonard didn't seem to mind about his uncertainty either.

That old farmer and what Mr. Leonard and his friends did to him had bothered Mercer in a way he didn't expect. Mercer wasn't stupid. He knew what the consequences would be for the old farmer once he lured him away. He'd lived his whole life in the South and he knew how things worked—who came out on top and who fell to the bottom. But sometimes Mercer felt as if he was living as bad off as the coloreds. And that wasn't how the hierarchy was supposed to work. He wanted to be like Dewey, driving the big fancy car around town and wearing new clothes. Wasn't he just as white as Dewey Leonard? So why was he living like a colored? Sometimes Mercer thought maybe if there were fewer coloreds, there might be more for people like himself.

Whatever was wrong with this country, no matter how hard he tried, Mercer hadn't moved the needle of his success very far. He had simply graduated from plucking random old farmers thought to be thieves to hunting down a colored woman running away from the police and her lovestruck boyfriend. He cut loose the one-man pity party. Instead of griping, he should be grateful. There was good money to be made on this job. And he might actually be saving her life. If Violet Richards killed that man and the police found her, she would find a noose around her neck before she even made it to trial. Dewey with his puppy dog love and orders not to hurt her might keep her out of harm's way. Mercer didn't know the woman. Frankly, it didn't really matter to him whether she lived or died. Again, less of them, more for him.

* * *

On the first day after Dewey hired him, Mercer drove past the house on Oakland, just to make sure there was life in there. He made a couple passes around the house after dark, too, hoping the Violet woman would show up and he could collect on the rest of his money. *Easy money.* On this particular day, his third drive-by of the day, he had an idea. He parked his car down a few houses from Violet's house. He eased into a threadbare plaid sports jacket, the only one he owned. He didn't have a tie, never liked them ever since he was a kid. Mercer tried to flatten the cowlick in his hair before he slipped from the car. He straightened his shoulders and strode up the street, right to the front door of the house on Oakland. He gently knocked a couple times before a colored woman, probably the sister, Marigold, peeked through the curtains of the door.

"Yes?" she asked.

"Hello. I'm looking for Violet Richards." Nothing like a good old-fashioned direct approach, Mercer figured.

"She's not here," she said through the windowpane.

"I'm trying to help her. Can you tell me when you expect her back or where I might find her?" Mercer asked, trying to put the woman at ease. He wasn't sure it was working.

"I don't know where she is."

Mercer fussed with the cowlick again. He smiled, tried to look friendly. "I see. It's just that I'm a lawyer. She came by my office looking for help. Even if she's in trouble, you can tell me. I'm trying to help her out of her . . . situation."

The woman behind the door gave Mercer a long stare. "I told you, I don't know where she is." She let the curtain fall back over the window and disappeared.

That hadn't gone as Mercer had hoped. *I should have busted that goddamn door down, scared some sense into her,* Mercer thought. He trotted down the street to his car. Mercer figured he was a hell of a lot smarter than a couple of colored women. And he wasn't about to let them stand between him and twenty-five hundred dollars.

He started up the old Fairlane and sped off.

13
Vera

Lilly, with the dimpled smile and the special eye, hadn't led me astray. There was only one yellow house on Washington Street. A bright, sunny sort of thing with white shutters and a white picket fence. It was like the house had jumped out of a picture book and landed straight in the middle of Chillicothe. I brushed the front of my dress for a bit of confidence and walked up the front steps. As I peeped through the screen door, I spied clutter, papers and the like, all over the living room. I pressed the doorbell. A few seconds later a petite white woman with pixie features and a bouffant hairdo stepped up to the door. She was barefoot, sporting a pair of black slacks and a white cotton shirt, the top two buttons open to show her cleavage. And if I wasn't mistaken, she had on a full face of makeup at this hour of the morning. Who was she expecting to see at this door?

"Yes?"

"Morning, ma'am. My name is Vera Henderson. I'm new in town and a friend told me you might be looking for help around your house."

The woman placed a hand on her hip and gave me a suspicious head-to-toe look. "You said you're new to town. Where you from?"

"Alabama." That was as close to the truth as I was willing to get. Besides, if Lilly was right about folks not wanting this job, it wasn't like she had a cause to be picky.

"Go on to the back and I'll meet ya' there."

I remembered Momma said white folks wouldn't let coloreds enter their house through the front door. Another reminder of our second-class status. The house was surrounded by dogwoods and peach trees against the neatly trimmed lawn. The woman was standing on the screened-in back porch by the time I made it around the house. I followed her inside the kitchen and the smell hit me before the sight of it all. The scent of burnt food had a hold of the entire place. The kitchen sink was full of dirty dishes and the floor looked as if it hadn't been mopped in a month of Sundays. The entire room looked like it hadn't been touched since their maid, Mamie, died two weeks before. Light beamed in through a large set of windows over the sink, throwing attention to all the dirt and mess on the kitchen table. The woman slid a few newspapers from one of the kitchen chairs and sat down at the table. She didn't clear a chair for me or ask me to sit, although in this kitchen and me in my good dress, I preferred to stand.

"My name is Bettyjean Coogler. Who'd you say recommended you?"

"Lilly Dukes. The two of us board over at Miss Willadene Mason's place."

"Oh, Miss Willa." Bettyjean's demeanor softened. "She's a nice lady. Real nice. Just move that stuff and sit down."

"Yes, ma'am." Every other chair at the table was filled with some kind of junk. I picked the one across from her, which had the least amount of clutter, and removed a pair of work gloves and some flower seed packets and sat down. If she wanted to pretend like her house wasn't a nightmare of a mess, I could pretend too.

"What'd you say your name was?"

"Vera. Vera Henderson."

"So you ain't ever worked for nobody around these parts, huh?"

"No, ma'am."

She stared at me for a beat. "Then how am I supposed to know if you're any good?"

"I figure you'll have to trust me." I gave a big smile. She didn't. "Hmm . . ."

Lilly was right. Bettyjean Coogler must not have had a whole bunch of folks lining up for this job. From the looks of the kitchen, I could see why. It all made me second-guess being here. But me and Bettyjean was both out of options.

"My husband is pretty particular about who works in our home. Maybe you could get a letter from the last family you worked for, a reference letter? Or maybe there's someone I can speak with?"

"Ma'am, with all due respect, I made my way to town hoping to stay at my cousin Birdie's place. But she ain't got room for me. I gave Miss Willa near the last of my money for room and board. I don't think I have much time for waiting on a reference letter from the last family I worked for to come in the mail. I need a job right now. I understand if you prefer to hire someone else." I stood from the chair and peered down at Bettyjean.

She glared back up at me for a moment before she stood from her chair. "You'll need to work six days a week. You need to be here by 8:30 every morning, and you can leave shortly after cooking dinner. My husband sometimes comes home for lunch, and he likes his meals hot on the table when he gets in for dinner at five o'clock. You'll do all the cleaning, laundry, and lunch and dinner. That includes shopping if I don't have the time to. Any questions?"

"How much you paying?"

"I'll pay you ten dollars a week."

I spied a bit of nervousness in her when she said it. That meant she paid her last maid more. "I don't mean no disrespect, Miss Bettyjean, but that won't be enough to cover my room and board and leave me money to send back home to my family. Seems to me fifteen dollars is a might fairer wage to pay. I don't mind working six days a week, but I have to have Sundays off. I aim to spend the Lord's Sabbath in church."

Bettyjean cinched her eyebrows together. I suspect she'd never bargained with a colored woman before. I needed a job, but I wouldn't grovel for it. Papa taught me a cup of confidence will take you a lot further than a bucketful of begging.

"Twelve dollars. You can take it or leave it."

"I suspect I'll take it then."

"You can start tomorrow morning, 8:30. Don't be late, either."

"Yes, ma'am."

I walked out past the white picket fence of the Coogler house. I could work for a few weeks or so and earn a little extra seed money to get me started in a new city. Maybe even head up north or out west like I'd originally planned.

* * *

I stepped onto the back porch of the Coogler household at 8:25 the next morning, now well versed in the expectations of my job as a maid in the South. I didn't know what a maid was supposed to wear, so I dressed in a plain brown skirt and white blouse. I didn't want to wear my nice things while I spent the day cleaning.

Bettyjean Coogler was already standing inside the kitchen, behind the screen door, when I arrived. "Nice to see you're prompt."

"Yes, ma'am." In that moment, shame washed over me. Momma would be so disappointed if she was here. She always said she cooked and cleaned for white folks so me and my sisters wouldn't have to. And now here I was, running from the law, hiding out from the police, and about to go clean up a white person's house. Here I was, repeating the cycle she worked so hard to break. Momma was dead, and I was still a living disappointment to her.

"Well, come on in here. Stop dawdling. There's work to be done."

I stepped inside the house. The kitchen was still filthy, of course. But this time, there was a man sitting at the kitchen table, reading the *Tolliver County Register.*

"Butch, this here is the *new* Mamie. This here is my husband, Sheriff Butch Coogler."

Sheriff!

Butch Coogler lowered the paper. The first thing I laid eyes on was his green police uniform and the bright shiny badge pinned on his chest. This was the same man I'd spotted the day I walked to Birdie Mae's house with Lilly.

I was hoping against hope that the knot in my throat wouldn't choke me dead. "Good morning, Sheriff," I said nervously. "My name is Vera . . . Vera Henderson."

He scoped me from head to toe. "Mornin'." He returned to the newspaper without another word.

Like most men, I suspect he left the business of running the household to his wife. Bettyjean handed me a dingy white apron and left the room. I slipped the apron on. It looked like the kitchen hadn't been touched since I left the day before, but at least the burnt smell was gone. It was replaced by the thick smell of tobacco. But I didn't see any remnants of cigarettes, not even an ashtray in the room. I started in on the dishes in the sink. What I really wanted to do was bolt from this kitchen. Standing this close to the law after what I did had me shaking inside, but there wasn't nothing I could do without looking suspicious. I just kept after them dishes.

I didn't mind the silence between me and the sheriff. The less I had to say, the better. But my mind was running a mile a minute. *Why the hell didn't Bettyjean tell me her husband was the town sheriff!?* I couldn't work for the town sheriff! What if the Jackson police had found a picture of me and sent it to all the other police stations? I didn't exactly know how all the police departments talked to one another, but if the police were looking for me in Jackson, working right under the nose of the Chillicothe police wasn't the smartest thing for me to do.

Finally, Sheriff Coogler cleared his throat. "Bettyjean tells me you not from around these parts."

"No, sir." I didn't turn around to face him. I just kept at those dishes.

"Where you say you come from?"

"I came here from Birmingham." It was the truth, although I don't think that was the answer he was looking for.

"I see. Why you in Chillicothe?"

I stared out the kitchen window gathering my thoughts. I rinsed a glass and gently placed it on the drying rack before I turned around to face him. "I buried my daddy a few years back. Did the same with my momma last year. I didn't have much else to keep me back home. I thought I'd start somewhere fresh. Maybe the pain of death might not hurt so much if I didn't have to look at them same walls."

"I see." The sheriff folded his newspaper and tossed it on the kitchen table. He stood from his chair and I was surprised to see that he wasn't much taller than his wife. But what he lacked in height, he made up for in width. His black belt, pistol and nightstick holster included, formed a tight circle at the bottom of his round belly. What was left of his blond hair was combed over the tight pink skin of his scalp. He reached in his back pocket and pulled out a small brown pouch. He dipped a thumb and forefinger inside and brought out a pinch of chewing tobacco, which he placed inside his bottom lip. He folded the pouch and slipped it in his back pocket.

"Tell Bettyjean I've gone to the station."

"Yes, sir."

I wasn't keen on the local sheriff digging into my background. I'd made a mistake taking this job. Maybe my explanation was enough to settle the Cooglers down about my past, but I couldn't be sure. I needed to leave town sooner than I'd planned.

After I finished the morning dishes, I set about cleaning up the living room. It seemed like every room I walked into, Bettyjean Coogler was hovering somewhere just beyond a wall or a doorway, peeping in, checking up on me to make sure I either did my work or didn't steal anything. From the looks of things, the Cooglers weren't rich. They were just about what you'd expect from folks who lived with all the favor life readily handed to white people, like a nice home, an icebox full of food, and the ability to come and go as they pleased. Meanwhile, colored folks was left with cleaning up their messes and standing last in line behind them for everything from food to furniture.

Back home, Papa had worked hard to shelter his girls from the harshness of life in the South—the ugly comments and the hard reality of being colored in a white man's world. But how do you shelter a child from what was inescapable? We weren't blind. We knew that the books we used in school didn't look like the ones the white kids used. We knew we couldn't use the local libraries or swimming pools like the white kids. How do you tell a child that life will be better for them, when everything in the world told them something different? I had to force my mind to stop thinking on those things because they always took me to a bad place.

After I made the beds, Bettyjean called me in the kitchen and pointed me to a bowl of ground beef and a couple cans of green peas. She said Sheriff Coogler wanted meatloaf for dinner with mashed potatoes and peas. It was my job to make it.

"And not too much milk in them potatoes, Mamie. Butch don't like soggy potatoes," she said.

She must have called me "Mamie" at least ten times since I stepped foot inside her house. And every single time, I corrected her with the name "Vera." Even though it wasn't my real name, it was the name I told her to call me and I wouldn't give up until she did.

When it came to dinner, I might finally show my true weakness as a maid. I could wash dishes, make a bed, and sweep a floor. But when it came to cooking, I was in trouble. Cooking never interested me and try as she might, Momma could never get me to follow her around the kitchen the way Rose and Marigold did. I preferred to be outside with the sun on my face, skinned knees, and my hair tangled full of leaves and dirt.

Shortly after lunch Bettyjean left the house. It was only after she did that I realized how tiring she could be. If she wasn't creeping around behind me, she was barking orders at me. With her gone, I decided to give that meatloaf a shot, but I can't say I woulda ate it if somebody sat it down in front of me. The shape of it was more like a big meat patty instead of a meatloaf, and if I was starving and them potatoes was the last thing on earth to eat, I wouldn't touch them, either. By the end of the day, I'd done the best I could and left it all on the stove. I took off the apron and headed out the back door for Miss Willa's boardinghouse.

My feet hurt something awful. All I wanted to do was get to my room and fall into bed. I crossed over the wooden bridge for the other side of town. By the time, I strolled past Periwinkle, I got an odd sensation, like somebody was following me. I turned around and spied an old man, bearded, late forties, walking behind me. Thinning gray wisps of hair along the sides of his head left the round bald top of it glimmering in the afternoon sunshine. A ragged pair of overalls and a faded plaid shirt hung off his thin body and his shoes had seen better days. I slowed down waiting for him to pass me. He slowed down. I sped up a bit, he did too. I finally turned around.

"What you up to, old man?" I said, my voice rumbling down the street. The man stopped in his tracks.

"I'm sorry, miss. I didn't mean no disrespect. I was

hoping you could spare a bit of change. I ain't eat nothing all day."

I felt a little bad at my having been gruff with him. "Sorry, I got nothing." I turned around and continued toward the boardinghouse.

"You new around here?" I could hear the old man's footsteps pace a bit faster to catch up with me. I didn't respond. By the time I turned the corner for Miss Willa's house, he was neck and neck with me. He smelled like he'd drank his last few meals, and a bath and a bar of soap wouldn't hurt him none either.

"You staying at Miss Willa's place?" he asked.

"That ain't for you to know." I never slowed down.

"I know some stuff. I know where it's at." He shook his head, wide-eyed and excited. "I do. I know."

"G'on now!" I kept a steady pace.

"Yeah, I know things," he said, sadly this time.

Just as I was about to take off running, a pickup truck pulled alongside me.

"Hey! Bankrobber, what are you up to?"

I peeped inside the truck at the most beautiful golden-brown face I'd ever seen in my life. His smile lit up the entire truck. I stopped cold. The man he called Bankrobber stopped too.

"Bankrobber, you're not giving the young lady any trouble are you?" the man asked.

"No, sir. I was just escorting this beautiful lady to her house."

I turned and rolled my eyes at Bankrobber. When I peered back in the truck, the man inside was chuckling. Obviously having a laugh at my expense.

"It's awfully hot out here. Can I give you a lift, miss? I'm not sure Bankrobber is the best company for a nice lady like you."

I threw him a suspicious glance. I didn't care if he did have a face like an angel. "I don't accept rides from strangers." I turned to Bankrobber. "And I don't need an escort!"

"I won't be a stranger if you let me introduce myself. My name is—"

I spun away from the truck and strutted off before he could finish his sentence. I heard him chuckling again before he drove off.

* * *

By the time I reached the boardinghouse, Bankrobber was still on my heels, even walked right up the steps beside me. I stopped on the porch. He sat down on the stoop, out of breath a bit. "You sho walk fast, lady."

Before I could say anything, Miss Willa appeared at the screen door. "Bankrobber, what you doing around here?"

"How you do, Miss Willa. I see you got a new boarder. I was just escorting the young lady back to your place."

Miss Willa looked at me, then back at the old man. "You eat anything today?"

"No, ma'am, and I sure would appreciate anything you could spare."

Miss Willa opened the screen door and I walked inside. "I didn't ask him to walk with me," I said.

She scrunched her face up like she was frustrated with me *and* the old man. "I know you didn't." She disappeared into the kitchen. I stood inside the screen door and watched the old man everyone called Bankrobber. He adjusted the strap of his overalls that had fallen from his shoulder before he knocked a bit of dust from the toe of his shoe. Oddly, he seemed to care about his appearance. Maybe he was a wino or maybe he'd just fallen on hard times like so many other folks do.

Miss Willa returned a few minutes later with a couple pieces of chicken and two slices of bread wrapped in a piece of Cut-Rite Wax Paper. "Bankrobber, take this and g'on about your business now. Leave my boarders alone."

"Thank you kindly, ma'am. I appreciate this." He

scuttled down the stairs, the food tight between his hands.

"Who is he?" I asked.

Miss Willa gave me a sad look. "Just another lost soul." She walked back into the kitchen without another word.

14
Vera

*F**ast decisions.*
  I lay across the bed still second-guessing everything I'd done between here and Jackson. Had the police found Huxley's body yet? Did Dewey return to Jackson and tell the police what I'd done to him? How long would it be before the police would start looking for me outside of Jackson if they weren't already? And I couldn't stay at the Cooglers. It was too close to dangerous.

I was lost in my thoughts when I heard a soft knock on my door. None of the rooms had locks on the doors. "Come in."

Lilly opened the door. She was dressed in a pair of pink capris and a flowered top. Her hair was plaited and tucked behind her ears. She looked like she should be outside, skipping rope or playing jacks instead of working in a funeral home and living in a boarding-house.

"Hey, Vera. You coming downstairs for dinner?"

"Maybe later."

"Miss Willa don't hold dinner for folks. She say the kitchen closes at six thirty. If you gon' eat, you best to get after it."

I sat up on the edge of the bed. "Hey, I went over to that house on Washington Street. The one where they looking for a maid? Why didn't you tell me that's the sheriff's house?"

"Do it matter? Work is work. Did she hire you?" Lilly walked over to the window and peeked down at Miss Willa's garden.

"Yeah, she hired me. I'm the 'new Mamie,' as she called me all day, even though that ain't my name."

"That's the way they do. How'd it go?"

"She followed me everywhere I went inside the house. She could have cleaned it herself. The sheriff didn't have much to say. I barely saw him."

"Then it sounds like it was a good day." Lilly smiled, her innocent dimples sprung to life.

"I don't think I'm much cut out for cleaning and cooking, though."

"You ain't done domestic work before?"

I slipped on my bobby socks. "Afraid not."

"Where you work before this?"

Lilly and all her questions. If she had a special eye, why didn't she know the answers before she asked. "Just different places. Hey, you know an old man named Bankrobber?"

Lilly giggled. "You met Bankrobber?"

"According to him, he was my escort home today."

"He harmless. But you betta hide your liquor if he's anywhere nearby."

"I figured as much."

"He moved here from Chicago some years back. Said he robbed a bank up in Chicago and stashed the money all over the city. Say the police can't find it and he moved down here so they wouldn't find him, either. He walk around talking about where all that money is hidden. Like I said, he's harmless."

So it looked like me and Bankrobber had something in common. Both of us outlaws.

"Well, I guess we better get downstairs before Miss Willa closes the kitchen," I said.

* * *

After dinner, I sat in my room, missing Marigold, tortured by Huxley's murder, and haunted by Momma and Papa's disappointment in me. Papa had been good to us—his "girls" is what he used to call me, my sisters, and Momma. I don't think I'll ever forgive myself for what I did to my little family. I ripped apart Momma's little bouquet—Rose, Marigold, and Violet. Her three flower girls. Rose was just like her name, beautiful, a standout. She was Momma's favorite, always following her around, sitting knee to knee with her and soaking in all Momma's wisdom. Marigold, smart and ambitious, was Papa's favorite. And then there was me.

What was a violet good for?

I slipped Rose's diary from my bag. I read a random entry.

May 10, 1956

Dear Diary,

I had the best time at the school dance. The dress Momma made me was perfect. Even Annie Pearl Culver told me she liked my dress. Silas said I looked pretty. And yes! Silas kissed me!! It was nice but a little too wet.

Before Silas and I left for the dance, Violet came up to me and said when she grows up, she wants to be as pretty as me. Violet doesn't know it yet, but she's the prettiest out of all of us. But like Momma says, she's going to have to learn to control her temper. Violet doesn't back down from anything. Momma said Violet will find her own way someday, either the easy way or the hard way. Yesterday, she got into trouble for fighting at school. Momma and Papa put her on punishment. She acted like it didn't bother her. I know it did. Last night, after everyone was asleep, I heard her crying. I went over to her bed and climbed in beside her. When I held her close, she stopped crying and told me sometimes she just can't help herself. She said she feels like she's chained up inside and the only way to break free is to speak her mind. I think Violet might be onto something because I feel the same way too. The only difference is that Violet speaks up. I only wish I could.

I closed the diary. I couldn't bear to read another word. Rose was dead and gone and it was my fault. I tamped down the urge to bust out wailing. Why did I keep letting my anger and my selfish behavior hurt the people I loved? I shouldn't have left Marigold behind to face the consequences for my deeds. Marigold was all I had left.

I slipped on my shoes and tied my hair into a pony-tail before I started off for Birdie's house. She was standing out on the front stoop talking with a neighbor, an older woman with pink hair curlers and a cigarette.

"Hey, Vee!" Birdie called out as I walked up.

I nodded at the neighbor. "Can I use your phone? I need to call Marigold. *Collect*. I promise."

"Sure, g'on inside."

I walked inside the house. One of Birdie's twins was asleep on the sofa. The other kids must have been outside because the house was quiet. I paced up to the phone on the kitchen wall and lifted the receiver. I hesitated 'cause I didn't know what was going on back in Jackson. I didn't even know whether Marigold would accept my call. I wouldn't blame her if she didn't.

I dialed zero and prayed.

"This is the operator. How may I help you?"

"My name is Violet Richards. I'd like to place a collect call to Marigold Richards." I rattled off the phone number and continued to pray. Then I realized I'd said my real name out loud. What a *stupid* thing to do. What if the operator found out the police were looking for me and they traced me back to where this call was coming from? Before I could hang up, I heard Marigold's voice.

"Hello," Marigold said on the other end.

Now I couldn't hang up even if I wanted to.

"I have a collect call from Violet Richards. Will you accept?" the operator said.

"Yes! Violet, is that you?"

The operator dropped off the line. "Marigold. Hey, I just wanted to hear your voice."

"Are you okay? Where are you?"

"I'm fine. I'm fine."

"Violet, what happened? The police were here at the house looking for you, and a white man showed up looking for you too."

"A white man?" *Dewey?* That didn't make sense. He wouldn't want anyone to find out about us.

"He said he was a lawyer and you were looking for his help. I work with lawyers every day and he didn't look like much of a lawyer to me."

"I didn't talk to no white lawyer. What did he look like?" *Could it have been Dewey?*

"Like I said, white man, dark hair. Cleft chin and a scar over his eye. Creepy eyes, too. Scary looking."

That didn't sound like Dewey. "You didn't tell him anything, did you?"

"I *couldn't* tell him anything. I don't know where you are."

"I'm in Chillicothe, Georgia. That little town where Birdie Mae lives."

"Chillicothe? What are you doing there?"

I didn't answer.

"Violet, did you kill Huxley?"

"Marigold, don't ask questions you don't want to know the answers to. The police ain't giving you no trouble, is they?"

"No. Like I said, they came by the house once. I haven't seen them since. But, Violet—"

"And I don't go by Violet no more. I go by the name Vera. Vera Henderson."

"*Vera?!* Like Grandma's name?" The phone went quiet for a moment. "Okay, *Vera*, I'm glad you called. I need to tell you something." She hesitated. "I wanted to tell you I'm getting married."

"Married?" My heart stopped and I hoped she wasn't about to say what I thought she would say.

"Yeah. Roger and I are getting married on Friday. We're moving to Cleveland, up in Ohio. Roger got a brother, Frankie. He thinks we can get a fresh start there."

I didn't say nothing at first. Marigold was smarter than this. Roger Bonny wasn't right for her and we both knew it.

"Violet? I mean, *Vera*. You there?"

"Yeah, I'm here. Why you doin' this, Marigold? You can do so much better. You work with them big-shot lawyers and folks down on Farish Street. Why you wanna hitch up with a knucklehead like Roger?"

"Violet, you've got the police banging on the front door looking for you! What if they think I had something to do with this thing? I have to leave town too."

"But you don't have to marry Roger to do that!"

Marigold was quiet for a moment before she spoke again. "It's just better this way. Let's just let it be. Do you have a phone where I can reach you when I get to Ohio?"

"You got a pencil? Take down Birdie's number. Call me when you get up to Ohio." I rattled off the phone number. "She'll know how to reach me. But why y'all got to move all the way up there? What about your job? You said you love that job and doing important work for our people."

Marigold went silent. I almost thought she'd hung up. "It's time to move on and do important work somewhere else," she said quietly.

We was both quiet for a few seconds. Something wasn't right. I could just tell. I had what Momma used to call a God sense, something deeper and more spiritual than common sense. And right now, my God sense told me there was something else going on.

"I'm sorry about all this. You sure you okay, Marigold?"

"I'm fine."

"What about the house? Momma and Papa's things?"

"You know we don't own this house. I gave notice. The moving truck is coming on Friday."

"But you just leaving everything behind?"

"Like you didn't?"

I didn't say a word. I deserved that. Marigold was right. Why was she supposed to stay behind in Jackson after the mess I'd created? Police and lawyers looking for me. If she wanted a better life up north, how could I begrudge her that? I just wasn't sure she'd find it with a man like Roger.

Marigold piped up again. "Roger said I could even take college classes up there. It's going to be fine, Violet— I mean, Vera."

"I know, it takes a little getting used to."

"Why are you staying down there? Come up north with me."

"Hmm . . . that's not a bad idea. Maybe I could do that. It's gotta be better than being down here."

"At least there's no Jim Crow up north. Come be

with me in Cleveland. I'll let you know as soon as we get settled in Ohio and you come on up."

"Okay, I will. You be careful up there. I hear things move pretty fast up north. I love you, sis."

"I love you too," Marigold said.

I hung up the phone and cried. I didn't get a good feeling about her moving up north. And I had an even worse feeling about the Jackson, Mississippi, police and some white man posing as a lawyer looking for me.

15
Vera

I showed up at the back door of the Coogler household the next morning, on time and loathing it. I studied the kitchen. How two grown people without a child or a pet could manage to trash one house in twenty-four hours was well past my understanding. Or maybe they did it just because they could, because "the new Mamie" would clean it all up.

As I cleared the dishes from the table, I noticed the *Tolliver County Register* newspaper on the table. I unfolded it and glanced at the first page—a small distraction from all the day's work ahead of me. From the looks of the headlines, nothing much happened in this small, dead-end town. A local election for town commissioner. The mayor cut the ribbon for some new building we would have to walk through the back door of. But down near the bottom of the page was a small article about those civil rights workers that had gone missing back home in Mississippi. The article wasn't more than a couple paragraphs, but it described how their bodies had been found buried on an old farm not too far from where they'd gone missing in Neshoba County.

Every time I thought about those young men, my heart ached. One was from Mississippi and the other two were from up north. They were someone's sons, brothers, a husband. They were loved. All three of them here in the South fighting to help us get the right to vote. And they were dead, fighting for something that is rightfully ours to have. When would people put aside all their hate and do what's right?

I scanned the rest of the page and spotted another article. This one reported on a young woman who was accused of stealing fifteen dollars from her employer. The all-white jury of twelve men found her guilty, and the judge sentenced her to twenty years in the women's state prison. A chill ran through me. If the Jackson police ever caught me, I'd rot in jail for killing Huxley. If they didn't do worse to me.

How long did I have before they found me? How far could I run?

16
Mercer

F riday morning, Mercer cruised past the house on Oakland. He'd made up some excuse to Mary Lou for getting out of the trailer early and headed over to the house. Through bits and pieces, he learned the woman's sister, Marigold, worked downtown with all those people fighting to get Negroes the right to vote. Mercer had never voted a day in his life and didn't really understand what the big deal was. As far as he was concerned, politicians were nothing but a bunch of crooks, skimming the cream off the top for themselves and leaving the little guy to scratch and survive on what was left. It was all a ploy to keep the powerful in power. Folks like Mercer were still kept out of the real action.

On his daily drive-bys, Mercer sometimes parked nearby to sit and watch for any comings and goings.

He dismissed his initial thought to go to Birmingham to look for her. The rich little bastard hadn't paid him enough for all that trouble. Thus far, the only people he'd seen anywhere near the house were Marigold and some man she appeared to be friendly with, probably a boyfriend. A small piece of him thought about taking the money Dewey had given him as a down payment and leaving town with Mary Lou and Randy. Dewey could find the woman the best way he could. But it wouldn't be nearly enough to get them through the end of the year unless he could find a job in the new town. And holding down a steady job was always hit or miss for Mercer.

The better part of him wanted to do something decent for his wife and kid. That's why he decided to finish the job, find the woman, collect all his money, and be done with the Leonard family forever. Ever since he'd met Mary Lou, she made him want to do better. She talked about her dream of living near the beach. She talked about it so much that living in a little house near the beach and watching Randy splash and play in the ocean had become Mercer's dream, too.

On his third drive past the house, he noticed a small moving truck out front and a couple of colored men standing on the porch talking to the sister and the man he'd spied before. One of them, dressed in a T-shirt and work pants, collected money from the sister's friend, who was dressed in a suit jacket and pants, no tie. Mercer made a quick U-turn at the end of the street and parked his car a few houses down. He watched as the moving truck pulled off. The well-dressed man headed back inside the house. Ten minutes later, he came back out with the sister. They climbed inside a busted-up Plymouth with another young colored man and pulled off. Mercer pulled off behind them.

* * *

Mercer followed the Plymouth to the edge of the parking lot at the train station. The place roared with the whistles of Pullman porters hailing taxis and travelers squealing welcomes or exchanging farewell embraces. Mercer watched the young couple climb out of the car. They hugged the driver and said their goodbyes. Mercer parked and followed them inside, careful to keep a reasonable distance. He'd shown his face to the sister. That was a colossal mistake. If she spotted him and remembered, he'd have to make up another lie to cover the first one he told.

Mercer pulled down the brim of his misshapen felt

hat as he stood back from the coloreds-only line. He watched the couple purchase their tickets. When they were done and walked off, Mercer dashed to the front of the line, cutting off a colored woman and several other customers behind her.

"This is official police business," Mercer said to the woman without an apology, as if he believed it himself. He leaned in toward the clerk. "Sir, can you tell me where that young colored couple is headed? The ones you just sold tickets to."

The clerk looked confused until Mercer pointed at them as they walked away. He reached in his pocket and pulled out a five-dollar bill and slid it across the counter to the clerk.

The clerk took the money and eased it in his pocket as he leaned in the direction Mercer pointed. "Oh, them? They just bought one-way tickets to Cleveland, Ohio."

Mercer thought for a second. "What time is that train scheduled to arrive in Cleveland?"

The clerk scanned a timetable posted on the wall behind the counter. "Let me see. That train has a few stops to make. Looks like they'll arrive in Cleveland tomorrow evening, seven o'clock."

"Thanks."

Mercer hustled back to his car, mentally calculating whether he could beat a locomotive train to Cleveland by car. With his car and the engine inside it that was just getting by, he'd barely make it across the Mississippi state line.

He needed to make a phone call.

* * *

Mercer stood inside a pay phone booth outside the train station. He dropped a coin inside the phone and dialed. Two rings later, Dewey answered, all confident and smug. It rattled Mercer just hearing his voice. He suddenly realized how much he hated this guy.

"Dewey. It's Mercer."

"Did ya' find her?"

"That's why I'm calling. I think I got a lead."

"A lead? What does that mean?"

"Her sister is headed out of town. Depending on how bad you wanna find this woman, I can follow her. It might lead me to the woman you're looking for."

Dewey was quiet for a moment. "Yeah, go ahead and follow her."

"Well, to do that, Imma need more money *and a plane ticket.*"

"A plane ticket?!"

"The sister is headed to Ohio."

"Where in Ohio?"

"Now if I told you that, you could go find her your-self and I would be out of twelve hundred bucks." Mercer let his words hang in the air between them. How long Dewey stayed quiet might tell him how bad he wanted to find Violet Richards. It might tell him how much this guy was in love with a colored woman.

"More money, Bugsy? I don't know. I already gave you over a thousand dollars. Like I told you, I'll pay you the rest when you find her."

Mercer resisted the urge to correct Dewey on his name. He needed the money. Mercer comforted him-self with the thought that Dewey was an asshole and he deserved the likes of whatever trouble this colored woman brought him.

"That woman is nowhere to be found in Jackson. It seems to me, there's a good chance the sister is traveling to see the woman you want to find. And I don't think they're coming back. The sister packed up the whole house and bought a one-way ticket. Your choice."

Dewey went silent. Mercer was smart enough to wait him out.

"And you said they're headed up north, huh?"

"Isn't that where they all head? I'll need another

thousand to trail her up there. And I'll need it fast. She's leaving in about an hour."

Dewey gave a long deep sigh into the phone. "Okay. Meet me in an hour. I'll get you the money."

Mercer hung up and headed for the supply store.

17
Mercer

This would be the hardest part of this whole job.

Mercer pulled up to the front of his trailer and cut the engine. What kind of man forces his family to live in a busted trailer with no hot water? What kind of man was he, serving as an errand boy to the likes of Dewey Leonard and chasing some colored woman across the country? He dropped his head against the window of the car. Surely he could do better than this.

The first thing he saw when he stepped inside the trailer was Randy lying across the sofa. A small sick thing of a boy. He had Mercer's cleft chin, and it always made Mercer proud when people fawned over the boy and commented about how much he resembled his dad. A tumble of strawberry blond curls fell across the little boy's eyes as he slept. Mary Lou wouldn't let Mercer take him to the barbershop, not when he was sick. He walked over to the sofa and laid his hand across the boy's forehead. Fever. Flushed cheeks.

"Mercer? That you?"

"Yeah, honey, it's me," he said quietly.

Mary Lou walked into the living room. "You hungry? I got some fried Spam and baked beans in the kitchen." Then she looked down at Randy. "I couldn't get him to eat. The fever's back."

Growing up as an only child, Mercer dreamed of having a pretty wife and a bunch of kids. The plan started out all right when he met and married Mary Lou. But Randy had always been a sickly sort of kid. Ear infections. Colds. Right after his fifth birthday, he came down with rheumatic fever. But Randy was as tough as he was sick, and he got through the worst of it. Over the years, Randy's illnesses had become like another kid in the house, something else they had to attend to with all the worry, medicines, hospital visits, and doctors' bills. *The bills.* They nearly swallowed up Mercer and Mary Lou both. Their plans to have another child fell by the wayside in their effort to keep this child alive.

Mercer motioned for Mary Lou to follow him back into the bedroom.

"What is it?" she asked. Mercer could read her face

like a road map, and right now it told him she knew bad news was on the way.

"Listen, I need to go away for a few days."

"Go away? We can't go anywhere now. Randy's not feeling well."

"Not *us*. Just me. I need to go to Ohio, honey."

"Ohio?! Good Lord, why are you going to Ohio? We don't know anybody up there."

"Dewey Leonard—"

"Dewey Leonard?! Mercer, why in the world are you getting involved with him again? I thought you were done with him and that whole family. I thought you said you were putting all that business in the past."

True, Mercer was tired of acting as an errand boy for the Leonards. But there was something about the lure of their money, the idea that maybe if he was in proximity to the Leonards and all their money, he could show them he was just as good as they were. After all, he was a white man just like them.

"Listen, Dewey asked me to handle some business for him up there. I promise I won't be gone more than a week."

"A week?! Does this have anything to do with that stuff that happened back a couple months ago?"

Mercer slipped an old gym bag from underneath the bed and unzipped it. "Nothing like that. Dewey just wants me to find some information for him. Once I get it, I'll be on the first plane home."

"Plane?! Mercer, you've never been on an airplane in your whole life. I thought you didn't like airplanes. What's this all about?"

Mercer dropped the bag and walked over to Mary Lou. He pulled her close. "It's the only way I can get up to Ohio and back home to you and Randy in a hurry. Look, he's paying me a lot of money. Enough money so we can buy that little house on the beach you been talking about. When I'm done, we can move out to Florida and be near your sister."

"Mercer, none of this sounds right to me. Airplanes, money. What's going on?"

There was no explaining to Mary Lou he was off to find a colored woman for Dewey. And he knew if he told her how much Dewey was actually paying him, he'd lose the argument that was sure to follow. It was best that she know as little as possible. He'd find Violet Richards, collect the money, and the three of them would be out of Mississippi and on to the sunny shores of Florida in a couple of weeks.

"Mary Lou, you know I love you. I wouldn't do anything unless it was best for you and Randy. You trust me?"

"I trust you. But—"

"Then let me pack this bag and get on my way."

Mercer reached in his pocket. He pulled out a thick wad of cash and handed it to Mary Lou.

"Landsakes! What are you doing with this kind of money?! There's . . ." She flipped through the bills. "Mercer, there's over five hundred dollars here."

"And there's more to come. Put it in a safe place."

Mary Lou stared at him for a beat. She was on the brink of tears, but she was softening. Seeing all that money was having the same effect on her as it had on Mercer. The money represented an answer to their prayers and freedom from the trailer park. The promise of something better made them both feel different.

"Mercer, I trust you. What you say goes in this house, but I do not have a good feeling about all this. Especially if it involves the Leonards."

"It'll be okay. I promise." He watched her shoulders slump under her cotton dress.

Everything in Mary Lou's face loosened, like a soldier surrendering to the fight. She slowly nodded. "There's clean underwear in the top drawer. I'd better go check on Randy."

She walked out of the bedroom. Mercer decided he'd give Dewey one week. After that, he could find his girlfriend on his own.

18

Vera

I was playing with the devil by continuing to work for the Cooglers. I debated long and hard with myself about whether I should return at all after that first day. On my second day working for them, I made up some excuse about having to return home to Alabama. I told Bettyjean she would have to find someone else. I figured after that meatloaf I left on the stove, she wouldn't be too broken up about finding another maid. Boy, was I wrong! First, she cried big old crocodile tears, telling me "how fond" she had grown of me—in one day! When that didn't work, she pitched a hissy fit, screaming and calling me everything but the child of God. She said she would blackball me in town, and I'd never get a job with another white family in Chillicothe. I wasn't none concerned about that, since

I was leaving town, but I decided I was tired of listening to all her tears and threats. I finally agreed to stay on. I figured maybe I was out of the woods, since the sheriff hadn't asked me any more questions. I still planned to quit. I just didn't tell Bettyjean as much.

Each day I worked for them was worse than the day before. Every morning started out the same. As soon as I stepped inside the kitchen, Bettyjean laid into me with a vengeance. No *Good morning.* No *How you doing today?* Just her barking orders at me.

"Mamie, you ever cooked a pot roast before?" Bettyjean said when I stepped in the house on this particular morning.

"It's Vera, and no, ma'am, but I'm sure I can figure it out." I went about putting on my apron and stashing away my lunch bag. I brought my own lunch and took up the rest of my meals at Miss Willa's house because Bettyjean Coogler said she would deduct from my pay the cost of any food I ate from her house. She also told me I couldn't use the toilet in her house, that I should use the one at the gas station around the corner. I ignored her and used it whenever she wasn't nearby.

"Now if you're going to stay on around here, you've got to learn how to cook." She lifted an old book covered in dust from a cabinet. "I found this cookbook somebody gave us as a wedding present. There's a recipe in here for pot roast. Follow it to the T, and it can't be like that meatloaf you made. That thing was a raggedy mess."

"Yes, ma'am. I'll do my best." I cleared the breakfast dishes from the table.

"Well, you might want to try harder this time. If you ruin Butch's dinner again, I can promise you he won't be happy. And by the way, Butch told me to ask you again, where you from?"

I didn't flinch although my stomach went to fluttering. "I'm from Alabama."

"I know you told me that. But what part of Alabama?"

"Well . . . Birmingham. All due respect, you mind my asking why, ma'am?"

"I don't know. He said he just wanted to know. Now listen, I need you to clean the back room. Everything in there's a jumble of clutter."

She rambled on, talking and barking orders at me, but I wasn't listening none. Sheriff Coogler was asking a bunch of questions about me again. What if he asked just enough questions to reach all the way back to Jackson, Mississippi?

I thought about Marigold living up north and never having to see the inside of a white person's house that she had to clean. I thought about her finally getting to take them college classes. She was so smart. Maybe she and Roger would work out after all. And like she said, maybe I'd move up to Ohio too. Thinking on Marigold's happiness and my moving up north to join her made me feel better. Pleasant thoughts about my sister was the only way I held my anger at a woman talking to me as if I was a child. It was also the thing that kept me from thinking too long about Sheriff Coogler and what would happen if he figured out his maid was a murderer.

". . . You know Butch and I are good people, and we treat our help a far cry better than some of the other folks here in town. Mamie, you listening to me?"

I sighed. "It's Vera, and yes, ma'am, I'm listening." I was still bound and determined to make her call me Vera. I wouldn't back down just because she had decided she wanted to call me some dead woman's name.

She finally walked out the room. No sooner had I started to enjoy the peace and quiet of her being gone before she was back in the kitchen. This time, with a friendly little voice.

"Looka here! I got something for you."

I stopped washing the dishes and dried my hands. Bettyjean came skipping toward me with a big paper sack in her arms. "I got a few things I can't use anymore. I thought you might like 'em. You're much bigger than me, but maybe there's something in here that might fit you."

"Thank you, Miss Bettyjean," I said as I took the bag. I didn't bother to look inside. Instead, I set it beside the back door. I picked up my dishcloth and began wiping down the kitchen table.

She stood staring at me for a moment before she spoke. "Well, aren't you going to look inside?"

Bettyjean Coogler was like a small child always looking for attention. I didn't have the extra strength to coddle her and clean up her dirty house, too. "Ma'am, I just thought I'd better tend to my work first."

"But look at this." She pulled a pink-and-green skirt from the bag. "This used to be my favorite skirt. You just need to fix the hem and patch up this hole in the front."

"Yes, ma'am."

"I bought this over at Cullum's in Augusta a few years back. They have the best things. You ever shop there?"

"No, ma'am."

"I tried to get a charge account there, but if you're a woman, they won't let you get credit unless your husband cosigns for you. And Butch . . . well, he's not interested in me having nice things."

I didn't say a word. How was I supposed to feel sorry for her not getting store credit when she was barely paying me enough to live on? Some days it was more than a notion with Bettyjean Coogler. The silence between us got awkward. I picked up the dish towel and proceeded to wipe down the kitchen table.

She dropped the skirt back into the bag. "Well . . . okay. Listen, I'm going to get dressed. I'm going out for a breath of fresh air." She scurried back to the bedroom.

Going out for a breath of fresh air was her way of saying she was leaving the house. Sometimes she'd be gone for hours, always arriving before her husband got home. And she always made me wash the clothes she had worn.

When she left the kitchen, I peeked inside the paper sack. It was worse than I'd imagined. The bag was filled with a bunch of junk that was better suited for the garbage can. In addition to the skirt, inside was a pair of old shoes, one of them missing the heel. There were several blouses and dresses with underarm spots and stains, along with two old bras and three pairs of soiled panties.

I remember Momma used to work for a white family back in Jackson. The woman would give Momma things for her "little flowers." I can't recall ever wearing a thing out of those bags. Momma forbade it. Instead, she would cut the clothing into strips and weave a throw rug out of it. She said the things weren't going to waste and walking around on a soft rug under her feet made her feel better. A few minutes later, Bettyjean clattered back through the kitchen, fussing around for a pair of shoes she'd misplaced. She finally left. *Thank God.*

I finished up the dishes and headed to the bedroom. The bedroom was worse than the kitchen, everything disheveled, dirty underwear and hosiery left on the floor, blouses and dresses pulled from the closet and scattered across the bed. Clusters of clothes bulged from opened drawers. If poor Mamie had to do this every day, she must have suffered an early death from working for the Cooglers.

I always saved the hardest task of the day for last. The only thing worse than the kitchen and the bedroom was having to clean the Cooglers' bathroom. Between the hair Butch left in the sink from shaving and the unflushed toilet and the soiled sanitary napkins Bettyjean left around, it was enough to make me want to throw up. I didn't even like cleaning the bathroom at my own house back in Jackson.

But cleaning without her around was still a far sight better than when she was in the house. If Bettyjean didn't go out, she followed me from room to room, commenting on some little thing I hadn't cleaned or some spot I missed, and always with a threat not to pay me my week's wages if I didn't correct it.

Whenever I stepped inside the *back* door of the Coogler household, a little piece of my soul crumbled off and made me feel a smidge less human. Every time I flushed their toilet after them or picked up some piece of garbage Bettyjean intentionally tossed on the floor when I entered the room, I fought back the rage. Since I decided today was my last day, the anger and shame of working for the Cooglers was replaced by the fear and uncertainty of what to do next.

* * *

I was just finishing up the bathroom when I heard the screen door at the front of the house slam shut. Bettyjean must have forgotten something. I didn't bother to seek her out. If I did, she'd find something else for me to do. I mopped the bathroom floor and emptied the dirty water down the commode.

A few minutes later, I stepped inside the kitchen. Sheriff Coogler was sitting at the kitchen table watching the doorway, as if he had been waiting for me to enter. My stomach did flips. All of a sudden the house got burning hot. Or maybe it just felt that way to me.

"Make me a sandwich, Vera."

"Yes, sir."

I was stunned two times over. First, that he called me by my name and not Mamie, the way his wife did. And second, because he was here. Although Bettyjean had mentioned her husband might come home for lunch, this was the first time he'd come home in the middle of the day since I started working for them. In fact, it was well past the lunch hour, nearly quitting time for me. I hadn't seen Butch Coogler since my first day working for them. I made it my business to be gone from the house long before he got home from work.

If you was a maid, the best thing you could do was to stay clear of the menfolk, especially if you was in the house alone with them. I didn't have Papa's pistol with me either. But I was close enough to a butcher knife or something hard enough to crack him over the head if he tried something.

I set the mop pail out on the screened porch and proceeded to the Frigidaire for the leftover ham and a few slices of cheese. I didn't say a word but went straight about the business of making his lunch. I prayed he wouldn't try to make small talk with me. *Just eat and go back to work.*

"Toast the bread too."

"Yes, sir."

I kept my back to him, lest I up and catch his eye. The silence between us was suffocating. No voices, only sounds in the room. The toast popping from the toaster. Metal against glass as I opened the mayonnaise jar. The clink of the knife against the plate as I sliced his sandwich in half. The sweet tea hitting the bottom of the glass as I poured his drink.

I walked across the kitchen and sat the plate and glass in front of him. I was already thinking ahead. The butcher knives were in the drawer next to the sink. The cast-iron skillet was sitting in the dish rack. The toaster was still hot and right on top of the counter. His pistol was in his holster. Right side. I had enough things close by to make it out of this house alive. I eased away from the table to go back to my work.

"Vera."

I froze.

"Where'd you say you was from again?"

"Alabama, sir. Birmingham," I said. "If you don't need me for anything else, best I get after my work, sir."

"Hang on."

I felt the roar of my blood rushing through my ears. My heart a pounding mess.

"I could use a little company while I eat my lunch."

I didn't have Papa's pistol with me. But I'd leave

him dead, too, just like Huxley, if he tried to lay a hand on me.

"Sir, Miss Bettyjean admonished me this morning about making sure that back room is clean before she gets home this afternoon."

"Sit."

"Yes, sir." I eased into the chair across the table from him, trying to put as much distance between the two of us as possible.

"You say your momma and daddy both dead, huh?"

"Yes, sir."

"You come a long way from home. Why you decide to come all the way to Chillicothe from a big city like Birmingham?"

So Coogler was trying to put the pieces of my background together. Had he heard about what happened back in Birmingham? Had Dewey called the police after I stole his wallet and now Coogler was on my scent?

"Birdie Mae Hudson is my cousin, and she live here in town. I thought it'd be nice to live near some kin."

"Mm-hmm . . . I see." He bit into his sandwich, breadcrumbs and a stray piece of ham falling onto the girth of his belly.

I didn't say a word. He didn't either. He just stared at me as he chewed. He didn't want my company. He was trying to catch me in a lie, to trip me up. All my bullheaded ways had led me down paths that were treacherous to walk. Running from the law, lying to the police, and murder.

"What'd you say your daddy's name was?"

I tried to control the butterflies all tangled up in my stomach. "John Henderson." John had been my grand-daddy's name. I never knew him, since he died before I was born. And Sheriff Coogler could go off looking for a John Henderson in Birmingham who was related to me. That should keep him busy for a good long while.

Coogler stared at me for a bit longer before he turned his attention back to his sandwich. With no more questions, I headed to the back of the house and tried to un-clench my hands from the two sweating fists I'd made at the kitchen table. I waited until I heard the screen door slam again. I scrambled to the front of the house and peeped out the living room window. I watched Coogler start up the engine and pull off from the front of the house. I stood at that window and stared until his patrol car turned off Washington Street and was out of sight.

Sheriff Butch Coogler was asking more questions than a body ought to. What made me think I could hide out in a town where people spent their free time nose-deep in other people's business?

I hustled back to the kitchen and quickly removed my apron. I had to get out of this house and this town. *Now.* I reached under the cabinet and grabbed my purse. I scrambled to the back door and out the screened porch. And who do I run smack-dab into? *Bettyjean.* I nearly ran her over I was moving so fast. She was panting and racing to get to the house just as I rounded the corner.

"Where are you going, Mamie?" she said.

"Well, I . . . I finished all my work. It's near quitting time for me."

Bettyjean looked down at her watch. "You still owe me almost an hour of duty. Come on back inside, Mamie. Imma need you to do a load of laundry before you leave for the day."

"Uh . . . yes, ma'am." I followed her back inside the house. I hated this job, and I hated this woman. I silently called her a name Momma would have scolded me for even thinking.

In the few days I'd been working for the Cooglers, Bettyjean always came back from her "breath of fresh air" right before her husband got home from work, tossing her dirty clothes at me. But I did not have time for this routine today. I had to get out of town.

Bettyjean raced through the kitchen and back to the bedroom. I followed her. I had originally planned to leave without collecting my wages—the price I'd pay for working for the Cooglers. But since Bettyjean decided to make me stick around for another hour, I'd collect what was owed to me. Bettyjean was halfway out of her blouse by the time I made it to doorway of the bedroom.

"What is it, Mamie?"

"It's Vera, and I wanted to ask about my pay for the week."

Bettyjean scrambled out of her pants. "Can't you see I'm in the middle of undressing? I'll be out in a few minutes. G'on, get out of here."

A couple minutes later, she scurried back into the kitchen in a bathrobe. She handed me her dirty underwear, a blouse, and a pair of white pants soiled with grass stains. "Get these in the machine and on the line before you leave. And put on a pot of coffee." She shook her head in exasperation. "You haven't even started dinner. What's going on? Get that coffee on and get started with dinner. Now. I'll pay you when you've *finished* your work!"

I shook my head and walked out to the old wringer machine on the back porch. Her blouse smelled of cigarettes and her underwear had a familiar funky, musty odor I recognized immediately: Bettyjean had been with a man. And it was highly unlikely that the man was her husband, since she needed them clean before he got home. I set the clothes inside the washing machine and started it for a five-minute cycle. I didn't care whether they were clean or not. She could explain her cheating ways to her husband if the smell didn't come out.

* * *

Nearly an hour later, I collected my pay and headed out the back door.

"Mamie! Wait a minute."

Oh God, what now?

Bettyjean handed me the bag of broken shoes and soiled clothes. "You forgot your things."

"Thank you."

I walked out the back door of that house for the last time. As I did, a little piece of my dignity was restored. Bettyjean and Butch Coogler assumed every colored woman was born to cook and clean for white folks. But I ain't like every other colored woman. I hate it when people try to put me in some little box because of who I am or what I look like. Anyway, I relished in the fact that I didn't have to step foot inside that big sunny house no more. And as for that paper sack of broken shoes and soiled clothes, I dropped it in the garbage can out behind the Piggly Wiggly on my way back to Miss Willa's.

Being so close to the town sheriff was a dangerous game I wasn't willing to play anymore.

I was leaving Chillicothe and headed to Ohio to join Marigold up north.

19

Vera

Back at Miss Willa's, I tidied up my room and left everything as neat as I'd found it the day I moved in. Then I packed up my things in my bag and crept down the staircase. I was headed to Ohio to be with Marigold. I heard Miss Willa in the kitchen humming and the sizzle of something frying on the stove. From the smell of it, pork chops woulda been my guess. I tiptoed to the front of the house and slowly opened the screen door, trying not to let the squeak of the rusty hinges reach Miss Willa back in the kitchen. I felt bad not saying goodbye to her or Lilly, but it might have been hard. I was getting used to Miss Willa's gruff way and Lilly had become like the little sister I never had. But both of them wouldn't understand and I couldn't explain the real reason why I needed to get on the road. It was time.

Outside, I hustled down the street and over the bridge headed for the bus port at the Piggly Wiggly. A few minutes after I arrived at the bus stop, a buxomly colored woman with finger waves in her hair pulled her small car up alongside me. She couldn't have been much older than me. I didn't recognize her. She honked her horn lightly.

"Miss? You waitin' on the Greyhound?"

"Yes."

"You'll be waiting awhile. I'm afraid you got the wrong day. The bus only comes through Chillicothe three days out of the week. Next bus won't be through here till Monday. Didn't you check the schedule posted on the wall of the store?"

"What?"

The woman pointed to a small gray sign on the side of the store's front door. It was a bus schedule. I'd been so stupid. I hadn't even bothered to check the schedule. Momma was back in my head: *Quick to act, slow to think.*

I walked over to the sign. She was right. Only two buses—one headed east and the other headed westbound—and both of them wasn't scheduled until Monday. I turned around. The woman sat in the car staring at me, her face full of pity for me.

"Thank you," I said as I gave a weak wave to the woman and started to walk off. She honked her horn again before she eased the car up beside me.

"You stay over to Miss Willa's place, don't you?"

"Yeah."

"Hop in. I'll give you a lift back."

I was tired. My conversation with Sheriff Coogler, the way I had hustled over here, my anxiousness to get out of town, and now the disappointment of there being no bus had worn me down. How could I run when I was so tired? And so stupid.

"Get in, honey. I won't bite." She smiled at me.

I stared back at the bus port like I was leaving an old friend. I slid inside the front seat, my bag tucked up against me on my lap. I wanted to crawl into a ball and cry.

She pulled the car out of the parking lot. "My name is Pauline Toney. I stay around the corner from Miss Willa."

"My name's Vera Henderson."

"Oh, I know who you are." My stomach tumbled. Did she know me from Jackson? Did she know what I'd done? "Miss Willa's a friend of mine. But it's nice to meet you formally, Vera Henderson."

"Thanks for the lift." I was still suspicious of her. What had she and Miss Willa been saying about me?

"No problem. So . . . you not too fond of our little town, huh?" she said with a chuckle.

"No. It's nothing like that."

Pauline gave me a side-eye glance. Then she smiled. "Honey, I've lived here for most of my life. You're the first person to move to Chillicothe in a long time. So where you off to in such a rush? Who you running from or what you running to?"

"What?"

Pauline pulled up to a red light and hit the blinker. "Look at you. Beautiful, with all that long dark hair. You could be anywhere you want to be. But you're here in Chillicothe because I suspect you need to be."

"What do you mean by that?"

"Oh, nothing." The light changed and Pauline turned into the intersection. "So where you headed . . . on Monday?"

"Washington, DC."

"Ahh, the nation's capital. You got family there or something?"

I replied, "No." Pauline was just like everybody else in this dreadful little town, full of questions that didn't concern them. "Just looking for a new place to land. I'm getting tired of the South."

"I can understand that." Pauline honked the horn

again, this time at an elderly couple sitting on their front porch. She waved and they waved back. "Can I give you a little piece of advice?"

I didn't say anything. Who was this strange woman to give me advice? Just because Miss Willa had gossiped to her about me moving to town didn't give her the right to think she could climb all inside my business like she was my momma or something.

"Well, you didn't say no, so I'll take that as a yes. If you're in so much of a rush that you didn't bother to look at the bus schedule, I'm thinking the rest of your plan to move to Washington, DC, might have a few holes in it too. You just told me you don't have family in Washington. You got a job lined up or a place to stay?"

I shook my head no.

"How much money you got saved up?"

I thought about Dewey's wallet. Again, I didn't answer.

"How old are you?"

I stared down at my hands. "Twenty-one," I said softly.

"You gotta be careful about moving to a new town with no family, no job, and no money. There's people out there that'll give you a job. The kind of job a nice girl like you wouldn't really want. And with no family and no other means of support, you wind up doing things you never thought you'd do." Pauline went silent and stared at the road, no words, her face blank.

"I don't know what you talking about."

"I think you do. Don't make the mistake I did when I moved up to New York."

I turned and stared at her. "What happened?"

"No need for details. I did some things I ain't proud of. But I had to eat, keep a roof over my head. I did what I had to do and I didn't hurt nobody in the process except myself." She gave me a quick glance. "A pretty girl like you, them pimps out there would have a field day. Look, I know Chillicothe ain't Washington, DC. I don't know what you're running from, but take your time and figure out your next move. Washington will be there when you're ready."

"If you was all the way up in New York, why you come back here to Chillicothe? Why didn't you go somewhere else?"

She stared straight ahead before she smiled. "For all the hate and hellfire in this town, I came back because there's people here who love me. They accept me for who I am. I don't have to ask anybody to love me or look out for me. They just do."

Pauline pulled up to the front of Miss Willa's house. Miss Willa was standing behind the screen door. Her brick bungalow perch where she watched over all the lost souls of Chillicothe. If I didn't know better, I woulda thought the two of them had cooked up this whole scheme. Miss Willa discovered I was gone, and she sent her friend to go retrieve me.

"Thanks for the lift."

"I'm rooting for you, sugar. We womenfolk gotta look out for one another."

I gave her a weak smile before I got out the car and closed the door. I walked up the front steps and stared through the screen door at Miss Willa. Neither of us said a word. Finally, she pushed open the door with a long loud squeak. I stepped inside.

"There's pork chops, rice, and beans for dinner. Don't let it get cold."

"Yes, ma'am."

Miss Willa and Pauline's scheme to keep me in Chillicothe wouldn't work. Come Monday morning, I would be back on that bus.

20

Vera

U pstairs in my room, Pauline Toney's advice rambled around in my head, busting up all the reasons I had for leaving this town. In a way, Pauline reminded me of Rose, giving out advice and trying to tell me what was best for me. Deep down, I knew Pauline was right, though. Just like Rose was always right too. Me trying to hide out from the police and run willy-nilly all over the country at the same time was a recipe for disaster. Killing Huxley gave me some justice, but it took away my freedom.

June 9, 1956

Dear Diary,

Sometimes Violet can be so bullheaded. Momma

told her to stay away from those woods. Again. But she didn't listen and because of it, I had to go out there to retrieve her. Again. Sometimes I think Violet does stupid stuff just to get Momma's and Papa's attention. Or maybe she does it because she's just like me and Marigold. All three of us want to be out of Mississippi and living where we can be like any white girl, free to roam around the streets without worrying about some white man grabbing us or some white lady accusing us of something we didn't do. We just want to be like any other girl. Why does the world have to work this way? What must it be like to wake up in the morning and not think about how different you are or to not have to think about what stores you can't go into and what streets you can't walk down because of the color of your skin? I can't remember a time when I didn't worry whether Momma or Papa would return home at the end of the day because someone had falsely accused them of something and decided to lynch them to set an example for everyone else.

Maybe Violet just wants to be free of all this too. Just like me and Marigold. All three of us like little birds, our wings clipped by life in Mississippi.

I'd made a mess of everything since I shot Huxley back behind that store. Now what was I supposed to do? I'd made a new name for myself, but my life was still the same quick-to-act-slow-to-think mess it always was. Pauline was right, I needed a plan. Especially since I was running from the police. But what about Butch Coogler and all them questions he was asking?

I ate dinner and then told Miss Willa I was headed over to Birdie Mae's house to sit for a spell. I left the house, but I walked toward town instead. I needed to clear my head. Thank God, no sign of the sheriff. I strolled down Church Street and past the Starlight Diner like I'd done every day on my way to the Cooglers' house. But the sign in the window made me stop: COOK WANTED. I couldn't cook a lick. And I didn't need another job. What I really needed was a way out of town. But something about that sign made me stop. I thought about Pauline's advice. *Take your time and figure out your next move.*

I refused to go back to the Cooglers'. Working under the sheriff's nose was like soaking my hands in gasoline before playing with matches. So that meant I either had to find another white person's toilets and nasty panties to clean or get an altogether different job, because I was certain I couldn't just lie around Miss Willa's place, not with her and Pauline Toney watching over me like a hawk.

A small bell hanging over the door tinkled lightly as I stepped inside the diner. Red leather booths lined two walls of the restaurant with small tables in the center. There was a row of red stools along a counter at the back and what I guessed was the kitchen beyond that. The smell of fried meat floated across the entire diner.

The place was mostly empty. I figured if I could talk my way into this job, maybe I could get Miss Willa to teach me how to cook and I could earn enough money to get myself settled properly in a new town. If I followed Pauline's advice, I'd move up to Cleveland with Marigold and be with people who cared about me. A tall, lean white man with a pompadour stood behind the counter. Two large ears stuck out from either side of his head and made him look like one of those characters from the funnies in the newspaper.

I stepped up to him. "I'm here to apply for the job you posted in the window, sir." The guy looked me over from head to toe, stern and all serious like. He didn't say a word.

"Order up!" a colored man called from the kitchen behind him.

The man with the pompadour turned and picked up

a plate with a hamburger and french fries and hustled over to a booth in the far corner. He exchanged a few words with a white couple in the booth before he slid a bottle of ketchup from his apron pocket and left it on the table. As I watched him interact with the couple, it occurred to me that I hadn't noticed another sign on the door. There wasn't a COLOREDS IN THE REAR sign. I looked across the diner. In the small table near the door, a colored woman sat with a young girl drinking milkshakes. I looked across the restaurant at the couple in the booth and then back at the woman and her child. I'd never seen the races sitting in a restaurant, nearly side by side, eating, talking, the way the world was supposed to work. I stood there like a statue staring at them, like it was the first time I'd ever seen people eating in a diner.

"Miss?"

I turned back to the counter. The man had returned and stood in front of me. "Where'd you work last?" he said without a hint of a southern accent.

My stomach sank. "Oh . . . well, I worked for Sheriff Coogler and his wife. But I've left that job."

The man pinched his brows together. "Did they fire you?"

I straightened a bit. "Sir, is the job taken?"

He shrugged. "No, the job isn't taken. Did you show up on time when you worked for the sheriff?"

"Yes, sir. I was never late or sick a day in the time I worked for them."

"Look, I'm in a tight situation here. Maybe we can try it for a week or two. One of my cooks on the day shift headed up north without telling me beforehand. Alma's the only cook I got out back and she can't handle the lunch crowds by herself. She can teach you what you need to know. You can't be late, and you have to work weekends."

"I can't work on Sundays. I take the Lord's Sabbath serious. But I don't mind working any other days."

"Do you want the job or not?"

"Yes, sir, I do. But I can't work when I'm supposed to be worshipping the Lord."

He stared at me for a beat. Then he started to talk like he was thinking out loud to himself. "Okay, tomorrow's Saturday. I can't be without a second cook. You'll have to work the Sunday thing out with Alma. She's the cook on the day shift you'll be working with. I can only pay you fifteen dollars a week."

I did a quick calculation and reasoned a couple weeks at this pay would be enough for me to head up to Ohio to be with Marigold, with a bit to spare. "Sounds fine."

"Okay. What's your name?"

"Vera Henderson."

"Nice to meet you, Vera Henderson. I'm John Palmer. I try to run a nice restaurant. I try to treat everybody fair. I've never required a Negro to go around to the back of my restaurant to get served and I treat them no different from any white person that comes in here to eat. I treat people the way I expect to be treated. Understood?"

"Understood."

Marigold and I had talked about that new law that said colored folks can come and go as they pleased now. But most white folks was still refusing to follow it. From the way Mr. Palmer talked, he followed it before anybody told him he had to. I was shocked.

"I don't want no trouble in my place. Be back here tomorrow at seven A.M. We open at eight. Alma can show you the ropes when you get here."

"Yes, sir." All of a sudden, I felt like a little kid on Christmas morning.

"Like I said, don't be late."

I started for the door when Mr. Palmer called after me. "Hey, Vera! I'm just curious. Let me ask you something. How did you like working for the Cooglers?"

His question caught me off guard. "They were fine people."

"They were fine people, but you don't work there anymore. Why?"

I thought for a moment. What I said to one white man could get me in trouble with another one. I smiled back at Mr. Palmer. "They were fine people. I just wasn't very good at cleaning, is all."

He shook his head and smiled back.

I left the diner. As I did, I felt something lift inside me. I was finding my own way. I knew the police might still be looking for me, so I wasn't out of the woods yet. But at least I had a plan. As long as I steered clear of Sheriff Coogler, I could earn some money and be up in Ohio with Marigold in a couple weeks.

21
Mercer

Mercer Buggs had never been on an airplane in his entire life. He'd traveled on a train a few times when he was a little boy living in South Carolina. Up until he was ten years old, he spent his summers in North Carolina with Grandpop, his mother's father. It was the one thing he looked forward to every year. He longed for those three months away from his father and all the booze and beatings. His mother had died giving birth to him. He'd heard the grown-ups talking about her losing so much blood it caused her to die. According to his father, he'd killed his own mother. "What kind of baby does that?" his father used to ask him. And Mercer never had a satisfactory answer as to why he'd killed his father's "dear, sweet Helen."

Whenever Mercer felt particularly bad about something, he would snatch a memory or two from the well of his heart. Memories of the train ride, the small towns and green farmland whizzing by in the window. Or the days when they went fishing and hunting wild rabbit. How Grandpop taught him how to play checkers and read him stories about Tom Sawyer or the Arabian nights. Grandpop used to tell him what a kind girl his mother had been growing up.

After that last summer, he and his father moved from South Carolina to Mississippi. Whenever Mercer asked about going to visit Grandpop, his father would slap him or hit him across his head hard enough to teach Mercer to stop asking. He never saw his grandfather again, didn't even know whether he was dead or alive.

Mercer learned to stop asking a lot of questions and just accept some things were out of his reach, beyond his grasp. Eventually, he dropped out of school and decided to live among the shadows. Odd jobs and day work were enough to keep him alive. But they weren't enough to keep him out of bars on those nights when all he wanted to do was get hammered and get into a fight. The nights when he wanted to feel the kind of physical pain that might erase the emotional ache.

And he might still be living that haggard life, in and out of trouble, if he hadn't met Mary Lou Stanton at a malt shop he'd wandered into looking for a pay phone.

She was everything he always told himself that he didn't deserve. Pretty, smart, and funny. He was right, too, except Mary Lou saw something in him that gave him another shot at living a different life. They didn't have much and Mary Lou, orphaned at two years old, didn't seem to mind. Once he met her, the timeline of his life was cut in two—"before Mary Lou" and "after Mary Lou." And they were happy; that is, until Randy got sick. Mercer knew he needed to do better. He wasn't as bad as his old man, but still, he needed to do right by his family. Finding that colored girl would give him enough money to be the kind of father to Randy that his old man never was to him.

Mercer had asked a neighbor to drop him off at the airport. Mary Lou didn't want to drag Randy out with a fever. He figured it was best that way. He and Mary Lou said their goodbyes on the front stoop. She couldn't talk him out of this trip with their neighbor waiting in the car. She couldn't even if she tried because the only thing that Mercer wanted now was a chance at making Mary Lou happy somewhere along a beach in Florida.

* * *

Mercer's flight arrived at the Cleveland Hopkins Airport at 12:30 in the afternoon. That gave him enough time to get a cheap used car, a 1958 DeSoto, off the lot of Cam Halladay's Used Car Emporium, with some of the cash Dewey had given him. The engine worked but the radio was busted. A shame, too, because music had a way of calming Mercer. Listening to Hank Williams or Elvis Presley always soothed him. He told himself, they were men like him, who'd made something of themselves. He could do the same thing too. He grabbed some lunch at a nearby diner and by five o'clock, he was sitting inside Cleveland Union Terminal, waiting for the seven o'clock Silver Crescent to arrive from Mississippi. The train was over an hour late. But even after arriving, there was no sign of the couple. He started to panic. What if the clerk in Jackson had given him the wrong city? What if they'd decided to get off the train in another city? This wasn't like the jobs he'd done for Mr. Leonard, Dewey's father. He couldn't just pluck some colored girl, any colored girl, and haul her off to Dewey. Dewey had specific instructions—he wanted to know exactly where Violet Richards was. Knowing Dewey, he'd probably want a picture, too, something to prove he'd found her.

Mercer waited for a few minutes more, watching passengers exit the tunnel. He assured himself with the thought that if they sat in the colored section of the train in the back, it might take them longer to reach the terminal. A couple minutes later, still no Marigold Richards and boyfriend. He started down the tunnel where their train unloaded. He spied a few more stragglers and there, all the way at the end of the platform, he spotted a man, stooped over, tying his shoe, the woman waiting. *Marigold.* Mercer hustled from the tunnel and back inside the terminal before they spotted him.

He lurked along a corner of the terminal until they headed out the door. He was out of the station like a shot, back to his car to get ready to tail them. He crouched down behind the wheel of the DeSoto, watching them as they waited in front of the station. Outside, the evening air felt a bit cooler than back home in Jackson. It was refreshing. The couple chatted. The guy was a loud, laughing mess. The woman, Marigold, seemed timid and less attractive than her sister. Mercer was still kicking himself for the stupid move he'd made to show up on the sister's front door pretending to be a lawyer. What in blue blazes made him think he could pull that one off? What if the sister had alerted someone? He couldn't worry about that now. The better option was to focus on the task at hand, to follow the couple until they led him to Violet.

Mercer sat watching them from behind the wheel of his car. About fifteen minutes later, a late-model

Buick pulled up to the front of the station. He watched the couple climb inside as he turned the key in his ignition. And off the Buick went, with Mercer on their tail. With any luck, Violet Richards was their destination.

22

Mercer

This job hadn't been as bad as he thought it might be. He had a new car. As new as a 1958 DeSoto could be. He was in a new city, and he'd hunt down that colored woman in two shakes. This might be the easiest money he'd make off the Leonards.

Dewey getting sweet on a colored girl—he was a bigger idiot than Mercer thought. A part of him tried to imagine Violet Richards, the one with the pretty mouth and cute little figure, killing Huxley Broadus. Mercer never cared for Huxley, even thought the guy might be on the slow side. Mercer chuckled to himself at the thought that the big dumb goof had been felled by a colored woman. And then he stopped chuckling when he realized Huxley had been shot. Did Violet still have a gun? No worries, though. The Smith & Wesson snub nose in the glove box would be his calling card if she tried any funny business when he found her.

* * *

Mercer decided he preferred the cool breeze of the air rushing in off Lake Erie instead of the sweltering heat of Mississippi. He rolled down his window and allowed the wind to blow over him. He was on the tail of the Buick, close but cautious. The car moved down a wide and busy street, Superior Avenue. Everything here seemed faster, the cars, the way people moved about. Or maybe he was missing Jackson already. After about fifteen minutes, the Buick finally turned off onto Sixty-Fifth Street. There were more colored people along this section of town. He worried whether his presence, a white man lurking about, would draw attention. The car carrying Marigold Richards finally came to a stop in front of a house—a duplex—paint peeling and the front yard in need of some attention. Mercer eased over to the curb, far away enough not to be detected but close enough to see what was going on. He cut the lights and the car engine. The falling darkness of the evening provided ample cover.

A heavy colored woman, wearing pink hair curlers and a flowered print house dress like Mary Lou sometimes wore back home, stepped out onto the front porch of the lower duplex. Unless she'd packed on about fifty pounds and dyed her hair red since she left Jackson, that was not Violet Richards. The woman waved and smiled as the couple climbed out of the car. The driver and the other man hustled around to the trunk to unload the bags.

"Marigold!" the woman said.

"Lurlene!"

The two women hugged and spoke quietly for a few seconds before they both roared in laughter. Mercer couldn't make out what they were saying. The men joined them on the porch before they all walked inside the house.

Marigold and Lurlene. Where was Violet?

Maybe she was holed up inside. She was running from the Jackson, Mississippi, police after all. Mercer felt more confident now that he knew where she might be. At least he had a start—he had an address. With little else, he decided to go find a hot meal to eat and a warm place to stay. He could come back later with a plan.

* * *

Mercer found the Lucky Hotel & Arms, which rented rooms by the week. It wasn't the Ritz, but it was clean and about ten minutes away from the duplex on Sixty-Fifth Street, far away enough not to draw attention to a white man hanging around a colored neighborhood. The North wasn't much different from the South when he looked around at the neighborhoods and how everyone lived according to skin color. There wasn't a colored person within miles of his rooming house. He'd heard the races mingled together more freely up here. But you wouldn't know it at first sight of the city.

He tried to settle in his room a bit, but the lights from Lenny's Deli across the street were like a beacon calling him. Mercer grabbed his hat and headed out toward the lights.

Inside the restaurant, things were quiet, only a few people sitting at tables sprinkled across the room. All the booths were empty. He eased inside the one farthest from the door to have a bird's-eye view of the entire place. A waitress with blue cat eyeglasses and graying hair covered by a hairnet walked over and handed him a menu and a stained-tooth smile. He quickly glanced at the menu and ordered something called a "Rueben sandwich."

"And a shot of Seagram's." He was on Dewey's dime now. He might as well live it up.

The waitress was back pronto with the shot glass. Mercer turned it up and let the warm liquid float through him. "Hey!" he called out as the waitress walked away. He raised his glass. "One more."

If Violet Richards was in that duplex, why didn't she come out to greet her own sister? Mercer was sure he trailed the right couple. No more mistakes like he'd made for Mr. Leonard and the feedstore theft. Maybe Violet lived somewhere else. Mercer decided he'd need to stake out the duplex for a few days to find out.

The waitress returned and sat another shot glass in front of him. "You new around here?"

"Yeah."

"Where you from?"

Mercer wasn't big on small talk, but something ached inside him. Maybe missing Mary Lou and Randy already. "Florida." In a few short days, this wouldn't be a lie.

"You're a long way from home. What brings you up here? Can't be the weather." The waitress giggled at her own joke.

"Work." Mercer looked around the room. "You got a pay phone around here?"

She nodded. "Sure. By the cigarette machine in the back. Your sandwich should be up in a minute."

"Thanks." Mercer walked to the back of the restaurant. He gathered what he could in strength and gumption before he slipped a coin inside the phone and listened to the clink of the money the operator told him to deposit as it fell to the bottom of the phone box.

Mary Lou answered on the first ring. "Hello."

"Mary Lou, honey, it's me. How you and Randy doing?"

"'Bout the same I suspect. Mercer, where exactly are you? You left me with more money than we've seen in years and now I don't even know where my own husband is. Mercer, tell me what's going on."

He hesitated for a moment. It was wrong to keep something like this from his wife. But he didn't want to drag Mary Lou into the middle of it. After all that business back in June up in Neshoba County, it was best to keep her clear of worry.

"I told you, I'm just running an errand for Dewey Leonard up in Ohio. That money I left with you is a down payment. He'll pay me the rest after I finish the work."

"What kind of work, Mercer? What's all this about?"

"Listen, I'll be home in a few days. Don't tell anyone about this. I agreed to keep it under wraps. But when I'm finished, we'll have enough money to move down to Florida near your sister in Daytona. You been aching for us to be near family. Everything's gonna be fine. You kiss Randy for me. I'll be home soon."

Mercer hung up before Mary Lou could say another

word. Hearing her fuss all over him might have made him rethink this whole job. Chasing some colored woman for a man he didn't take much shine to was crazy. And Mary Lou could always talk him out of the crazy stuff. But what was he to do? He was a desperate man. He'd been blacklisted all over Jackson and they were knee-deep in debt with all the medical bills.

Mercer picked up the receiver again and dialed zero. This time, he told the operator he wanted to place a collect call and gave her Dewey's number.

"Hey, it's me." Mercer inhaled deeply and released. "Just wanted to let you know I'm in Ohio. I've got a tail on the sister."

"You find Violet?"

"Not yet. But I'm pretty sure her sister will lead me straight to her. I'm just curious. Why is it so important for you to find this woman?"

Dewey hesitated before he cleared his throat. "She took something that belonged to me. I really need to get it back."

"What'd she take that you're willing to pay thousands of dollars to get it back?"

"Just find her."

Mercer hung up the phone and shook his head. Dewey was pining after some colored woman who stole something from him. The rich kid was even stupider than Mercer imagined.

He ambled back to his booth. He took a big bite of his sandwich and decided to make a plan to find this Violet woman and get back home to the woman he loved.

23
Marigold

Lies and secrets can drain you dry. I felt guilty for having kept the baby a secret from Violet. I felt guilty for planning to pass the baby off as Roger's. I felt guilty for not being strong enough to tell everybody to go to hell when it came to my pregnancy and whether that meant I was a good girl or not.

By my best estimate, I was at least two months pregnant, and still within the window to pass the baby off on Roger and everyone else as a preemie. I tried not to think of James anymore. But that was hard to do. Every tall, brown-skinned man I saw with tortoiseshell glasses made me think of him. Every time I watched a movie with two lovers caught up in an embrace on Lurlene and Frankie's black-and-white set—James. Every time

I picked up the *Call & Post* newspaper to read of how the Mississippi Summer Project was going—James.

Our last conversation before he skipped town rolled around in my head like a nonstop pinball. Did I tell him about the baby the wrong way? Was I too pushy? Did I sound too needy? What could I have done differently to make him marry me and take me back to New York? When I really wanted to torture myself, I imagined tracking him down and showing up on his Harlem doorstep, big pregnant belly and all. I imagined him opening the door and begging me to forgive him, telling me he had made a mistake and had been looking for me but he couldn't find me because I moved. But the daydream always turned into a nightmare when I imagined a woman opening the door to his house and telling me she was his wife. Why did I keep doing this to myself? I'd made a mistake. *Just move on, Marigold.*

And all the while, I kept telling myself this baby was Roger's and there was never anyone else but him. The first time Roger and I had sex, I pretended. I did everything the same way I had when I was with James, just like it was my first time. Roger was so excited about getting between my legs after his "forever wait" as he called it, he was never the wiser. I let him climb on top of me as many times as he wanted so I wouldn't get any suspicious pushback when I told him he was going to be a father. But having sex with him was neither pleasant nor enjoyable, not like it was with James. There were no soft kisses or gentle hands. No slow, deep breaths falling into my ear. With Roger, it was a quick peck on the lips and then a blur of pounding flesh and fast moves like he was racing to get to the end, to call "winner" against some unseen rival.

* * *

Roger and I had moved into the upstairs apartment of the duplex over Frankie and Lurlene's. By the end of our first week in Cleveland, Roger had yet to find a job, but it's hard to find something you're not looking for. We had a bed, barely, more like a couple mattresses on the floor. In the living room, a lumpy sofa sat up against the wall. The left back leg was missing and replaced by a couple Yellow Pages phone books. In the kitchen, an old scratched-up Formica table and three chairs, the plastic seat of two ripped down the middle, provided our dining accommodations. All of it was furniture left over from the previous tenants. There were no curtains to cover the windows, just yellowed paper roller shades. Roger liked to talk about the day we'd live in a big house with a hi-fi stereo and a mink coat in the closet for me. It was as if he never looked around the place where we currently lived. The distance between here to there was the width of an ocean. I was never sure who Roger was trying to convince of his big dream—me or himself.

Roger had hired a couple of his friends to drive my furniture up to Ohio and paid them up front. We never saw them or the moving truck again after they pulled off from my house in Jackson. Roger kept saying they would be here any day now, but they left Mississippi before we did. I knew I'd never see my things again. Furniture that Momma and Papa had worked so hard to afford. It wasn't fancy or expensive, but it was mine. Half my clothes, and sentimental things like my high school diploma, family pictures, Momma's Bible, obituaries from the funerals of Momma, Papa, and Rose— all of it picked through and probably dumped along the side of the road after Roger's "friends" fished out what they wanted. And we were also out the up-front money Roger had given them to drive the truck up north. I don't know why I expected something more from Roger. I knew he wasn't as smart as James. I just didn't know how wide the intellectual gap was.

Back in Jackson, we got married in the pastor's back office at the church. Roger's mother refused to attend.

Violet wasn't around for me. The only witness we could scrounge up was Roger's friend Buster, the same *friend* who drove the moving truck. As soon as I said "I do," I knew I'd made an awful mistake. But what was I supposed to do, pregnant and no husband? Gossipy women and judgmental men would make me an outcast. I'd be labeled a slut, forever branded as "one of those kinds of women." Being Roger Bonny's wife was better than being the mother of a bastard child.

I was clearing away the breakfast dishes, a few chipped things Lurlene had given us to tide us over until my things arrived from Mississippi. To add insult to injury, I felt bad every time Lurlene headed off to the grocery store and returned with an extra chicken or a dozen eggs, telling me to hold them for her because her icebox was running hot. She and I both knew what she was doing. I heard Lurlene's footsteps lumbering up the back staircase.

"Marigold, you home?"

"In the kitchen."

"Whew! You gon' hafta start coming down to my place. These stairs ain't no joke."

I giggled. Lurlene was what men called "thick" and doctors called overweight. She had this big bubbly personality that always swept up everyone around her. And she had the prettiest face you ever laid eyes on.

Soft features and a smile that could land her a Colgate toothpaste commercial if Negro women were allowed.

"Hey! I thought you'd be asleep. Didn't you have a set last night at the club?" I asked.

"I did, but the club was quiet last night. We broke early, so I got to bed before two o'clock."

"Look at you, getting all that shut-eye." We both laughed. Lurlene sang with the Fats Johnson trio at the Tip Top Club. Fats owned the club and did a pretty good business.

"Girl, I got so much sleep, I even remembered my dream. Dreamed about fish last night. What's the number for fish? 527? Maybe I'll play it, maybe box it." Lurlene let out a huge laugh and plopped down in one of the three chairs at the rickety table. "Funny thing . . . every time I dream about fish, somebody pop up pregnant. You're not pregnant, are you?" She laughed again.

I tried to laugh, too, but I just got nervous and turned away to look out the window over the small sink.

"Maybe I'll go see Sister Glory this afternoon and get a reading," she said.

"Sister Glory?"

"She's a reader over on Quincy. For two dollars, she'll read your palm and tell you what's in your future."

"Hmm . . . sounds like Sister Glory is looking into people's pockets instead of their futures." Sister Glory, Sweet Daddy Grace, and a host of other people who had traveled to the North to flee the Jim Crow South had found myriad ways to make a living in the segregated tenements of places like Cleveland, New York, and Chicago. Charismatic people who dabbled in one thing or another to make a fast buck. Palm readers. Faith healers. Numbers runners. Hustlers. Con artists. You didn't have to be smart to live up north. For some, you just needed to talk a good game.

Lurlene shrugged. "You might be right, but she gave me a couple numbers two weeks ago. I hit for $500. By the way, I called the landlord about the back door downstairs. The lock's busted again. Just make sure you push that two-by-four up against it when you come in at night."

"Okay. So . . . when does it start snowing up here? I've never seen snow before."

"We got a few months before that, but it does get coolish by late September."

"I would offer you something to eat, but we don't have much here. We're still looking for jobs. Roger left out of here with Frankie this morning. I hope he can get on at the steel mill with Frankie. We really could use the money."

Lurlene went quiet and started fiddling with a box of salt on the table, avoiding eye contact with me.

"Lurlene, you okay?"

"You talk to Roger . . . I mean about the job at the steel mill?"

"What are you talking about?"

Lurlene hesitated. "It ain't my place to get caught up in married people's business, but I don't think Roger is trying to work at the steel mill, honey. He asked Frankie to drop him off at some place downtown. Said he's got a lead on some kind of business venture."

"Yeah, him and his big dreams. He's always talking about opening up a nightclub." I couldn't figure out what was sadder—a man too inept to handle his dream or one unwilling to work for it. Either way, Roger Bonny's dream was doomed from the start. "Roger's gotta give up that dream for a while. We need money, groceries."

"Running a club ain't no easy thing. It's fly-by-night and then you got the Mafia that wanna come in and get a cut of the profits. I'm surprised Fats is still open. But I'm damn sho glad he is, 'cause I don't know where else I can go sing and make enough to pay my bills."

Silence fell around us. I stared out the window again. I thought about the baby, a child that hadn't even come into the world and there was nothing but chaos surrounding it. I wished Violet was here. I missed her so much. I should have told Violet about the baby. She would have known what to do. Now here I was, in a city with no one to talk to, to confide in. Maybe Lurlene was my next best thing.

I was still staring out the window. "You said you dreamed about fish, huh?"

"Yeah, why?"

I turned around to face her, but I didn't answer.

Lurlene sat the box of salt on the table with a light thud. Her eyes narrowed on me. "Marigold, you pregnant?"

"Please don't say anything to Frankie. I'll tell Roger soon enough. I'm just waiting until he gets a job, you know. So everything won't seem so overwhelming."

"How far along are you?"

"Not far." I didn't answer Lurlene's question directly. I didn't need her counting backward on her fingers, trying to guess when Roger and I had sex. I looked down at the dishcloth in my hands, ashamed of everything, and now more lies. "Once I start showing, I'll never get a job. Who's going to hire a pregnant woman? And even if I got one, how long could I keep it?"

"Oh, Marigold. I don't know whether to congratulate you or feel sorry for you." Lurlene walked over and hugged me. "Well, don't get down just yet. Maybe when Roger knows he's gonna have another mouth to feed, that job down at the steel mill is gonna look a lot better than that nightclub idea, huh?"

I leaned into Lurlene's girth. It offered small comfort against what was really going on right above Lurlene's head. What she didn't know was that I *couldn't* tell Roger about the baby. Roger had no plans for a family. All he talked about on the train and since we'd arrived in Cleveland was *my* getting a job. "If you got a job, I could make plans for the club . . . If you got a job, I could scour the city for a great location . . . If you got a job, you would be showing so much support for my dream." It was almost like he had this whole plan to marry me just to support his dreams. What about *my* dreams? He hadn't mentioned the college classes he once dangled out in front of me before we got married, telling me we needed to "put all that on hold" until after the club was up and running.

Lurlene patted my back. "It's gonna be okay, sugar. The Lord always work out things the way they oughta be."

"Thanks."

Lurlene smiled at me. "I tell you what, go grab your purse. Let's go get something to eat."

"No . . . I'd better stay here. Roger might be back soon."

Lurlene looked at me and shook her head, the same way Rose used to do whenever she tried to pull my nose out of a book and get me to go outside to play. "Come on, you need to get out of this house. We can go over to Scatter's Barbecue. It's my treat. Well, I ain't got no money, either, but Scatter is friends with Fats. He'll slip us a couple red hots just for dressing up his joint."

We both laughed. I nodded okay.

"Besides, you eating for two now. We gotta keep up your strength."

* * *

A few hours later, I sat on the sofa in the living room, leafing through an old copy of the *Call & Post* left behind by the previous tenants. The local newspaper informed Cleveland's Negro denizens about everything from the city's efforts at urban renewal to an early morning knife fight between a group of men in a back-alley crap game.

I heard Roger plodding up the back steps. A good wife, a wife who looked forward to seeing her husband at the end of the day, would have gotten up off the sofa to greet him with a kiss. But sometimes I felt like Roger didn't deserve my kisses. The way we were living, his refusal to get a steady job didn't leave me much to work with. I was now relegated to getting my meals courtesy of some strange restaurant owner's kindness. This was not how I wanted to live my life. Tonight, I decided I would put my foot down and demand that he get a job. I'd held my tongue for as long as I could.

Roger waltzed into the living room, whistling as if we didn't have an empty icebox or a light bill due at the end of the month. "Hey! What's going on?"

I didn't even look up from the paper. "Nothing."

He chuckled. "Well, I can tell that from the cold stove with no pots on it."

This time, I looked up from the newspaper and rolled my eyes at him. I deserved better than this man.

"So what's the matter with you?" he asked.

"Nothing." I dropped the paper on the sofa and got up, headed into the bedroom.

"Marigold?"

I didn't respond. I stepped in the bedroom and opened a suitcase to get a clean nightgown. It was shameful that I had a house full of furniture back in Jackson but here I was, still living out of a suitcase and practically sleeping on the floor because of his stupidity.

"What's the matter? No luck job hunting today?"

"Did *you* have any luck job hunting today?"

He jerked his head back slightly. "What's that supposed to mean?"

I didn't respond. He knew exactly what I was talking about.

"Look, I know I'm late getting home. I told you I'd be out all day today meeting with people. I think I might have a lead on some seed money for the club."

I pulled out a blue nightgown and shook the wrinkles from it. I heard him blow an exasperated sigh. "What we gonna eat tonight?"

I stared at him, debating whether to answer him or just go to the bathroom and get ready for bed. Maybe I didn't want to get into this with him. I was angry and tired. But against my better judgment, I decided to bring things to a head. "From the looks of what's in the icebox, Roger, nothing."

"I haven't eaten since this morning. Can't you go downstairs and grab something from Frankie and Lurlene? Just tell 'em we'll pay 'em back when a job comes through."

"No! I'm tired of asking for handouts from them. They have their own bills to pay."

"Look, my brother said he'd help us out until we get on our feet. Just go downstairs and grab some tuna fish or something."

"I said no. I didn't marry you to come all this way to live off somebody else. We're both grown. We should be supporting ourselves. We're already eating off their hand-me-down dishes." I could hear my voice rising, my anger curling and whipping up inside me. "You got Frankie acting like your personal chauffeur. And my things still haven't arrived from Jackson!"

"Marigold!" Roger stepped over to me. "I'm tired of hearing about your damn things from Jackson. Wasn't nothing but rags and a few sticks of furniture anyway. If you would back me up on this club idea, I could make enough money to buy you stuff ten times better than that shit from Mississippi!"

"I'm not working to take care of a grown man. Or have you forgotten how things are supposed to work? You're supposed to take care of me, remember?"

"We're married. We're in this together. Marigold, I got dreams."

"I got dreams too! But you have to work for a dream. No one is going to hand it to you. You can meet all day with whoever you want, but until you get a job and are willing to invest your own money, your dream is going to remain just that—a dream."

Roger stared at me. "I don't want an argument. Just go downstairs and grab something for me to eat."

"No."

"Frankie and Lurlene are family. We help each other out." Roger slipped off his shirt. He tossed the shirt on the mattress and stood in front of me in his undershirt and slacks with a menacing grin. "See, me and Frankie, we're brothers. We support each other. But you wouldn't know nothing about that, seeing how you got one sister who killed the other, huh?"

A chill ran through me. "What did you say? What did you say about Violet?"

"Oops, I mean it was an accident, right?" Roger laughed, a loud, ugly sound. "Go'n, Marigold. I'm tired of playing with you. Go get me something to eat."

Rage whipped up inside me like a ferocious beast. "Go get it your damned self!"

Before I even realized what was happening, Roger reared his hand back and slapped me across the face so hard I saw stars. It must have shocked us both because Roger spent the next hour apologizing. He offered all sorts of reasons for his abhorrent behavior—he was tired, he didn't know what got into him, he had never laid a hand on a woman in his life, he was sorry. He was so sorry. The horror of everything fell onto me like a concrete wall. The plan I had for marrying Roger had fallen through because Roger had a different plan.

I was pregnant and living with a man who would try to beat me into submission.

24
Mercer

S till no sign of Violet Richards.

Only a few days in town and Mercer had learned how to navigate the city easily, even though Cleveland was far bigger than Jackson. Everything worked in big blocks of stores and businesses on the main streets and houses tucked along the streets off the main drag. He'd even found a few shortcuts and an alley where he'd park to watch the back of the duplex on Sixty-Fifth Street to monitor the comings and goings of the two couples.

Mercer stalked all four of them and, after a week, had picked up a pattern on everyone who lived in the house. He even picked up a few names just by listening in on their conversations he could hear from the street. The heavyset woman with the box-dyed hair and the loud laugh was Lurlene. She was married to the tall, lanky fellow. His name was Frankie and he looked just like the wavy-haired man married to the Marigold woman. His name was Roger. As far as Mercer could tell, Frankie left every morning, headed off to his job at US Steel. Lurlene stayed close to home during the day, occasionally leaving to go to the A&P supermarket down the street. Frankie dropped her off at the Tip Top Club in the evenings where she sang with the house band. Marigold would leave the house at different times of the day. Sometimes she would leave early in the morning, catch a bus downtown, and head into a different office building every time, probably looking for a job. She went into a grocery store once. Her husband, Roger, was the only one who didn't seem to leave the house with any purpose. Some days, he wouldn't leave the house during the day except to stand outside and smoke a cigarette. From what Mercer could tell, he spent his evenings out, mostly at bars, and once Mercer saw him in the company of a tall, attractive colored woman. His own experience told him, a man who didn't get up regularly every morning was a man without a job. Unlike Frankie and Lurlene who ventured out together, he hadn't seen Roger and Marigold together since they arrived from the train station.

And still, he hadn't seen Violet.

It was now the first week of August, and he hadn't

seen hide nor hair of Violet Richards. She hadn't come out of the duplex once. Maybe she wasn't in there. If she wasn't, she had to be somewhere, and he was pretty sure her sister knew where. Mercer parked his car and lit a cigarette just before he caught sight of Marigold dressed the same as always—navy skirt, white blouse, and sensible-looking shoes. She headed out the back door.

Mercer flicked his cigarette out the window. He'd had enough of watching from afar. He reached over and pulled the Smith & Wesson snub nose from the glove box.

Today would be the day to find Violet.

25
Marigold

By eight o'clock in the morning, I was dressed and standing at the bus stop. I was barely talking to Roger since he slapped me. I guess he interpreted my silence at his apology as forgiveness. He tried to pretend like everything was okay, talking and spinning lies about how close he was to wrapping up a deal for the club. And still, I was expected to work and support the two of us while he ran all over Cleveland chasing a dream he had no intentions of working for. The irony of it all was that I was pregnant, which meant if I was lucky enough to talk my way into a job, I would be asked to leave or fired once I got late into my pregnancy. And we would be right back where we started. Broke. Violet was right. I was smarter than this. Why did I keep making so many stupid decisions? Sleeping with a man

I hardly knew and marrying a man I knew too well. I was standing on wobbling legs of emotion—trying to be the dutiful wife to an incompetent dolt of a man and the quiet keeper of a bastard child.

Times like these, I wished Rose were here, doling out sisterly advice and telling me what was best for me. What kind of woman would she have been as a writer living in some big city like New York or Chicago? Would Violet and I have made all the mistakes we did if Rose had lived? And would Violet have been different if she didn't carry around all that guilt for Rose's death?

The bus pulled up to the stop with a loud hiss. The driver opened the door, but for whatever reason, I couldn't move from the spot where I stood.

"Miss?" The chubby white man behind the wheel stared at me. "You getting on?"

I blinked a few times willing myself to move.

"Miss, I have to get on with my route. Are you getting on?"

I stared back. "Uh . . . no."

The door closed with a soft thud and the driver pulled off. I could not go inside another office building and beg for a job I knew I could only keep for a few weeks before I started to show. It was impossible for me to wrap my mind around going out to work every day while I was pregnant and there was a full-grown man living in my house who was not working. If we were "in this together," as Roger liked to say, why was I the only one working toward *his* dream? This situation I was living in had become a hell of my own making. How could I have been so stupid?

I walked down the street before I finally wandered into the library. A refuge. I got lost in the rows of shelves and the unmistakable scent of books and paper. Hushed voices floated through the space, along with the occasional sound of the librarian's date stamp as she checked out books for people. This place was like a safe harbor that might keep me from drowning in the chaos of my life. It was the first time since I moved to Cleveland that I felt at peace, no worries or concerns while I roamed the stacks. A librarian walked over and asked me what kind of books I like to read. She helped me find a few titles she thought I might like.

"Would you like to check them out?" she asked.

"Excuse me?" Back home in Jackson, Negroes were only allowed to check out books if they were doing so for a white person. We weren't allowed to have library cards. "Uh . . . yes."

She signed me up for a library card, stamped the card in the back of the books, and reminded me of the due date. I scooped up my books and thanked her before I left. I practically floated toward the front door. To hell with Roger and job hunting. I planned to spend the rest of the day reading. I stepped outside. A few sprinkles of rain fell and I unsnapped my umbrella. A car sped by, laying on the horn, and I looked up to check out the commotion. That's when I saw him. A white man sitting in his car across the street.

The same man who stood on my front porch in Jackson looking for Violet!

My heart thrummed inside my chest. I did a double take. Why would a man looking for Violet back in Jackson be here in Cleveland? And why was he parked outside the library where I was?

My first instinct was to bolt from the library and run back home. This man had followed me all the way from Jackson. Had he followed me looking for Violet? And if so, why? I started to go back to the librarian, to ask her to call the police. But she would think I was crazy. Maybe I was. I stepped inside the library's vestibule again, to get another look. It was definitely the same man. The same dark eyes and creepy, odd-looking face.

I backed away from the library door, bumping into another woman who was leaving. "I'm sorry," I said. The woman glared at me before she walked out the door. I peeped out the window again. He was still there. I hustled back to the service desk and the librarian who'd checked me out a few minutes before. "Excuse me, miss." My voice trembled. "Can you help me? I think there's a man following me . . . Can you call the police?"

"A man?" The woman looked over my shoulder, her eyes darting back and forth. "Where?"

"He's outside in a green car."

The woman walked from behind the desk. "It's okay. Come, show me."

I was almost too afraid to move. I took a few timid steps toward the door and stood behind the woman.

"Where is he?"

I stepped into the vestibule and peered through the door. "He's right—" The car was gone. The man had driven off. "He was parked right there," I said as I pointed to the spot where the car was before, now just an empty space across the street from the library.

The librarian opened the door and stepped outside. She looked both ways up and down the street. She stepped back inside. "I don't see any green car, miss. Are you okay?"

I scrambled outside. It was as if the man and car had disappeared into thin air.

The librarian followed me. "Are you okay? Do you need me to call someone?"

I nodded. "I'm fine. Thank you."

She returned inside. I stared across the landscape of the street. There was no sign of the man. Maybe I had imagined it all.

The light drizzle from a few minutes before broke loose into a full downpour. I hustled through the rain back home. I kept a watchful eye for the green car the entire run home. No sign of him. I made it home safely.

26
Marigold

I was a wet, nervous wreck by the time I made it back home and wedged the two-by-four against the back door. I figured if Lurlene or Frankie needed to get inside, they could go through their front door. And I was happy if Roger never made it back in the house. I changed out of my wet clothes and tried to talk myself out of the fear. What was the likelihood that the man on my porch in Jackson was the same man outside the library? Perhaps I was just being a nervous Nellie. Papa used to tell me, the only way I'd ever be able to go anywhere in life was to walk courageously. He said being brave didn't mean you had no fear. Bravery meant acting even in the face of fear. I realized it was fear that had landed me in a pregnancy and a marriage I never wanted.

I headed back into the kitchen. I'd asked Roger to take out the garbage twice, but he was hell-bent on getting out of the house at daybreak to meet with some people. He had more meetings than any legitimate businessperson I knew.

I snapped up the paper sack of garbage and headed down the steps. I peeped through the back door. No sign of anyone, including the man from Jackson. I stepped out onto the back porch. The neighbor's dog barked a few times. The rotted picket fence that bordered their house was missing at least three boards. I paced over to the gaping hole and peeped through. In the yard, a poor German shepherd was chained to a tree in their backyard. I reached down inside my garbage bag and pulled out the remnants of a hot dog I hadn't finished and tossed it through the hole. My aim was pretty good and the dog managed to reach it and gobble it down in one bite. I headed to the row of garbage cans a few feet away, yanked the metal top off one, and tossed in the trash. I replaced the lid and peeked back through the fence at the dog. He stood eager, waiting for me to toss another hot dog.

"Sorry, buddy, I don't have anything to eat, either," I whispered to the dog.

I turned around to go back inside and there it was.

The same green sedan parked in the alley. And inside, the man from Jackson!

I gasped and took off running for the back door. My heartbeat pulsed in my ears. I raced inside the house and up to Lurlene's back door. I had to get to a phone to call the police.

"Lurlene! Open up! It's me!"

I banged again. No answer. I peeped over my shoulder out the back door. The man was out of his car and heading toward the house.

I banged on her door again. "Lurlene!"

I raced up the back steps to my house. I got inside and locked the kitchen door. I snatched up a kitchen chair and wedged it under the doorknob. I stood there waiting. Panting. Desperate.

Who was this man?

A few seconds later, I heard him enter through the door downstairs.

The lock! I forgot to push the two-by-four up against the back door! He was inside the house. *Please God help me.*

I heard his footsteps coming up the stairs. I looked around the kitchen for something to protect me.

The footsteps were getting closer. I raced to the kitchen drawer and pulled out a butcher knife.

The footsteps stopped. Everything went quiet. All

I could hear was the thumping of my heart and the racing pants of breaths as my body struggled to breathe through the fear.

He knocked twice. I backed farther away from the door. He tried turning the metal doorknob a couple times. Thank God, it wouldn't give way. Could the cheap wood door hold if he wanted to get inside bad enough?

Things went quiet again.

I was sweating. It felt like it was a hundred degrees inside the kitchen.

Finally, the footsteps retreated down the stairs. I raced to the bedroom that overlooked the alley. The man was back in his car. I couldn't see his license plate from my vantage point. I waited to see if he would drive off. He continued to sit in his car.

I walked back to the kitchen, dropped the knife on the table, and slid into a chair. I dropped my head in my hands and started to cry. What kind of evil had followed me all the way up north from Jackson? God only knows what he would have done to me if he got inside the house.

A couple minutes later, I heard footsteps again. *He's back.* Maybe with a crowbar this time, something to force his way into the house. My entire body buzzed with fear. I grabbed the butcher knife again. I could barely hold it, my hands were trembling so. I quietly eased beside the kitchen door. If he got in, I'd have the advantage and could attack him from behind. I had only one chance to save myself.

The steps grew closer until they were right outside the door. I raised the knife above my head and waited.

Two quick knocks this time.

"Marigold? It's me, Lurlene."

I released every bit of air inside my lungs and opened the door. Lurlene stood in front of me, holding a paper sack of groceries.

"I just got back from the A&P . . . Marigold, are you all right?"

I fell into her arms and started to weep.

"Marigold, what's wrong?"

"A man followed me home!" I managed to blurt out between tears. "He tried to get inside the house."

Lurlene's eyes grew wide. "What?"

"Out back! There's a white man parked in a car in the alley."

"Come on!" Lurlene dashed down the stairs and inside her back door. I crept down the stairs, still holding the knife.

She came back out of her house a few seconds later with a baseball bat.

"Shouldn't we call the police?" I asked.

"The police won't show up around this neighborhood unless we tell 'em there's a dead white man in the house. Let's go."

"What are you gonna do?"

"Chat with him for a minute, and Imma let this Louisville Slugger do all the talking."

We hustled out the back door to the porch. The white man from Jackson and the green sedan were gone. We both scanned the entire alley. Again, he disappeared into thin air.

"Well, whoever he was, he's gone now," Lurlene said.

We stepped back inside the house. "Lurlene, I need to use your phone. I have to call my sister."

27
Mercer

Mercer Buggs was smart enough to realize the stupidity of his mistake. He'd followed Marigold right up to her back door. *Idiot.* He should have driven off as soon as she stepped outside the library. But what choice did he have once she spotted him in the alley behind her house? Twice she'd seen him now. That meant she was likely to tip off her sister if she hadn't done it already. Since he was no closer to finding Violet than he had been when he was back in Mississippi, Mercer was starting to doubt that Violet Richards was here in Ohio. But she had to be somewhere on the face of the earth. And someone had to know where she was.

Back in his hotel room, he lifted the picture of Violet from the bedside table and studied it. Violet and Marigold were sisters. They looked alike but different.

Marigold was heavier, with a plain sort of appearance. All colored women looked plain to Mercer. All except Violet. She was softer looking. For a minute he almost understood why Dewey was sweet on this girl. Had she really killed Huxley Broadus? And what had she taken from Dewey to make him want to pay a king's ransom to find her?

Mercer got up from the bed, got dressed, and headed downstairs to the pay phone on the street corner.

* * *

"Dewey, it's me, Mercer."

"Yeah, you find her?" If Mercer wasn't mistaken, he could hear a twinge of anxiety in Dewey's voice. What the hell did he have to be nervous about?

"I think I'm close. I got a tail on the sister up here. I should have something soon."

"Soon?! Bugsy, you gotta find her right away."

"Don't call me that!" Mercer's disgust for this guy was starting to overtake him.

"I'm paying you a lot of money!"

"Unless you forgot, she's hiding out from the police, not just you. She's not the easiest person to find."

Dewey blew a deep breath in the phone. "You read the newspaper lately?"

"Yeah, I just told you, the police think she might be involved with that Huxley murder. Which makes me wonder why you're so anxious to find her."

"No! They found them boys up in Neshoba County. Dug 'em up out at Old Jolly Farm. The FBI is sniffing around, rounding up everybody that was there that night."

"Wait a minute. I didn't kill them boys. They were already dead when we got there."

"Are you listening to me? The FBI is involved. This is bigger than Bickford and those idiots that work for him. Nobody's sweeping this under the rug this time. Not with the government and Hoover's boys involved."

"I just drove the car for your daddy. I didn't have nothing to do with whoever killed those boys."

"That's fine, Bugsy-boy. You hang on to that excuse and let's see if it'll keep you out of the electric chair. I need you to put a fast foot on this and find Violet now!"

"Why? What does she have to do with this?"

There was a long pause. Mercer heard Dewey breathing, but he didn't utter a word. Mercer decided if his ass was on the line, he'd wait Dewey out as long as it took to get some answers.

"Listen," Dewey started up. "Me and Violet was planning to get married. I suspect with all this business about Huxley Broadus, she got scared and ran. But she took something from me, and I need to get it back. That's all."

"What'd she take?"

"I don't have time for a bunch of questions and neither do you. Just trust me. She's got something that could send me, you, all of us straight to jail."

Mercer scratched his head. "What are you talking about?"

"Just find her and don't do a thing to her until I get there. We clear?"

"Yeah."

"Remember, don't harm her. I'll take care of her."

Mercer hung up the phone. Olen Leonard—the head of the Mississippi Citizens Council and big-shot proprietor of Leonard Feed & Supply—had a son that was secretly paying him to chase down a colored woman he was in love with. Mercer had half a mind to call Mr. Leonard and tell him what his son was up to.

28
Vera

Marigold had left word with Birdie for me to call her, that it was urgent. Birdie proceeded to ask me a bunch of nosy questions, so I decided to call Marigold from the pay phone at the Piggly Wiggly instead of Birdie's house.

"Marigold, is everything okay? Birdie said something about you needing to talk to me right away?"

"He's up here," Marigold whispered in the phone.

"Who's up there?"

Her voice went even more quiet. I could barely hear her. "That man I told you came to the house back in Jackson looking for you. I think he's followed me here to Cleveland."

"Oh my God. Did he hurt you?"

"No, but he's been following me. He followed me

from the library and then I saw him parked in the alley behind my house. He tried to get inside! Are you sure you don't know him?"

"No. He must be following you to get to me."

"I know you talked about moving up here to Ohio. If he's looking for you up here, I don't think that's a good idea."

The operator returned to the line. "Please deposit twenty-five cents to continue this call."

I scrambled around in my pocket for another quarter. I had a dollar bill and a couple pennies. I decided to keep talking. "I guess you're right. Did you tell Roger? Maybe he can scare the guy off."

"Roger's not good for much, but I'll tell him."

"Sis, I'm sorry about all this. I didn't mean to bring no trouble to your door."

"I'm more worried about you," Marigold said. "It's obvious he's not a policeman. And he's not any kind of lawyer like he told me. Maybe a private detective? Maybe someone one of Huxley Broadus's friends might have hired?"

Dewey?

"Please deposit twenty-five cents to continue this call."

"Oh, blessed savior, I don't have another quarter." I tried to keep talking. "Listen, tell Roger—"

Silence.

"Marigold, you there? Marigold?"

The line was dead.

* * *

May 20, 1956

Dear Diary,

*I am so happy for my little sisters. Marigold
made straight A's again, just like she always
does. And Violet won first place in the school's
horticulture contest. She grew a batch of steak
tomatoes that beat out all the other kids' projects.
Her teacher told her they were good enough to
enter into the Mississippi State Fair. But Papa
immediately cut off that idea. He never takes
us to the state fair. It's always held in Neshoba
County and Papa said it isn't safe to be in those
smaller towns. We never venture outside of
Jackson. He always says if you think it's bad
here in Jackson, try going outside the city limits
and see how you fare.*

*I think Momma and Papa were more excited
for Violet than they were for Marigold. I was*

too. Maybe Violet is starting to come around.
Momma said maybe she is losing her "wild child"
ways and has decided to do things the easy way.

I closed the notebook. Rose couldn't have been more wrong about me. I was still lost and catching the rough end at every turn.

Now some man was looking for me and threatening Marigold. The police were looking for me too. And it was just a matter of time before all Sheriff Coogler's nosy questions would lead him back to me. This time for murder. All the jagged lines of my life, the fits and starts to try to do better, to be a good girl, to do what was expected of me—I never could measure up to what everybody wanted. And I always told myself that what I did, who I was with, was okay as long as I wasn't hurting nobody. But like Pauline Toney, I hurt myself in the process. I hurt people I loved and brought trouble right up to Marigold's back door.

I needed to move on. It was time for me to leave Chillicothe. Even if I couldn't catch a bus at the Piggly Wiggly, I'd hitch a ride into Augusta. There was likely to be more buses going in and out of there since it was bigger than Chillicothe. I pulled Dewey's wallet from underneath the mattress of my bed. I counted out the rest of the money in it. Twenty-seven dollars. That didn't include the seventeen cents on my bedside table. Here I was, twenty-one years old. I'd killed a man, stolen a wallet from another one, and I was running from the law.

God, please help me.

I stared down at the brown leather wallet. It was practically brand-new. Like everything else Dewey owned. His daddy didn't let Dewey want for much. New cars, new clothes, everything. All he had to do was ask. Then it occurred to me, if Dewey was so rich why did he have so little money in his wallet? How was he going to whisk me away to a new life on forty dollars?

I unfolded the wallet again. Maybe he had tucked away some additional cash in a hidden pocket. The right pocket held Dewey's driver's license. The long insert held the same twenty-seven dollars I'd just counted. The left side pocket contained a AAA membership card. I slid the AAA card out. Nothing. I slid his driver's license out. There was no money, but underneath the license was a piece of paper. I slid it out of the wallet and unfolded it.

I had to do a double take just to make sure I was seeing what I was seeing. The paper turned out to be a photograph. A black-and-white picture of what looked like three dead bodies in an open grave. One man was colored. The other two bodies were white men. Why in the world would Dewey be carrying around a picture of three dead men in his wallet? I studied the picture for a minute.

Standing in the background behind them bodies—Olen Leonard, Dewey's daddy!

I suddenly remembered the newspaper article and those three civil rights workers, two white and one colored, who went missing up in Neshoba County. Marigold said it was all they talked about at her job at the Summer Project. When I left Jackson, the FBI was crawling all over the county looking for those men.

Did Dewey and his daddy kill them?

I slowly slid the picture back inside the wallet and covered it over with Dewey's license. I didn't realize it until I closed the wallet and tucked it back under my mattress that I was trembling.

Who was Dewey Leonard and what had I got myself into?

29
Marigold

To say things were tense between me and Roger was an understatement. He'd slapped me, something no other human on this earth had ever done to me. My own parents had never laid a hand on me. And he expected me to cook and clean for him as if it had never happened. To make matters worse, he barely batted an eye when I told him about the man from Jackson who'd followed me home from the library. His response was that I needed to make sure the two-by-four was wedged against the door whenever I came home. I wanted to lash out at him. But what good would that do? I hadn't seen the man from Jackson since the day he tried to get in the house, but I moved through my life like a frightened rabbit, watching, terrified of being alone. And being married to a man like Roger didn't ease my fears. Now that I knew who he really was, I was at risk inside my own home, just as much as I was outside of it.

When I stopped speaking to Roger completely, he decided that we needed a night out on the town to lift our spirits, even though we had almost nothing in the icebox to eat and neither one of us had found a job yet. We were going to Fats's place, the Tip Top Club, to hear Lurlene and the band.

I stood at the bathroom mirror applying eyeliner. I could never get the cat eye straight, and Violet would always help me back home. Lurlene helped me once when I went downtown in search of a job. But she had to leave early to meet the band to rehearse. I kept at it anyway. I wore my green chiffon dress with the gold brooch. The dress was far too tight to call myself a lady and my bosom nearly burst from the top of it. If Roger hadn't noticed my weight gain, he must be blind. Or maybe he was trying to be nice after that slap across the face.

I stared into the mirror and wondered, *What am I doing with my life?* College? Law school? Those things seemed like someone else's dream now, like something I could watch a friend do but never do for myself. If Papa had lived, maybe I'd be doing something other than dreaming about college. I'd be a graduate of one. He used to tell me, I could do anything I wanted as long as I was willing to step out in courage and go after it.

I believed him, too, as long as he was around pushing me forward. But after he died, Violet and I had to get jobs to help out with the bills. College seemed like some silly folly. Now I was married to a man like Roger and carrying someone else's baby. And once the baby arrived . . .

I did about the best I could with the makeup. I tossed the tube of eyeliner back inside my makeup bag and headed across the hall. Before I stepped into the bedroom, I noticed Roger fussing with his beloved brown-and-white Stacy Adams alligator wingtip shoes in the back of the closet. I watched him slip twenty dollars from the left shoe into his pocket.

I cleared my throat. "I'm ready."

He jumped from the floor of the closet. "Oh hey!"

"I'm all set." I stood in the doorway, quiet. Perhaps I was stupid enough to stand there waiting for either a compliment or an insult. I got neither.

"Okay. Let me get Frankie. He should be back from dropping Lurlene off at the club."

Roger slid past me without another word.

* * *

The Tip Top Club was alive with clinking glasses and laughing voices. The wail of Walter "Fats" Johnson's saxophone pleading in high A-flat filled the entire club. Lurlene always talked about how Fats's saxophone could make a woman drop her panties faster than a roller coaster going downhill. The drummer driving the jazz beat and the bass player plucking the strings, his eyes closed, lost in the music. The whole room was loud and raucous in a happy, toe-tapping sort of way.

Roger, Frankie, and I walked through the small club, past couples huddling together in booths and small groups of people at tables, swaying to the sound of the music. All kinds of people were packed in the club. Negroes and white people, hunched over the little brown tables laden with glasses and beer bottles. We took a table at the front, so close to the stage we might catch the sweat off Fats's forehead if he shook too hard.

I'd only been inside a club a few times back in Jackson, when Violet begged me to keep some friend of one of her boyfriends company. Me, acting as a convenient placeholder instead of a real date for some guy who was usually expecting Violet's twin. And without fail, the guy's silence throughout the evening told me he was greatly disappointed. Instead of getting some long-haired beauty like Violet, he got the plain-Jane sensible sister.

We weren't seated at the table more than two minutes when an alluring young woman in a tight blue dress walked over to our table to take our drink orders. She was all legs and bouffant hairdo. I watched Roger as he scoped the young woman from head to toe. He smiled at her and watched her melt at the sight of his hazel eyes, the way most women did. She leaned in especially close to Roger as she took his order. When she finished, Roger turned in his chair and watched her walk away from the table.

Frankie gave me an uncomfortable smile before he tapped Roger on the arm. "C'mon, man. Lurlene is coming up next. The band always warms up the crowd before she comes on." Frankie looked toward the stage and grinned like a proud father at his child's Easter pageant. Frankie was in love with Lurlene, and he was not afraid to show it, no matter where they were. I couldn't imagine Roger, or any man for that matter, beaming at me like that.

"This is a nice place Fats got here. How long he had this club?" Roger asked.

"'Bout five years. Lurlene say he run a clean place too. No dope running in through the back door, none of them girls hanging around after closing. You know what I mean?"

Roger grinned and nodded. "See, that's what I'm talking about. I wanna place like this. I'll bring in cats like Miles and Trane. Maybe something with a dance floor and I can bring in Ray Charles and Jackie Wilson, so folks can shake their tailfeather."

"Man, you broke as a joke! Them cats charge big money. Where you gon' get that kinda cash?" Frankie asked.

"You ever heard of investors? Seeing as you my brother and all, I might be willing to let you in on a cut."

Frankie laughed. "Shit, I work too hard down at that steel mill. I ain't handing off my hard-earned money to some Mississippi clown to burn through on a pipe dream. Even if he is my own brother."

Roger waved Frankie off and turned to me. "See that, baby. Small minds live small lives."

I knew Roger wanted me to back him up, to give support to his "dream." All I could think about was the empty icebox back at home and the light bill that would come due at the end of the month. People couldn't eat dreams. Roger stared at me for a few seconds, no expression. The waitress returned to the table and Roger let it drop between us. She sat a couple beers on the table for Roger and Frankie, along with a 7-Up for me.

Fats brought the saxophone to a crescendo and the crowd cheered. Then the music slowed and the lights dimmed, with a single empty spotlight onstage.

Frankie leaned forward and whispered across the table excitedly. "Here she comes!"

A hush fell over the crowd. Lurlene stepped into the spotlight. Her crystal earrings and necklace twinkled.

The sparkle from her red sequined dress caught the light and made her look like a red-hot flame. She was like a movie star up on that stage. I looked across the table at Frankie. His entire face was lit up like he thought the same thing too.

Roger leaned over and whispered in my ear. "I'll be back in a minute."

I glared at him. "Lurlene is just about to sing! Where are you going?"

"I'm just gonna run to the back and grab a pack of cigarettes." He was gone from the table before I could say another word.

I tried to forget about Roger. If he dragged me here to have a good time, I might as well do it, regardless of him. Lurlene began singing "My Funny Valentine." Every word spilled from her lips like lyrical nectar into the human ear. Everyone in the club was mesmerized by her voice. Her high range and the skittering of words as she sang made her something of a cross between Dinah Washington and Ella Fitzgerald. I'd never heard anything so beautiful. She stopped and Fats began a saxophone solo.

I suddenly realized Roger hadn't returned to the table. The club was only so big, so he didn't have to go far for a pack of cigarettes.

I nudged Frankie. "Roger said he was going to buy

a pack of cigarettes. He's not back yet." Frankie and I looked toward the back of the club. We both spotted it at the same time—Roger stood at the back, near the bar, nuzzling and whispering into the waitress's ear as she giggled up against the back wall.

I wanted to walk back there and break it up, but I didn't want to cause a scene. My next thought—to get up and walk out of the club—fell flat, too. I didn't even have bus fare back home.

"I'll talk to him when we get home, Marigold," Frankie said quietly.

I spun back around in my seat and watched Lurlene continue as tears slowly slid down my face. When she finished the song, everyone in the club went wild with applause. I turned toward the back of the club again. This time, the waitress was gone, but Roger stood near the door beside a white man. I couldn't be sure with the dim lighting inside the club, but the man looked awfully familiar. I didn't know any white people in Cleveland. I squinted.

The man from Jackson!

He stared back for a moment before he grinned at me and slipped out of the club.

30
Marigold

The next morning, I slipped out of a dream so vivid I was still seeing all the vibrant colors of it as I opened my eyes. It was a dream about me, Rose, and Violet. We were all together playing in a sunny field of flowers. Violet and I were grown women, but Rose was still fifteen. She looked the same as she did the day she died, right down to her blue Bermuda shorts and tan sandals. All three of us held hands and laughed, running across the field like we did when we were girls. And then, in that weird way dreams always seem to go, Rose melted away from the dream. Violet and I continued playing until a white man stepped in front of us. He pulled Violet away. I fought with everything inside me to keep her with me, but she was gone as fast as Rose had disappeared. Before he dragged Violet off, I saw his face. It was the man from Jackson.

I sat straight up in the bed. *Who is he?*

I threw back the sheets and dashed over to the bedroom window. I raised the roller shade and peered down into the back alley. The green car and the man from Jackson weren't there. He'd followed me home and followed me to the club last night. He was getting bolder. I gazed back at the bed. Roger was gone. I knew better than to think he might be out looking for a job. And then it dawned on me that I didn't even care where he was. I enjoyed my own company better than being in his. I got up and used the bathroom and brushed my teeth. The morning sickness was starting to ease, but that just meant I was further along and would need to tell Roger about the baby soon.

I walked down the hall to the living room. Surprisingly, Roger was sitting on the sofa in his undershirt and boxers, shining his shoes. I just walked past him into the kitchen.

"What? No good morning?" I heard him yell from the living room.

I didn't respond. Maybe he'd forgotten about the waitress at the Tip Top Club. I hadn't.

I opened the cabinet and retrieved a glass to get some orange juice from the icebox, about the only thing we had left in there. I opened it expecting to see the same stray jars and emptiness, but instead there was eggs, bacon, milk, and butter inside. I was shocked. I opened the freezer on top. There was ground beef, steaks, and pork chops. I slowly closed the freezer door. On the countertop sat a fresh loaf of Wonder Bread, bags of oranges, potatoes, and rice. And right beside them, a box of gingersnaps.

"*Now* can you say good morning?"

I turned around. Roger was standing in the doorway of the kitchen, his spindly pale legs and bare feet falling from beneath his boxers. I didn't say anything. I was still in shock that this kitchen held more food than we'd ever had since moving to Cleveland.

Roger walked over and kissed me on the cheek. "And it didn't come from Frankie and Lurlene, either."

"Where did you get all this food?"

"I went to the A&P! Where else you gonna get food from?" He laughed like his joke was funny.

"I guess I meant, where did you get the money?"

"Don't worry about that." Roger hustled over to the counter and lifted a box. "And look, I bought you a box of gingersnaps. I noticed you always ate them back in Jackson."

I cautiously took the box from him. "Thanks."

"Now surely you can do better than that." He pulled

me in and kissed me. Nothing soft or sincere. Just him shoving his tongue into my mouth in an effort to put things back together between us.

He released me and slapped me on my backside. "Hey, can you make me some breakfast? I gotta get dressed. I'm meeting a cat to talk about the club."

I sighed. We were right back in the same place again. The only thing that had changed was the status of our icebox. Roger had decided to tap into his shoe bank to feed us. It wasn't the same as getting a job, but at least I wouldn't have to beg Lurlene for something to eat any time soon. I reached under the counter and pulled out a frying pan.

A few minutes later, Roger was back in the kitchen dressed in slacks and an open-collared shirt. *A business meeting?* He sat down at the table, and I placed his breakfast in front of him. I sat down beside him.

"You're not eating?" he said.

"No, I'm not hungry." Roger shrugged his shoulders. He was in a good mood. There was food in the house. Maybe I'd chat him up a little and then tell him about the baby.

"Are you sure you don't know that white man that was standing beside you in Fats's place last night?"

"What?"

"The man I asked you about after we left the club

last night. When you went to the back of the club, you were standing near a white man. That's the man I told you followed me home. Do you know him?" I decided not to mention the waitress, although I could tell from Roger's nervous expression when I mentioned the back of the club, he thought about her too.

"Baby, it was a lot of people in there last night. Fats's club is hopping these days. But I don't remember a white man standing beside me. Sorry." He gobbled down the last of his eggs and wiped his mouth with the back of his hand. Was Roger lying to me? It was no coincidence that a man from Jackson, looking for Violet, would follow us to Ohio and stand beside Roger in a nightclub. None of this was right.

"But, Roger, that man—"

"Look, I gotta go. I'm late."

"But wait. I wanted to tell you something."

"We can talk later. Gotta run." He jumped up from the table and kissed me on the top of my head before he scurried down the back stairs.

I stood up from the table to clear the dishes.

"Hey!" Roger was back in the doorway. "You still going out job hunting today, right?"

"Yes."

He smiled and winked. "We're in this together." Then he hustled down the back steps, whistling as he went.

31
Vera

I had decided to let that Greyhound bus pull off from the Piggly Wiggly without me. Again, I knew I was taking a big risk by staying in Chillicothe. Especially now that Coogler was sniffing around and asking about me. But I couldn't go up to Cleveland like I had planned with some man following Marigold all over the city looking for me. I felt awful every time I thought about how my stupidity put Marigold in danger. When would I learn to stop hurting the folks I loved? And on top of everything else, that picture in Dewey's wallet haunted me. Dewey and his daddy was all mixed up in the murder of three civil rights workers. I was squeezed in on every side, trapped in a cage of my own making.

But Pauline, and even Rose in her own way, were like little voices in my ear telling me to slow down.

Think first. Something I hadn't done much of lately. No one in town was on to me yet, not even that wretched Sheriff Coogler. I had a job, and I was lying low. *Slow down. Think first. Move later.*

Alma had showed me the ropes around the Starlight Diner kitchen on my first day. It seemed like working in this kitchen was a lot better than working in Betty-jean Coogler's kitchen. Even still, I had enough sense to know I didn't want to do this for the rest of my life either. This job was just a means to an end.

I showed up at the diner bright and early, even before Alma did. She gave me a look like I had slapped her momma when she saw me in the back starting up the biscuits for the morning breakfast run. Mr. Palmer was out front taking down the chairs from the tables and readying the place for morning customers.

"Mornin', Alma," I said with a rosy tone in my voice.

"Mornin'. How much flour you use?"

"Enough." I smiled.

"Humph," she said as she ambled back to the sink to wash her hands.

I heard the bell jingle over the door and peeked through the pass-through. In walked that golden-brown angel man in the pickup truck from the day Bankrobber followed me back to Miss Willa's. He was as tall as a tree, with shoulders that spanned forever.

My God, he was more gorgeous than I remembered. He stepped up to the counter and rested a couple boxes on top.

"Mornin', Mr. Palmer," he said. "I brought by those tomatoes and green beans. I also threw some squash and onions on the back of the truck if you're interested."

Mr. Palmer moved to the counter. "Hey, Hank. Let me see what you got there." The man waited patiently while Mr. Palmer sifted through the vegetables, before he gazed up at me. I realized I was staring and darted my eyes back down at the biscuits. I looked back up, and this time he was smiling at me. I smiled back and pretended to go about my work.

I nudged Alma. "Who's that?" I whispered.

Alma glanced up. "Hank Cummings. He owns a farm on the outskirts of town. Sells vegetables to the folks around here." She walked off.

"Hank, business been a little slow lately. I can't give you more than three dollars for this stuff. Besides, the tomatoes look a little soft today."

"Mr. Palmer, with all due respect, I know you got a business to run. I do too. But I ain't never brought you nothing but the best of my harvest. My vegetables twice as good as the white farmers' and half the price. I don't try to slide nothing by you or any of the other folks I sell to. And all I ask for is a fair price. Six dollars.

If you think my vegetables ain't right for your business or you think my prices too high, I'll understand and take my business elsewhere."

The two men stared at each other. In all my life, I'd never seen a colored man stand up to a white man the way Hank Cummings did. For a minute, I wondered whether I was really in Georgia.

Mr. Palmer finally broke the staring match. He hit a couple keys on the cash register. It jingled open and Mr. Palmer counted out six dollars. "Go'n take 'em in the back."

I quickly turned my gaze from the pass-through and tried to look busy when Hank Cummings walked back into the kitchen.

"Good mornin', ladies."

"Mornin', Hank," Alma said, not even bothering to look up from the eggs she was cracking. "Sit them boxes over there and don't knock over my pots."

"Yes, ma'am." Hank smiled at me as he walked toward the counter where I was working. He set the boxes of vegetables down and stood so close to me, it made me nervous. For the first time in my life, I was nervous around a man. *This* man.

"I don't think we've properly met, although it wasn't for my lack of trying the other day. My name is Hezekiah Cummings. Everybody around here calls me Hank."

My face went hot. "Vera . . . Vera Henderson."

"Well, it's nice to meet you, Vera Henderson."

I smiled. "Same to you."

Alma walked over and wedged her way between the two of us. "Hank Cummings, unless you got some other business back here, Imma ask you to leave. This here kitchen is too small for all three of us."

"Yes, ma'am. I'm leaving." Hank nodded at Alma and winked at me before he left the kitchen. For a minute, my knees buckled. I ain't never buckled over some man before.

He stood at the counter with Mr. Palmer. "You sure you don't want some of these squash and onions I got out in my truck?"

"I can't afford them," Palmer said with a wry smile.

Hank laughed. "I'll see you in a couple days, Mr. Palmer." Hank glanced back at me, and I laughed a little too.

* * *

The end of my shift seemed like it had taken a lifetime to come. I was taking off my apron when I heard the bell jingle. Me and Alma peeked through the pass-through. Hank Cummings walked inside, wearing a white dress shirt and, if I wasn't mistaken, a fresh crease in his pants. No boxes of vegetables this time. He looked like he was going somewhere special.

"Hank! I didn't expect you back here today." Mr. Palmer stopped wiping down the table in one of the front booths. "I bought all my vegetables this morning."

"Yes, sir. I'm not back here to sell vegetables. I was hoping I could speak with Miss Henderson for just a brief minute, sir. If that's all right with you."

Mr. Palmer stared at Hank for a beat. "Vera, somebody's out front here to see you." He went back to cleaning the booth.

I glanced at Alma. She shook her head with a slight smile. "Well, go on and see what he wants. Although I suspect I have some idea."

I hung my apron on the hook and grabbed my purse before I walked out into the restaurant. "Hi, Hank." I had that buckling feeling in my knees again, and I hated it. "You got some business with me?"

"I was hoping I could speak with you outside for a minute."

I glanced back and both Mr. Palmer and Alma were staring at us. Hank opened the door for me. We stepped outside into the late-afternoon sunshine. The street was nearly empty.

"I'll get right to the point." Hank slid his hands inside his pockets. "I was hoping I could call on you sometime. I own my own farm and I ain't one for tailing around a lot of women. I'm a good man just looking to spend my time with a good woman. Will you let me call on you?"

He was nervous, and I thought it was kinda cute, especially after the way he handled Mr. Palmer earlier in the day. "Well, Hank—"

"I understand a woman like you might be partial to a man with fancy ways and all."

For the first time in my life, I didn't have a comeback for a man. Not a word. I didn't know what to say, so I turned and looked down the road, but I could feel his eyes burning through me. When I looked back at him, he was smiling at me. That beautiful pearly smile parting his handsome face.

"You trying to think of a reason to tell me no, but you ain't got one. You new to town, so you ain't got another beau. So why you wanna say no to me?"

"And who said I wanna say no?"

"Well, you taking your good old-fashioned time to say yes."

I giggled. "Look, Hank, I'm sure you're a nice man and all, but I'm just not looking to hitch up with anybody right now."

"Miss Henderson, I'm not asking you to marry me. We'll get to all that a little later. I'm just looking to spend some time with you. Maybe go over to Augusta and see a movie sometime."

"Well, ain't you the charmer?"

"Is it working?" He laughed, a big, booming sort of sound that filled me up inside.

I laughed too.

"So can I call on you?"

He was so damn handsome, and I swear I started to tingle between my legs.

"Well . . ."

"Looks like you're off duty. Let me give you a ride home and you can think about my offer along the way. And remember, I'm not a stranger anymore, so you can accept my ride this time."

"You move fast, don't you?"

Hank grinned and opened the door to his pickup truck. "It's either me or Bankrobber. I figure I better work quickly before he gets the upper hand."

I giggled before I climbed inside.

Hank Cummings. Yeah, I liked Hank Cummings.

32
Mercer

Like Mr. Leonard said, Mercer Buggs was dogged. And now that he knew Violet Richards had something that could implicate him in a murder, he wouldn't rest until he found her. He wasn't going to jail for murder, especially for one he didn't commit.

He devised a new plan. This time, he'd trail Marigold's husband, Roger. And he'd started by following him into the Tip Top Club a few nights ago. He didn't say anything to Roger, just stood near him to see if his wife had accurately described him as the man who'd followed her home from the library. Either her description was off or she hadn't told her husband, because Roger didn't seem to notice him when they stood shoulder to shoulder in the nightclub. But Mercer knew Marigold recognized him when she spotted him standing next to Roger. He simply smiled at her and left the club. Risky, he knew, but he could squirrel out of it if he was cornered by Roger. Or he'd snuff him out if he had to.

Mercer stayed clear of the alley now, since the day he'd chased Marigold into her house. He'd also returned to Cam Halladay's Used Car Emporium and traded in the DeSoto for something smaller, less noticeable. He bought a used Ford Fairlane, like his car back home. This one in black, and the radio worked this time. He also picked a new spot to stake out the duplex.

Watching the couple's comings and goings, he'd already figured out Roger was a man without a job. There had to be a reason why. Mercer sat in his car near the front of the duplex. Roger usually left the house around seven o'clock in the evening. It was 7:45 and there was no sight of Roger. All of Sixty-Fifth Street was quiet, and a light summer rain had started to fall. Mercer eased out of his car and slipped up between Roger's duplex and the house next door. A dog in the yard next door barked and he hesitated for a beat. The dog settled down. Mercer quietly crept up to the back porch and peeked in the window.

The hall was empty, but there were voices coming from the upper floor. A man and a woman arguing. Then the crash of glass and a hard thud. *Marigold and Roger arguing?* The voices were muffled. He couldn't make out what they were saying. Another thud. Mercer thought about Mary Lou. They never argued much. Whatever Mary Lou said was usually right and there wasn't much use in arguing with her. Besides, Mary Lou had saved his life and turned him around. He couldn't say a cross word to her if he tried.

"I don't need this shit! I'm going out."

Roger.

He heard the door on the upper level open. Mercer dashed down the back porch steps and raced around the side of the house, back to his car. Inside, he scrunched low in the seat, peeping over the dashboard to watch Roger storm between the houses and down the street. Mercer watched for a few moments before he turned the ignition and followed at a distance. He tailed Roger a couple blocks to a place called Jake's Bar Tap and watched him walk inside. He parked the Fairlane and gazed across the neighborhood. The light rain on his windshield reflected the headlights of an oncoming car. What to do next? A white man openly moving around in a colored section of town was brazen and might arouse suspicion. But this might be his only chance to get Roger alone. Better to approach him without a lot of people around. Mercer had had enough foresight not to strike up a conversation with Roger in the nightclub. No more stupid mistakes this time.

Mercer slinked out of his car and trotted through the rain up to the door of Jake's. Inside, the place was nearly empty, a few customers scattered across a couple dingy-looking booths. Jake's Bar Tap had the same dreary imprint of a dozen other bars he'd been in. The only difference was the color of its customers. The bar's lighting was just dim enough to hide the stained floors, the wrinkles on the women, and the bloodshot eyes of the men who spent too much time inside. No one looked up when he entered. So far so good. Mercer recognized James Brown's gravelly voice belting out "Prisoner of Love" from the jukebox. He liked James Brown, but he never told his friends back home. The kind of friends he had back in Jackson didn't think much of a colored man making a living on talent instead of muscle. Two men sat at the far end of the bar laughing and chatting. The bartender was clearing glasses from an empty table. Roger sat by himself near the middle of the bar, nursing a beer.

Mercer eased onto a barstool near Roger. The bartender walked behind the bar and put a couple dirty glasses somewhere underneath the end of the bar before he strolled up to Mercer. He was a wide man with a road map of moles on his face that marked his age like rings on a tree stump.

"What'll you have?" the bartender said. No smile. No friendly banter.

Mercer could never get used to colored people speaking to him without a "sir" or downcast eyes. But so was the way of the North.

"A Pabst."

The bartender waddled away. The jukebox changed songs, another slow, sad one this time with a woman crying out into the night for a lost lover. Mercer glanced at the two men at the end of the bar, still laughing and crowing like long-lost buddies who'd just found each other again. He peered over at Roger who was staring into the bottom of his beer.

"Is it always this quiet?" Mercer asked Roger. Roger didn't respond. The bartender returned with a glass of Pabst, placed it in front of Mercer, and meandered off. Mercer pulled a cigarette from his shirt pocket and leaned in toward Roger. "You got a light?"

Roger turned to Mercer with the kind of expression that said he was either lost in thought or slow on the uptake. "What?"

Mercer held up his cigarette. "Light?"

"Um . . . yeah, sure." Roger reached in his pocket and pulled out a pack of matches. He slid them across the bar.

Mercer picked up the matches, struck one, and then gave a long look at the match cover. "You from Mississippi?"

Roger turned slightly on his barstool. "Yeah. How you know that?"

Mercer sat the matchbook on the bar and tapped it a couple times before he slid it back across to Roger. "The Honeycomb Motel. It's in Jackson, Mississippi. It's right there on the cover."

"Oh. Yeah." Roger picked up his beer and took a long sip, rested it on the bar, and pulled a cigarette from his pocket. He picked up the matchbook and lit up.

"How long you been up here?" Mercer asked.

"Not long." He took a long drag on his cigarette, creating a half inch of red ash at the end of it.

"Cleveland's pretty nice. You still got family in Mississippi?"

"Hey, look, I just came in here for a little quiet, you know. A little time away from the wife to think," Roger said.

"Oh . . . yeah. Sure. I didn't mean any harm." Mercer turned on his barstool. The last thing he wanted to do now was to alienate Roger, his one good link to Violet Richards.

Roger took another drag on the cigarette. The door opened and a bluster of wind and rain whipped through the entrance to the small bar. Roger and Mercer looked toward the door. A thick colored man entered the bar. He recognized the man as the sax player from the club the other night. The guy's hair was pressed and slicked back—a "process," Mercer had heard someone in a store call it—and he was decked out in a gray sharkskin suit. Fats Johnson looked like a man of means. Mercer had never seen a colored man dressed so fine.

"Jake! What you know good, man?" he bellowed to the bartender.

"Fats Johnson! How you doin', man? Thought you had a set tonight?" the bartender asked.

"Yeah, everything's copacetic." The man called Fats strolled up to the bar and slapped Roger on the back. "On my way now. Just looking for this cat right here."

Roger gave a tired grin. "What's up, Fats?"

"Marigold told me I could find you here. She looked a sight when I stopped by. What's going on with you, man?"

"Nothing." Roger polished off the last of his beer. "We just got into a little argument. Nothing big. Did you talk to your friend? What did he say about the club?"

"It's not gon' work out. I told you, Roger, man. Ain't nobody investing in nightclubs but them Mafia guys. The margins are too thin."

"Did you tell him it's just a loan?"

"Yeah. Look, man, you gonna have to find another way to find the money. Frankie told me—" Fats stopped talking and glanced over his shoulder at Mercer. "Come on, let's go get a booth." The two men walked off from the bar.

Mercer eased slightly on his stool and watched them as they sat down in a booth on the other side of the room. They talked in low voices. Mercer strained against the music trying to hear anything the two men discussed. Nothing.

"You need another?"

Mercer looked up. Jake, the bartender, was standing in front of him pointing to his empty glass. "You need another or you ready to settle up?"

"Oh . . . yeah. Let me have another one."

The bartender gave him a long, pinched stare before he rolled off for the beer. Mercer figured he must be giving off a vibe and decided he'd better lie back before anybody got suspicious.

So . . . Roger is looking for an investor for a nightclub.

The bartender was back with the beer and more questions. "Where you say you from?" He leaned across the bar, looking Mercer directly in the eye.

"Uh . . . me? Florida."

"I don't get a lot of white folks from Florida in here. What made you want to leave the South and head to Ohio?"

Mercer hesitated before he figured old Jake might be of some help. A found opportunity. If he played this thing right, Jake might help him make some headway with Roger. "I've been here for a while. I'm an investor in private businesses, you know."

"Hmm . . . what kind of businesses you got?"

Mercer glanced over his shoulder. Roger and the man they called Fats still had their heads together, their voices so quiet they looked as if they were miming their conversation to each other. Roger seemed to be trying to convince Fats of something. "You know, a little bit of this and that. Mostly restaurants and clubs. What about you? You looking for an investor to go in with you on this little business of yours? I could help you with some money to fix the place up."

"I do just fine, thank you."

"Well, if you know of anyone looking for a partner, maybe you'll direct them my way."

He stood erect and shot a look at Mercer. "I'm nobody's middleman. Find your own trouble." Jake sauntered over to a booth. The two old men who occupied it were standing to leave. One of the men slapped Jake on the back. Mercer glanced back at Roger's booth.

Fats and Roger were laughing now. The serious conversation they were having before was replaced with what looked like friendly banter. If Mercer was lucky, maybe Jake would pass along his invitation to Roger, but judging from Jake's reaction, he couldn't count on it. Mercer polished off his beer in one long sip. He dropped a dollar on the bar and left.

Back at his car, Mercer realized he still didn't have much. But he had more than what he had when he walked into Jake's Bar Tap. Because now, he knew two things. First, he knew Roger and his wife, Marigold, weren't getting along. And second, and more importantly, he knew Roger was hard up for money to open up a nightclub of some sort. He didn't know how all this would lead him to Violet Richards. But what he did know was that a man desperate with a dream might do anything to see it come true.

This was just a start. And for Mercer, all he ever needed was a start.

33
Vera

In just a few short days, Hank had practically become a fixture on Miss Willa's front porch, making me laugh and stealing kisses after dark. I knew from that first ride home Hank was a good man—honest, decent, and everything I didn't need in my life while I was trying to outrun my past.

Hank had just left the boardinghouse and I was upstairs in my room listening to Ray Charles on the radio and nursing a couple mosquito bites with some Mercurochrome when I suddenly heard a commotion downstairs and a woman crying. I sat straight up, trying to make out the voices. Miss Willa was consoling someone. I jumped off the bed and eased to the top of the stairs. I was never one for getting mixed up in other folks' business, 'cause they was likely to wanna get mixed up in mine too.

Miss Willa's voice drifted upstairs, full of impatience and concern. "Stop crying and just tell me what happened."

The voice whimpered to a halt. And then I heard the words. "He beat me."

Lilly.

I raced down the stairs. Miss Willa had her arms around Lilly. I slipped into the parlor. Both women looked up at me. I almost didn't recognize Lilly. Her face was bloody with one eye swollen to the size of a baseball.

"Lilly! What happened? Who did this to you?" I asked.

Lilly composed herself and looked up at me. "My daddy," she whispered. Miss Willa rubbed Lilly's back.

"Your daddy? Reverend Dukes did this to you?! Why?" I eased onto the sofa next to her. I couldn't imagine a father doing something so awful to his own daughter. And a pastor at that.

"It don't matter," she said.

"Let me get a cold towel for your face." Miss Willa stood from the sofa. Before she could move, Lilly threw up all over the floor and Miss Willa's shoes, too. Then Lilly commenced to gagging something awful,

Miss Willa didn't bat an eye. She hustled off to get towels to clean it up. I eased closer to Lilly, rubbing her back.

Miss Willa returned with a couple wet towels and a fresh pair of house slippers. She gently sponged the cloth across Lilly's face. After a couple minutes, there was nothing coming up, but Lilly was still gagging as if she would throw up a lung. Just dry heaves.

"Something's wrong," Miss Willa said. "Stay here with her. I'll be right back."

A few minutes later, Miss Willa returned with Pauline Toney, the same woman who'd given me a lift from the bus port when I tried to leave town. The two of them helped Lilly to her feet and guided her to the front door.

"Where are you going?" I asked.

"We're gonna take her over to the colored hospital. You stay here. And don't say nothing about this or Reverend Dukes."

I watched the women pile Lilly into the car and drive off. I used the towels to clean up the floor. Lilly's daddy was Reverend Rudolphus Dukes, pastor of the Full Gospel Baptist Church, the only colored church in Chillicothe. I'd attended with Birdie last Sunday. I tried to imagine the raspy-voiced preacher telling folks they ought to follow the word of the Lord, love one another, treat your fellow man with kindness, then beating his own daughter to a bloody pulp.

* * *

I was sound asleep when a knock on my door jolted me awake. I sat up in the bed. "Come in."

She opened the door and stood there, her silhouette like the shadow of a small child.

"Lilly?"

"I'm sorry to wake you. I'm scared," she whispered.

I jumped out of the bed. "It's okay, honey." I closed the door and ushered her over to the bed. "Everything's gonna be fine. We not gon' let him lay another hand on you. You can be sure of that. What did they say at the hospital?"

"They pumped my stomach."

"What? They pumped your stomach. Why?"

Lilly didn't respond.

"Come on. You sleep in here with me tonight." I climbed in the bed and reached out for Lilly's hand. "Come on."

She slowly climbed in beside me. I spooned her, the same way my sister Rose used to do to me whenever I slept in the bed with her. I had this overwhelming urge to protect Lilly. But protect her from what? Her own daddy? We lay there quietlike for a few minutes.

I felt Lilly's body tense up. "He kicked me out 'cause he found out I like girls. That's why I moved in here at Miss Willa's place."

I held her closer. What she said didn't bother me none. My friend Arlene back in Jackson liked girls and boys. People should be able to do whatever they wanna do as long as they didn't hurt nobody. Folks do a lot worse things than love somebody.

"I'm sorry he did that to you."

"Sometimes I feel so . . . I don't know. It's like everybody else in the world fit together. Boys like girls. Girls like boys. But me? I'm the one that don't fit in nowhere. It's like my daddy say, I'm somethin' unnatural and spawned from hell."

"That's not true, Lilly. God made us all and God's got a place for all of us in this world." I'd told myself that a thousand times before, despite what the other people told me I was, including the church. Poor Lilly. Fighting like me against the push-pull of not fitting in and all the world telling you where you're supposed to go, who you're supposed to love, how you're supposed to love. I'd never been the type for dwelling in the shadows. And if I had a say in it, I wouldn't let Lilly do it either.

"My daddy told me I'm gonna burn in hell for all eternity." She started to whimper again. "Sometimes I think burning in hell would be better than living on earth like I do."

How could Reverend Dukes call himself a man of God, spewing hate at his own child? Lilly was quiet again for a long while. I thought maybe she had drifted off to sleep. But then she started talking, so low I could barely hear her.

"He told me I could come back if I ever gave up my sinful ways. I missed home so much. I thought if I did things his way, I could move back." Lilly started to cry.

"Shh . . . it's okay. Everything gon' be okay."

"I started keeping company with Alvin. That's my daddy's best friend. I didn't really like him, but I knew it would make my daddy happy, so I pretended I liked him. I pretended with Alvin, too. I let him—"

Her special eye didn't see that her plan with Alvin was doomed from the start. Lilly went silent. I didn't want to press her none. She didn't need me beating on her for answers after tangling with her daddy. We lay there together in the dark. I was just drifting off to sleep when Lilly started up again.

"My daddy want me to marry Alvin."

"Why?"

"I'm gon' have a baby. I told my daddy 'cause I know

Miss Willa won't let me stay here with a baby and no husband. I thought he would let me come back home. But he said I had to marry Alvin. I don't want to marry Alvin. So we argued and he beat me."

"Oh, Lilly. I'm so sorry. You don't have to marry nobody if you don't want to." I held on to Lilly like letting her go might mean certain trouble for her. I'd only known this girl for a short while, and yet I wanted to protect her. I wanted to heal all her hurting, but my arms weren't equipped to do that. Her pain ran too deep.

She wept in my arms like a baby. I almost started to cry myself.

Lilly grabbed my hand. "I don't want no baby, either. That's why I was so sick tonight." Then she whispered, "I took some turpentine. My friend told me it would take away the baby."

"Oh, Lilly, you could have died!"

"Maybe it would have been better if I did. I don't want to marry Alvin and I don't want this baby."

"Did you tell the doctor at the hospital you was gonna have a baby?" I whispered.

"No. I was too scared."

"Good. Everything's gonna be okay. No more talking now. Get some rest."

Lilly was smart not to tell the hospital about the

baby. If they figured she'd taken poison to get rid of it, she could have gone to jail instead of returning to Miss Willa's place. My friend Arlene once told me rich women could get doctors to get rid of their pregnancies, as long as they had enough money. Even though it was against the law. But women like me and Lilly didn't have that kind of money or know those kinds of doctors. I could have told her turpentine was too risky. I used a different method back in high school; it was more painful but more certain too. All that was in the past now, though. The thought of Lilly or any other woman risking death to decide how to live her own life broke my heart. As I lay in bed that night, I firmed up in my mind that the next time a woman was in trouble like this, *I would help her* instead of leaving it to a bottle of poison.

Lilly slept in my arms like a baby all night long. It reminded me of the times I'd got into a row with somebody back in Jackson or when Momma and Papa scolded me for something. I'd climb in the bed with Rose, and she would hold me, consoling me and telling me all would be well in the morning. I drifted off to sleep holding Lilly and missing Rose.

34
Vera

The next morning, I slipped out of bed without waking Lilly. I suspected she was so wore out from the beating her daddy give her and the poison she drank, she didn't have the strength to get out of bed even if I had woke her up. Poor Lilly.

By the time I got to the diner, Mr. Palmer was out front sweeping the entry to the restaurant. I waved and hustled inside. Alma was already in the back.

"Mornin', Alma," I said as I tied on my apron.

"Mornin'." She was kneading dough for the biscuits. "You can slice up them potatoes and start the grits."

"Yes, ma'am." I picked up a bag of potatoes from the floor and started to pick through them, avoiding the soft ones or the ones that were starting to go bad.

"I went to Sunday services over at Full Gospel. Reverend Dukes seem nice."

"Mm-hmm," Alma responded without looking up from the dough.

"My cousin Birdie told me his wife ran off and left the reverend and his daughter."

"Your cousin didn't tell you the whole story, did she?"

"What you mean?"

Alma's wide hands stretched out the dough, still not looking me directly in the eye. "Maybe you best to ask Birdie, since she got so much to say about Reverend Dukes."

I made a note in my head to ask Birdie Mae what all that business was about. The bell jingled and Mr. Palmer walked inside holding the door open for Eva, the white waitress who worked at the diner. As usual, she was giggling and flirting with Mr. Palmer. He ignored her as usual, too. It was shameful and sad to watch. She was a heavy woman with pockmarked skin and ankles as thick as tree trunks. The silly little blue dress and white apron she wore as a uniform could have used a good ironing. She never talked to me or Alma unless it was to complain about an order she said we messed up for one of *her* customers. Alma ignored her completely. I was learning to do the same.

"So do you know Lilly Dukes, the reverend's daughter?" I asked Alma.

"Yeah, I know her." Alma pulled out a rolling pin and began flattening the large wad of dough. "Why you asking 'bout her?"

"No reason. She stay over to Miss Willa's place where I stay. She seem like a nice girl."

"That ain't what her daddy say. The reverend say that girl is a wayward mess. Her daddy can't do nothing with her."

"You ever knowed him to hit her?"

"What?! Reverend Rudolphus Dukes?!" Alma scrunched her face up like she was eating lemons. "Shut your mouth, girl. Reverend Dukes is as fine a man as ever walked God's green earth. If somebody beating on Lilly, you might wanna check with that girl she's friends with on the other side of town."

"What girl?"

"Johnnie Mae." Alma stopped rolling the dough and turned to me, wagging the rolling pin between us. "Why you asking all these questions about Lilly Dukes? What business is it of yours?"

"Like I said, she stay over to Miss Willa's like me. She seem like a sweet girl, a little naive. Just wondering why she live in a boardinghouse when she got a daddy live right down the road." I pulled a couple potatoes toward me and started to peel them.

Alma gave me a long look before she picked up a teacup to shape the biscuits in little circles of dough. "You new in town. You'd be wise to watch the company you keep. I heard Lilly Dukes is kinda funny." She leaned in and raised her eyebrows. "Some folks say she like girls instead of boys."

I decided to give up on Alma. She was part of the "some folks say" crowd. The same kind of people back in Jackson who always knew I was a slut or a whore or crazy or whatever else they thought they knew about me. Shoot, most of the men who said they'd been in between my legs was lying. The few who I really had been with wasn't nothing to brag about. Seem all them people back in Jackson that talked bad about me was the same folks who went tipping in and out of back doors, sleeping with their neighbors' husbands or turning tricks when their own husbands were off at work. That's why I tell people, believe half of what you see and none of what you hear.

* * *

The lunch rush was dying down. Alma was prepping vegetables for the next shift, and I was on dish duty.

My hands were near raw from all the scrubbing and hot water of washing dishes. Seem like Alma always had me on dish duty. I guess if things were turned around and I was the one in charge, I'd have Alma on dish duty too. But I didn't complain none because I didn't want to go back to cleaning the Cooglers' toilets. I took off Momma's old Timex and slipped it in the pocket of my apron. I filled the sink and started on the dishes.

The bell over the door tinkled and I didn't even bother to peek out the pass-through, figuring it was a late lunch straggler.

A few seconds later, Eva yelled through the pass-through. "Mr. Palmer, Sheriff Coogler's out front to see you."

I perked up. I looked out into the restaurant and caught Butch Coogler's eye. He didn't smile, just looked a hole right through me. My God sense told me Coogler was toting bad news. I didn't know whether to run or sit tight and wait for him to put handcuffs on me. My head started hurting and I could feel the blood rushing around through my body like electricity.

"He's out back emptying the trash," Alma said flatly through the pass-through.

I watched Coogler waddle out the door, headed to the trash bins around back. Coogler had never stepped foot inside the diner until now. Had he gotten word from Jackson that the police were looking for me? Wouldn't he have just arrested me on the spot? Why'd he ask for Mr. Palmer and not me? I smelled a rat—the two-legged, balding kind.

I eased over to the back door and watched as he approached Mr. Palmer. They exchanged pleasantries about the weather before Coogler lowered his voice. All I could make out was my name and something about "shoes" and a bazaar.

I needed to get closer to hear their conversation. "Alma, I better empty this trash can while Mr. Palmer's out back."

"Why you need to do a fool thing like that now? Go'n finish up them dishes. I'm not staying any later than I need to tonight. I got Bible study at church tonight and—"

I was halfway to the back door with the garbage can in my hand before Alma could finish her thought.

Coogler was still whispering to Mr. Palmer when I stepped outside on the back stoop. The two men stopped talking and looked at me. My heart nearly jumped through my chest. "I thought I'd bring the last of this garbage out, Mr. Palmer."

"That's fine, Vera. Leave it right there. I'll get it."

I set the bin down. Both men continued to stare at

me. None of us said a word. My stomach was tangled up in all kinds of knots. If they was talking bad about me, then they could do it to my face.

"Vera, why don't you go on back inside with Alma," Mr. Palmer said.

"Yes, sir." I headed back into the restaurant. The two men picked up their conversation. I continued peeking through the back door. Mr. Palmer nodded his head in agreement as Coogler continued talking. I couldn't hear anything, but I figured I'd find out soon enough, since bad news don't tarry.

"Vera! Get back to them dishes."

I gave one last look back through the door. Was this the end for me? There was no waiting bus like back in Birmingham. I didn't have a car. I had no way to get out of town in a hurry.

Calm down. Think.

If Coogler were here to arrest me, he would have done it. He wouldn't have talked to Mr. Palmer first. This is about something else. But what?

* * *

A few hours later, I found out what Mr. Palmer and Coogler had their heads together about. Alma was taking off her apron and handing off things to the evening shift cook. Mr. Palmer walked into the kitchen. "Vera, can I speak to you before you leave?"

"Yes, sir." My stomach tumbled.

Alma gave me a funny look and shrugged before she walked out the back door. I removed my apron and followed Mr. Palmer to his back office. It was a small room with a desk and chair and a lumpy settee. I stood at the door. He hadn't invited me to sit down and I was too nervous anyway.

"Vera, I'm going to have to let you go."

"Let me go?!" I was as confused as that settee was lumpy. "Why? What did I do? I ain't ever been late or missed a day of work."

Mr. Palmer rubbed his forehead then looked down at his shoes. "Sheriff Coogler said his wife said you stole a bag of clothing and shoes she had set aside for the church bazaar."

"*What?!* I didn't steal nothing from them. I don't steal." I suddenly thought about Dewey's wallet. "I wouldn't steal from you, Mr. Palmer."

"I told you the day I hired you, I try to run a nice place around here. I try to treat people fair. So I expect the same thing in return."

"Well, this ain't fair. Bettyjean Coogler gave me a big bag of old rags and—"

"Listen, Vera, I don't want any trouble with the sheriff. He told me he won't arrest you. He said his wife won't press this thing as long as he can be sure you won't be . . . They just think it's best that I let you go. I think so too." Palmer reached inside his pocket and pulled out a week's wages and handed it to me. "Here's your pay through the end of the week. I'm sorry. I just don't need any trouble."

I didn't need no trouble either. I took the money. I glared back at Mr. Palmer. "You know I didn't steal from Bettyjean Coogler." I walked out the office and back into the kitchen.

The evening shift cook was standing at the stove. "What was that all about?"

I removed my apron and hung it on the hook on the wall. "Ask Bettyjean Coogler."

* * *

When I got back to the boardinghouse, I told Miss Willa I was feeling poorly and not to hold any dinner for me. I headed straight to my room. I fell onto the bed and cried and wallowed in pity for hours. I was like a bad penny, dragging trouble everywhere I went. I'd done every stupid thing possible and now I was stuck in this town without a job and a way to get out. I cried until I realized crying wasn't gonna do me any good. I needed a plan. I couldn't go north to Ohio to be with Marigold because some man I didn't even know was looking for me. And I couldn't stay in Chillicothe without a job, not with Miss Willa and Pauline on me like two bloodhounds on the fresh scent of a rabbit. And every time I thought about Dewey's wallet with a picture of three dead men in it, I wanted to run. But run where? Everywhere I went I made a mess of things and opened up another can of trouble.

I decided it was best to get some rest. Momma always said things look better in the light of day. I'd make a plan when I was fresh and sitting on top of a good night's sleep. I started to get undressed. I removed my headscarf and earrings, a pair of cheap dime-store fake pearls some guy back in Jackson had given me. I didn't even remember his name. I sat them on the table. I reached for my watch on my wrist. It was gone! Momma's old Timex watch. I panicked for a few seconds till I remembered I'd left it in the pocket of my apron at the diner. I glanced at the alarm clock on the table. It was after nine o'clock. The diner closed at nine, but maybe I could race back before Mr. Palmer locked up and left for the night.

I wasn't much on walking through dark streets by myself ever since Huxley attacked me back in Jackson.

The streets were dark and empty back then, too. And just like that night I killed Huxley, I slipped Papa's pistol in my skirt pocket; this time for protection, that time for vengeance. No man would hurt me again. Ever. I dashed back to the restaurant as fast as my legs would carry me. As crazy as it seemed, I wished old Bankrobber was around. My escort. But I kept a sharp eye out and prayed the entire walk back to the diner. By the time I made it to the front door of the Starlight Diner, the red-and-black CLOSED sign greeted me at the door. The restaurant was dark inside. I tugged on the door like it might magically open just for me. No such luck. I looked around. The entire street was dark. The whole town shut down over an hour ago.

Maybe Mr. Palmer was in his office counting up the day's receipts. I hustled around to the back door of the restaurant and spotted a light coming from his office. I was in luck!

I climbed the back stoop and peered in through the back-door window. At first I couldn't make out exactly what I was seeing. I blinked a couple times and then everything came together. Stretched across the desk in the back office was Mr. Palmer, naked as a jaybird, his pink ass gyrating and pumping up and down. And lying there underneath him, on the receiving end, enjoying it all—Bettyjean Coogler.

35

Mercer

He told himself this would be the last time he'd ever work for the Leonards. They were trouble. Every single one of them. Now those assholes had roped him into a murder. A big one.

Mercer had escaped prison time once before after he got into a fight at Rally's Roadhouse and punched out the mayor's son. The only reason he didn't go to jail then was because Mercer had served as the driver last June for Olen Leonard; his son, Dewey; and their cousin, Sheriff Bickford, when they decided to go hunt down those boys from up north, and all that business about colored folks getting the right to vote. Mr. Leonard had a lot of clout around Jackson, being friends with the mayor and serving as the head of the Mississippi Citizens Council. Olen Leonard had intervened and gotten the mayor to back off on pressing charges. But even with Olen Leonard vouching for him, Mercer was blacklisted all around town unless he wanted to do the slop work the coloreds did. Even Mr. Leonard wouldn't let him come around and do any day work at the supply store anymore, telling him to let all the dust with the mayor's son die down before he came back around the store.

But Dewey was right, the FBI wouldn't handle this Neshoba thing the way Sheriff Bickford and his deputies usually did, by pretending it never happened and turning a blind eye to the colored family's pleas. A couple of those boys that were murdered were white, from up north too. This was bigger than that old farmer and the feedstore theft. And he'd be damned if he was going to prison for the Leonards or anybody else. He decided he had another plan for what to do when he found Violet Richards, and what he'd do with her boyfriend, Dewey, too.

By eight o'clock in the morning, Mercer was already staked out at the corner of Sixty-Fifth Street, with a vantage point of Roger and Marigold's house. Ever since he learned Roger and Marigold were having problems, he decided to focus all his attention on Roger. One thing Mercer knew for sure, whether a man loved his wife deeply or hated her and the ground she walked on, either way, he was likely to talk about her at some point. Men usually talked about the women in their lives, whether singing their praises or cursing them to the heavens. If he could get this Roger fella talking about Marigold, maybe he could get him to talk about his sister-in-law too.

As usual, Frankie left early in the day. Marigold left the house shortly after, and she was sporting a shiner she tried to cover by combing her hair over one eye. Mercer figured it was probably from the thud and clanging he'd heard the night before outside their house. He couldn't imagine ever laying a hand on a woman. He despised any man who did. The more time he spent lurking and following this guy, the more he started to hate him. Maybe after he found out where Violet Richards was, he'd do her sister a favor and knock off the Roger guy.

Mercer lay in wait for Roger. It was nearly noon by the time Roger strolled out of the house and up to the corner bus stop. Mercer started up the ignition, waiting to follow Roger when he got on the bus. Roger waited for exactly five minutes before he strolled away from the bus stop. Mercer let the engine hum while he waited. Watching. Two blocks later, Roger was back at the same spot Mercer had left him the night before, Jake's Bar Tap. Mercer drove his car the couple blocks and parked. He eyed Roger as the guy paused at the doorway, like he was trying to decide whether to go in. Yep, this was a man with problems on his mind.

Mercer cut the engine. He had an instinct about Roger and he decided to take a chance on his gut. Mercer hopped out of the car and headed toward the bar. When he got close enough, he pretended to bump into Roger as he approached the entrance to the bar.

"Oh, excuse me," Mercer said. Then he stopped. "Hey, you look like a man who could use a drink." Mercer nodded toward the door. "I'm buying."

Roger gave him a suspicious look. "Do I know you?"

"I don't think so. I'm just a friendly guy willing to buy you a drink. C'mon."

Mercer opened the door, stepped aside, and waited for Roger to enter in front of him. Roger gave him another suspicious look, still not recognizing Mercer from the other night, and walked in ahead of him. Inside, the place was empty except for Jake, who was taking down the last of the chairs from one of the tables, setting up for the early patrons like Roger, and now Mercer. Jake didn't even bother to look at the men. Someone was always wandering in as soon as Jake unlocked the doors.

"I'd like to buy my new friend here a drink. Anything he wants," Mercer said.

Jake didn't stop his task of removing the chairs, didn't even look at them.

"A Pabst for me and . . ." Mercer smiled at Roger.

"Jake, let me get a Seagram's, neat."

Mercer was sharp enough to notice that every other time he saw Roger—at the Tip Top Club, here at Jake's—the guy was nursing a beer. Now he decided to upgrade to Seagram's on Mercer's dime. He smiled because his gut instinct about Roger was right. The guy was broke.

Jake pushed the last chair up to the table with a loud scrape against the linoleum floor before he waddled behind the bar. Roger and Mercer ambled up to the bar and sat in stools next to one another. Both men sat quietly waiting for their orders.

Finally, Roger asked, "Why are you here?"

"What?"

"What's a white cat like you doing hanging around Jake's?" Jake sat the drinks in front of the men. "Sorry, Jake, no harm meant."

"None taken," Jake muttered as he rested his elbows on the bar and gave a wary glance at Mercer. "I was wondering the same thing myself."

Mercer flushed red. He had hoped his friendly manner might have saved him from an encounter like this. He'd spotted a few white people around the neighborhood a couple days ago. And the Tip Top Club had almost as many white people as coloreds. Had he made a misstep by coming inside this bar again? What if these guys tried to rough him up? All the bartenders Mercer had ever known usually kept some form of heat behind the bar. And he'd left his gun in the car. Could he take them both on?

Mercer took a deep breath and rested his palms on the bar. Roger and Jake glanced at each other before a smile eased across Jake's face. Both men laughed out loud.

"Come on, man, we just pulling ya' leg," Roger said. "Drink your beer."

Mercer let out a nervous laugh, partly relieved, partly pissed off. "You guys had me for a minute there."

"Don't get a lot of guys like you in here." Roger pulled out a pack of Camels and tapped the package against the back of his hand before he removed one. "Hey, now I remember, you were in here the other night. What you doing around here anyway? I thought your type preferred the west side of the city."

Mercer scrambled for an answer. "I think people oughta be free to go wherever they wanna go. What's that line that old-timey guy said? Give me liberty or give me death."

Roger struck a match from the same Mississippi matchbook Mercer had borrowed the last time they sat at the bar and lit his cigarette. "Well, that's fine for folks that look like you. A cat that look like me can't walk around Little Italy or certain parts of the west side. But white folks go anywhere they damn well please. Look at you right now. Here you are sitting in a bar, chatting as free as you want. You see any other white folks in here? If this bar was on the west side of town, full of white folks, and I stepped inside, my ass would be hauled off before I could sit it on a barstool. Let's just say Jim Crow has a Yankee cousin up here in the North. Must be a nice feeling, all that liberty or death stuff, huh?"

Mercer didn't say anything at first. How was he supposed to defend what he didn't know? "But this is the North. It's not as bad as back in Mississippi, right?"

Roger laughed out loud. "Well, you'll fit right in up here. You'll get first dibs on all the best places to live and the best jobs. All of it waiting for you. Then you can pass out your leftovers to cats like me. Maybe I don't have to go around to the back of a restaurant to order a meal. But it's all just about the same as back home."

Jake nodded in solemn agreement.

Mercer chuckled nervously. "I guess everybody's still trying to figure it all out, huh?"

"Yeah. Whatever, man," Roger said with a shrug and a frown. He flicked the ashes off his cigarette. "So where are you from?"

"Florida." The same lie he'd told Jake and the waitress back at Lenny's Deli when he first arrived in Cleveland. If this job worked out the right way, soon enough he wouldn't be lying.

"So how long you been up here?"

Jake strolled away and started arranging bottles on the shelf behind the bar.

"About a year," Mercer lied again.

Roger held the cigarette between his thumb and forefinger, then took a long drag before he inhaled and let two long plumes of smoke fall from his nostrils. He stared at Mercer like he was trying to read his mind. "Now why would a white man wanna leave Florida and everything y'all got down there, including all the money and warm weather, to come up north?"

Mercer took a sip of his beer to collect his thoughts. He had to make his story believable or he might lose this thin thread of trust he had going right now with Roger. "I work with a group of guys and we invest in real estate. My partners and I decided we might like to venture out into other kinds of deals."

"Oh, yeah? Like what?"

Mercer took another quick sip. "Restaurants, night-clubs, stuff like that. Lots of good jazz bands up north."

Roger's eyebrows flew up in surprise. Mercer knew his story had landed. He decided to pedal slow now and let his words marinate in Roger's mind for a bit. Mercer calmly polished off his beer. But still, not a word from Roger. Better to leave him with his thoughts. Mercer raised his empty glass in the air toward Jake. "Another one of these, please."

Jake poured another Pabst from the tap and sat it in front of Mercer. "Roger, you need another? Diamond Jim here said he's buying."

"Yeah." Roger took another drag on his cigarette before he stubbed it out in a nearby ashtray.

"You look pretty deep in thought there," Mercer teased.

"Yeah, I got a lot on my mind."

"Maybe talking it out might help." *Easy, Mercer, boy.*

"The kinda problems I got, you can't help me with. Not unless you and your partners are willing to part with five thousand dollars."

"Hmm . . . that's a lot of dough. Must be a pretty big problem."

Roger chuckled. "Not really a problem. More like a solution."

"A solution, huh? My daddy used to say there's a solution to every problem. Keep talking and let's see if you can make me part ways with my money."

Roger turned on his barstool to face Mercer. "So you sayin' you got five thousand bucks? But you up here in Jake's place in the middle of the day. No suit. No job probably. Man, get the fuck outta here." He turned back and polished off his drink.

"If you think investors in nightclubs all wear suits and ties, you got a lot to learn about the business. But your choice if you wanna take a chance with me or wait for someone else to come along and part with five thousand dollars. I guess you could always go get a loan at the bank."

If the banks in Cleveland worked anything like they did back in Jackson, Mercer knew Roger's chances on a business loan were as slim as a knife's edge.

There was a stretch of silence between the two men as long as a river. For a moment, Mercer thought Roger might get up from his stool and leave the bar. What would he do then? His new plan could fall apart. Jake sat another shot glass down in front of Roger. He kicked back the second shot of Seagram's. Mercer wasn't sure whether he'd said so much it made Roger suspicious or not enough to get his interest up.

"So, you looking to invest, huh? Invest in what?"

"I don't know . . . like I said, a restaurant, nightclub, something happening, you know. Music, dark lights, fancy clothes." Mercer shrugged.

Roger gave him a suspicious side-eye. "And what do you know about running a restaurant or a nightclub?"

"Well, to be honest, not much. But I know what I like and I know what people like."

"You do, huh?"

"People here are stuck in the house because of all the cold weather. I think they might wanna get out sometimes. Listen to some live music. Eat some good food. No disrespect to Jake, but I think they wanna do all those things in a nice place. Big fancy booths, cute little dolls in some skimpy little outfit. That's what I think."

"So why haven't you opened up a place like that?"

"I work the business end of things with my partners. We invest up front and get our cut out of the profits. We let the lawyers work out the details."

Roger nodded as if he had this sort of conversation every day with investors.

"What about you? You ever thought about opening up your own business?" Mercer asked.

"Jake!" Roger yelled toward the back door where Jake was bringing in a garbage can. "You got some peanuts or something around here?"

Jake ambled back to the bar and tossed the garbage can underneath. "This is a bar. Ain't no damn diner. Go on across the street if you want something to eat."

Roger laughed. He turned back to Mercer. "If you still buying, I know where we can get the best barbecue in town. Maybe I can talk you out of that five thousand dollars."

Mercer smiled before he reached in his pocket, pulled out a ten-dollar bill, and tossed it on the bar. "Keep the change, Jake." He knew leaving a big tip would impress Roger more than it would Jake. "Let's go get that barbecue."

"My name's Roger Bonny," Roger said as he extended an open palm.

Mercer gave a big broad smile and pumped Roger's hand. "My name's Dewey . . . Dewey Leonard."

36
Marigold

Roger cared absolutely nothing about me, and now I was shackled to him through marriage. Every time the thought crossed my mind, it made me cry. And I still hadn't gotten around to telling him about the baby. I just had a feeling if a man didn't care about his wife being followed by a stranger, what was the likelihood he would care about a baby? Especially if he figured out the baby wasn't his.

What would I do now? I couldn't feel a baby yet, but I sure could see one—in the fullness of my face and the plumpness bursting against my bra. Nothing big, since I wasn't showing yet, but enough to make someone do a double take if they hadn't seen me in a while. Roger even had the nerve to make a joke the night before about my behind getting big and round. And every day Lurlene asked me if I'd told Roger about the baby yet.

I gave up the hope that he would ever look for a job. Last night, he came home talking about opening up a nightclub with some man he met at Jake's place. Who goes into business with somebody they met in a bar?! Part of me wanted to tell him about this baby. Maybe that would knock some sense into him. Better yet, maybe someone needed to knock some sense into me. Why was I staying with Roger? And then, the answer that I always fell back on—I was pregnant with no money and no job. Where would I go?

I stood at the kitchen sink staring out onto the back alley. I hadn't seen the man from Jackson since the day he followed me home from the library. *Thank God.* The summer breeze tumbled up dust and a few leaves across the backyard. I heard the next-door neighbor's German shepherd bark. Not the strong bark of a ferocious animal but more like a sad lonely howl. It was shameful how much they kept that poor animal chained to that tree. Sometimes I wanted to go over there and set him free, but I was scared he might bite me.

"Hey."

I turned around. Roger stood in the doorway of the kitchen, the scent of Aqua Velva aftershave floating through the air around him. He was dressed in his Sunday finest, a sky-blue suit, holding his porkpie hat in his hand, at eight o'clock in the morning. His hair was slicked back, the way he used to wear it when we first started dating. It looked like he'd used a whole jar of Duke's Pomade on it. He didn't look as distinguished as James or the other lawyers I used to work with at the Mississippi Summer Project. But at least he put in some effort like he really was about business today. For a fleeting moment, I got excited. Maybe he was on his way to a job interview.

"Hey, it's early. You going somewhere?" I asked.

"I'm meeting Dewey. We gonna go take a look at a couple places . . . for the club." Roger cleared his throat. "I might not be home before dark. Don't wait up for me."

"Roger, wait."

He looked down at his hands and ran a forefinger along the brim of his hat. "I already told you, I gotta try this thing, Marigold. I know you don't take a shine to it, but I gotta make this work the best way I see fit." He finally looked up at me, his eyes cold, hard with anger. "A good woman would stand by her man while he was trying to make a better life for them."

"I just don't know about all this. What makes you think some man you met in a bar is going to part ways with his hard-earned money just because you're a nice guy? That isn't how the world works. You always say you're smart when it comes to business, but, Roger, this is not smart. Maybe go slow, find out something about this man."

"Marigold! I don't want another argument with you!"

"But none of this makes any sense! What do you know about this Dewey guy anyway? What white man do you know from the South who's willing to give a Negro thousands of dollars to start a business?"

"Let's just drop it, okay?"

"Okay, so you bought a few groceries. But we still have rent, and the light bill coming due at the first of the month!" I trembled, the anger rising in my voice. I didn't want to start something that might lead to another bruise or black eye. But I couldn't stop myself. I couldn't hold back the hatred and loathing I felt for this man. "We can't keep living off handouts from Frankie and Lurlene. They've got their own bills. Can't you just find a job? Something to bring in a little money in the house and work on the club thing at night? Lurlene said her sister told her the post office is hiring. It's good money too."

"Damn it, Marigold! That's enough!"

"Roger, you have to find a job. I'm—" I stopped

myself. I didn't want to tell him this way. I didn't want to talk about the baby in the middle of an argument.

"You're what?"

I turned my eyes away from him. I knew where this was headed. "Nothing."

"You're what? Go on and say it. You're gonna leave me? Is that what you wanna do?" Roger tossed his hat on the counter and rushed across the kitchen before I could move. He snatched me by my arm, his grip so tight I knew it would leave a mark.

"Let me go!"

"Where the fuck you think you're going, huh?"

"Let me go!" I squirmed, trying to free myself from the heat of his anger. But it was too late. He wrapped his left hand around my neck and slapped me across my face so hard it made my ears ring. He pushed me up against the cabinet.

"Where you going, huh? Who's gonna take your fat ugly ass?" He raised his hand again.

"Don't!" I pleaded. "Lurlene's home. She'll hear us. Please don't!"

He stared at me for a second, his eyes hot with anger. He finally released his hand from around my neck and pushed me to the floor. He kicked me in the stomach, a kick that knocked the wind out of me. He grabbed his hat and hustled out the door.

Stupid as it was, a small part of me expected him to come back through the door and apologize for what he'd just done, to tell me this wasn't the real him who'd hurt me. To apologize and utter all the usual excuses he gave all the other times before. But he didn't.

I cried, right there in that spot where he left me, for what seemed like an eternity. And then I stopped. No more tears. No more sadness. Only anger was left. I got up from the kitchen floor and calmly headed into the bedroom. I pulled my suitcase from against the wall and packed up everything I owned or wanted from that house. When I was done packing, I went to the closet and found Roger's brown-and-white Stacy Adams shoes. I reached inside. Fifty-three dollars was stuffed in the toe of the left shoe. I pulled out every single dollar. I checked the right one, too. Empty. I stuffed the money in my purse and threw the shoes out the bedroom window.

I was leaving Roger.

I had no choice. Either I continued to stay in that house and take Roger's abuse or risk a run to Georgia. If the man from Jackson was still following me, I might bring trouble straight to Violet's doorstep. An impossible dilemma. But I decided to take my chances with the evil-looking white man following me around Cleveland before I'd let Roger lay another hand on me.

* * *

Thirty minutes after I packed my bags, I was dressed and headed down the back stairs to Lurlene's car. I had told her I needed a ride and asked her to pull the car around to the alley. No sign of the man from Jackson. As soon as I climbed inside Lurlene's car, I started silently praying. *Please God, do not let the man from Jackson follow me.* I still continued to look for him, even after Lurlene pulled off from the house. I peered out the door window and behind me through the back seat window.

"Marigold, are you all right? What are you looking for?"

"I'm fine. I just want to make sure we're not being followed. How much farther to the bus station?"

"Not much," Lurlene said. "Marigold, tell me what's going on. Where are you going exactly?"

"I'm just going to visit my sister in Georgia. She's sick. I'll be back in a couple weeks," I lied. My hands trembled as I took another look through the back seat window.

"Why Roger ain't going with you? Seems like he got the time. You shouldn't be traveling alone in your condition."

"He said he and that Dewey guy from Florida got a

lot to take care of to get the club open. He can't spare the time." I was talking fast, trying to keep up with all Lurlene's questions and make sure we weren't being followed. I glanced back out the window.

"This ain't got nothing to do with them noises I been hearing from y'all place?"

I looked at Lurlene and she gave me a sad look of pity.

"Sweetie, I know Roger can be a handful and he ain't got no right to put his hands on you. But don't you think he got a right to know he's gonna bring a child in the world?"

"So you've heard the noises. You've seen the bruises and you think telling him about another mouth he has to feed will make everything better between us?" I turned away and stared out the window. "Listen, Lurlene, I appreciate you giving me a lift to the bus station. Roger and I just need some time apart."

We pulled up to the front of the station. Lurlene put the car in park and turned toward me. "So what should I tell him when he comes home looking for you?"

I hugged Lurlene. "Thanks for the lift." I carefully peered out the windows before I opened the door. No sign of the man from Jackson. I hustled out of the car, grabbed my suitcase from the back seat, and slammed the door.

Lurlene yelled through the passenger window. "Marigold! Marigold, what should I tell Roger?"

I leaned back inside the window. "Tell him his Stacy Adams are out back in the bushes!" I headed inside the bus terminal.

I hadn't thought much beyond a bus ticket to Georgia. Violet didn't even know I was coming. But one thing I did know for sure. I wasn't going to sit around waiting for a man to come home and beat me again. Ever.

* * *

I sat in the bus station waiting for the call for my bus. I was a wreck. Every white man that passed by me made me jump. What if the guy was here in the station right now? Maybe he was looking at me right now and I just didn't see him.

Calm down, Marigold.

I loved my baby sister. I just prayed I wasn't bringing trouble to her door by heading to her house with this man on my tail. But I was desperate. Roger had left me no choice.

The loudspeaker announced my bus and I gathered up my suitcase. I darted my eyes in every direction. No sign of him. I stepped onto the bus and took a seat right at the front. It felt good to sit up front for a change.

I hoped I could keep this seat for the entire ride. I also took this seat so I could see every single person who got on. When the driver closed the door and started up the engine, I finally relaxed. I stared out the window. No sign of the man from Jackson. I released a deep breath and leaned back for the ride.

I was headed to Chillicothe, Georgia.

37
Mercer

M ercer sat on a stool at the end of the counter at Jake's Bar Tap and wondered why men chase dreams they can't ever have. Take Roger Bonny, chasing after some kind of Hollywood-movie dream of owning a nightclub with famous entertainers. Or Dewey Leonard, wanting some colored girl so bad he was willing to pay someone to go halfway across the country to find her.

Mercer had dreams too. All the other things he once dreamed of doing or having had fallen apart. The mechanic shop he wanted to own, the taxicab service he wanted to run—everything always crumbled around him in the aftermath of a barroom fight or a misunderstanding over money. It seemed like he was always falling back and losing ground. It was because of Mississippi. He wished his father had never brought them to that hellhole. And now his new dream—of owning some property on a beach down in Florida, where he could take Randy on fishing trips and Mary Lou could romp around in the Atlantic Ocean—might fall apart, too, if he didn't find Violet Richards. According to Dewey, he'd be in prison soon if he didn't find Violet Richards and whatever information she had that could send them all to jail.

What if Dewey was lying? Or what if he wasn't? It didn't matter. Mercer had another plan for keeping his dream alive. But even with his new plan to take care of this whole mess, Mercer was confused and homesick. He'd spent hours listening to Roger Bonny rattling on about some harebrained scheme to open up a night-club. Roger planned to call it Cleveland's Cotton Club, like that old-timey club up in New York City. That made absolutely no sense to Mercer. He was convinced the guy was all bluster and brag, in addition to being a coward for bashing his wife around. And through all that talk, Mercer hadn't been able to find out a thing about Roger's sister-in-law. Of course, Mercer was all bluff too. He'd made all sorts of promises to invest in the club, all in an effort to keep Roger Bonny talking.

It had been well over the time that he'd told Mary Lou it would take him to finish up this job for Dewey.

He was lonely and he ached for his own bed. No colored woman was worth all this. He loved his wife and kid and he needed to be home with them.

To hell with it. He was done with chasing Dewey Leonard's monkey girlfriend. The rich boy who'd flunked out of college up north had returned back to Mississippi and was now dating colored women because a decent white woman wouldn't touch him. Mercer ambled to the phone booth at the back of the bar. He closed the door, picked up the receiver, and dialed the operator. She patched him through to Jackson, Mississippi, announcing his name before he heard Dewey on the other end.

"Mercer? That you? What'd you find out, buddy?"

"Hey, Dewey. I thought I had a lead on that woman you're looking for. I tracked her sister up here to Ohio, but no sight of the woman. Nothing."

"What d'ya mean, nothing?"

"Looks like the sister moved up here, but there's no sign of that gal you looking for. Look, I'm heading back to Mississippi. I was thinking I could just keep the money you already paid me and we can call it square." It wasn't what he had hoped to make on this job, but it was a solid start on getting his family out of Jackson. They could find a small place to rent until they could afford to buy that house by the beach.

Mercer stopped talking. The phone was quiet. All he could hear was Dewey's breathing on the other end.

"Listen, Dewey, I need to be home . . . with my family." The last three words were designed to elicit some sympathy from the other end of the phone.

"What?!"

Mercer let the phone go silent for a beat. He didn't want to rile Dewey up. He thought back to the night he introduced himself to Roger posing as Dewey. That was all by design. Better to leave Dewey's prints all over this job rather than his own. If Dewey knew what he'd done, he'd really get upset. It was better to back out of all this now.

"I'm sorry. That girl has disappeared into thin air."

"Have you lost your fuckin' mind?!" Dewey yelled through the phone.

Mercer sighed deeply. Best to let Dewey get it all off his chest. By the time Mercer got back to Jackson, Dewey might still be mad, but it might not be as bad.

"Let me tell you somethin', Bugsy boy. Your ass is hanging on by a thread."

"Look, Dewey, I know you're mad about the money, but I had expenses to get up here. I can't give it all back."

"You idiot! You're going to prison if you don't find

this woman. We all are if you don't find her. She's got evidence that puts us all at that murder back in June."

Mercer felt stupid and trapped for taking this job. "Look! I told you. That gal ain't here. Maybe she went off to a different city."

Dewey let out an exasperated sigh. "So what did you find out so far?"

"I'm in Cleveland. The sister, Marigold, is married to some goofball named Roger Bonny. He's from Jackson too. You know him?"

"Bonny . . . Bonny. No. I don't know him. Have you followed the sister? Maybe she can lead you to Violet."

"What do you think I've been doing all this time?! I've followed them both. I'm telling you, that woman ain't up here."

"Then find her. That's what I paid you for."

"Dewey, I got a sick kid at home. I need to get back to Jackson. I'm sorry I couldn't help you."

"You find her or don't bother to bring your sorry ass back this way. Find Violet or go to jail. Think about how hard it is to see your sick kid from a prison cell. Now get back to work."

Click. The line went dead.

"Dewey? Dewey?"

Mercer slammed the phone down on the hook. What the hell was he supposed to do now? He picked up the receiver again before he dropped coins inside the phone. He and Mary Lou couldn't afford the reverse charges.

"Mary Lou? It's me."

"Mercer, where are you? I've been worried sick."

"I know you have, honey." He wished he could climb through the phone and hold her. "I'll be home soon. How's Randy?"

There was no response.

"Mary Lou?" Mercer heard her whimper softly on the other end. She sounded like she was a million miles away. "What's going on?"

"It's not good. The doctors are talking about heart surgery now. The rheumatic fever, it . . ."

Mercer fell against the wall of the phone booth.

"The doctor said it did something to his heart. If he doesn't have the surgery . . . It's expensive, Mercer. It's gonna cost thousands." She started to cry softly into the phone. "Just come home, Mercer."

"It's okay, Mary, baby. Everything's gonna be okay. Give me another week. I'll get the money and I'll be home."

"What are you gonna do?"

"Don't worry. I'll call you back."

Mercer hung up the phone and stared back out into the bar. A few seconds later, Roger walked in and took a seat at the counter. Roger was dressed in what looked like a clown suit, bright blue with matching shoes and a spit shine in his hair. This guy was a buffoon. Mercer had promised Roger they would scout a few places for the club today. But Mercer was ready to tell Roger the deal was off. Better that he scrap this whole idea and head back to Jackson. Especially now that Randy had taken a turn. He left the phone booth and walked up beside Roger.

"Hey, partner," Mercer said.

"Hey, man."

"You look down. Everything okay?" Mercer asked.

"The wife again."

Mercer perked up. "What's going on?"

Roger grunted. "Same old same. Except this time, she left. My sister-in-law said she's headed to visit her sister in Georgia."

Mercer's stomach did a somersault. *Is Violet Richards in Georgia?* "Maybe a little time apart ain't so bad, huh?"

Roger nodded at Jake, who was standing nearby. "Seagram's, neat."

"Make it two." Mercer eased onto a barstool beside Roger. *Georgia.*

"Maybe you're right. A few days and hundreds of miles apart might do us both some good."

"You give her a couple days, then drive down to . . . Where exactly is she headed?"

"My sister-in-law said she's been calling some small town outside of Augusta . . . Chilly something. Chillicothe, I think. Yeah, Chillicothe is what it's called."

"All right, give her a couple days, then you drive down to this Chilly town. Give her your best begging and pleading routine, she'll be back up here with you in two shakes." Mercer patted Roger on the back.

Both men laughed. "Yeah, my sister-in-law said I ought to go down there and plead for her to take me back. Oh, and here's the kicker. My sister-in-law also told me I'm gonna be a father." Roger shook his head sadly.

"Well, congratulations!"

"Humph. I just hadn't figured on kids so soon. Gotta get this club up off the ground first."

Jake returned with a couple shot glasses and sat them on the counter.

Mercer thought about Randy, the best thing that had happened to him after meeting Mary Lou. He couldn't imagine loving another human being as much as he loved his son. "You might not believe it right now, but having kids can be better than you think. They have a way of making you see the world differently. Come on, let's toast."

The two men clinked their glasses.

"To getting your wife back and a kid to boot. Cheers!" Mercer said with a chuckle.

They kicked back their drinks. Mercer could hardly contain the excitement roiling through him at the knowledge that he finally knew where Violet Richards was.

"Jake, another round. We're celebrating over here," Mercer said.

Roger's demeanor brightened a bit after he downed his shot. "So we all set to take a look at the club over on Carnegie?"

"Absolutely. But give me a few minutes. I'm gonna hit the can and make a phone call. Be right back." Mercer walked back to the phone booth.

Chillicothe, Georgia.

Now that he knew where Violet Richards was, Mercer had another idea. A better idea. He had a way to get his money fast and get back home to his family. He placed another phone call to Jackson, Mississippi, this time to a different man.

He called Dewey's father, Olen Leonard.

"Mr. Leonard, this is Mercer Buggs, sir. Sorry to bother you at your office, but I wanted to talk to you about your son, Dewey."

"Mercer Buggs?"

"I used to do odd jobs around the supply store. I drove you and your son up to Neshoba County—"

"I know who you are. I wanna know why you're calling me," Olen Leonard said, his southern accent strong, his patience short.

"Yes, sir, I just thought you might wanna know, Dewey hired me to find a colored gal for him. I suspect this girl must be pretty special to him if he wanted me to find her, but he didn't want me to tell anyone about it."

"What's all this about? What colored gal?"

"Violet Richards. Like I said, he wants me to find her and told me not to touch a hair on her head. This girl is pretty special to him. Even offered to pay me twenty-five hundred dollars if I just let him know where she is."

"Would this have anything to do with why I had to go over to Birmingham to collect Dewey?"

"Yes, sir, I think it does." Mercer didn't have a clue what Mr. Leonard was talking about, but he knew he had the old man's interest.

"That jackass must have followed her over to Alabama. I suspected something was up when he said he *lost* his wallet. I wouldn't put it past that dirty mongrel to have stolen it from him."

"Yes, sir," Mercer said, continuing to play along.

"Do you know where she is?"

"Yes, sir. I've got a tail on her. Should I let Dewey know where she is? I mean I'm only coming to you because I was surprised that you approve of Dewey dating some colored gal. With you being on the Citizens Council and all, I wasn't sure how your colleagues would feel if they knew your son was involved with . . . Well, I just thought you should know. Especially after the way things panned out up in Neshoba County last June. I just thought *you* might want to know where she is, instead of my telling Dewey."

The phone was quiet for a moment. Mercer was playing a game with big stakes now. When the FBI started investigating the disappearance of those civil rights workers, the Leonards and a few other men from the Citizens Council rounded the wagons, running scared and getting their alibis together, trying to convince themselves why they couldn't be charged. Dewey was the most scared out of all of them. College boy implicated in the murder of some civil rights activists. He imagined that wouldn't go over very well with his colored girlfriend.

Mercer almost wanted to say something, just to smooth out his nerves that were dancing on edge. He knew he had to be careful or this whole plan could fall apart.

"Hmm . . . and you say he told you this girl is special to him, huh?"

"Yes, sir. He said they planned to marry up north. If you want to know where she is, I can tell you, but . . . I had expenses finding her and—"

"If Dewey thinks he's gonna bring some monkey bitch in my house, he's crazy. I tell you what. You find this girl and kill her."

Mercer's eyes grew wide. "Kill her?! So . . . you don't want me to just find her. You want me to kill her too?" Mercer held his breath. Olen Leonard had just upped the stakes to an entirely different and dangerous level.

The phone was quiet before Mr. Leonard chimed up. "Yes, kill her."

"Sir, no disrespect, but Dewey just asked me to find her. I don't think he wants any harm to come to her."

"You kill this girl and I'll pay you ten thousand dollars."

"Sir?"

Click. The phone went silent.

"Sir? Mr. Leonard?"

What the hell had just happened? Mercer had only wanted to get a few thousand bucks more out of the old man. He thought it would go down like that job with the old farmer—point Olen Leonard in the right direction and let Olen and his buddies take care of the rest. But Olen had a different plan.

Mercer stared at Roger Bonny out the window of the phone booth. Roger sat at the bar, all dressed up, a clownish buffoon that Mercer had used as a pawn. Were the Leonards doing the same thing to him? Did it matter? Ten thousand dollars would solve every problem he had in the world. Mercer placed the receiver back on the phone and took a deep breath. He'd been stupid to agree to anything Dewey Leonard asked and now he had gotten himself knee-deep in a mess of his own making.

He exited the phone booth and strolled up to Roger at the bar. "Hey, man, I gotta take care of something for a friend. It shouldn't take more than an hour. How 'bout I meet you back here then we can take a look at that place. What you say, partner?"

"Uh . . . I could ride along with you if you want. You know if it's on the way."

"Sorry, buddy. It's for a lady friend." Mercer smiled and winked at Roger.

Roger smiled back. "I get it."

"All right. See you in an hour." Mercer slapped Roger on the back with a sly grin before he left Jake's bar, and Ohio.

He was headed to Chillicothe, Georgia.

PART II

Headed South

38
Vera

I woke up from a dream. The details scattered from my brain like little mice scampering away from the light of day. But Rose was there. Rose was always around me. Haunting me at night and tumbling into my thoughts during the day. My ghostly reminder that I was the wilted flower in Momma's little bouquet. I was different from the others, my petals loose and tinged with dirt. My roots fragile with no depth. I hadn't peered into her diary since the night I discovered that picture in Dewey's wallet. That picture, Rose's diary, the things I'd taken that were now like little reminders of what I really was—a thief and a murderer.

I opened my eyes and stared out at the fields. I thought back over the last few weeks. I'd killed a man, stolen from and ditched another one. I'd left

Jackson, my sister, and the only home I'd ever known to move to this small town. About the only thing I'd done right during this whole time was to date Hank Cummings. Miss Willa offered to let me stay on after I told her what happened at the diner. She agreed that Bettyjean Coogler's tricks were childish and designed to hurt me. But Hank offered me the opportunity to stay at his place, probably thinking it would guilt me into marrying him so people around town wouldn't think I was a woman with "loose morals," as the old folks say. I wouldn't marry Hank or any other man for that matter. Especially not now. But I did take him up on his offer for room and board. As it all turned out, I was doing a far sight better living on the farm with Hank.

Hank's farmhouse was head and shoulders above Miss Willa's boardinghouse and my six-dollars-a-week room on the second floor. Hank and me, we worked out a little deal. I helped him sell his vegetables at the little sell shed at the bottom of the driveway, and he would pay me. He said everybody who worked hard for him ought to earn a decent wage. He treated me different from all the other men I'd been with. He respected me. He treated me like I was as smart as he was.

Here at the farm, I woke up in a big iron bed with blankets and sheets that were soft. There was a closet, small, but big enough that I could hang up my things. Sturdy pine floors and walls that seemed like they'd stand forever. I loved Hank's house. Even though it lacked a woman's touch—no curtains on the windows, just roller shades, and no rugs on the floors—still it felt like being home. It felt safe.

Hank's house was solid, like he was. I could tell almost as soon as I met Hank, he was a good man. Probably too good for me. That's why I turned down his marriage proposal he made just days after he stepped inside the diner. I couldn't be tied down. Especially not now.

* * *

"Vee! Come quick!"

Hank?

I turned off the spigot at the sink where I was washing dishes.

"Vee!"

Oh Lord, what was wrong? I quickly dried my hands and ran off to the front of the house. I hustled through the screen door and stood on the porch looking for Hank.

"Hank?"

"Over here."

I rushed to the side of the wraparound porch. And there he stood, beaming with eyes bright as new coin money, beside a car I'd never seen before. Some big shiny thing in silver with a bright white stripe across the side of it.

"What in the world?" I said.

"I bought it from a used car dealership over in Augusta. I figure we just got the one truck between us and you might want to get around during the day while I'm out making deliveries. So what do you think?"

"Well . . . it's beautiful, but . . ."

"But what? You don't like the color? I know it's about five years old and it's not the fanciest car—"

"No . . . no, nothing like that. Hank, I don't know how to drive a car."

"Oh, well, we can rectify that—"

"No, Hank. I mean, I appreciate the gesture, but I don't need a car."

Hank gave me a long unblinking stare, like he was sizing me up. "You scared, huh?"

"Hank Cummings! I ain't scared of driving no fool car."

"Okay, so prove it. C'mon. Hop behind the wheel. The key's already in the ignition."

I hesitated. I'd never been behind the wheel of a car. Maybe I was scared a little. Or maybe I was more afraid of accepting such an expensive gift from Hank. I knew I would have to leave soon. This was too much. But it would be nice to have a little freedom and not have to walk everywhere. And then the thought that really made me feel guilty crossed my mind. If I learned to drive, could I get out of town with this car?

"Well, okay," I said. I climbed into the driver's seat. Hank raced around the front end of the car and climbed in beside me.

"All right, down below, pedal on the right is the gas, makes the car go. The pedal on the left is the brake. You step on that to stop the car."

I was confused as all get-out trying to take in everything Hank was telling me about gas pedals and gearshifts and such. Maybe this car wouldn't be my getaway car, after all, since I couldn't make heads nor tails of it. I started the car up like Hank told me. I had a death grip on the steering wheel. Just sitting behind the wheel of something so big and powerful set my nerves on edge.

"Your foot's still on the brake?" Hank asked me.

"Yes."

"Good. Now put the gear into Drive and ease off the brake."

I did like he told me. I put the car in Drive and it slowly started to creep forward.

"Okay, slowly push down on the gas pedal," he said.

I hit the gas pedal. The car flew straight down the driveway like a rocket.

"Lord Jesus, Vee! Ease up on the gas!"

I hit the brake. The car screeched to a stop. Me and Hank jerked forward, then back fast as lightning. Hank shook his head like he was trying to right himself from the shock.

He rubbed the back of his neck and chuckled. "Whew!"

"See, Hank. All this driving business ain't for me."

Hank patted my arm. "Listen, first you gotta relax. We're in no rush here. Loosen up on the steering wheel. Come on. Do it."

I relaxed a bit and loosened my hold on the wheel.

"Now, when we start up again, I want you to touch that gas pedal the same way you touched me last night. Slow and easy."

I turned to Hank. He gave me a devilish wink. I giggled.

I tried it again. It was better. Just like he said it would be. We spent the next couple hours with him teaching me. I took out somebody's garbage can sitting along the curb, and I couldn't help but smile when a couple people hustled across the street after Hank yelled out the window, "Driver in training!" As far as I could tell, I didn't do no real damage. Hank told me I was a quick study. But he was the most patient teacher I'd ever known.

We drove all over Chillicothe. I even swung by Birdie's place and Miss Willa's house, laying on the horn until they had no choice but to come outside to see what all the commotion was about.

We finally made it back to the farmhouse. I cut the engine and just sat there, rubbing the steering wheel. I'd never felt such freedom in all my life.

"You okay, Vee?"

I smiled at Hank.

"Vee?"

"I don't know how to thank you for this." I felt myself getting overwhelmed. The way I felt about Hank I'd never felt about any man before. "I don't mean the car. I mean . . ."

"Shh . . . I know what you mean." He brushed a piece of hair from my face. "I love you, Vera."

"I love you too, Hank."

He leaned in and kissed me. Slow and easy.

39

Vera

The next morning, Hank rolled over in the bed and slipped his arm around my waist. He gently kissed my neck. "So you changed your mind yet?"

I wondered if I'd made a mistake telling Hank I loved him. I've never uttered those words to any man except Papa. Now Hank would expect me to marry him and give him the happily-ever-after he was looking for and rightly entitled to. But I was a woman on the run. I had too much baggage for a man as good as Hank. I'd already stayed in Chillicothe far longer than I needed to. I told myself the only reason I hadn't left yet was because I didn't have all the pieces of my plan together. Deep down, though, I knew I would miss this place. Figure that!

I wriggled slightly under the weight of his arm. "We already talked about this."

He chuckled. "Maybe I need to show you again what you missing out on."

"Oh, I think you showed me just fine last night."

Hank kissed my shoulder and turned my body to face him. "I knew from the first time I laid eyes on you, you belong here on this farm with me. In this house with me."

"I'm here with you now. Ain't that good enough?"

"You know that ain't what I'm talking about."

"Hank—"

"Vee, I know what you gon' say. We ain't known each other for that long. But I'm twenty-six years old. I had my pick of a lot of other women. I ain't bragging. Just speaking plain facts. I been waiting for a woman like you. I don't need no long courting."

"Hank, I'm not the marrying type."

"Every woman is the marrying type if she find the right man." He stretched out his arms. "Take me, I'm yours."

"Ha!"

"Come on, let me make an honest woman outta you."

"Hezekiah Cummings, my honesty ain't got nothing to do with where I rest my head at night." I got up from the bed, naked as a jaybird. I didn't even have to turn around to know he was staring at my backside. He grabbed my arm and pulled me back into the bed. I pretended to fight him off until he kissed me. Softly. For a man as big and strong as Hank, his kisses were as soft as a spring breeze.

He released the kiss, and I still had my eyes closed, like doing so would keep the taste of him inside me. I finally opened them, and he looked back down at me. His eyes were gentle, but the rest of his face was serious.

"Ain't it enough that I moved out of Miss Willa's place and I'm here with you now? Most men would think this is just fine."

"That's what I'm talking about. You a good woman, Vee. You got the whole town talking about how you out here with me and no wedding ring between us. Everybody talking 'bout you. I hear the things they whisper behind your back."

"Hank, I couldn't care less what folks say about me. The last time I cared about what somebody said about me was when my momma and papa said something. And that's 'cause they put food in my belly and clothes on my back. I don't care 'bout no folks in Chillicothe, Georgia. What other people think about me ain't none of my business."

Hank stared at me for a few seconds. "Why don't you ever talk about your family? Your momma or daddy?"

"I told you, Momma and Papa passed. We oughta respect the dead."

"Both my folks gone, too. Just me and a couple uncles over in the next county. But that don't stop me from talking about them. Talking about the people we love who've passed on ain't a sign of disrespect. It just means we miss 'em and love 'em. Especially if we remembering the good things about them."

I sighed. "Why we always gotta talk about me? When do I get to ask all the questions?"

Hank's easy smile slid across his face. "Go ahead. I ain't got nothing to hide."

"Okay, so how you come to work on this farm all by yourself?"

"I got the guys that help me out. Linc. Delroy."

"No, I mean . . . how a colored man come to own twenty-five acres of land with a big pretty house like this on it? Your family rich or something?"

Hank laughed. He rolled over on his back and rested an arm behind his head. "Hardly. My granddaddy's momma was a slave. She was born on this farm. Her daddy owned this farm."

"What? I don't understand."

"My great-grandmomma's daddy was a slave owner.

I heard tell, he was as mean and evil as God make a man, too. But he loved my great-grandmomma. All his kinfolk died off little by little. When he died, he left this farm and everything on it to her. For a while, she was richer than most white folks in this county. My daddy used to tell me stories about how it damn near split this town in two. That's why me and my daddy and his daddy before him is used to fighting with our fists and in courts. After my folks died, everything fell to me. Seem every few years somebody pop up talking about this land belong to them. But it's been a heap of years since anybody tried to take me on. Everybody within two hundred miles know this is Cummings land. Always has been. Always will be."

"I don't think I've ever known a colored man that own his own house."

"Enough of all this talking," Hank said before he grinned and pulled me on top of him. "I need to handle a little something before breakfast." He nuzzled my neck and kissed me. Then he let out a deep belly laugh. "Woman, Imma marry you if it's the last thing I do." He kissed me again before he ran his hand along my thigh and up between my legs. When he rolled on top of me, I knew I was done for. Breakfast would have to wait. We was still going at it a few minutes later when the phone rang.

Hank murmured in my ear, "Whoever it is, they can call back."

The phone rang a couple more times. "You better get it. This early in the morning, it might be something important."

Hank smirked as he pulled on his pants. "Just don't forget where we left off," he said with a sly smile.

I perked up and listened as he padded down the hall. Who was calling Hank's house this early?

"Hello? . . . Who? . . . Yes, I'll accept the charges. Yes, she's here."

My heart gave a thud. I shot straight up in the bed. Someone was calling for me. Had the police found me? But they wouldn't call first. That didn't make any sense. They'd come out here and haul my ass straight to jail. How could anyone have found me out here at Hank's place? I eased out of bed and slipped my night-gown over my head. Something inside me—my God sense—told me there might be trouble on the other end of that phone. I wanted to bolt straight outta this house. I sat on the edge of the bed waiting for Hank to say something else. I heard Hank put the receiver down on the table.

I froze.

Hank walked back up the hall and stood in the doorway of the bedroom with a funny look on his face.

"Vee, there's a woman on the phone for you. She say she's your sister."

"Marigold?" I sprang from the bed and dashed past Hank into the living room. I picked up the receiver. "Marigold? Is that you, Marigold?"

"Violet . . . I mean, Vera. Hey, it's me. Please tell Hank I'm sorry for reversing the charges."

"Don't worry 'bout that none. Hold on." I turned around and Hank was standing in the hallway, staring at me, trying to figure out what was going on. I'd only told Hank I had a sister but not much else. I covered the mouthpiece and whispered, "Everything's okay. Go put some clothes on." He shrugged before he turned around and walked back to the bedroom.

I turned my attention back to Marigold. "Where are you? You still in Cleveland?"

"No. That's why I'm calling. I needed to get away for a few days. I was hoping I could come to visit you."

"Of course you can. When were you thinking of coming?"

"Well . . . actually I'm at the Greyhound station now. I know I should have called before I left . . . but . . ."

"Marigold, you okay? Is that man from Jackson still following you? Oh my God, did he hurt you?"

"No. It's nothing like that."

"Then what's going on? Is Roger with you?"

"I'm fine and Roger's not with me."

Marigold wasn't running from the man in Jackson. My God sense told me she was running from Roger.

"I'll meet you at the station. What time your bus get in?"

40

Vera

I don't know what it was, but something about my big sister coming to visit me seemed like it was worth throwing a party. I told Hank I wanted to throw a good old-fashioned fish fry. I wanted her to meet all the people that I knew. Maybe in my own stupid way, I wanted to impress her. I wanted her to know that I had met some nice people and I had my own money, even if it was in a place as small as Chillicothe.

The next morning, Hank picked some collards from the back end of the farm, and we rustled up some fresh catfish he'd caught over at West Lake the day before. Me and Birdie spent half the day scaling and cleaning them. I invited Alma, Miss Willa, Pauline, Lilly, and her friend Johnnie Mae, and even old Bankrobber. He wasn't likely to get a decent meal if everybody was at me and Hank's place eating and having a good time. Hank invited Delroy and Linc, the farmhands who helped out around the place. They weren't much to look at, with Delroy and that lazy eye of his and Linc with his love affair with apple pie and a round belly to show for it. But they were good men, like Hank. They treated me with kindness and courtesy. They respected Hank and they respected me too.

I pulled the car up to the farmhouse. Bankrobber sat out on the front steps as me and Marigold approached the porch. He wore his same overalls but had a different shirt on underneath. He was humming and whispering to himself as usual.

"Bankrobber, did Birdie give you something to eat?" I asked.

He grinned. "She did. Yes, ma'am. You think I could trouble you for a cigarette, though?"

"Now, Bankrobber, you know Hank don't like no smoking in his house." We climbed the front steps.

"I tried to tell Miss Birdie where they hid it."

"Okay, Bankrobber. That's fine," I said.

Bankrobber looked at Marigold. "Excuse me, miss, did you see it too?"

Marigold shot a look at me. I said to Bankrobber, "This here is my sister, Marigold. And she don't know where that money is buried either." I whispered to

Marigold, "He's harmless. I'll tell you about it later. Come on, let's get inside."

By the time me and Marigold stepped inside the farmhouse, the whole place was teeming with a good time. Hank had moved the kitchen table out into the living room and set it up against the wall. Miss Alma had brought out some roses from her garden and covered the table in a bright yellow tablecloth. On top, the table was covered in food. Everybody was sitting around on the sofa and in chairs laughing, eating, and talking. Sam Cooke's smooth voice was flowing from the record player in the corner. The smell of nothing but good food—fish, greens, black-eyed peas, pound cake, and pies—floated through every room in the house.

"Marigold, I want you to meet my friends. This here is Lilly and her friend Johnnie Mae. Over there is Pauline. That's Alma and Miss Willa." All three women nodded. "And over there at the table is Hank's buddies, Delroy and Lincoln, but everybody call him Linc." Both men stood and smiled. "They help out around here on the farm. Now, come on, let me show you where you can drop your bag."

We headed inside the bedroom just off the living room. It was small, but it had everything a body would need for a visit—a soft bed, a dresser, a lamp and table.

Hank's house wasn't the fanciest, but it was inviting. I closed the door. We could still hear the muffled sound of the music and people roaring in laughter and chatter on the other side of the door. Marigold peeped through the window overlooking the front porch and out across the yard.

"You'll sleep here." I turned on the lamp next to the bed. "It kinda reminds me of home, Hank's place."

"This is nice," Marigold said as she looked around the room. "I think this is nicer than Papa's Palace."

We laughed. I took her bag and placed it near the dresser. "You know I ain't one for pressing grown folks on their personal business. But you come all this way alone, without your husband. You sure you okay?" Marigold stood looking at me all sad-eyed. It reminded me of when we was little and Papa had scolded her about something.

Marigold tried to smile. "We can talk about it later. Right now, I'm hungry and it smells good out there."

"Marigold?"

She hugged me real tight. "I missed you so much. You had me worried sick that I might not see you again. Let's just have a good time for now. We can talk about everything else later, okay?"

"Later then." I kissed her on the forehead. "Come on, let me introduce you to Hank."

I grabbed Marigold's hand and hustled her through the living room into the kitchen. Hank was pulling a couple beer bottles from the icebox.

Birdie stood at the stove, stirring a pot of greens. When she saw Marigold, she dropped the spoon and barreled in for a hug. "Marigold!" The two of them hugged and Hank smiled at me.

"Marigold, you ain't aged a day since I left Jackson. Ya' face just a little fuller. You must be living high on the hog up in Ohio." Marigold smiled like it might hurt her to part her lips. "Well, I better get these collards out on the table. We'll talk out front. It sure is good to see you, Marigold." Birdie swooped up the pot and headed into the living room.

"Hank, this here's my sister, Marigold. Marigold, Hank."

"Well, looka here. The Henderson sisters strike a right gorgeous picture."

Marigold gave me a side-eye glance and smiled at Hank. I suspected she was just getting used to calling me Vera instead of Violet, and now Hank had thrown in a new last name too. I tried to cover up Marigold's suspicious glance.

"Hank, I thought I told you Marigold is married. Her name is Marigold Bonny now."

He looked at me with a smirk. "You don't tell me

much. No disrespect, Marigold." Hank walked over and hugged her. "Maybe I could spend some time with your husband one day and he can give me some tips on how to get a Henderson woman to walk down the aisle with me."

I tapped him on his arm. "Hush up, Hank Cummings."

"What's that?" Marigold said with a real smile this time.

"Pay him no mind."

"Oh, your sister didn't tell you? I asked her to marry me, but she must be holding out for a better offer."

"Maybe you oughta get them beers out to the living room before you have an uprising on your hands," I said as I shook my head. "Come on, sis, help me get this potato salad out front."

"I'm glad you're here, Marigold," Hank said before he headed out of the kitchen.

Marigold nudged my arm and giggled. "He seems nice. Handsome, too. So why won't you marry him?"

"You mean a man I've known for less than two months? Besides, can't women do something other than grow up and marry a man? Maybe I want to do something else with my life."

"Oh yeah, like what?" Marigold asked.

I walked over to the sink and pulled a spoon from

the dish rack. "I don't know . . . the president talking about sending people up in outer space. Or maybe I'll move up to New York and become a famous actress like that lady . . . what's her name . . . Ruby Dee." I stirred the salad and giggled at Marigold.

"Mm-hmm . . . well, you're pretty enough to do whatever you want. But don't be so quick to look past what good you got in front of you. You said Hank own this farm outright and he make a decent living running his business."

"Blah, blah, blah . . . grab the napkins. Let's get back to the party."

* * *

Back in the living room, the party was really jumping. Jackie Wilson's "Baby Workout" was spilling from the record player. Birdie was in the middle of the floor doing the twist with Hank's buddy Linc. Lilly and Johnnie Mae were up on the floor, too, doing something called "The Fly." I loved seeing the two of them together. It was the only time they truly seemed happy, when they was in each other's company. Turns out, the turpentine *had* gotten rid of Lilly's baby, and nearly killed her in the process. But she was happy now. And that was all that was important. And if anybody didn't care for Lilly and Johnnie Mae, they never spoke a word about it to me. Lilly was my friend and I wouldn't tolerate a bad word about her.

Lilly spotted me from the makeshift dance floor and skipped over to me. "What did I tell you? See, I was right!"

"Right about what?" I said.

"My special eye! I told you we would get visitors to Chillicothe the first day I met you. And now here's your sister. But she won't be staying." Lilly shook her head slowly. "She ain't meant for Chillicothe. I can just tell."

I chuckled. I didn't have the heart to tell Lilly that Marigold was just visiting. I just smiled at her. "I'll never doubt your special eye again."

"One day y'all will learn to listen to me."

"Come on, Lilly. Let's finish dancing," Johnnie Mae called from the dance floor. Lilly scurried back.

Everybody was having a good time. I even saw Alma tapping her toe to the music. And without fail, it happened again, the same way it did whenever I was having a good time: Rose slipped in. Just like she always did, creeping around in my head telling me how bad I was, how good times lead to bad things. Sometimes Momma and Papa would crawl in there too. Or maybe it wasn't Rose telling me I was bad. Maybe it was my own guilt at playing a part in her death that made me feel that way. When I was back in Jackson and she slinked around in my head, it made me wanna party that much harder just to quiet her voice inside my mind.

"Vera?"

In that moment, I realized somebody was calling my name. It was Hank.

"Yeah."

"You okay? Look like you was a million miles away." Hank slid his arm around my waist. "Your sister here was just telling me something about you."

I looked at Marigold standing in front of us with a big Cheshire cat grin on her face. "Oh, really? Well, as long as she not confessing all our family secrets, that's fine by me."

"She was just telling me how headstrong you are. That can't be no family secret. Anybody talk to you for more than two minutes can figure that out."

Hank and Marigold laughed.

"Oh, you two are a regular barrel of laughs, huh?" I gave Marigold a playful smile.

Delroy walked over to the table where we was standing. "Miss Marigold, would you like to dance?"

"Well, I'm—"

"Marigold, go'n dance. We put this party together for you," I said.

Marigold gave me the same kind of expression Momma used to give me when I spoke out of turn at the dinner table.

Hank tried to come to her defense. "Delroy, now this here is a married woman."

"She married. She ain't dead. It's just a dance," I said. "Why everybody around here so old-fashioned?"

Hank let out a huge belly laugh. Marigold shook her head at me and giggled before she walked to the middle of the living room floor with Delroy.

"Come on, woman!" Hank pulled me to the floor, and we danced too. I was actually having a good time. My sister was here. My friends was here too. It all felt so right.

Jackie Wilson's fast number ended and the next song to fall off the stack of 45s was Jerry Butler's "For Your Precious Love," a slow mournful ballad about a man confessing his undying love to a woman. Hank said it was his favorite slow song. Everybody started to walk back to their chairs or grab food from the table. I started to walk off too.

"Where are you going?" Hank swooped me up in his arms. "Come on, just one more."

He pulled me in closer and kissed me real tender on the cheek. I heard Delroy and Linc hoot and holler behind me.

"That's right, Hank, lay on the old Chillicothe charm," Delroy yelled across the room. Everybody laughed and Linc walked by and slapped Hank on the back.

Hank smiled and winked back at Delroy.

"The Chillicothe charm? So, I'm not the only one you've danced with in the middle of the living room, huh?"

"Maybe not the first, but you'll definitely be the last." He pulled me in closer.

"Mm-hmm."

I closed my eyes for a moment and just enjoyed this man's arms around me. The bulk of his body and the scent of his clothes. I'd never felt this way about any man before. I had fallen hard. This was not what I had planned. This wasn't supposed to be.

"Your sister is nice."

"She's a nice girl. Always has been."

"She told me something else about you."

My heart sped up. I pulled back a bit. "What else did she tell you?"

"She told me you was the prettiest girl back in Jackson, Mississippi."

My heart went to pounding something ferocious. I stared up at Hank, but I didn't say a word.

"I thought you said you came here from Alabama?"

I glanced back at Marigold. Delroy had her all tied up in some silly conversation they were giggling about at the edge of the hallway. What else had Marigold blabbered about to Hank? When I looked back at Hank, he was still staring at me, waiting for an answer.

"Well, I was born and raised in Jackson, but I headed to Alabama before I made my way to Georgia. Why all these questions about me again? Ain't it enough that I'm here with you now? Why does it matter where I been?"

"It don't matter. That's what I'm trying to get you to understand."

I took my eyes off Hank and looked around the room for something else to land on. Should I have made up some story about my past to go along with my new name? Staying here in Chillicothe was a mistake.

Hank leaned down and whispered in my ear. "One of these days, you'll realize I'm always going to love you and you won't have to run anymore."

His words ran through me like I'd stuck my finger in an electrical socket. Marigold would never tell another soul about what happened in Jackson. How did he know I was running from something?

I stopped dancing. "I'd better go check on the table, make sure everybody got enough to eat."

Hank wouldn't let me go. "Let's just finish this dance. Let's finish what we started."

"But what about—"

"Shh . . . Listen to the song, Vee." He held me tighter as he started to sing the words into my ear, his deep bass voice haunting me. *And of all the things that I want . . . is just for you to say that you'll be my girl . . .*

I'd had dozens of men whispering and singing in my ear, thinking that was the key to unlock my legs, to make me do something folks told me I wasn't supposed to do. I did what I *wanted* to do. I did what gave *me* pleasure. But here was a man touching me in a place I'd never let a man reach—my heart—and it was making my head spin. This wasn't the way things was supposed to go.

But *this* time. *This* man.

My eyes went to stinging. I wanted him to let me go and hold me tighter all at the same time. I wanted to run straight out of Georgia in that very moment. And at the same time, I didn't want to be anywhere else in the world but right here in Chillicothe, in this man's arms. I was all mixed up in my head. Things that used to make sense didn't make sense anymore. Rose was back in my head, along with Momma and Papa. And now Hank was in my head, too, jumbling things up and confusing me.

When the song finished, I looked up at Hank. His eyes bore a hole straight through me before he softly whispered, "Marry me, Vee."

I backed away. "I better go check on the food." I rushed off to the kitchen before anyone could catch me crying.

41
Vera

By eleven o'clock, everybody started talking about the early day they had tomorrow and how they had to get home. Of course, they stayed for another hour beyond that. Delroy followed after Marigold like a lost puppy the whole evening. Roger Bonny might have something to contend with when Marigold got back to Ohio. Finally, after the longest round of goodbyes, folks piled into their cars and trucks. Me and Marigold cleaned up the kitchen while Hank got ready for bed. He was planning to take a haul of vegetables over to the farmers' market in Augusta in the morning.

After the last of the dishes was done, I turned to Marigold. "How about me and you go outside for a breather before heading to bed?"

We sat on the big wraparound porch, swinging back and forth in the wooden rockers. The air was cool and clean. It was a good ending to what had been a good day. I had just ushered off my little band of friends, and now I had my big sister with me. We were both quiet for a few minutes. The beam on the porch ceiling offered the only light in the night darkness.

"Your friends seem really nice," Marigold said. She looked at me and smiled. "Especially Hank."

I chuckled. "Mind your business, Marigold. Oh, and in case I forgot to mention it before, stop talking about Jackson. Folks in this town work at gossiping like it's a part-time job."

We both went quiet. A coyote howled, long and low, off in the distance. Then quiet again.

"It's so peaceful out here," Marigold said. "I take it you haven't heard anything from Jackson?"

"Nope. And I'm hoping it stay that way, too." I thought about the way I left Jackson, and guilt washed all over me. "Hey, look . . . I'm sorry I ran off without telling you first."

"You had good reason to." Marigold leaned across her chair and patted my hand. "Huxley was a despicable beast. I would have done the same thing if I was as strong as you."

"Spilling a man's blood. It ain't nothing to be proud of. Look where it got me." I peeped through the window to make sure Hank wasn't nearby. "I'll be running for the rest of my life. As a matter of fact, I got plans to leave soon."

"Vera . . . no." She gave me a solemn expression. "Is that why you won't marry Hank?"

I glanced toward the door of the house again.

"Vee, you can't keep running."

"I can't go to jail, either," I whispered. "Hank's a good man. He deserves better."

"He is a good man and you need to appreciate that."

"How's Cleveland?" I said, trying to change the subject. Maybe we could spend a few minutes poking around in her business for a change.

"Well, it ain't Jackson, that's for sure. Fast cars, fast talk. But it is nice not to have to sit on the back of the bus or use separate facilities."

I smiled. "So that's your opinion. What does Roger think?"

Marigold sighed deeply. "Do we have to talk about him?"

"The fact that you hightailed it outta Ohio without him makes me think we should. That and the bruise on the side of your neck."

Marigold gently touched the side of her neck. She

never looked at me before she started to speak. "We're not going to work out after all. I guess you were right."

"All right, send another sermon from the mount. So what happened?"

"Doesn't the bruise speak for itself?"

"True."

The silence between us unfolded again like a slow-moving train. And neither one of us got in the way. We rocked and waited and rocked some more. Some words just take time.

"I'm pregnant," Marigold finally said.

I stopped rocking.

"Probably about two or three months."

I didn't say anything, and Marigold went silent. I could tell she needed some space. Everything comes in its own time, including words.

"All Momma's warnings about being a good girl and look at me—knocked up and married to an idiot."

"Well, you coulda been like me, ignored Momma's warnings and end up on the run from the law. Damned if you do and damned if you don't."

Marigold smiled. "They expected so much from us girls. Remember we were supposed to be teachers now."

"Ha! They expected a lot from you and Rose. Momma and Papa knew better than to think I was ever gonna be somebody's teacher."

We got quiet again. I heard that coyote howling off in the distance again. Marigold finally stopped rocking. "So you're not going to congratulate me?"

"Should I?"

"I guess not. Don't congratulate Roger, either."

I stared at her for a piece. "What's that supposed to mean?"

Marigold stared back at me with tears in her eyes. "I think you're only supposed to congratulate the father."

Everything inside of me sort of melted into sadness for my big sister. "Who's the daddy?"

"It's not important. He ran off when I told him."

"Does Roger know?"

Marigold shook her head no.

She was the smartest person I've ever known in my whole life. Her, with all her ten-dollar words and straight A's in school. It broke my heart to see her in trouble. "Are you gonna tell him?"

"I've already made one stupid mistake. No need to make matters worse. I guess it's never been in the cards for me to have a good man."

"You don't have a good man because you act like you don't deserve one."

Marigold looked at me, her mouth gaped open. "What's that supposed to mean?"

"You're smart, pretty. But you sit around waiting for some man to tell you that instead of telling the man you want all them things. Beautiful things don't ask for attention. They command it."

Marigold smiled at me.

"So what are you gonna do? Don't you think Roger has a right to know if he got another mouth to feed?"

Marigold sighed deeply. "Roger can't even feed himself. We've been living off his brother ever since we moved to Ohio."

"He can't find no job?"

"He doesn't *want* to find a job. He's got some crazy idea about opening up a nightclub."

"He got nightclub money?"

Marigold giggled. "What do you think? He met some white man in a bar who's supposed to put up the money. His investor, he calls him." Marigold shook her head.

"You know how men are. Maybe you let him stick his hand near the stove. Once he gets burned, he'll find another way to keep warm."

Marigold laughed this time. "Maybe you're right. For the past week, all he talks about is Dewey's gonna do this and Dewey's got enough money to—"

My stomach tumbled when I heard his name. "Wait. What did you say?"

Marigold looked at me all surprised-like. "What do you mean?"

"Who's the man Roger's partnering up with?"

"Dewey. Why?"

"What's his last name?"

"I don't know."

My head told me to calm down. There had to be more than one Dewey in the world. "Did Roger say where this Dewey fella is from?"

"I think he said Florida. Why?"

I stood from my rocker and walked to the edge of the porch, staring into the black night. Surely it couldn't be the same person. But a strange white man following my sister, looking for me, and now a man with the same name as Dewey Leonard was more than a coincidence.

"Vee? You okay?"

I turned to face Marigold. "What this Dewey fella look like?"

She stood and met me at the edge of the porch. "I don't know. I've never seen him."

"What about that man you said was following you around Ohio?"

"You think they might be the same person?"

"I don't know. But it ain't no coincidence that a man is following you at the same time someone named

Dewey is partnering up with Roger. Oh, heavenly Father."

Marigold slid her hand inside mine. "What's going on, Vee?"

"Nothing good."

"What does that mean? You know somebody named Dewey? Just tell me, Vee."

"Marigold, I need to show you something, but you can't tell a soul."

"Of course."

Marigold followed me back inside the house and down the hall to the bathroom. I closed the door behind us. I reached under the sink and pulled out a box of Kotex. I reached down in the bottom of it and pulled out Dewey's wallet wrapped in a white handkerchief.

"Look at this," I whispered. I handed the picture from Dewey's wallet to Marigold.

She took one look before she slapped her hand up to her mouth and gasped. "Oh my God!"

"Shh . . . don't wake, Hank."

Marigold looked like she'd seen a ghost. "Where did this come from?"

"This wallet." I showed her Dewey's wallet. "It belonged to a fella I was keeping company with back in Jackson. His name is Dewey Leonard. His daddy own Leonard Feed & Supply."

"*Olen Leonard!* You were messing around with Olen Leonard's son?! You know Olen Leonard is the head of the Mississippi Citizens Council, right? Vee, what in the world are you doing fooling around with a *white man*?!"

"I swear to you, I didn't know his son was like him. He told me he didn't believe in that segregation stuff. He was really nice to me. As a matter of fact, he wanted me to run away to Boston with him and get married."

"*What?!* Are you crazy? Why didn't you tell me about dating the son of the head of the Citizens Council?"

"Because I didn't want to disappoint you," I said.

"Disappoint me?"

"I know what those people are trying to do. But I promise you, his son isn't like that."

"So what are you doing with this man's wallet?"

"Shh . . . keep your voice down. It's a long story for another time."

I watched Marigold study the picture. Then she got a look on her face like she'd seen the devil himself, her eyes as wide as saucers.

"Vee . . . I think this is a picture of those three men from up north who were killed in Neshoba County. These were Freedom Riders."

"That's what I think too. Marigold, I swear on

Papa's and Momma's graves, I didn't know nothing about this." I started to cry.

"Shh . . ." Marigold rubbed my arm, trying to calm me down.

All I could think about was how I had missed this side of Dewey Leonard. "I knew who his daddy was. But Dewey told me he wasn't like his daddy. He even told me when we got to Boston, he had something planned for his daddy. I didn't know what he meant by that. Maybe his plan had something to do with this picture."

Marigold leaned in real close to me. "We have to get this to the police. The FBI is investigating this as we speak."

"I can't go to the police. Have you forgot about Huxley Broadus?"

"Oh dear God. Okay, let's hide this for now. Maybe I can make a call to one of the lawyers where I used to work. Maybe they can help us."

I took the picture back from Marigold and placed it back inside the wallet. I placed it all back inside the bottom of the Kotex box. "Between this picture and that man you said you saw in Jackson and Cleveland, I'm scared."

"I am too," Marigold said.

42
Mercer

Mercer felt a little bad for Roger, his wife leaving him and all. But once he found out where Marigold was headed, he peeled out of Cleveland so fast, he didn't even have time to make up some excuse why he wouldn't be "investing" in the nightclub. Roger Bonny wasn't that bright, but he could talk pretty good. He would find some sucker to foot the bill for his nightclub dream.

Chillicothe, Georgia.

Mercer was closer than he'd ever been to getting his payday and realizing his own dream of getting Randy healthy again, a house on the beach in Florida for his family, and a lifetime away from Jackson, Mississippi. Finally, he was within sight of living like a real man, even if it came at the cost of a woman's life.

He knew how much Olen Leonard hated Negroes. Where Mercer mildly tolerated Negroes—could take them or leave them—Olen Leonard hated them with something that slicked through his bloodstream and settled in the marrow of his bones. Mercer remembered once watching Mr. Leonard at the feedstore talking with such disgust about them that the old man started to froth at the mouth. As far as Mr. Leonard was concerned, they were only good for cooking, cleaning, and hard labor. Anything else was a waste of a good body.

Mercer thought back on this past June when he drove Dewey, Mr. Leonard, and Sheriff Bickford up north to Neshoba County. Olen Leonard and his Citizens Council buddies wouldn't be outdone when it came to all that business about equality and the right to vote. Mercer wasn't keen on coloreds, either, but Olen and his Citizens Council friends were adamant that those people would never share a restaurant or bus seat next to a white person in the state of Mississippi. And they'd orchestrated their share of murders to make sure of it.

And now Mercer himself was on the hunt for Violet Richards—not just to find her, but to kill her, too.

Violet or Randy? Was the cost to save his son's life worth snuffing out Violet's? Mercer didn't have to spend more than two seconds thinking about that question. He already knew the answer.

* * *

Mercer arrived in Chillicothe on a slow Monday morning. By the looks of it, everyone was still in bed. He pulled his Ford Fairlane into a filling station at the center of the small town. A greasy-looking man in a pair of worn overalls eased up to the side of the car, wiping his dirty hands with a rag.

"Fill it up for ya', mister?"

"Low test and check the oil, too," Mercer said. "You got a phone around here?"

"Ova' to the side of the building," the man said as he pointed.

Mercer walked to the phone booth, slipped some money into the phone, and called Mary Lou. She picked up on the first ring.

"Hello." Her voice sounded different. Breathy, like she'd been crying.

"Mary Lou, it's me, honey. What's going on? Everything okay?"

"Mercer?" She sounded weird. Something was wrong.

"Yeah, how's Randy?"

"He's back in the hospital." She sniffled. "It's bad. Mercer, when are you coming home? Where are you? What do I tell the doctors?"

"What happened?"

"He ran a high fever. Baby aspirin. Cool baths. Nothing worked. Dr. Finlay told me to take him to the hospital. He's got some kind of infection."

She started to cry, and Mercer hated the sound of tears coming from a woman. "Okay, honey. Just slow down. What kind of infection?"

"I don't know. Those doctors talk so fast at me I can't understand half of what they're saying. They said they'd treat him for the infection, but things can get worse if he doesn't get the surgery. They asked me where's the boy's father. Randy's asking about you too. What is going on?!"

"I'm so sorry. I'm working on getting the money we need."

"Forget about that. Mercer, you need to be here. You need to be home with your wife and sick boy. You know I can't do this alone."

"You're right . . . you're right. Give me a couple days. I'll be home. You kiss Randy for me. I'll be home real fast."

"Where are you, anyway?"

"I love you, honey. I'll be home as fast as I can."

Mercer hung up the phone. Mary Lou was right. He should be back in Jackson. Every time he called home, he felt like a low-class piece of trash. Randy might die while he was down in Georgia chasing some colored woman. He felt even worse, not just for being away, but because sometimes he wished he didn't have a kid that was sick all the time. Maybe he might be better off if he and Mary Lou weren't fighting to keep Randy alive. He wanted to pound something, a wall, a door, another person.

He had half a mind to ditch this whole job and head back home. He and Mary Lou could just figure out the money another way. But what if they couldn't? What if Randy died while they were trying to figure out the money?

Maybe there's another way out of this mess.

He'd tell Olen Leonard he *had killed* Violet, even though he still hadn't found her. He would collect his money right away, pack up Mary Lou and Randy, and be out of Mississippi. What was the likelihood that anyone would ever see her again, a woman on the run from the law? And if Violet Richards did show up, Olen and Dewey Leonard could fight over what happened to her. Olen could kill her or Dewey could save her, but either way Mercer would have his money and be out of Mississippi and done with the Leonards. He smiled to himself as he thought through his new plan.

But he had to get the money from Olen Leonard first.

Mercer dialed the operator to place another call to Olen Leonard; Olen accepted the charges.

"Mr. Leonard, I'm calling back to square up our deal. I found that colored woman." It wasn't exactly the truth, but Olen didn't know that. This wasn't the first lie he'd ever told.

"Where?"

"There's a little matter of payment for my services before I give you all that information."

Mr. Leonard hesitated for a beat. Mercer wouldn't stumble. He had a sick kid and a terrified wife, all alone without him. Mercer had to do this just right so that Mr. Leonard would pay for his son's surgery and Dewey's errant ways.

"Listen, Mercer, I was just downtown here in Jackson and a friend of mine tells me the police are looking for this Violet Richards woman. Think she might be involved in that Huxley Broadus murder. Maybe we ought to let the police handle all this."

Shit! He hadn't planned for this new wrinkle. Mercer could feel sweat start to pop along his brow line. He had to think fast. He might lose this whole deal, and that could mean losing Randy.

"All due respect, sir, you could do that. But I recall you saying you were cutting Dewey off after all that business with them Freedom Riders up in Neshoba, how he wasn't really supportive of the Citizens Council mission. So I figure if Dewey's willing to pay me money he doesn't really have, to find a colored woman, and he don't want a nappy hair on her head touched, he must have some pretty strong feelings for this woman. He's pretty adamant that nothing happen to her. Remember, he was planning to marry this girl."

"I'll be damned if he's gonna marry some mongrel bitch."

"If he can help her get out of all this, what's to stop him from carrying out his plan to marry her?"

Mercer stopped talking. He knew he'd laid enough breadcrumbs to lead Mr. Leonard into the trap of cleaning up another one of Dewey's messes. Mercer had a son too. He knew the lengths a man would go for a child he loved. The phone was quiet for what seemed like an eternity. The elder Leonard was trying to decide how to handle the mess his son had created. Mr. Leonard was only slightly smarter than his son.

"You might have something there, Mercer. Yeah, go on ahead and take care of her the way we discussed. But *first*, I'll need proof that you've handled the job."

"What?"

"I need a picture, some evidence that bitch is dead."

Mercer felt his pulse speed up. His plan might fall

apart. He'd come too far. He'd be damned if he let that happen.

Mercer cleared his throat. "I'll get you a picture. Then you can compare it to the one your son carries around in his wallet. Now, like I said, we need to discuss my payment first."

"Uh-huh," Leonard said suspiciously.

"I'll need you to deposit ten thousand dollars into my account at Jackson Trust & Savings by tomorrow noon."

"Now wait a minute—"

"Mr. Leonard, I've worked for your family for a number of years now. You know you can trust me. And I can trust you. I didn't speak a word about that business up in Neshoba County. I've never uttered a word about that sharecropper you said stole feed from you. My word is my bond. Now, I don't have a problem killing a colored woman. But I won't do it for free. The bank closes at two o'clock. I need to be certain it's in there, so I'll need you to deposit the money by twelve noon. Once I'm certain the money's there, I'll call you back with details."

Mercer was trembling, but he let the silence float across the phone line. The less he talked, the less chance he'd stumble.

"And how do I know you really found her? How do I know this ain't some kind of scam?"

"Well, you could always check with your son, but that's probably not the wisest course if you want her dead. Mr. Leonard, I'm a man of my word. Remember that trust we just talked about? I'll call you back tomorrow after you've made the deposit."

"Trust and your word are good. But not good enough. How's your wife these days? She's a pretty little thing the last time I saw her."

"Sir?"

"Remember, I know where you live, Mercer. And if you try to run a scam on me, Violet Richards won't be the only woman in danger. I want that dirty mongrel bitch dead."

"What?"

"Kill Violet Richards and get me a picture. I'll keep an eye on your wife until you get back to Jackson."

Click.

"Mr. Leonard? Mr. Leonard?"

Mercer slammed the phone. His guts tumbled inside of him. He was playing an awfully dangerous game and now Olen Leonard had changed the rules.

43
Vera

Me and Hank had settled into a sort of routine. He headed out early in the morning, delivering vegetables to his restaurant customers across the county. I spent my days working around the farm and helping Hank out by selling vegetables in the small shed at the edge of the driveway until dusk. I was bone-tired by the time we packed up the sell shed at the end of the day. But working outside in the sunshine all day filled me up inside. I can't rightly say why. I was working harder than I had ever worked in my entire life, and wonder of wonders, I was enjoying it. The smell of the earth, the feel of vegetables that I had plucked from the ground—it was all new and different to me. Hank taught me how to work the tractor and taught me about rotating where the vegetables were planted to get the best life out of the soil. He even showed me how he handled his books, how to keep track of things like his revenue and his payables. I learned so much from Hank. Like the Bible says, as iron sharpens iron, so one man sharpens another.

Working here in Chillicothe was different from working back home in Jackson, sweeping up the mess in the back of the Leonards' feedstore or trying to keep a bunch of bratty kids happy. Here on the farm, I was making decisions about what to sell and for how much. That made me feel good and feel in charge of myself.

Or maybe working with my hands all day left my mind free to wander. Ever since Marigold mentioned the name Dewey, I hadn't felt right. *My God sense.* It was like the Lord was climbing inside my spirit, warning me. Maybe I was worrying over nothing. My Dewey couldn't be the only Dewey in the world. But still, how many men named Dewey just happened to make friends with my brother-in-law? I kept telling myself, now was the time to go. I needed to leave Chillicothe. The longer I stayed, the more risk I was taking. And I didn't want to bring no trouble to Hank's doorstep.

Marigold hadn't uttered a word about returning to Cleveland. And I was glad too. She never should have married a man like Roger in the first place. She deserved so much better. Maybe, if Marigold was up for it, we could move east. I'd nurse on that idea for a bit before I mentioned it to her.

* * *

It was the end of the day and I started to pack up the remaining vegetables at the sell shed. Hank strolled down the driveway from the farm, smiling at me. I watched the orange glow of sunset falling around this tall, brown angel man. Everything inside my head told me it was time to leave, but deep down inside my heart, I didn't want to be anywhere else in the world except right here on the receiving end of this man's affection. I had really fallen hard for Hank. If I had met him back in Jackson, I might never have given him a second thought. But now here I was, giddy and looking forward to another day with the man with the big broad shoulders and the wide smile and all that gentle heart he gave me.

It would be tough when it was time for me to leave him.

Hank walked up to me, slipped his arms around my waist, and held me close. No kiss, no smile. Just a simple request. "Marry me?"

I stared back. I couldn't keep telling him no. I needed

to tell him something until I left. "Let me think about it."

"You been thinking about it since the first time I asked you, but I'll take what I can get." He laughed. "Let's lock up for the day."

Hank went behind the shed and pulled the wheelbarrow around to the front so we could load up the vegetables and cart them back to the house. We'd bring them back down in the morning, along with anything fresh Delroy and Linc picked.

"I think I'm gonna rip this thing down," Hank said. He broke off a piece of the rotted wood board on the side of the shed. "It's barely standing anyway. I think I'll pour a concrete foundation and build something sturdier."

He gave the side of the shed a shake and I thought the whole thing would come crashing down around my head. "Hey!" I yelled.

Hank laughed. "We doing pretty good business out here. It must be your winning ways with the customers." He gave me a playful little grin and slapped me on my rear end.

"Stop it, Hank Cummings!"

We both laughed. We began to pack up the few remaining vegetables from the baskets and then loaded them into the wheelbarrow. I started to push the empty baskets inside the shed. We wasn't even two minutes into clearing the shed when we heard the sound of loud music and the roar of a car engine rushing down the road. Hank and I watched the pickup truck approach.

When Hank spotted who was inside, he turned his back and continued cleaning up. "It's just some kids. Ignore 'em."

I watched the old red pickup truck slow to a crawl in front of us. There were two white boys, no more than sixteen or seventeen years old, inside the truck and two others sitting in the flatbed of the truck.

"What you monkeys selling today?" the fat one said from inside the truck.

Hank pushed the wheelbarrow toward me. I lifted a small basket of green peppers and placed them into the wheelbarrow. Momma's warning to me and Marigold about interacting with white folks kicked in.

Don't make eye contact. Be polite, yes sir and no sir. Never give them a reason to harm you.

The music blared from the radio. The greasy-looking one in the back of the truck leaned over the side of the truck. "Hey, nigger! He's talking to you."

"We're closed," Hank said over his shoulder, his back to the boys.

"Well, maybe we can have a taste of that ass on her," the greasy one shouted. All four boys hooted and laughed.

Hank turned in a flash, his eyes full of anger as he lunged toward the truck. He was headed for the greasy boy who had insulted me.

"NO! Hank, don't!" I stood between Hank and the truck. "Like you said, ignore them."

Hank settled back. The boys howled in laughter. We went back to the vegetables. One of the boys slapped the outside of the truck with his hand. It startled me so that I jumped. And then I got angry with myself for showing fear in front of them boys. They all yelped again before the truck sped off. Neither me nor Hank said another word. We filled up the wheelbarrow. Hank rolled it up the driveway to the house and I followed behind as the evening sun kissed the horizon.

* * *

Marigold insisted on cooking and cleaning around the house for us, saying it was the only way she could repay me and Hank for the hospitality. My cooking had come a long way from that meatloaf I made for the Cooglers when I first moved to Chillicothe, but I was still grateful for Marigold's fussing about after long days of working around the farm. After dinner, Marigold headed off to bed. She said the baby was making her more tired than usual. I think that baby was making her feel a lot of things lately, whether she wanted to admit it to herself or not. I knew she would come to some decisions in her own time.

Later that night, Hank lay in bed staring at the ceiling. I could tell his mind was somewhere else. Maybe on them boys who had come by the sell shed. But I couldn't sleep, and if I wasn't sleeping or making love to Hank, I loved lying in the bed talking to him.

"Hank, you okay?"

He turned over to face me. "Long day, I guess."

"What's on your mind?"

"Vee, maybe it ain't such a good idea for you to be out at the sell shed when I'm not around. I can get Delroy or Linc to mind the business."

I sat up on one arm and faced Hank. "I don't need no man protecting me. I can handle myself."

He reached up and stroked my face. "I know you can, Vee. Heaven help the poor soul who runs up against you the wrong way. But every now and again, we get some rowdies like them peckerwoods that drove by today, and I recognized one of them boys. His daddy heads up the local Klan around here. I couldn't live with myself if something happened to you."

"Listen to me, Hank. I'll be fine. I can smell trouble when it come around. And besides, if I'm not working for you, where else Imma work? Mr. Palmer fired me. And now you firing me too?!"

Hank looked at me, then chuckled. "Come here." He kissed me. "I'm not firing you. You the prettiest employee I got around this farm. You seen what Delroy and Linc look like?!"

We both burst out laughing.

I snuggled up in his arms before we both drifted off to sleep. I guess we would have stayed that way all night, too, if we hadn't woken to the sound of screams from the front bedroom.

Marigold.

"FIRE! FIRE!"

44
Marigold

All I could do was back away from the window, screaming at the top of my lungs. By the time I had enough presence of mind to run out of the room, Hank was racing down the hall, zipping up his pants; Vee was on his heels, barefoot and in a nightgown. I just pointed toward the door. Hank opened it and rushed onto the porch. Vera and I stepped out behind him. The first thing that hit me was the smell. Then the heat. Then the bright orange glow and the crackle of burning wood. There it stood at the edge of the yard. The biggest cross I'd ever seen in my life was covered in burning flames.

"Get back inside!" Hank yelled as he rushed past me and Vera.

"Hank! Oh my God!" Vera yelled.

He hustled to the hall closet and pulled out a shotgun. "Get back inside the house and don't come out!"

Hank ran back through the front door. After a couple minutes, Vee and I eased back out onto the front porch. I couldn't take my eyes off the flame. I'd heard stories about the KKK burning crosses in folks' yards, but I'd never seen it for myself. I felt Vee grab my arm.

"Hank, what you gonna do?" Vee asked.

"Protect my property. Now you and your sister get back inside . . . *Now!*"

"Maybe we should call the sheriff," I said.

"That's useless around here. Hell, he was probably under one of those robes with the rest of 'em. Now you two go'n back inside."

Hank stood on the front porch staring at the roaring fire. The reflection of the flames lit up his face, making his skin look like it was twinkling. Vee and I watched him as he stepped off the front porch and cautiously walked around to the side of the house, his gun lifted and ready to shoot. It seemed like an eternity waiting for him to come back. I held on to Vee. Her eyes were wide with fear, but she didn't say a word.

After a couple minutes, Hank returned to the porch. "The cowards are gone."

"You think it was them boys from the truck earlier today?" Vee asked.

I looked at Hank and Vee. "What boys?"

"Who knows? Y'all get on back in the house. Everything's all right now."

Hank slid a rocker to the center of the porch, right in front of the door. And he sat, rocking with the shotgun stretched across his lap, staring at the roaring flames. We watched him from the doorway. My feet felt like they were nailed to the floor.

A few minutes later, Vera went to the bedroom. She came back with a shirt and a blanket. I watched her as she went out to the porch. She lifted the shotgun and held it while Hank put on his shirt. When he'd finished buttoning his shirt, she handed him the gun and the blanket before she walked back into the house.

"I'm gonna go make a pot of coffee," Vee said. "You best get back to bed and get some sleep. I suspect there's not much else we can do now."

Sleep?! I wouldn't be able to sleep the whole night. I lay in bed peeking through the bedroom window until I finally dozed off to the sound of crackling wood.

I was born in Jackson, Mississippi. The Ku Klux Klan burning crosses in front of our houses was nothing new to me. What was new was the fierce way Hank Cummings dared a white man to step foot back on his property. He barely blinked as he sat on the porch with that gun across his lap, his finger on the trigger. He had every intention of firing that shotgun if one of them showed up again. He reminded me of Papa and the way he kept his pistol close to protect his family.

The last time I checked on Vee and Hank, he was still in the same spot on the front porch, wide awake. Vera had pulled a kitchen chair into the living room and perched it right up to the front door directly behind Hank. And sitting on the floor beside the chair, Momma's old carpetbag. I knew what was inside of it. She had every intention of helping Hank protect his property too.

45
Marigold

When I woke up the next morning, the first thing I did was peep out the bedroom window looking for the burning cross. It was gone. Hank, Delroy, and Linc stood quietly talking in a small circle around the ash and remnants of that hateful symbol. What if they returned and did something worse than burn a cross? I prayed to God to keep a hedge of protection around us. A few minutes later, Vee burst into the room.

"Get up! Get dressed."

"What's going on?" I asked.

"We're going shopping."

"Shopping?!"

"Yep! I'm getting married and I need a dress. Come on, lazybones. Get some clothes on. Hank's gonna drive us over to Augusta."

"Married?!"

"Yep!"

I jumped up from the bed and hugged Vee. Apparently, Hank's reaction to that cross the night before must have made some impression on her. It was almost like moving to this small town had worked some kind of magic over her. She was more responsible, more in control. Maybe she had really left all that fast living behind her. A fresh start had made a new woman out of my baby sister. After all the late nights worrying whether she would make it home, she'd finally figured it all out. I just prayed everything she left behind in Jackson stayed back there.

Later that day, Hank drove me and Vera over to Augusta to shop. It was the closest place she could go and find anything resembling a fancy dress. Colored women weren't allowed inside bridal salons, so that was out of the question. Hank was beaming like a little kid on Christmas morning the entire drive into Augusta, holding her hand and goosing her. They even made a playful pact that Hank couldn't look at the dress before the wedding. That man was in love, and so was my baby sister. It was like everything that happened the night before was a distant memory. Thank God, too. We had to find some joy in the midst of so much pain in the world.

Hank dropped us off at the store and said he'd pick us up later, since he had an errand to run while he was in Augusta. Vera picked out a gorgeous cream organza dress with a full tea-length skirt. Of course, the store wouldn't let her try it on and we knew we wouldn't be allowed to bring it back if it didn't fit. It would have been considered "soiled" and the store couldn't resell it after a Negro bought it. That's the way it worked when shopping in the South. I was too broke in Ohio to shop for clothes and see if it worked that way up north.

* * *

A couple hours later, we were back in Chillicothe. Hank decided he needed to stop at the store and get some spark plugs for his truck back at the farm. Vera and I decided to wait in the car. Neither of us would be caught dead anywhere near auto supplies.

A hot summer wind blew into the car through the open windows. I sat in the back seat of the car, admiring the dainty white gloves bejeweled with small pearls and rhinestones that Vera picked out to go along with her wedding dress. I wanted to ask her about the cross burning from the previous night, but every time I looked at her, she was practically glow-ing, and I didn't want to do anything to spoil her happiness. These days should be focused on her and Hank.

"Honey, you are going to look gorgeous," I said. "I can press your hair for you, if you want."

"Oooh, will you?" Vera said like a gushing teenager. It reminded me of when we were girls back in Jackson and getting ready for Easter Sunday. Momma would wash our hair on the Saturday before. After it dried, the three of us girls would sit around the kitchen laughing and talking as Momma stood at the stove with the straightening comb and the red jar of Royal Crown hair dressing, pressing our hair before we put it up in pin curlers for the night.

"You should wear your hair down. You always look so pretty when it's down around your shoulders."

Vera giggled again. All those hasty thoughts about running off and leaving Hank were behind her. And I prayed that all that business with Huxley stayed back in Jackson. I knew Vee was happy, and I was happy for her. I even managed to tamp down the niggling bit of jealousy that rose up in me on realizing that my sister was marrying a decent man who really did love her. She deserved some happiness; we both did. I folded the gloves and returned them to the small box.

"I'm so glad you put away all those thoughts of leaving Hank."

"You were right about me not being so quick to dismiss what good I have in front of me."

"I've made some decisions too."

Vera turned around in her seat. "You have? Decisions about what?"

"I'm going to divorce Roger. I'm going to raise the baby on my own."

"Marigold, that's great."

"Of course, I'm not sure how I'll do it. But it can't be worse than raising a child in a house full of violence."

Vera grabbed my hand and squeezed it. "You're a lot stronger than you think."

Perhaps she was right. I guess I'd find out soon enough.

Vera pointed out the window at the diner we were parked in front of. The Starlight Diner. "You know, I used to work at that diner."

"Really?" She had never mentioned working for anyone but Hank. "Why'd you quit?"

"I didn't. The owner fired me."

"Why?"

"I used to work for the sheriff and his wife as a maid when I first moved to town. Well, you know about how well that went, huh?" I just shook my head and grinned. "Anyway, I quit and got a job at the diner. The sheriff's wife got mad and made the owner fire me. You know what else?"

I leaned forward in my seat. Vee always could tell a good story. "What?"

"The owner was gettin' some trim from the sheriff's wife!"

"Oooh . . . shut your mouth! How do you know that?"

"The night he fired me, I left Momma's watch at the diner. I came back up here to get it and I seen it with my own two eyes. The two of 'em going at it like a couple dogs in heat."

We giggled. "Did the sheriff ever find out?"

"Not from me. Ain't my place to tell him." Vera hesitated for a moment. "Not unless she give me reason to tell him."

"Vee! You wouldn't?"

Vera turned around toward the back seat and gave me a wicked smile.

I laughed. "You are a handful. Always have been."

"Made me mad, though, 'cause I had to come back up here the next day to get my watch. I didn't wanna interrupt the two lovebirds and all that foolishness they was engaged in. Sheriff Coogler is an idiot. Doesn't surprise me one bit his wife tips around behind his back."

Vee turned back around and stared out the window for a beat. "I wish Momma and Papa were here. You know, to see me get married," Vera said.

"I do too. They would be so proud."

She went solemn and I hoped she wasn't getting cold feet about the wedding. Maybe she was sifting through the pieces of how she'd come to be here, ready to get married and live a different life from the one in Jackson. We had come a long way from our days back in Mississippi. And while Momma would be proud of Vee, she might not feel the same way about me. I had made a mess of my life, pregnant by James and getting kicked around by Roger. Vera, for all her partying ways, was smarter than me when it came to men.

"Marigold, you ever think about Rose?"

Her question caught me off guard. We hadn't talked about Rose since Momma's funeral last year. "Yes, I do."

"Yeah, I think about her a lot too. I think about her so much, sometimes I can't get her out of my head or think about anything else."

"That's okay, Vee." Vera just continued to stare out the window. "That's a good thing, remembering someone we loved so much."

"You know Rose should be here. I shoulda been the one to die that day."

"Don't say things like that. It's not true."

Vera turned around in her seat again and looked at me. Her face was grim, the same broken and sad way it looked the day Rose died. "Why you think God took Rose that day?"

"Only God himself knows, honey. He always has a plan."

She stared at me for a moment, her eyes filled with tears. "You was the only one didn't blame me for Rose's dying."

"Vee—"

"You didn't blame me for Momma and Papa either. Why?"

"Vee, stop this crazy talk. You had nothing to do with Momma or Papa dying, and you weren't responsible for Rose's death, either. It was an accident. A terrible accident. Now, I won't hear another word about it."

Vera turned around in her seat and stared back out the window. I watched her wipe away tears with the back of her hand. I reached up and squeezed her shoulder. My beautiful, headstrong baby sister. A few minutes later, Vera opened the car door and climbed outside.

"Where are you going?" I asked.

"Just stretching my legs. Come on out and get some of this sunshine." She looked across the town square, shielding her eyes from the sun with her hand.

I climbed out too. We stood against the car, watching people milling about. Everyone—white folks and Negroes, too—moved slower here than they did up north, or even in Jackson. No hustle and bustle. But what was there to rush around to in a town as small as Chillicothe? I wondered how they went about their lives in this false contentment. Less than twenty-four hours ago, someone, maybe even some of these very white people walking around on this street, had lit a symbol of hate on Hank's property while we slept. I wondered if Negroes here in this little town were allowed to vote. Of course not. And who was fighting for their rights? Would Dr. King's work reach as far as this dusty little town in Georgia too?

Vera finally broke my trance. "Birdie said she'll bring a cake and Alma said she'll bring me some flowers from her garden to make a bouquet for me to carry."

As Vera talked, I felt the first stabbing pain in the bottom of my stomach. It nearly took my breath away.

"Can you imagine? Me? Somebody's wife. I never thought I'd get married."

The next cramping pain made me gasp and bend over.

"Marigold? Marigold, you okay?"

The baby. "Something's wrong, Vee. Something's wrong."

Vera swung open the back car door. "Come on. Sit down. Sit right here."

I just wanted the pain to stop. The cramping seemed to pulsate and radiate down through my groin. Vera gently lifted my legs into the car. As she did, another sharp pain hit. This one made me moan. "It's the baby!"

"Okay, sweetie. You stay put. I'll run and get Hank. Just hang on."

Vera ran inside the auto parts store. It seemed like they were back in less than a minute. Hank climbed behind the wheel. Vera climbed inside the back seat beside me. She held my hand and I leaned on her shoulder as Hank revved the engine and sped off.

46
Mercer

Mercer Buggs sat inside the booth at the Starlight Diner on Church Street, trying to figure out how to force down the greasiest hamburger he'd ever tasted. He lifted the bun and nearly gagged at the sight of the meat, dull and soggy, like a round, wet lump of clay. He tossed the bun back on the plate and peered around the small restaurant. The jukebox blared Frank Sinatra's "Bim Bam Baby" louder than he cared for. Horns wailing and ole Blue Eyes crooning about going home to his girl.

He wondered what Mary Lou was doing at that moment. Was Randy getting any better? Calling home now to check on them would only make him feel worse than he already did. Every time Mercer thought about Olen Leonard's threat to harm Mary Lou, his blood pressure spiked. He wanted to drive back to Jackson just to wrap his hands around Olen's throat and squeeze the life out of him. He toyed with the idea of heading to Jackson straightaway. He'd pack up his family and get out of town on the money they had. Even if it might not get them to Florida. The only problem was that Randy was in the hospital now. He couldn't get Randy out of the hospital and risk making the boy sicker. Mary Lou wouldn't have it. And if he didn't kill Violet, Olen Leonard would hurt Mary Lou.

What the hell was happening? How did he wind up in this mess?

He'd been in town for a few days and still he hadn't spotted Violet Richards or her sister, for that matter. And on top of everything else, he had a bad feeling about this place. Even though he was searching for Violet, he felt like eyes were on him. Watching. Waiting. Small towns like this had their unfriendly types too. And they didn't like strangers, no matter what color they were. What if that idiot Roger had given him a bad lead? Mercer tried asking around town a little, but he didn't want to drum up suspicion. He'd even driven through the colored section of town, but no luck. All the luck he had found tracking down the sister and following her to Ohio had run out.

Or maybe not.

He gazed out the window of the diner. And poof! Violet Richards.

The woman from the picture with the lipstick bow of a mouth stood right across the street from him. Violet was leaning up against a car with the sister from Ohio. Mercer slid across the seat of his booth, craning his neck toward the window, doing a double take. Was it really her? Violet Richards was even prettier in person than she was in the picture Dewey had given him. He watched the women as they talked. Then the sister bent over like she was in pain. He watched Violet help her sister back into the car before she hustled inside the store, probably to get help.

Mercer tossed a dollar on the table and hustled out to his car. A couple minutes later, Violet Richards ran outside the store with a colored man in tow. Both of them rushed inside their car and took off down Church Street. Mercer turned the ignition key and was off like a shot behind them.

Adrenaline coursed through him. He had traveled for days, crisscrossing the country, and now he was a mere two car lengths behind Violet. Weeks spent lurking in cars, shadowing and trailing people all over some strange city was finally paying off. No more slipups like back in Ohio. He wasn't sure where they were going. If the sister were sick, perhaps they were headed to a hospital. He hoped not. He'd be spotted in a New York minute walking around a colored ward at a hospital.

He followed the car as it sped through the town and onto the two-lane road. Much to Mercer's surprise, luck was still on his side. No hospital. Instead, the car turned onto a long driveway that led to a big yellow house. He slowed his car and watched them. The man jumped out of the front of the car. He and Violet carefully helped the sister from the car. All three rushed inside.

Mercer raced off to the nearest telephone booth.

* * *

It was exactly 12:15 in the afternoon. Olen Leonard was supposed to have the money in Mercer's bank account by now. He pulled the car over to the Phillips 66 gas station and placed another collect call to Mr. Leonard.

"Did everything go okay at the bank?"

"The money's all there. Remember, I want a picture. No tricks. By the way, I heard your boy's in the hospital. I stopped by to see him."

"What?!" The thought of Olen Leonard being anywhere near his family incensed him.

"Yeah, I saw your wife there. She sure is pretty. Be a

real shame if something happened to her. Now handle it like we discussed!"

Click.

The phone went silent. Mercer immediately called Mary Lou. He prayed she would pick up the phone. If Olen Leonard touched his wife, he'd kill him with his own two hands when he got back to Jackson.

Mary Lou, pick up the phone. She finally picked up on the fourth ring.

"Mary Lou, it's me, honey. You okay?"

"Of course. When are you coming home?"

"Now listen to me carefully. I need you to go to the bank—"

"Mercer, where are you? You said you were coming home."

"Listen to me. Go to the bank. We should have ten thousand dollars in the account. It's more than enough to pay the hospital bills and move to Florida when Randy's all better."

"Landsakes! Where did you get that kind of money?"

"I told you, I'm doing some work for the Leonards."

"What work pays that kind of money? Mercer—"

"Mary Lou, *please!* I just need you to go to the bank right away. I'll call you back in half an hour. You let me know if the money's all there, okay?"

Mary Lou was quiet for a moment. He knew she smelled trouble all over this money. But she was well aware of what their life was like and how this money could change it, too. "Okay. Then will you come home?"

"If the money's all there, I'll be home tomorrow. And, honey, make sure you lock the door whenever you're home."

"What?"

Mercer rubbed his forehead, frustrated by this entire situation, including all his wife's questions. "Just be careful, Mary Lou. I'll be home soon."

Mercer hung up the phone. He walked up to the attendant at the gas station and purchased a gas can and a couple gallons of gasoline.

"You know where I can buy an Instamatic camera around here?"

The attendant removed his cap and scratched his head. "Well, you might wanna start at Madison's Pharmacy just down the road a piece. They might carry that kind of stuff."

"Thanks."

Mercer had already hatched his plan for killing Violet, but since she was in the house with her sister and that man, he needed to make some adjustments. If killing that colored woman would get his son healthy again and his family out of Jackson forever, then Violet Richards was as good as dead.

He loaded the gas can into the trunk of his car. He'd make a stop at the drugstore and then head back to the cheap motel on Route 278 to wait for nightfall.

47
Vera

"The good Lord work out everything exactly as
it's supposed to be. We best to leave Him to
his work," Emma Raines said as she stood on the front
porch between me and Hank.

She was a midwife from nearby Grovetown. Emma
was pushing hard on seventy-five, with golden-brown
skin and thinning silver-white hair. Her hands were
covered in veins, gnarled and twisted from holding all
that life had thrown at her. From what folks said, she
had helped bring into the world almost every colored
baby in Tolliver County for the past forty years. Not
a lick of medical training, and she'd never lost a one of
'em. She lost some of the mommas, though, the ones
not strong enough to bear a breech baby or the ones
who was just too tired from all the babies that came

before. Emma said she knew everything there was to know about bringing new babies in the world, but she didn't know much what to do when they decided to come before they was fully formed and ready to show up.

"I imagine she might be about three months along, gauging from her pain. But she's losing the baby. Nothing much we can do now. Her cramping likely to continue anywhere from a few hours to a few days. Can't rightly say. She'll start to bleed until the baby pass and it's all over."

Emma stopped talking and watched Hank as he eased to the edge of the porch. Most men hate to hear anything about a woman's issues with blood. Maybe they're afraid they might learn something useful.

Emma started up again. "Like I said, ain't much anybody can do now. Keep her comfortable and let God take care of the rest. Just remember, if she start to run a fever, you and Hank get her over to Augusta. Maybe you can get her into one of the colored wards at the hospital. I know Collier Hospital is closer, but they don't take Negroes. Not yet at least."

"Thanks, Miss Emma."

"I'm sorry about all this. But your sister looks like a strong girl. I suspect her body will be fine in a few days. But her heart'll need some healing. Losing a baby can be tough," she said as we walked to the edge of the porch and joined Hank.

Hank pulled a couple bills from his pocket. "We appreciate you driving over. Here's something for your trouble."

Emma took the money, folded it, and slipped it inside her bra. She returned to the Pontiac in the driveway where her granddaughter waited to drive her back to Grovetown.

Me and Hank stood on the porch and waved her off in silence. We stood quiet like that for a couple minutes longer, until he started asking a bunch of questions about things he had no business poking around in.

"Don't you think we oughta call Marigold's husband? What's his name again?"

"Roger," I said as I stared off at a passing car on the road.

"A man got a right to know if his wife is sick."

"Men ain't got to know everything. Y'all just think you do."

"That's his wife. That's his baby."

I turned to face Hank. "He don't know about the baby. And it ain't our place to tell him either."

Hank opened his mouth to protest but instead closed it and pinched his brows, like he was thinking through the reasons why Roger wouldn't know about the baby.

He must have finally landed on the right one, because his eyes grew wide. He cleared his throat. "But, Vee, what if she gets worse? You heard what Emma said."

"Marigold traveled a long way, just her and that baby. She'll be fine. She's pretty tough. A lot tougher than people give her credit for."

We stood in silence again.

"I'd better get back down to the sell shed," he said. "I'm near done digging up the foundation. I gotta pour the concrete."

"I'll go check on Marigold."

* * *

I peeped through a crack in the door to Marigold's bedroom. She was sound asleep. I walked back to my bedroom and closed the door. I dropped to my knees and prayed to God to bring Marigold through this, to not take her away from me. Then I walked over to the closet, reached in the back, and dug through Momma's carpetbag until I laid my hands on Rose's diary. I was worried something awful about Marigold. And like I always did whenever I was scared, I ran back to Rose. I sat right there on the floor and opened the journal. I read the very last entry she ever wrote, the one she wrote on the day she died.

August 15, 1956

Dear Diary,

Silas kissed me again. He said I'm getting better at it, like he's some kind of expert. But he is really so cute. The cutest boy in class.

Miss Lawrence, my English teacher, said she knows I'll be a famous writer someday. Momma and Papa would kill me if they knew I wanted to become a writer instead of a teacher. Teacher. Teacher. Teacher. That's all they ever talk about. But that's not for me. I have to write all these stories that float around in my head. There has to be a place in this world for all the words I write but dare not speak.

Oh shoot! I gotta go. Momma's yelling for me to go find Violet again. I swear this is the last time I'm going out into those woods to get her. If she wants to risk her life playing out there, then somebody else is going to have to get her. I hate going out there.

Gotta go. Momma just yelled my name again.

I started to well up thinking about Rose's last day on earth. It was burning hot that day. I just wanted to be someplace cool. I really wanted to go swimming like all them white kids at the local pool. They had swim lessons, a lifeguard, and a place where you could buy ice cream and popcorn. But colored people weren't allowed to swim at that pool. And the pool they had assigned for the colored people had been drained for years because the city said it needed repairs. The law said we could have separate but equal facilities to what the white people had. A drained-dry public pool was separate enough but hardly equal.

Whenever I walked by their pool, I always stopped at the chain-link fence and watched them white kids splashing and having fun. I wanted to have fun like that. Sometimes I thought about defying Momma and Papa and everybody else and jumping in that pool anyway, just to see what would happen. But I didn't really know how to swim. Rose and Marigold didn't know either. None of us ever learned. I guess if I had jumped in that pool, I woulda just drowned and none of them white people would have tried to save me either.

Some of us colored kids found a bluff in the woods that backed up to a small lake. A hedge of cypress trees shaded the water and gave us a break from the heat of the sun. We would dunk and play around in it. The bigger boys would stand on the cliffside and jump into the water. Some kids said it had snakes in it. If it did,

I never saw them. And I probably wouldn't have cared either. Just having that water splashing up against me on a hot day was worth the risk of a snakebite. Momma had told the three of us girls to stay away from that swimming hole. But I was hardheaded. I snuck off one day with my friend Nettie. When we got to the lake, there was some bigger boys already there. But me and Nettie didn't care. We played at the edge where the water was shallow. The boys kept horsing around and trying to dunk my and Nettie's heads underwater.

Then I heard Rose calling my name. She was standing at the edge of the cliff by the lake, telling me I was in trouble 'cause Momma said we couldn't be there. I tried to ignore her, but she just kept yelling my name over and over. She kept yelling that I would get my hair wet and Momma would be mad if she had to press it again. Rose was always bossing me. I just laughed and splashed about in the water. When all her yelling didn't work, Rose threatened to come down and pull me out. I knew she wouldn't. She was too afraid of the water.

"Violet! You better get out of there right now! I mean it," she said.

I laughed again and started to goad her. "Come in here and get me, Miss Goody-Goody!"

"Violet, if you don't come out, I'm going to leave you. I mean it. I'm leaving you!"

I just kept splashing about, holding my nose and dunking my head underwater, laughing at her for being a Goody Two-shoes. The last time I dunked under, I came back up for air and looked for Rose at the top of the cliff, but she wasn't there. I looked up the side of the hill; maybe she was headed down to pull me out. No Rose. I thought she'd gone home until I heard some boys on the other side of the creek screaming and all kinds of commotion. Me and Nettie climbed out the water to see what was going on. The next thing I saw was one of the boys trying to hold or pull on something.

It was Rose's leg!

I spotted Rose's tan sandal floating in the water. My heart raced. I turned back to where two boys were clamoring to pull Rose up from the lake. I heard another talk about her slipping and falling off the cliff. I wanted to scream. I opened my mouth, but not a sound came out. I swallowed and opened my mouth to scream again. Nothing.

"Go get help!" one boy yelled to another.

I was frozen. I couldn't think. I couldn't move. I just stood there, dripping wet and silent, while my big sister drowned to death.

By the time they pulled Rose out, she was gone.

I was gone too.

From that day on, the Richards family started to

unravel. Papa and Momma weren't ever the same. It was like the light went out in their eyes. They had lost their beloved Rose. Grief and loss so deep that Marigold and I sadly watched from the corners of the house, tiptoeing in and out of rooms with hushed voices, trying not to get in the way of their pain. Our parents were not our parents anymore. They had become the parents of the late Rose Marian Richards.

Everyone blamed themselves for Rose's death. Marigold blamed herself for not going along with Rose to bring me back home. Momma blamed herself for sending Rose to get me out of the swimming hole. Papa blamed himself for not protecting his family better, second-guessing his decision to keep the family in Mississippi instead of moving up north as Momma had wanted.

Other people talked about how it was an unfortunate accident. Nobody's fault. Some people in town blamed the city for not repairing the pool assigned to us so that we kids didn't have to play in such a dangerous place. But none of that mattered. Rose would never have died if I hadn't been at the lake.

I spent the last eight years haunted by Rose's last words to me: *I'm leaving you!*

I was just a thirteen-year-old colored girl who wanted to go swimming on a hot day. But instead, I lured my sister to her death and destroyed my family in the process.

I was the flower in Momma's bouquet that started the ugly, sad chain of death in the Richards family.

Papa grew weaker and Momma spent her days trying to help him. By the time of his heart attack, I think everybody expected it. Wasn't nobody in Jackson surprised. When Papa died, we were broken, his "girls" waist-deep in grief and loss. We trudged through the routine of life without our leader. Until one day, Momma woke up and declared, "Enough." She propped us all back up. She said there were bills to pay and lives to lead. Me and Marigold got jobs babysitting and helping her clean to keep food in the house and a roof over our heads. And we were doing fine until Momma just dropped down dead on the kitchen floor just a few short years later. There was no one around to tend to what was left of Momma's bouquet.

All those deaths. All those ghosts. And all because of me.

I closed the diary. I'd lost Rose. I lost my parents. If I lost Marigold, too, that would be the end of me.

I put the diary away and went off to the kitchen to put on a pot of tea and fix up a tray for Marigold. When I entered the room, she was still asleep. She looked like Momma lying there with her deep-set eyes and the little mole on her chin she'd hated ever since we were little girls. I eased the tray onto the table beside the bed and started to leave.

"Violet."

I smiled down at her. "I told you, that ain't my name."

She gave me a weak smile. I sat on the edge of the bed and pressed my palm to her forehead. She was warm. Was this the fever Emma warned us about?

"I'm sorry I came all this way to cause you and Hank so much trouble, right before your wedding, too," she said.

"Hush up. That man ain't going nowhere. We'll get married when you up and feeling all better."

"You didn't tell Roger, did you?"

"What you think? Roger Bonny is not the first person I would call for anything."

Marigold smiled again. "You think I'm stupid for marrying him, don't you?"

I patted her hand. "That ain't for me to judge."

"I think the real father would be happy to know what's happened. He asked me what *I* was gonna do when I told him about the baby."

"And you decided it was better to marry Roger than anything else you could have done?"

Marigold stared at me for a bit. "What would you have done if you were in my situation? You would have gotten rid of it, huh?"

I patted Marigold's hand again. I'd never told anyone what I'd done in high school. "I'm not sure. But like I said, Roger Bonny wouldn't be the first person I'd call for anything." I smiled at her. "Every woman has to figure that out for herself. What's good for me might not be good for another woman. Every woman is different. Every woman has to make her own decision." I folded down the blanket she was under, hoping that was the reason for her warm forehead. "You get some rest now. I'll leave the tea and crackers here. Try to eat a bite when you ready. You gotta keep up your strength."

I walked to the door.

"Violet."

I turned toward her.

"He was a lawyer," Marigold whispered.

"Who?"

"The baby's father. He was one of the lawyers I worked with at the Summer Project."

I sat back on the edge of the bed. I figured she had something to get off her chest.

"I don't know why I slept with him. Maybe it was because he wanted to sleep with me."

"Marigold, hush up with that kind of talk. Any man would be lucky to have you. And Roger Bonny hit the damn jackpot when he found you."

"Roger only married me because he wanted me to work and take care of him. I was never like you. Boys always flocked around you. Everybody wants to be around you."

"Okay, let's not start that stuff again."

"It's true. You've been in this town less than two months and you have more friends in Chillicothe than I've had my whole life."

I just shook my head. "Here we go again with you. Let's not do this, okay? You need to rest."

"I'm not like you, Vee. I'm not the pretty one with all the boyfriends."

"And I'm not like you, either. I wasn't Momma's favorite like Rose was or Papa's favorite like you. I'm not the good one. So what?"

"Oh, Vee! Momma and Papa didn't play favorites among us. They loved all of us. You know that."

I could feel myself slipping again, falling apart. All the guilt and ghosts coming back to haunt me. "I gotta get dinner started."

Marigold grabbed my arm before I could move from the bed. "Listen to me. What happened at that lake wasn't your fault."

I started to well up because Marigold had been telling me this since the day Rose died. And it didn't make a bit of difference. Every time I thought about Rose, it was like I was right back at that swimming hole in Jackson. My stupidity had caused all those deaths.

"Vee . . . are you listening to me?" Marigold said.

I didn't look at Marigold. I just grabbed her hand and squeezed it. I killed a piece of her, too, by killing her dream of going to college. What good comes of violets?

"I'm so, so sorry," I whispered.

"For what?"

"You better get some rest." I leaned over and kissed her on her forehead. Still warm.

The next thing I heard was a loud scream and a thud before the sound of wheels peeling off on the street.

I jumped up from the bed and rushed out to the front porch.

All I saw was Hank's brown body sprawled in front of where the sell shed used to be. Broken wood and the dented wheelbarrow were left in its place. And blood.

All that blood.

48
Mercer

Mercer settled into his motel room, a bleak, wood-paneled, brown sort of place that could have used some fresh paint on the outside and a total gut job on the inside. The bed sank in the middle and the massaging-hands machine attached to it didn't even work. He'd purchased three cold beers, the condensation from the bottles spilling onto the peeling veneer of the bedside table. He turned on the radio, stretched out across the bed, and tried not to think about home. He also tried to resist the urge to go out to the motel lobby and call Mary Lou again. He had already confirmed with her that the ten thousand dollars was in the bank. Another call would only lead to more questions. More tears.

He leaned over and opened a bottle of beer with the

bottle opener affixed to the table. He chugged it down while he massaged visions in his mind of Mary Lou in a bathing suit sunning herself as he chased Randy along the beach. He smiled to himself, trying to guess how much a house on the beach in Florida cost. He polished off a second beer, went to the bathroom, and relieved himself. When he returned to the room, the sunny pictures of Florida overwhelmed him. He stood in the center of the room, frustrated with himself that he was standing in the middle of a fleabag motel instead of a hospital room with his wife and sick boy.

Shit!

He grabbed his room key and marched down to the motel lobby. Inside, an older man with gray hair sprouting from his ears looked up from his newspaper.

"What can I do for you, Mr. Leonard?"

It took a few seconds for Mercer's brain to register that he'd checked into this motel under Dewey Leonard's name. Again, if anything went wrong, like Roger Bonny blustering on about their "deal" or even this motel clerk talking around town about a stranger who checked in that no one knew, all roads would lead back to Dewey Leonard. Dewey, the smart-ass college boy in love with a colored woman that his own daddy had put a hit on. Mercer thought his plan was pretty damn good for a man with a tenth-grade education. It was good, at least, until Olen Leonard threatened his wife.

"You got a pay phone around here?" Mercer asked.

"Sorry. Our phone's busted, but there's one at the filling station about a mile down the road. I suspect all that business is over by now. You should be able to get through the road free and clear."

"What business?"

"Hit-and-run down at Hank Cummings's farm. Somebody come along and hit him as he was working his roadside vegetable stand. Shame, too. As niggers go, he was one of the good ones. Pretty friendly."

That explained all the cars Mercer had seen back at the house. "Yeah, that's pretty bad. Anybody else hurt?"

"I don't think so. He was living with some woman, but I don't think she was around. Folks said they could hear her screams all up and down Route 278."

"Well, I'd better get down to the filling station. Thanks."

"Sure thing, Mr. Leonard."

Mercer wasn't sure what all that was about. But at least his job was easier with that Hank fella out of the way. And with only two women inside the house, he really could wrap this job up tonight and be back on the road to Jackson.

49

Marigold

Between the cramping in my stomach and my bare feet, I couldn't run as fast as Vera, so she made it to the road before me. By the time I caught up to her, she was down on her knees, gripping Hank's bleeding head. I couldn't decide what broke my heart more—the sight of Hank's blood streaming out of him or the sharp, piercing sound of Vee's screams as she held on to what was left of him.

"Oh my God . . . Oh my God!" I just kept repeating. I didn't have words for what I was seeing. Blood streamed out of his head and chest. Only when I looked closer did I realize that somehow Hank had been impaled with the sharp end of a pine board from the old sell shed. The rest of the shed was splintered and scattered all over the ground. Blood was everywhere, including all over Vee.

"What happened?!"

Vee just kept screaming his name over and over. *Hank . . . Hank . . . Hank.*

Delroy and Linc came running from the field, shock plastered all over their faces. A colored man in his car with his family pulled over. I tried to bend over, but the cramping pain was too great. I couldn't even help my little sister.

The man and woman jumped from their car, telling their kids to stay inside. The man said, "I think I saw who hit him. White man in a pickup truck. He nearly hit me speeding from this direction."

A few more cars started to pull over. People got out and formed a small circle around Hank and Vee.

"I have to call the sheriff," I said.

I headed back to the farmhouse when I heard the wail of a police siren. Someone else had taken care of the task for me. I moved back to Vera, still cradling Hank. Still crying.

The sheriff pulled his squad car up to the edge of the small crowd. People parted to give the short, squat white man with a fleshy red appearance room to walk up to Hank's body. "C'mon now," he said as he moved through the gathered bystanders. "Y'all back up. What's going on here? Is that Hank Cummings?" He seemed surprised.

"Somebody hit him, Sheriff. Hit him and sped off," a man from the middle of the crowd shouted. Another man: "The man nearly ran me off the road trying to get away after he hit poor Hank."

The sheriff knelt down beside Vera and pressed a couple fingers against Hank's wrist. "Jesus. Did one of you boys see what happened?"

The first man repeated his earlier statement about being nearly hit by a pickup truck.

"What'd he look like?"

"A white man . . ." He lowered his eyes to the ground. "He was driving a red pickup truck with some kind of writing on the side of it, sir."

"Did you see him actually *hit* Hank?"

"No, sir, but like I said—"

"Then you don't know whether he was the one who hit Hank, boy." The sheriff turned to the rest of the small crowd. "Anybody else see anything?"

The man persisted. "Sheriff . . . sir . . . that truck was speeding so fast. Coming from this here direction."

The sheriff let out a deep sigh and rested his hands on his hips. "What'd he look like? This white man in a red truck."

The man went blank for a second. "Well . . .

I couldn't rightly say. He sped by so fast. But the truck."

"Listen, boy, you got anything else besides a white man in a speeding truck? A license tag, a description?"

The man said nothing.

"That's not much to go on now, is it? I got other stuff going on in town. Somebody better call the funeral home. Ain't nothing else we can do around here."

The sheriff ambled back to his patrol car and climbed inside. He made a U-turn and drove back down the road. I'd never seen such disregard for another human life. And just like that a Negro bled out in the street while a white sheriff drove away.

Someone in the crowd came forward with a blanket and covered Hank's body. Word must have spread through town because at some point, Birdie and Lilly showed up. The man with the *not much to go on* description stood off at a distance, talking quietly with Delroy and Linc. Birdie and Lilly tried to get Vera up on her feet. She refused. She didn't want to leave Hank in the street like an animal, she said. White folks in cars that drove up honked, trying to force us out of the street, but Vera wouldn't budge. And she wouldn't let anyone touch Hank either. I finally fought through my own pain to help Vera with hers. I lowered myself to the ground, and the three of us—me, Vera, and

Hank—stayed in the street until a black hearse with the words GRESHAM'S MORTUARY on its side pulled up beside us. The attendants gently pried Vera away from Hank's body before they laid him across a stretcher and placed him inside the hearse. Birdie and Lilly helped me get Vera inside the farmhouse. People quietly got back inside their cars and pulled off as Hank's blood was left to dry in the evening sunset.

* * *

Me and Birdie finally got Vera cleaned up, into her nightgown, and settled into bed. I sat in the living room with Birdie, Lilly, Delroy, and Linc. Alma, Pauline, and Miss Willa showed up soon after. And before I knew it, Hank's house was full of people. Even white people showed up with food and kind words about Hank. A white man named Mr. Palmer showed up and told me he considered Hank a friend. Birdie said people from all across the county knew Hezekiah Cummings. The trail of people seemed to be unending, all of them so fond of Hank. People sat around speculating about who would want to kill Hank. Some thought it was one of Hank's competitors who couldn't match Hank's prices or quality. Most thought it was the Klan who'd come back to finish the job they'd started. My guess was on the Klan. The image of the burning cross was seared in my mind. Maybe it had started with all that business with the boys in the truck down at the sell shed.

Everyone finally left after nightfall. With the cramping, it was becoming nearly impossible to stand. I was exhausted. I'd been so busy with Vera and everything that had happened to Hank that I hadn't had time to grieve my own loss.

I was losing the baby. A baby I didn't think I wanted, but now I couldn't stop crying over. Every decision I'd made since I realized I was pregnant had been in the interest of protecting me and this baby. Soon it would just be me again. Alone.

I changed into a nightgown and fell into bed and into a deep sleep.

A few hours later, I was startled awake by a sound.

Loud.

Sharp.

A single gunshot.

50

Vera

I think the hardest part about losing someone is the small way you die inside when they die. Everybody I ever loved who died took a little piece of me. Rose, Papa, Momma. And now Hank. There would be nothing left of me now. Too many pieces of me gone. Buried with all the bodies I'd left in my wake. I didn't even know I loved Hank as much as I did until I felt myself dying out on that road alongside him. I cursed myself for dabbling with Hank's affection for me. I'd squandered time we could have spent together. I know Lilly's girlish folly was just that, but now I wished she and that special eye of hers coulda told me that these were the last precious days I'd have with Hank.

Small swatches of the whole day kept flashing in front of me whenever I closed my eyes. Driving to Augusta to buy a wedding dress. Me and Hank arguing about whether to call Roger to tell him about Marigold losing the baby. Hank's scream from the road. The blood. The police siren. The hearse. And then all the people around us.

Earlier in the evening, I'd heard Marigold and Birdie and Hank's friends talking about how the KKK had come back to finish the job they started after they burned that cross on the front yard. But I knew it was them boys from the other day when me and Hank stood at the sell shed. When they came back, I would be ready for them. And if they didn't come back, I vowed to God, I would find them. Whoever did this to my Hank would pay dearly. I would make sure their blood would spill down the side of the road just like Hank's had done.

Somebody—Marigold or Birdie, I couldn't remember who—drew a bath for me to wash away Hank's blood. They helped me get dressed and into bed, like I could sleep or think or be. I didn't want to exist anymore without Hank. I heard people out in the living room talking about who killed my Hank. The house was filled to the brim with people who loved Hank, too, and didn't know what to do except stand around inside his house, helpless. And that Sheriff Coogler was useless. Like Hank said, maybe he was part of the Ku

Klux Klan. Coogler didn't want to find the people who killed Hank because he knew who they were—his buddies. I stopped listening to the voices after a while. I couldn't stand to hear everybody talking about Hank's killer but nobody with any power to do anything about it. They was sweet to pour out all that love and sympathy for Hank, but that wouldn't fix anything.

It was nightfall when I heard the last of the people leave the house. Marigold came and stood at the door of my bedroom. I pretended to be asleep. I didn't have the strength to talk and be strong. When I was sure she was fast asleep, I eased out of the bed and slipped into the living room. I turned on the lamp and sat on the sofa. Hank's dungaree jacket was still slung across the arm of the sofa where he'd left it the last time he wore it. I pulled it close to me and waited for the heavy musk smell of him to float over me. As it did, I prayed to God to take me too. I'd had enough of watching people I loved die all around me. I prayed for the peace and ease of death.

I gazed up at the clock on the mantel. It was almost midnight. It dawned on me how different my life was since I'd moved in with Hank. There was a time I was sneaking out of the house at midnight to hang at Snooky's Joint, thinking dancing and drinking all night might put back all the little pieces of me that died with all those funerals and all that death in the Richards household. It didn't.

As I sat on the sofa in the quiet of the night, I could hear the rustle of the trees and all the night sounds that let me know there was life outside. In the midst of all the death inside the house—Hank, Marigold's baby—there was still life outside this farmhouse.

I was so tired, like everything was draining out of me. Exhaustion wrapped itself around me like a thick blanket. I grew heavy and still. And then . . . maybe it was all the excitement of the day, but for a minute I thought I heard voices. A man's voice. Was it Hank? *Is my Hank nearby?* I was so tired. Oh God, I was so tired. I couldn't keep my eyes open. I finally surrendered to the comfort of a deep sleep.

I'm not sure how long I'd been asleep before I heard it.

Loud.

Sharp.

A single gunshot.

51
Mercer

Mercer drove past the house at least three more times that day. Whoever this Hank fella was, he must have been pretty important or something because it seemed like nearly the whole town poured in and out of that house. He even saw white folks swing through there.

It was after eleven o'clock by the time the last car pulled away from the house. Mercer drove by a couple more times just to make sure there were no other visitors. On his last drive-by, every room was dark. He cut the headlights on his car and slowly pulled to the side of the road, near the farmhouse. The slow crackle of gravel underneath the car seemed like a roaring blaze of firecrackers, and he was scared he might alert the women inside. His plan was simple. Shoot the two women, take a couple pictures, and set the house on fire. Luck had been on his side and if it was still running good, the sheriff would think whoever offed that Hank fella came back and finished the job.

To avoid alerting the women, he parked his car behind some trees down the road from the house, eased the gas can from the trunk, and started the short walk to the farmhouse. Just as he arrived at the porch, a light popped on in the front window. He stopped cold. Did they hear his car? Had someone inside spotted him? Mercer crouched down at the side of the house. He waited, barely breathing. Nothing. Not a sound came from inside the house. A few minutes later, he eased up the porch steps and peeped inside the living room. Violet Richards lay on the sofa holding a jacket. Asleep. Everything was quiet.

Then Mercer felt the hard round barrel of a gun pressed against the back of his head.

"Drop the gun and the gas can," a man whispered in his ear.

52
Dewey Leonard

"**D**rop the gun, Bug-a-boo, or I'll splatter your brains all across the side of this house."

Mercer slowly eased down and dropped the gun at Dewey's feet, along with the gas can.

"Dewey?" No one else on earth called him Bug-a-boo. "I don't understand," Mercer said.

"I bet you don't. There's something I don't understand either. Now, I thought we had a little deal. You find Violet. Keep it just between the two of us and you don't lay a hand on her."

"Listen, Dewey—"

"Shh . . . from the looks of things, you had another plan in mind, huh? Cut a little side deal with my daddy, did you?"

Sweat started to creep along Mercer's hairline and upper lip. "Let me explain . . . I got . . . I got a sick kid at home. He's gonna need some expensive surgery."

"And you thought a little side deal with the all-powerful Olen Leonard would solve all your worries, huh?" Dewey chuckled and thought Mercer was as stupid as his daddy. "Guess what? My daddy was dumb enough to brag to me about how he paid you to kill Violet."

"Look, just let me go. I'll go get my wife and kid and be out of Jackson. Nobody will know a thing. Promise."

"Hmm . . ."

"Dewey, you can trust me. I didn't say a word about what happened up there in Neshoba County with them boys. Not a word, remember?"

"Well, Bugsy, you didn't say a word 'cause that would have been your ass too. Who was our speed-demon driver? Besides, I didn't pull the trigger on them boys. Matter of fact, it made me sick to my stomach. The sight of what they did to those men made me vomit. Or have you forgotten all that?"

"How did you find me? I mean . . ."

"See, that's where you messed up, Bugsy. You were supposed to call me every day with a report. But you stopped calling. And my daddy slipped up. Made some ugly comment about Violet. Now, all that got me to thinking. Who would want to find Violet? Someone who loved her as much as me or someone who hated her as much as my daddy? Bug-a-boo, you forced me to go up to Ohio and look for Violet myself. And lo and behold, I found Violet in half the time it took you. Or maybe you were just stringing me along to get at all my daddy's money, huh?" Dewey pressed the gun harder against Mercer's temple, just to make him sweat. "Did you know I've been following you around this dead-ass town for days, just to see if you would live up to our little deal? And what do I find? You, standing on Violet's front porch with a gun and a gas can. I think you was aiming to break our little deal, because you made a better one with my daddy."

The sight of Mercer Buggs was starting to disgust him. Guys like Bugsy came a dime a dozen. The ones who always wanted more than they were capable of handling. Guys who wanted to run the world, but didn't have the brains to run around the corner without screwing it up. Dewey worked himself up into a rage thinking about Mercer trying to make a fool of him. Mercer, his daddy, even Violet, all tried to play him for cheap. He'd show them.

"Wait. Just let me get home to my wife and kid. I'll disappear. I promise."

"I have a better idea." Dewey calmly leaned into Mercer's ear. "I just hope your wife enjoys all that money my daddy gave y'all."

He took a step back and pulled the trigger.

Now it was time to take care of Violet.

53
Vera

The sound of the gunshot went right through me. I sat straight up on the sofa. *Someone is outside the house!*

Maybe it was them boys who killed Hank. I was ready for them this time. I raced from the living room to the bedroom to get Papa's .38 from the closet. As soon as I hit the bedroom, I heard someone busting through the door. I was terrified; my hands shook as I scrambled through my carpetbag for the gun. I could hear Papa's voice in my head as clear as if he'd been standing next to me: *All that marching is fine and all. But if someone comes in here for me and mines . . .* I finally found the gun. By the time I raced back to the living room, everything looked like a nightmare I was having with my eyes wide open.

Dewey Leonard was standing in front of me holding a gun to Marigold's head.

"Vee . . . what's going on?" Marigold whimpered. "Dewey?"

Dewey grinned at me. "Surprise! I bet you thought you'd never see me again, huh?"

"Now, Dewey, honey, let's just calm down."

Dewey narrowed his eyes on me. "Don't you dare call me *honey*. Did you enjoy your little romp out here to Georgia? Living out here in the middle of nowhere. I was prepared to treat you like a queen in Boston. And here you are shacking up with some old farmer? Now put the gun down unless you want me to kill your sister here."

Poor Marigold was weeping as Dewey kept that gun against her head. I figured the only way I would get me and Marigold outta this mess was to keep him talking.

"Listen, Dewey, that's my sister. She ain't done nothing to you. It's me you got a problem with. Now let her go and let's just talk this all out. Okay?"

"Slowly slide the gun over this way," he said. "Maybe my daddy was right about y'all all along."

I knew I wasn't a good enough shot to take him out without hurting Marigold or him killing her first. She was still quiet, but I could see tears running down her face.

"Slide the gun over here, Violet . . . *NOW!*"

I didn't want to. Marigold was all I had left. But what could I do? I slowly bent down and placed the gun on the floor. I gave it a push and it glided across the pine boards of the floor. He kicked the gun under the sofa.

"Good girl. Now, I think you got something that belongs to me."

Marigold was still crying. Dewey could do whatever he wanted to me. But I would not go to my grave having been responsible for the death of another person I loved.

"Dewey, please let my sister go. This is between me and you. *Please.*"

He tightened his grip around Marigold's neck, the gun barrel still against her temple. "Where's my wallet?"

And now I knew what all this was about. Dewey Leonard had followed me halfway across the South for what was inside that wallet. "I'll get the wallet. Just don't hurt Marigold."

"Get my wallet, and then me, you, and your sister are gonna take a little ride."

I stood there for a few seconds, thinking. He was involved in the murder of those men up in Neshoba. Even if I gave him that wallet and what was in it, me and Marigold might well be dead the second after I handed it over.

"Let's just stay calm." I raised my hands to show Dewey I wasn't no threat. "How did you find me?"

"Wasn't too hard after I found that goofball your sister is married to, Roger Bonny," he said, tapping the gun against Marigold's head. "By the way, Marigold, no need to rush back home to your husband, not unless you looking to collect some insurance money."

"Dewey—"

"Oh yeah . . . and, Violet, I'm sorry about your farmer boyfriend."

"What?" My head started to pound. What did Dewey know about my Hank? "*You* killed Hank?"

"I had to. If I can't have you, nobody else will. I meant it when I said I love you. I couldn't stand the sight of you shacking up with some old raggedy farmer. You belong to me, Violet. I always told you that. Maybe now you'll believe me."

A sly grin slid across Dewey's lips. I looked at Marigold. Her eyes grew wide. Dewey had killed Roger and Hank, and he would kill her too. I stared at her, trying to keep her focused on me. And that's when I noticed the bright crimson streaks of blood across the middle of her nightgown. She was bleeding. The baby was starting to pass.

"Dewey, my sister's ailing. Look at there." I nodded toward Marigold's nightgown. Dewey looked down at the blood. "She's pregnant, but she's losing the baby. Now, let's not make things any worse than they already are. I'll go with you. I'll do whatever you want. Just let her go."

Dewey gazed down at Marigold's gown again, then back at me. I could see Dewey's grip loosening a bit on his gun.

"Listen to me. I was wrong to leave you back in Birmingham, but I was scared the police would stop us again. You know what they'd do if they caught us trying to get married."

"I had it all worked out, Violet . . . Just give me the wallet!"

"You killed them three young men in that picture?"

"So you didn't just steal my wallet, you went digging all through it, huh?"

"Let me and Marigold go. You can take your wallet and we won't say a word."

"That picture was my way out, Violet. I was gonna take care of my daddy and his Citizens Council buddies. I planned to turn that picture over to the FBI when we got north. But you ruined everything. You don't have a clue what I did for you, how I was willing to die for you. I stood up to my daddy for you! And you made a fool out of me."

Just keep talking. "But, Dewey, I was scared we

wasn't gon' make it. The two of us wasn't supposed to be in that car together. We caught a lucky break with that cop in Alabama. I was just scared, honey. Just let Marigold go get cleaned up and I'll get the wallet and I'll go wherever you wanna go. We can start all over again." Men always like to hear what they wanna hear. They just looking for a woman who'll tell it to them.

He stared back at me as if his eyes might cut a hole into my soul. He was probably trying to figure out what to do with me and Marigold. Whatever plan Dewey had in mind, I could tell Marigold had not been a part of it. He started to relax his grip on the gun, slowly lowering it from Marigold's head. A few seconds later, he nudged her away.

"G'on, Marigold. Go get a clean nightdress," I said. But Marigold must have been in shock or something. She just stood staring at me. "Go on, Marigold! Go in the bathroom and get cleaned up."

She gave a quick fearful glance at Dewey, then back at me before she walked down the hall to the bathroom. I waited until I heard the door close.

Dewey pulled the gun up and pointed it at me.

I saved Marigold, but who saves colored women like me?

"Okay, now let's just relax," I said.

"I ought to blow your goddamn head off. I loved

you so much and you just . . . Go get the wallet." His voice sizzled.

I inched backward toward the hall.

"Hey! Where are you going?"

"It's back here. Just stay calm." I kept moving down the hall, slow and steady, Dewey's eyes on me the whole time. "It's okay. I'm just going right down the hall here." I watched Dewey dart his eyes toward the window, like he might have heard a noise or someone outside.

I made it to the hall closet and slowly opened it before I peered back at Dewey. He stood watching me for a moment before he moved to the sofa and sat down, elbows on his knees. I could almost see inside his mind. He had no choice. He'd stood up to his daddy, killed Roger, killed Hank, all for the love of a colored woman. He had no choice but to trust me. He turned to look out the window, like he'd heard a noise again.

That was all I needed. I pulled Hank's shotgun from inside the closet and pointed it at Dewey. He finally turned back to me, his eyes wide as new quarters. Before he could raise his gun, I pulled the trigger.

Loud.

Sharp.

Another single shot.

54

Vera

Marigold came running from the bathroom, tears streaming down her face. "Oh my God, Vee. Are you okay?!"

"I'm fine. Go grab a blanket from the bedroom!"

"What are you gonna do? Shouldn't we call someone?"

"Who? The sheriff that wouldn't investigate who killed Hank? And then tell him what? A colored woman shot a white man. And then what we gon' do? We gotta take care of this ourselves. Ain't nobody gonna save a colored woman who just shot a white man. Go get the blanket, Marigold!"

A few seconds later, Marigold returned with a blanket. I spread it across the floor. "Help me roll him up in here."

Me and Marigold rolled Dewey off the sofa and onto the blanket.

"What are we gonna do with him?"

"I have an idea. Come on. Let's get him outside," I said.

We dragged Dewey's body through the front door, headed for the driveway.

Marigold gasped. "Vee! Who's that?"

We stopped and dropped Dewey's body to the ground. Both of us creeped up to a man's body lying on the porch. I bent down and rolled him over.

Marigold gasped again. "Vee! That's the man that came to the house back in Jackson looking for you." She leaned in closer. "That's the man that was following me up in Ohio."

"It don't matter. He's dead too. Come on. We gotta get these bodies outta here."

We dragged both men down to the foundation Hank had started digging for the new sell shed. First Dewey, then the man from Jackson. I'd never been so panicked in all my life. All it would take was a passing car, someone who might see us out in the middle of the night with large bundles. We managed to bury both bodies in the hole Hank had dug for the new shed. Then we made up a few batches of concrete and poured the new foundation. It seemed like there was a little justice in the fact that Dewey had killed Hank but not before Hank dug Dewey's grave.

It was nearly sunrise by the time we finished. The foundation for Hank's new sell shed was done.

55

Marigold

Three days after Vee and I buried those two white men under the sell shed, we buried Hank too.

The Full Gospel Baptist Church was packed with people from all over the county. Vera laid Hank out in a navy-blue pin-striped suit. The one he was planning to wear to their wedding. She even had Mr. Gresham from the funeral parlor put a boutonniere in his lapel made of flowers from Alma's garden. And not to be outdone, Vera wore her wedding dress to the funeral. She looked so regal in that silk organza dress and those jeweled gloves. The two of them would have made a beautiful wedding day picture if they had only gotten the chance. I could tell a few of the older women in the church thought it unseemly of a woman to wear white to a funeral, and a wedding dress at that. But Violet always said, what other people thought about her was none of her business.

Vera told me all about Dewey and how she had pretended to be in love with him so he would get her as far away from Jackson, Mississippi, as she could get after she killed Huxley. She said she would have gone to Boston or wherever else he wanted to go, but he started talking of marriage and kids. That's why she left him high and dry in that bus station in Birmingham. I could not fault her one bit. I left Jackson with a man who I thought would father my illegitimate baby. My plan didn't work out either.

It was a long time before I could get that image of those three young men in that picture out of my head. My heart ached every time I thought about them. They lost their lives for simply being the best that this country has to offer, young volunteers trying to help everyone get the right to vote. They died over something that never should have been up for debate if you read the Constitution of the United States. One man. One vote.

As for the picture of those young men, Vera and I thought about sending it to the FBI anonymously. I spoke to Walter Anderson, my former boss at the Mississippi Summer Project, and asked him how the investigation was going. He told me that after the bodies were found, the FBI had started to round up all the people who'd been involved in killing those young men. Olen Leonard and his cohorts from the Citizens Council were involved and would be charged with conspiracy to commit murder. If the Summer Project was successful, maybe they would be tried before a jury that didn't consist of all white men. Walter said the FBI was still looking for two men thought to be involved— Dewey Leonard and Mercer Buggs. The authorities thought they may have gotten away before they could be charged. Vera and I decided it wasn't worth the risk to send the picture on to the FBI. We burned it, along with Dewey's wallet.

As for the second dead man on the porch, the best we could determine was that he was some sort of detective. He had followed me and Roger up to Ohio and then must have followed me to Chillicothe to find Violet. I felt horrible for having brought all that trouble to Vera's doorstep. It was all still a bit of a mystery, one that would remain under that sell shed at the bottom of the driveway.

So I lost the baby, and Vera lost Hank.

Now we were both trying to reconcile with losing things we thought we didn't want. It's a funny thing about that sort of loss. Losing something you didn't think you wanted doesn't lessen the pain when it's gone. Losing the baby, me and James's baby, was raw and more visceral than I had imagined. That baby was as much a part of me as my lungs or a limb. And now it wasn't. It didn't matter that my options for bringing my baby into the world were horrible, raising a child with a man who would beat me or fathered out of wedlock by a man who left me. Neither one a fitting plan until I decided I would divorce Roger and raise my baby by myself. That was the plan I had decided on before God intervened with another.

The plans we make and the way they don't work out is a wonder.

I imagine Vera probably felt the same way. Her love for Hank and all he had meant to her had buried itself deep in the well of her heart. I could just tell. She used to say, she would never settle down with just one man. Watching the grief all over her face at Hank's funeral told me she would have spent her entire life with him if the good Lord had willed it so. My heart ached for her.

* * *

Two weeks after Hank's funeral, I decided I wasn't going back to Cleveland. Dewey Leonard had closed that chapter of my life. I called Lurlene. She said the police found Roger's body in an abandoned building that used to be a nightclub. He'd been shot in the head and Frankie suspected he'd gotten mixed up with some loan sharks. She said the police were looking for someone named Dewey Leonard from Florida. Of course, I didn't tell Lurlene what I knew. My baby sister and I would take those secrets buried under that shed to our own graves.

So, instead of returning to Cleveland, I boarded a Greyhound bus headed to Washington, DC. Vee gave me the bus ticket she bought but never used, along with some seed money to help me get settled. I'd lost all Momma and Papa's earthly belongings. I'd lost a husband and my baby. I'd lost everything, which gave me an opportunity to find something new. And Washington seemed the perfect place to find it. Once I found a job, I could enroll in college, and law school after that, like I'd always dreamed about.

I'd wanted to go back to Washington, DC, ever since I'd heard Dr. Martin Luther King's speech at the March on Washington the year before. I still had hope that one day we'd all be allowed to vote, that we'd live on equal footing with anyone else in this country. No more killing us for sport or taking away rights we had to fight tooth and nail for. And the thought of living in Washington, possibly continuing to work on behalf of my people, filled me with more excitement than I'd ever known. And I was doing all this on my own.

A month ago, I was too afraid to leave Jackson without a man. I thought I needed a man to help me figure out my life. Now I was off to figure it out alone, and this time it felt right. Admittedly, I was scared leaving for a new city where I didn't know a soul. But Vee told me something that I've hung on to ever since I left Chillicothe. She said God will not let you falter when He has set you up to soar.

That Violet always was smarter than me.

56
Vera

I sat on the front porch of the farmhouse. The bright
beam of sunlight was bearing down on my face.
And I couldn't imagine living anywhere else in the
world.

A few days after Hank's funeral, a lawyer from
Augusta came to the house. He had a leather briefcase
filled with a bunch of papers. He pulled one of them
out and showed it to me. It was something called the
Last Will and Testament of Hezekiah Cummings. It
was dated the same day Hank took me and Marigold
into Augusta to shop for my wedding dress. The same
day Hank was murdered.

The lawyer read the words and I didn't think I was
hearing him right. Hank left the farm and everything
he owned to me. I think I must have scared that old

white man with all the crying I did. The farm that had been passed down through Hank's family was now my property. This house where Hank and I danced, his strong hands at the small of my back; him humming James Brown songs in the morning as he shaved; the two of us making love as the sun came up—every glorious memory of my brief life with him was wrapped up in the walls of this house. My house.

Momma, Papa, and Rose still stayed in my mind, but not like ghosts haunting me. I know now Rose wasn't ever bossing me. She was guiding me, even after her death. All three of them, like angels surrounding and protecting me on all those dangerous roads I had carved for myself. They was simply helping me along on this new path I was forging. Sitting on this porch, tending to land that I own, is where they had been leading me all along. In my youthful stubbornness, I had taken the harder route to get here. I couldn't save Rose all those years ago, but I had saved Marigold. I think I mighta saved myself, too, in the process. Some of Momma's dirt-tinged bouquet was restored.

Who knows? Maybe someday the police might find me. Maybe Coogler might ask enough questions to figure out who I really was. But I'd decided not to spend my time worrying about the police and all that business back in Jackson. And unless I thought on it real hard, most times, I forgot about all that business under the sell shed, too. I was twenty-one years old. I decided to focus on my future. I'd spend my time loving on my family and friends and helping other women the way Pauline and Miss Willa had helped me. I decided to do what the old folks used to say. I'd run on along to see what the end is gonna be.

I didn't have Hank anymore, but he had given me the very best of everything he ever had: love, a business of my own, and a wonderful group of friends. Delroy and Linc still worked on the farm. Lilly would stop by and sit on the front porch, telling me the things she saw with her special eye. She even told me she could see Hank up in heaven and he was proud of the way I was taking care of the farm. Birdie told me Lilly's imagination had gone buck wild and I should make her stop all that foolish talk. But Lilly was harmless. Besides, she wasn't telling me nothing I didn't already know myself.

I'd never made a plan for my life before because I never knew where I belonged. Until now.

All those years as a young girl feeling caged and chained had only made me that much wilder and eager for freedom. I searched for it in all the wrong places with all the wrong men. There was a time back in Jackson that I thought I'd never settle down with one man. Right after Hank died, I didn't want to be in this house or on this farm without him. But Marigold said something that changed all that. She told me that Hank loved this land and he loved me. He wouldn't want the two of us—me and this farm—to ever be separated. I was supposed to carry on his legacy of love for this God-given earth.

That Marigold always was smarter than me.

Acknowledgments

As always, I thank God, for blessing me with the gift and the opportunity to tell stories. None of this would be possible without the Creator. This book has been a labor of love because I stand on the shoulders of strong women like the ones in this story, who were bound and shackled by the mores of an era that has passed but, if we are not careful, threatens to return.

There are so many people to thank for making this book possible. First, I have to thank my amazingly talented editor, Asanté Simons, for giving me the support and encouragement every writer should be so lucky to have. I treasure your insight and wisdom. Thanks to my incredible team at William Morrow, including Liate Stehlik, Jennifer Hart, Virginia Stanley, Lainey Mays,

Essie Li Ramirez, Kaitlin Harri, Danielle Bartlett, Ploy Siripant, Diahann Sturge, Laurie McGee, Bianca Flores, Jeanie Lee, and the HarperCollins sales team.

To the woman who works overtime holding my hand, covering my back, and pushing me forward, my incredible agent, Lori Galvin. You are simply the very best when it comes to agents and human beings! And to the rest of my incredible team at Aevitas Creative Management, including Allison Warren, Shenel Ekici-Moling, and Erin Files, I am incredibly blessed to work with such fantastic people.

I owe a huge debt to the librarians and staff at Auburn Avenue Research Library on African American Culture and History, located in Atlanta's Sweet Auburn Historic District. You have been a godsend of knowledge and patience. I daresay you all are warriors in your dedication to preserving our history, which is American history. Especially at a time when some threaten to erase it.

To Jonathan Shapiro, a living legend in the fight for civil rights, I could have talked to you for hours. Thank you for sharing your wealth of knowledge and for your own contributions to making the kind of history of which I am now the beneficiary. And huge thanks to Hank Phillippi Ryan for making the introduction and for all your support of this very green writer. You are a joy. I am lucky to call you friend.

To Brandi Wilson for always providing unflinching candor, sage insight, and huge belly laughs.

To the women of Gilmour Academy, Lesa Holstine, Pamela Samuels Young, Laura Zigman, Jumata Emill, and Irene Reed, you all lifted me up when I needed it most and gave me the confidence to know I can do this "writing thing" and stay sane in this crazy business. A thousand thank-yous.

To the librarians, booksellers, bookstagrammers, bloggers, podcasters, and, most of all, readers who took a chance on a new writer like me, you are my heroes for being so dedicated to these things we all love: books.

Always thanks to my sister squad, who keeps me sane and grounded: Cheryl Haynes, Angela Cox, Michonne Fitzpatrick Baker, Cheri Reid, Juli Harkins, Rachel Gervin, Key Wynn, Melloney Douce, and Elizabeth Robertson.

To my family—Myra, Herman Jr. ("Red"), Carolyn, Linda, Bertha, Paul, Michael, Sandra, and all the rest of the Morris and Hightower clans—I love you. Thanks for loving me.

As always, immeasurable thanks to my precious sweet peas: Alexandra, Mitchell, and Ashton. You light up my life. I love you three more than words can articulate.

To my guy, Anthony Hightower, you already know how much you mean to me. But just so the rest of the world knows—I love you.

HARPER
LARGE PRINT

We hope you enjoyed reading
our new, comfortable print size and found it
an experience you would like to repeat.

Well – you're in luck!

Harper Large Print offers the finest in
fiction and nonfiction books in this same larger
print size and paperback format. Light and easy to read,
Harper Large Print paperbacks are for the book lovers
who want to see what they are reading without strain.

For a full listing of titles and
new releases to come, please visit our website:
www.hc.com

HARPER LARGE PRINT

SEEING IS BELIEVING!